AN ENEMY'S FUNERAL

AN ENEMY'S FUNERAL

LORRAINE DUCKSWORTH-ROGERS

This is a work of fiction. Names, characters, places and incidents either are the product of the author's imagination or are used fictitiously, and any resemblance to any actual persons, living or dead, events, or locales is entirely coincidental.

This book was printed in the United States of America.

To order additional copies of this book, contact:
Xlibris Corporation
1-888-795-4274
www.Xlibris.com
Orders@Xlibris.com
76570

*"The sun will come up,
but will you be ready when it goes down?"*

I must at first and again thank God Almighty. Next, I would like to send special thanks to my parents, Elvie & Thomas Husband and my father, Dennis Duckworth Jr. Additionally, I bestow the privilege of thanking my husband, Kenneth D. Rogers Senior and my children, Mekale, DeAlvia and Kevin Ducksworth as well as Ahlandria and Bryce Norton. To my brothers, Thomas Junior and Jason as well as my sisters, Linda, Marie, April and Jessica, and all of my brothers and sisters on the other side, including you, Malcolm, I haven't forgotten you. You all are definitely my inspiration. To everyone else, I would just like to say, "Hello." Love you all, Lorraine.

Lord, I would like to thank you for all that you do and all that you will continue to do. I would like to thank you for extending my time, so that I can be closer to you. I would like to thank you for giving me the necessary understanding to forgive my trespasses as well as those who have trespassed against me. Additionally, I would like to thank you for my and my family's health and strength. I love you Lord, I will always continue to give you the honor, the victory, and the praise. Now I can truly say that I have myself together and that I would not have made it without you. Lord, I now ask that you bless this work and the energy put within. I ask now that you multiply its worth by the upmost power. Even before that Lord, I ask that you bless my immediate family, whom have stood patiently beside me during this endeavor and aided me. Please bless the children of the organization that I represent. Lord, bless the critics as I know with all works they exist. I ask that they pray for me, and when they pray that they will say to you Father that this one is for Lorraine; that she may be strengthened, healed, and always on God's side. I conclude this prayer by asking you Father to remind my critics to pray for themselves as well; that peace may reign: that back-biting may cease, and that every piece of animosity that they have toward me or anyone else, will vanish and be no more. Finally, I close this prayer asking that my readers forgive any errors they may find and knowing that you will do what you said you will do Lord. In your divine son Jesus' name, I pray. Amen

Sometimes, we as human beings do not know how many lives we are affecting with our negative verbal and non-verbal attitudes. Even more, we do not at times consider how we have physically harmed someone for a lifetime. However, it is important for all of us to know that 'no man is an island of his own'. All of us are affected one way or another by the actions of someone else, whether negatively or positively. However, it must be known that we must at sometime in our lives sit down and consider the consequences as a whole for our actions alone. Just because it does not look as though the incident that occurred was our fault, does not mean that it is not. Being vindicated by one or many is not total vindication. We as a people must learn to love one another as our Father in heaven loves us all. We as a people must do the right thing, even when it seems wrong, and vicariously observe life changing events from someone else's shoes. The bible says, "Judge you not, for in the days that you judge, you shall be judged'. So my questions to you are, "how can you criticize the behavior of someone else if you have not walked a mile in his or her shoes." Better yet, "How can you hate someone you never even knew?" Additionally, "how can you change if you never see what it is that is wrong?" God gives us the signs. It is about us accepting and correcting the warnings. Sometimes, all we have to do is stop, listen and possibly act.

Gospel recording artist, Donnie McClurkin said that "when there is nothing left to do, *Just Stand*". That's exactly what I did, and the Lord heard my cry as I cried much. I stood still, long and hard, even though, I was discouraged. I kept praying for those little problems, those little obstacles in my way. I made it up in my mind that sometimes you have to go through something to get to something, your blessing. I wanted to give up so many times, but I decided that I would just stand still and wait on God. That is what I said, until I was tempted yet again by Satan. He was trying to convince me to return to the same person that I use to be-that selfish woman who would not look past her sins and go to God, but God stepped in once again, and I pulled up my strength enough for me to tell Satan 'no'. You see, something on the inside of me just would not let me give up. I had come too far to turn around. Finally, I made it up in my mind that I was going to trust God. When I finally gave up everything, God saw that I was sincere, and He blessed me. I had no idea of what God was doing, but I could feel him doing. He opened my eyes to greater understanding and wisdom. All that I wanted to see was peace, and that is what I saw. You see, I had to give everything to God. I had to move out of myself, and now, I thank God that I did. Sometimes, we honestly do not know what is best for us. We continue to pursue the same path, thinking that it will lead to a different outcome. We tell ourselves that we are no one and that no one loves us. But realize this, the person who says these things has forgotten God's love, or never had a chance to experience it. Sometimes, as Donald Lawrence wrote in his song, "*Be Encouraged*," we have to look in the mirror and tell our self that we can make it. Sometimes, we have to speak over ourselves and tell the devil that he is a lie. Consider this when life gives you lemons, use them as the main ingredient in a great recipe and just watch how God will pull you through. Even at your worst of time, you can be your best. All you have to do is believe in God and have faith then He will see you through. Always remember to never take a problem back once you have given it to God. Let God have it and watch the change in the way he strengthens your life. As the Clark Sisters would say, "*Jesus brought the Sunshine*". If you want it, all that you have to do is ask for it and be content as well as sincere, and He will supply your every need. Your problems do not have to be your problems, for it does not hurt one bit to kneel down on your knees and say, Father, I need you. Will you say yes to Jesus today? Will you throw away all of your heartache and pain as well as all the heartache and pain you have caused and seek God? Jesus is waiting to save you. Don't think about what you have done or are doing wrong? Think about how bright your tomorrow can be? Just know that you are not alone, as Kirk Franklin may say, "we need each other to survive". I would like for it to be known for those of you who knew me before now; I would like to say that maybe you did. But for those of you who know me now, I have to say that you are getting to know the best part of me. My inspiration for writing "An Enemy's Funeral', comes from a literary work published by John Donne, which is titled, "*Meditation 17:From Devotions Upon Emergent Occasions*". My entire book is based on the words in the poem which state that "no man is an entire island of his own". The purpose of my work is for reader's to first recognize God, and second, inspire positive change. Enjoy the book, thank you for purchasing it, and may you be blessed.

Lorraine D. Rogers is a Laurel, Mississippi, native. She has earned numerous awards for her poetry and has been writing short stories since the age of 13. This book is her first published work. She is a college graduate of academic excellence and holds a degree in Arts. She is also an "All American Scholar Nominee", and the proud wife of Mr. Kenneth D. Rogers Senior. She has five children: Mekale, DeAlvia, Kevin, Ahlandria, & Bryce, and five additional children by marriage. She is also Co-Founder and Vice President of the *Better Boys and Girls Community Learning Center*. She volunteers her time with this Organization and assist with the important functions of this facility daily. She believes that hard work and dedication are key characteristics in making a dream a reality; but in order to keep that dream a reality, she believes that God has to the first, and HE has to be the main focus.

The Better Boys & Girls Center is a non-profit organization in the state of Mississippi with a mission to provide academic tutoring, physical and recreational readiness, as well as artistic and social outlets for youth progression. The Founder and President of this Organization is Mr. Kenneth D. Rogers Sr., the husband of Lorraine. This Organization was founded on November of 2007 and meet of all of the necessary qualifications as a non-profit. This Organization is new and has encountered a great deal of strength while trying to prosper. Lorraine would like to see something special happen for the underprivileged youth of Laurel, Mississippi; and with this said, she has decided to donate 20% of her funds generated through the sale of this book to the Better Boys & Girls Center. To learn more about the *Better Boys & Girls Center*, please visit the Center's website @ *www.bbgclc.com.*

Chapter 1

THE REASON

Sarah captured her breath and grabbed her purse before getting out of her car. She did not know once inside her home how she would tell her husband and her two daughters the bad news that she heard from the Reverend of her church. All she was sure of is that the news was bad and that she never believed in a million years that it would turn out this way. Once inside the house, Sarah found her husband in the bedroom watching television. He looked half asleep until she entered the room. "Well, James. I have some news—and I have some news." Sarah said as she laid her purse on the dresser by the door and walked over to the end of the bed. Her husband's eyes slowly came to view, waiting for her next few words. "Reverend Stevens said that James Junior can not be memorialized at that church."

"What?" James said in a gentle tone uncertain of what he had just heard. "That's what he said and so did all of the other churches that I went to." Sarah replied.

"What kind of talk is that Sarah?" James asked.

"It's just like I said James. In fact, all of the churches said the same thing when I asked. The first question they asked was, is he a member? Then they asked if he had been to church within the last ninety days, if he hasn't, then why? My responses to both questions were no and no, and it's a long story that offers no relativeness whatsoever in explaining why he hasn't been here." She replied while sitting at the edge of the bed before clutching her face in her hands for a brief second.

"Sarah, for years, I have been to and heard of funerals that were preached in churches and people hadn't been to church in years." James said looking at the back of his wife's head.

"I know, but not anymore." Sarah stated with a smile as she looked in the mirror at her and her husband's reflection looking back at her. "However, it appears that at convention gatherings within the last couple of years, churches discussed, particularly Baptist churches, how they were tired of offering memorials in their churches to individuals who hadn't been to church or offered some kind of charity to the church."

"What does that mean?" James asked.

"Exactly what I said James," Sarah said turning to look at her husband. "And that story ain't even the half of it or what else I have to tell you. After so many complaints from the Pastors of churches, a law was passed on the matter."

"A law!" James exclaimed.

"Yes, a law." Sarah confirmed.

"What do you mean a law? Since when did the government step in on religious decisions and make laws?" He asked his wife.

"Well a funeral isn't exactly a government matter. A funeral can be held anywhere."

"What? But you just said a law was passed—I don't understand." James said.

"This law was passed at last year's Religious Convention. The Pastors passed it unanimously." Sarah replied.

"What does all of this have to do with Jr.?" James said sitting up in the bed. "This sounds like a violation of the first amendment."

"Not exactly." Sarah said.

"Not exactly, what? People do have the right to assemble in a peaceful manner." James said.

"Of course they do, but only if it is safe and peaceful for all parties involved." Sarah said looking at James in the mirror. "Let me clarify something for you. It appears that gangs and violence are appearing in God's house a little too often these days, interfering with the lives of innocent people who want to bury their children or their friends in peace-not only gangs but different demonic spirits disturbing God's house."

"Hold up!" James exclaimed. "Ain't the church where you go to cast out demons, spirits and save lives?"

"James, before you start this question and answer survey, JJ was in a gang, and Reverend Stevens does not want that gang rhetoric in Saint Hope." Sarah said.

"My goodness gracious-so this is what this whole thing is about? The law ain't even relative to Jr. being memorialized." James replied.

"The law still stands. It is—what it is." Sarah said taking off her shoes. "You know for a fact that gangs and violence enter into churches easily. It causes a problem, and where problems exist, there is no peace, and JJ was apart of the problem."

"No, what I meant was that this is not a governmental law. It's only a consequence or rule voted on and executed by the church. Anyway, the boy wasn't in no gang, Sarah. Kids these days don't know the meaning of a gang. They just create stuff to take up some of they time. Besides, I'm his father. I would know."

"Know what? I'm his mother, and I know all to well. He was in a gang, and he has always been involved in one or more court cases than I care to remember. Reverend Stevens said that he will not tolerate gangs assembling in his church and destroying God's sanctuary and his members' lives. You know as well as I that gangs have been known to destroy churches in rivalry with other gangs because of dead gang members by another gang. JJ was in a gang—whether you care to admit it or not. And in refute to what you mentioned earlier, this is a new religious law."

"No, it's a rule-a consequence. Congress nor has the President of the United States voted on this matter or passed it into law, only the church. Besides, ain't the *Bible* the law that Christians should abide by. And if you haven't already realized, the Bible is already written. All this stuff about a law is not relative, Sarah. This stuff that you all are carrying on can't be right." James profoundly stated.

"Well, it is." Sarah replied while looking at her husband from the mirror again. "Besides, you haven't heard the worst of this story yet."

"Oh, I have heard the worst. Woman—why are you so naive when it comes to everyone else but me? You believe everything that is spoken to you from someone else and debate everything that I tell you. I'm your equal Sarah and so is the Reverend. Both of us put on our pants the same way. What makes his word more relevant than mine?"

"I don't want to hear that mess, and you might want to save all of that noise." Sarah exclaimed.

"My goodness—you dumb. I swear you have no understanding whatsoever," James said taking a deep breath.

"Whatever—I don't have to listen to you James. You don't even go to church. So you can't even relate to this subject. What has it been, fifteen years now?" Sarah asked him.

"Shut up! I ain't even going in that direction with you." He replied.

"The only decent place that would allow us to have a memorial for JJ is the train depot." Sarah stated, sarcastically. James looked as though he was about to explode.

"What in the hell . . . and just where did you get that idea from?" He asked before quickly getting out of bed.

"James, must you continue to use act foolish?" Sarah asked.

"Look at you!" James said grabbing his shoes, "Or whatever word that fits before you, Sarah! You and that preacher of yours, done lost yo minds. You coming up in here telling me this bull as though its April fools day—and I didn't know it or something." James stated out loud as he put on his shoes. "What it is wrong with you? All calm like none of this bothers you. Why you doing this Sarah? Why you acting this way?" He asked. Sarah could see the pain in his eyes.

"Doing what? Acting how? I haven't done anything but come in here and tell you the truth." She replied.

"I know why you acting this way. It's because Jr. ain't none of yo real son. If he were yo real son, you wouldn't act this way. You would feel the same way I feel. You would understand all the real emotions that I have bottled up inside of me." James confessed.

"What? He ain't my real son?" Sarah said not sure of what James had just confessed. She knew that she gave birth to JJ. After understanding her husband's words, she said, "of course he's my real son! Why are you creating a mockery in here and letting the flesh allow you to respond this way?"

"The flesh Sarah, what do you mean the flesh? Oh, I guess you all saved and sanctified now. Can't nothing piss you off. You so understanding about everything, huh?

Well let me break it down to you,—you don't know nothing-Sarah. And that's because you refuse to learn something. Afraid of change—you are—thinking that you will be controlled. When are you going to stand up and get some clear knowledge in that head of yours? You know beauty don't last forever. You got to know something to make it in this world." He replied.

"What is wrong with you? Why are you insulting my intelligence?" Sarah asked her husband as she stood up to look at him.

"Sit back down! Ain't that what you use too? Ain't that what you do when the Pastor say it or Mr. Winston at yo job say it. You listen to everyone else but me. Now all of sudden you don't know what's bothering me. Well, I'm gone show you what's wrong with me. Put yo shoes back on, in the flesh that is, cause we going down to Saint Hope and see Reverend Stevens bout this, in the flesh that is also. Oh, and you might want to pray before we get there, cause that ain't what I'm going to do. Now that's one for you in the spirit," he said pointing at his wife before continuing, "You got to be brain washed or something bringing that bull in here. The nerve you have to come in here like none of this concerns you or me and want me to behave passively. I tell you Sarah, the more I teach you how to fight, the longer you run."

"Whatever James, and the more I tell you to calm down, the louder you get! Being loud isn't going to change any of this." Sarah said picking her purse up from the bed after putting on her shoes.

"That's a lie. You got my mammy mixed up with yours." James said opening the bedroom door.

Sarah caught off guard by her husband's comment and shocked asked him, "What did you just say?"

"Oh suck it up Sarah—and let's go." James said walking out the bedroom door.

Chapter 2

THE LISTENER

Every family has a nosy member. Leesa Sidney was the one in the Sidney Family. She was this way from birth. As a baby, she observed every face and everything moving. She was fascinated by the human mouth and its sound ability. By the sound of any voice, she would hearken, and she would not proceed with her work until the last word was spoken. By then, she had made it up in her mind to run and tell somebody, anybody who would listen. Today was like every other for her. She had heard the whole conversation that her parents' were discussing on the inside, and she was headed in the direction of the front door and out to tell her sister, Lexe, what she was shocked to hear. Lexe, feeling that Leesa had to have come in contact with some gossip, could hear Leesa's footsteps up until the front door abruptly became ajar. In fact, she could almost figuratively see gossip in her sister's face even before her mouth came open.

"Lexe, Lexe, Lexe," Leesa called out to her sister before she sat down beside her on the steps.

"What?" Lexe asked her sister, disinterested as she watched cars passing by her parents' house. Leesa had a habit of moving mess but not her own.

"You will not believe what I was just given the opportunity to hear." Leesa replied.

"No I won't, but I am almost sure that you are going to tell me, but not before you say that you swear it is the truth." Lexe said looking at Leesa while chasing a disheveled piece of hair behind her ear.

"I swear—it is the truth." Leesa said hesitant by Lexe's last words before continuing. "Anyway, Mama just told Daddy that JJ's memorial service was gone be at the train depot. What do you think?"

"Man, you just don't quit, do you? Can't we just grieve in silence?" Lexe said with a smile after looking at her sister.

"The truth Lexe—I am serious." Leesa said. Lexe could tell that she was serious by her non-verbal behavior.

"And what do you mean what do I think?" Lexe asked her. "I think—no!" Lexe said with a slight laugh. She found humor in her sister's tattling of such a subject. "How can you say such words?"

Leesa shaking her head from left to right said, "Easy—from hearing them spoken, and not such words, the truth." Leesa said before she paused and engaged in thought for a moment, she then asked her sister, "whatever happened to peace and decency?"

"Nothing, both still exist, but the majority doesn't care about that. They're still alive like infidelity and chivalry," Lexe replied.

"I can almost see the truth in that, especially when momma talking bout having our brother's memorial at the train depot." Leesa said.

"I'm going to pretend that I did not just hear that for the second time." Lexe said getting up from a step to go sit in the swing on the porch.

Leesa turning to look at her sister said, "Ma just told Dad that. He's upset. No, he's past upset." She concluded while laughing after she saw the look on her sister's face.

Swinging back and forward gently in the swing, Lexe said, "Wouldn't you be? This is stupid, the whole thing. We gone look stupid if she and dad decide to have that memorial service there."

"Well, the church can't and ain't going to do nothing." Leesa said.

"Why they can't? We've been going there for years." Lexe said, stopping the swing abruptly.

"It's the reason why JJ has to be memorialized at the train depot according to Reverend Stevens." Leesa said.

"Explain?" Lexe asked Leesa.

"Ma told Dad that last year's Religious Convention past a new law for all churches. The law stated that if a member of the church hadn't been to church within ninety days, then he or she was no longer considered a member. And if the person is not a member, he or she can not be memorialized at the church. Something like that Ma said."

"You are lying?" Lexe asked Leesa.

"Nope." Leesa said while looking at a passing motorist.

"Now that's just rude," Lexe said swinging again. "I don't understand that," she said shaking her head and confused, trying to make sense of the matter. "If I had to write that law in a book at the rate I feel now, it would be right beside foolish rhetoric and right after stupid."

Leesa laughed at her sister and said, "I almost agree. When was the last time you been to church?"

"I went last Sunday with a friend in Shreveport." Lexe answered.

"But you don't belong to that church. Do you?" Leesa asked looking at her sister swinging in the swing.

"No. And I haven't felt much like I belong to Saint Hope either. I mean—I didn't feel exactly welcome there."

"Why?" Leesa asked.

"Just haven't. This feeling is nothing new. I have always felt this way since Ma and Dad chose that church when we were young. I always felt excluded—like I didn't belong, all of us for that matter. Our family was never the exception and always being judged even if some of us tried to do the most good. We were never credited for our greatest virtues. Now JJ is dead. This is only the typical behavior of Reverend Stevens and the congregation of Saint Hope. Whenever wrong comes, we always seem to be the mark." Lexe said.

"Wow Lexe, I never knew you felt this way. Why haven't you said anything before now?" Leesa asked. She could hear the hurt in her sister's voice.

"For what? To become the mockery that we are? For Dad, let along mom to scold me. I mean—its one thing above all else to believe in and worship God, but when the claimed saints of God treat you like crap, what do you do? What do you say? Not too much, and you know why? Because as soon as you respond, it suddenly becomes a problem and then here comes the bible quotes-the mixture of the spirit and the flesh-where they take from and add to God's word. Not only that—the very ones screaming I love the Lord, pretty much hate and despise you. They mock you, criticize and condemn you, instead of praying with you and for you. Honestly, they smile in your face and disgrace you behind your back, like the same God they serve, you don't serve. Don't believe me? For once act like you have spiritually grown and watch the eyes looking at you in the sanctuary. I mean, what is it? It's alright for me to confess my sins, but it's wrong for me to praise and worship when God has forgiven me? I'm like—make up your mind people. I read my bible too."

"So, all of this comes to mind when you think of Saint Hope? Because—it's deep." Leesa said.

"Yes, even more, pay attention to this? Many of the ones trying to help you move closer to God—never seem to go to the altar for prayer themselves. All of a sudden they have no problems and no sins. You are the sinner. You need the prayer. They are suddenly in a position where God blesses and excuses them where they sit. Think I'm lying? When was the last time you've seen Ms Mary, Ms Hampton, Ms Rose and the Pastor's wife stand at the altar for prayer or forgiveness when the benediction is extended?"

"I haven't-actually," Leesa said with a slight laugh. "Not ever as a matter of fact."

"Because they don't want you to know that they mess up—and that they are not absent from wrong doing or doing wrong. They have become too big to confess. Too many people look up to them. They will not endure any shame. Their job is to judge you and correct you. Anyway, have you ever paid attention to Associate Pastor Stanton in the pulpit?" Lexe asked her sister.

"Yeah," Leesa said unaware of where her sister was going with the question.

"What do you think?" Lexe asked.

"About what? What do you mean?" Leesa asked her sister, not sure of how to answer the question.

"Everything. His praying—his preaching." Lexe said.

"Nothing, sometimes he seems like a big impression of confusion—at other times and on a good day, I'll give him a C-minus." Leesa replied.

"Exactly, one big ball of confusion, do you think that God appreciates that?" Lexe asked.

"I think God's just molding him, getting him in the right perspective." Leesa replied. She didn't want to judge God's anointed.

"Girl please!" Lexe said. "It's been almost ten years. How long does it take to learn how to say the right prayer at the right time and preach? You are acting like Ma now. He dead in the pulpit; a tree that don't move—nothing in him is alive. He's lukewarm, and you know God's opinion of lukewarm behavior in the Book of Revelation. Besides that, he lacks the three P's." Lexe said.

"The three p's—what are those?" Leesa asked her sister with a slight laugh.

"He ain't gone pay and cannot preach or pray, and Reverend Stevens should tell him instead of mocking him. He knows that Reverend Stanton lacks the three P's, which hold truth to God's word that many are called, but few are chosen."

"Lexe," Leesa called out to her sister. "He don't pay his tithes?"

"Girl no! Reverend Kenton and Manning either. You remember when I applied to serve as church secretary and Reverend Stevens said that I was too young to serve after I was nominated for the position and was active in the position for over a month?"

"Yeah, when he told Ma that he felt like you weren't spiritually mature yet?" Leesa asked.

"Yeah, see you remember. Well—the real reason the position was taken from me was because I knew what they had been doing, and I told Ms Shelton about it. She told Ms Louis, who told Reverend Stevens about it. All of sudden, I was no longer the church secretary because I was too young. I was so happy that I didn't say anything to her about Reverend Stevens flaking on his tithes too."

"Get outta here!" Leesa exclaimed. "Are you telling me that he was cheating on his tithes too?" Lexe nodded her head up and down to answer her sister's question. "Honestly Lexe, you make Saint Hope look and sound ridiculous." Leesa said.

"Saint Hope is not the only exclusion. Other churches do the same mean things and more. I only speak of what I have witnessed and experienced hands on. No one sees wrong in anything until he or she is the wrongee. Don't believe me? Just wait until you graduate and see what happens at Saint Hope? One truth I know for sure, don't nobody have to tell me that God is good because I know of His goodness and grace. Every time they hindered me, God blessed me. And can't anybody do anything about that." Lexe said before her father burst opened the front door. Her mother was walking closely behind him.

"Where y'all going?" Leesa asked, surprised by her parents' mobility.

"We'll be back," her Dad said as he continued to walk past her and down the steps.

"I know that, but where y'all going?" Leesa asked, walking behind her parents toward the car. Lexe walked in the direction of her parents as well.

"Just stay here Leesa and Lexe. We'll be right back." Their mother said-going to the passenger side of the car.

"Ok, but where y'all going?" Leesa asked.

"We are going down to the church to talk to Reverend Stevens." Sarah said getting inside the car.

"Cause I wanna know what the hell is going on," James said starting the ignition of the car.

"We wanna go. We wanna know too." Leesa said. "Don't you wanna go Lexe?" Leesa asked her sister as she stood beside her.

"Heck yeah, I wanna go," Lexe said before realizing her parents' presence.

"Girl!" James exclaimed to Lexe.

"I did not curse that time. I promise I didn't." She said. James wasn't sure as he eyed his daughter heavily. Leesa agreed with Lexe by nodding her head from left to right at her father in order to reaffirm Lexe's answer. Lexe looked away from her father. James proceeded inside the car and so did his daughters.

Chapter 3

THE RIDE

James was upset, and he lashed out at his wife during the entire ride to Saint Hope. He did not believe that Sarah was doing a great job of convincing the Pastor to let JJ's Funeral be held at the church-for if she had, then Reverend Stevens would have said yes to the memorial. James knew this because his wife never debated anyone else when it came to having her way except him. If a stranger said no to her, then no would be the final answer. Meanwhile, Sarah knew that she should expect a long ride and a deep lecture all the way to Saint Hope. She was already convinced that James would open his mouth in a minute. Even before she thought of him speaking, he was already doing so. "Sarah," *here it comes,* she thought to herself as James called out to her before pulling away from the curb near their home, "I don't know what kind of foolishness this is. I just don't get it. Our son can't be memorialized down at that church, and he was a member. I don't care what you say-Sarah, Stevens and Mayor Davenport is up to something. You do remember that this year's budget again ruled out building a new train station on the South-Side. You reckon they trying to use Junior's memorial to get those gang bangers to completely demolish the train station this time so that the insurance will pay enough to build a new one?" '*The road is not occupying him enough'*, Sarah thought to herself.

"And where did all of that just come from?" Sarah asked her husband. It was something to consider, but she was not about to let him know that. James knew how to blow things out of proportion.

"My head and out my mouth," James said as he glanced at his wife for a second.

"Then, you need to void all of that. That makes no sense. Reverend Stevens doesn't own up to that kind of selfishness nor does he think that way." She said in her Pastor's defense.

"Maybe not as a Reverend but as Councilman, he is capable of some very sick compromises." James said. Leesa and Lexe seated in the back seat of the car, just listened to their parents. '*Yes,'* they thought, '*they are making some valid points together, but dad has something that definitely needs to be taken into consideration.'* James continued, "I honestly believe that our son's memorial is being used to pave the way for a new South-Side train station. I can't see no other reason for this foolishness with JJ and Saint Hope. We need to get to the bottom of this."

"There is nothing to get to the bottom about, and this has nothing to do with a new train station on the South-Side. Like I said at home, James, it's because JJ had not been to church in years, nor had he repented for his sins." She replied.

"Now, it's his sins. At home, you said a charity!" James exclaimed.

"Well, what better charity to offer than the soul of a sinner to God?" She said.

"Who's side are you on? You sound like a coached woman. Church is changing you, Sarah."

"I believe that's what it's supposed to do, James. You might ought to give it a chance to change you." Sarah said with certainty while looking at her husband. She was not sure about whose side she should be on. James did have some valid points to consider. *'Should I be on anyone's side?'* She thought. She did not know. Sarah was confused.

"I mean—its changing you for the worse." James replied. "Did you even offer to pay Reverend Stevens to preach the memorial in the church? The thought of some money would have bought you some time. You know preachers are always looking for you to hand some money down. You know how they love jewelry and nice suites and don't forget the women. In fact, I can't tell you of any Preacher that I know that don't like to look good."

"James—I can't believe that you just said that." Sarah replied as she was caught off guard by her husband's comment. "Anyway . . . Jesus didn't care about none of that."

"He different . . . I was talking bout in this world, anyway, I said Preacher man not Perfect man. Besides, Jesus has nothing to do with this. He's in an entirely different category of his own. I'm talking bout Reverend Stevens." James said.

"What's going on? Where is all of this coming from? I mean . . . are we talking about JJ or are you jealous-James?" Sarah asked her husband.

"Of Stevens. Hell no! He ain't no saint, Sarah. You just don't want to admit that I am right about him. If it ain't money and small accessories, then it's a new ride. You know, he always talking bout he could use a new Cadillac."

"What do you mean new? The church just purchased him a new Cadillac last year." Sarah replied.

"Oh, y'all fools done messed up. Next, he gone want a Mercedes, then a Lexus, and y'all gone be just the fools to buy it. Then he gone tell y'all they too small and he need a Hummer. Y'all gone rob the church's bank account to get that too," James said before he asked, "What he do to get that Cadillac—threaten to leave the church again?"

"No, and who are you kidding? Nobody wants a Hummer but you, James. Why do you continue to insult Reverend Stevens? He is a good man of God-and very unlike you." She responded.

"In your eyes, I know that snake, Sarah. Remember—I grew up with him, and he use to drank just as much as me and Robert drank and gossip at Will's Barbershop too. I'm telling you. He had many other concubines along with that wife of his back then-ain't nothing changed. Still do, everybody just in denial. Y'all can see . . . just scared to say something."

"James! All of this is nonsense, and it's also irrelevant." Sarah said.

"Why?" James asked looking over at his wife for a brief second.

"Because this isn't about Reverend Stevens, it's about Junior," Sarah said.

"Of course not, it's about Reverend Stevens—the snake."

"No, it's about Junior—the gang member." Sarah responded.

"Then I believe that we have reestablished relevance. See the relevance, Sarah, snake and gang member."

"You know what I mean." Sarah said.

"Yeah, and I also smell an enemy. Yeah, I said it. I smelled one way back at the beginning of this conversation." James said under his breath, loud enough for Sarah to hear.

"Whatever James! I did what I could do for JJ—if you had been home some of . . . ."

"Mom, Dad, can we please stop this commotion?" Leesa interrupted and said, tired of her parents arguing and tired of moving her head from her mother to her father. "Besides, are you two going to ever tell us about what's really going on here?"

"Girl, shut up." James said. "I know that you were in the bathroom listening to everything. You know everything that your mother and I know. Has she told you yet, Lexe?" James asked his other daughter as he glanced at her in the back seat from the rearview mirror.

"Is it all true?" Lexe asked her father.

"You now Leesa can't lie bout nobody else's business but her own. She and ya momma just alike." Sarah gazed at her husband after hearing his comment. "They ain't never got nothing to tell about them, but they can and will tell you anything you need to know about someone else. They the main two running down to that church every week and spreading that false witnessing that Reverend Stevens is dishing out. Now they ain't powered up enough to tell him that he wrong."

"Whatever James," Sarah said. "When did you obtain immunity from judging?"

"Whatever? I ain't the one accepting some Preacher's advice of allowing my son to be memorialized at a train station. He knows that it's tradition for Baptists to be memorialized in a church. Besides, that's the only place where we can get an excuse for showing out without getting locked up. Anyway, they said that Reverend Stevens was the main one who said last year that he was not going to allow no more funerals in that church for people who wasn't a member. You know what he meant, no money—no funeral."

"Now we back to money . . . and tradition—what could you possibly know about tradition and Baptists, and anyway who said that Reverend Stevens said that mess about not having anymore funerals for non-members? James, you haven't been to church in 15 years-fifteen—got it? How can anybody tell you anything when you don't care about what happens at Saint Hope?" Sarah asked.

"Ma—Dad, please." Leesa said. She was tired of the debate already.

James looked in the rearview mirror at Leesa and said, "Girl—the sad thing about you is you about to get that mouth of yours duck taped and you don't even know it. Yo mouth is always moving—mess that is. Just shut up. That means don't say nothing—not even yes Sir." Leesa, after hearing her father's words looked at Lexe. Lexe gave her a '*I told you to shut up look?'*

"Why are you on the Offensive so much?" Sarah asked her husband.

"Because defense ain't exactly working right now, and how is it that you would prefer me to be? Full of crack and spaced out through this whole ordeal? That would make you and Stevens convincing me of this a lot easier, don't you think?" James asked his wife.

"Look James, it all boils down to this. Junior lived a non-virtuous life. He clearly did not make the best decisions for himself and all of us. You know that as well as I. The streets are what he loved. The streets are what he leaves." Sarah said with no remorse and looking out the passenger window of her husband's car. Her two daughters in the back seat of the car just looked at each other, and James couldn't believe what his wife had just said. There was no way that he could understand because he never knew how afraid Sarah was of her own son.

"Lady, I can't believe what I just heard. You got to be crazy. Are you crazy-Sarah?" He asked in a low tone before yelling his next few words. "This is our child that we are talking about, Sarah. You do remember that don't you? I am your husband. You ain't talking to Sister Mitchell on the phone about Sister Linda's son."

"Do I look like a woman with amnesia? I know who you are, James. Park over there." Sarah said as they arrived at Saint Hope. "This is a handicapped parking space, and the last time I checked, I wasn't receiving your blue envelope in the mail on the first of the month." Sarah said looking out her husband's window.

James stopped for a second to stare at his wife to advise her that he receive the memo via her mouth. Sarah looked away. She knew that she had just insulted her husband. James stated while parking the car, "Imagine that. Well, I guess that excuses Sally's car, um! All the preachers of this church she done laid down with must have finally paralyzed her. Good Job Sally! You think she done got her blue envelope yet-Sarah? Or is she still able to work?" He said shoving the car in park. Leesa and Lexe laughed amongst themselves at their father.

"You are so sick," Sarah said, looking at her husband.

"And I guess Sally ain't," James said while looking at the church door from his vehicle. "Every time you come up here or pass by, Sally is up here at this church."

"She is only the church Secretary, James." Sarah said.

"Call girl, secretary, hooker, prostitute, I would say that other word, but you wouldn't like it—see where I'm going with all of this? I ain't going in 'til she comes out! You hear me?" He asked while looking directly at his wife.

"Hopefully that will be soon. I'm sure she's talking to the Reverend bout something." Sarah said.

"Sure, she's talking alright." James said looking at the church door as it was slightly opening now. "Sally doesn't know how to talk unless it's bedtime. She know that ain't no man listening to her unless she laying down. She is the main reason why y'all can't keep no preacher now." James said. Sarah looked at her husband. Leesa and Lexe looked away from the church door in amazement to see what their father was about to say next. "Every time you look around, she up in one of 'em . . ."

"James, don't start. Just don't start." Sarah said.

"Come on Dad. Give it a break?" Leesa asked.

"Didn't I tell you to shut up?" James turned around and said to his daughter, Leesa. "Just keep on talking and see how fast this millimeter temper of mine gone just drop everything and make you walk back home. Think it's a game? Try me, and see how fast you reap the result." Leesa turned her head away from her father and began to look out her window. Lexe wanted to intervene, but swallowed her comment abruptly. James then focused again on Sarah and said, "All I said was, I ain't going up in that church, Sarah."

"Yeah, I know-James," she said looking out the passenger window of the car again and shaking her head from left to right in shame, "until she comes out. No need to re-iterate it."

"Wit her nosy self. She ain't nothing but FOX, CNN, and NBC tied together." James said, looking out of the front window of the Cadillac at the church door. He then took a cigarette from his shirt pocket and put it in his mouth.

"James, bad enough you have to attack me, but must you attack everyone else? And please do not light up that cigarette?" Sarah asked with her arms folded. "Honestly, I just don't understand you."

Putting the cigarette back in the cigarette pack in his front pocket, James said, "I don't understand you—Sarah, letting some hypocrite preacher convince you to have our son's memorial service at the train station." Sarah could see the anger in his eyes.

"You should pray for understanding, and will you please stop with the name calling?" She abruptly said.

"My God, will you two quit already! Both of you are like the knat at the barbecue with the fly-fighting over the same piece of food. This whole ordeal is nonsense. Will one of you please just have sense enough to be quiet? We need to focus on fixing this whole situation concerning JJ." Lexe said from the back seat. She was fed up with her parents' arguing.

After her comment, her father said to her, "Girl, what's the name of that college you at? The name can't be James and Sarah University, cause at this college, we don't take orders, we give'em. Now unless you plan on sailing in the same boat as blabber mouth here," he said pointing to Leesa, "you might ought to shut up too."

"I was just saying Dad . . ." Lexe replied

"You was just saying nothing!" James responded.

"Hush James, here comes Sally." Sarah said to aid her husband in closing his mouth as well.

"I don't care about her coming. She shouldn't even be over here. I bet Lillian ain't in there with her and Stevens," he replied.

"Yeah, like you ain't in there with me on Sunday?" Sarah replied with a smile, catching her husband off guard before Sally said, "Hey James, Sarah, girls."

"Here ye, hear ye . . . did that Jezebel just speak to me? Did she just have the audacity to say my name?" James turned to his wife and asked. Leesa and Lexe waved at Sally.

"Hey Sally." Sarah said with a smile before directing her attention to her husband. "James, you are a sick man, a very sick man."

"Oh yeah, well that don't make me dead. Now, do it?" He replied.

"What are you implying? That I am?" Sarah asked. James looked at his wife. He was about to suggest that she was. She knew that he was going to say something ignorant, so she said while opening the passenger door of the car, "Never mind, let's just go in the church!" James said under his breath, *'she almost left her mouth open for a dumb response.'* On the other hand, Sarah had already figured that out.

Chapter 4

SAINT HOPE

James imagined that the inside of Saint Hope Church had changed, especially after 15 years, but it had not. Everything appeared the same to him. He witnessed the same smudges on the linoleum floor and the same pictures of various African Americans on the wall-like Martin Luther King Jr., Thurgood Marshall, Malcolm X and Rosa Parks-even more were the same three black crosses that hung on the right side of the wall away from the door. James was not the only one admiring the inside of the church. His daughter Lexe was looking as well. Staying away from home and mostly at Grambling State, Lexe had not attended church at Saint Hope for some time now. She only came home when her mother needed her most and on some holidays, even then, she avoided church because it was not interesting anymore and to mostly attend clubs in New Orleans. By Sunday morning, she was too tired for church. Meanwhile, James complained from the entrance of the church until he and his family reached Reverend Stevens' study.

"Well, I see nothings changed in here." He said after coming in the back door entrance through the kitchen and witnessing the large Lord's Supper picture across the room from the entrance. In contrast, Sarah said nothing. She kept walking, trying to avoid another argument with her husband. Suddenly, James stopped and grabbed Sarah by her right wrist. Sarah wondered why the sudden halt. James was looking at the picture of the Lord's Supper up close now. Sarah did not understand why as she gazed at him for a brief moment. In amazement, he said to Sarah, "And that's suppose to be Mary Magdalene sitting next to Jesus?" Sarah was confused. However, Reading Dan Brown's Book *'Davinci Code'*, James wanted for some time to know if there really was a woman sitting next to Jesus in the portrait.

"Where?" Sarah asked looking at the picture.

"There . . ." James replied while pointing, "here, to Jesus' right."

"No James. That's Judas, the one that betrayed Jesus." Sarah responded.

"How do you know? In the *'Davinci Code'* book, author, Dan Brown, says that that is Mary Magdalene and that she and Jesus had an affair."

"What!" Sarah said, laughing at her husband. "Stop playing."

"Where daddy," Leesa suddenly asked? She closely observed the picture to find the features of a woman.

"Right there." James pointed to the woman or man in the picture again.

"Are you serious, Daddy?" Leesa asked. She was still eyeing the picture up close before turning to her father and asking again, "Is that a woman?" James nodded his head up and down.

Sarah not happy with the heresy James said inside of Saint Hope and to their daughter said to her husband, "James that is a lie—that's a man, and you know it. Stop playing and carrying on with this nonsense," Sarah said. "This is serious."

"How do you know if it's not her?" He asked while looking at his wife.

"I just know." She said with no proof at hand to offer.

Lexe looking at the picture closely now asked, "Is that really Mary Magdalene, Ma?"

"No Judas!" Sarah said, thinking of what her husband had just said.

"Huh?" Lexe asked, confused by what her mom had just called her. "I'm Lexe."

"That's what I said, Lexe. I can't believe you just said that." Sarah replied.

"No you said Judas. Didn't she say Judas?" Lexe asked Leesa. Leesa nodded her head up and down. Lexe continued, "Anyway, daddy said that it was her—just bite me already." Lexe replied.

"What did you just say?" Sarah asked her daughter. "I've told you about talking out of line."

"Correction, Dan Brown said it." James said looking at Sarah as she awaited a response from Lexe. Lexe turned away. She didn't want any trouble.

In the meantime, Sarah replied to James, "That is only Dan Brown's theory. You shouldn't go around spreading lies-James."

James replied while folding his arms together-certain of himself as his small belly stood out.

"Why would he say it, if it wasn't true? He researched all of that stuff in that book, and the last time I checked-research was facts. I believe him."

"Because that's what writers do." Sarah responded. "They embellish their work to sell it."

"What," said James, confused by the word his wife used?

"And you read Dan Brown's, 'Davinci Code'. Let's go, you big dummy. I can't believe you brought that hear say in this church."

Chapter 5

SAINT HOPE

Several steps away from the kitchen and down a second hall of the church, James started to question Sarah again. He could not seem to keep his mouth shut. On the contrary, everything was up for debate. Sarah was planning a stupid funeral and was trying to convince him that it was as a result of every Pastor of every Baptist church telling her no to hosting JJ's memorial. Something was a miss, and James could sense it. Yeah, he had tendency to hate his son and his actions, but that did not mean that he didn't care about what was happening to him. Subsequently, James could not believe that so many people could be so literally rude, not even suggesting that he and his wife give them a little time to weigh out the matter. Yes and needless to say, JJ was a foolishly, terrible man, not child, but man because the Holy Bible clearly states that foolishness is bound in the heart of a child. But do we have a right to condemn, is the question? The answer all day and every day is no. Why, because all of us are yet sinners. Nevertheless, James was angry and upset and believed that someone should feel his wrath, and he decided that he would rather take it out on Sarah; someone he loved and would not hurt intentionally; rather than a stranger, he would almost kill, literally.

"So what happened to that loan y'all got to remodel this church? Everything still looks the same to me." James said to his wife as he walked behind her.

"No it's not." Sarah said turning to look back at him for a brief second. The girls were walking down the hall viewing the portraits on each wall.

"Yes, it is." He said with a slight gaffe.

"James Earl!" Sarah said as she stopped in her steps.

"Well, it is." James responded. "Martin's still here, Thurgood too, and I bet Malcolm's still around this corner along with Rosa Parks keeping up mess."

"What!" Sarah asked. She was shocked by her husband's comment.

"Mess, you heard me." James said before turning the corner and noticing what he said was true. "Low and behold, what did I tell you? And look, Reverend Steven's awards and degrees. Seems like the only one growing around here spiritually is Reverend Stevens. He got that Pimp Degree, yet?" James asked while observing the awards.

"James you know nothing. You haven't been here in 15 years. Remember?" Sarah replied.

"Oh yeah, then I can see that I haven't missed sh—much." He cut the profanity off and said with a laugh. Sarah gave him a hard stare. He knew that she was about to say something regarding the profanity. "I know. I didn't say it."

"Oh you do? Then consider it before we go in there to speak to the Pastor." She said pointing at the door of Reverend Stevens' study down the hall.

"So, his office is down here now?" James asked quietly.

"Yes." She replied as she continued to walk in the direction of the Pastor's study.

"So, that's where the money went. Y'all built him a new study—I see." James said holding on to the last word of his sentence in amazement.

"That's not all." She replied as she looked behind her at Leesa and Lexe. They were now looking at Reverend Stevens' degrees. "The Sanctuary and the Foyer have been remodeled as well." Sarah said.

"Well, I need to see that before we leave." James instantly stated." I need to know what you been spending my money on, talking about tithing and blessings. We ain't got rich yet. The house still ain't paid for, and yo car keeps breaking down."

"What? James—blessings are not just materialistic. You still have your health and strength, don't you? And as for the money issue, no you didn't go there. You know where your money goes. You are just too drunk to remember." Sarah immediately replied.

"Unless somebody stealing from me, you know, you might have a point there, Sarah." He suggested.

"I know and I do. Nobody's stealing from you." She responded. "Girls," she then called to Leesa and Lexe as she was about to approach Reverend Steven's door. But before she knocked on the door, she turned to James and said while catching him off guard as he was walking closely behind her, "Talking about I spent your money. The nerve you have to say that." She laughed. On a more serious note, she concluded by saying, "you barely give me any, and I work for my own money, and come to think of it, you haven't tithed in fifteen years." She then knocked on the door.

"Fifteen years, fifteen years, fifteen years, whatever Sarah," James replied. "Anyway, I don't even come to church and my car ain't breaking down, the mortgage is getting paid, and I still have my health and strength-so you ain't got to necessarily pay tithes to get blessed."

"Do you even know how you sound now? You sound stupid. You are only being blessed because of my favor with God. Imagine what will happen if I cut you loose. You'll feel the coming of hell on high water. Come on girls," Sarah said hurriedly while knocking a second time on the door before calling out, "Reverend Stevens." James stared at his wife. A knot had formed in his throat. He could not respond. Again, Reverend Stevens did not respond to the knocks on the door either. Sarah, suddenly, knocked a third time as Leesa and Lexe approached her side. This time she knocked more aggressively.

James paced back and forward as Sarah knocked. He soon became impatient with Sarah knocking and said with his hands in his pockets, "What is he doing?"

"He's probably in the bathroom." Sarah said not sure if Reverend Stevens heard the knock.

"Yeah," James replied while looking at Sarah from the opposite side of the study door. "I can imagine that—washing off the un-holy, holy ghost, I suppose." Leesa and Lexe laughed at their father's suggestion, but suddenly stopped when their mother gave them a hard stare. Sarah wondered that if now is what the beginning behaves like, then she could only imagine what the end would be like with James around.

Chapter 6

THE TALK

Reverend Stevens turned off the faucet in his bathroom as he thought he heard a voice calling out his name. He knew that it was not the Lord because he was just talking to him, mainly asking for forgiveness for the act that he had committed with his secretary. For some reason, he just could not tell Sally no when she came on to him, and for other reasons which were known, he did not want too, considering she knew how to please him in a way that Mrs. Stevens could not. As a consequence, he felt bad about the countless acts that he had committed with Sister Sally, but he did not regret them. Additionally, he only prayed that God would forgive him and make him stronger so that he would avoid her advances, knowing that he had to first get himself together, and he didn't plan on doing that anytime soon with the new tricks that Sally forged on him. Soon hearing a knock on the door again, he quickly dried off his hands and said to himself in a quiet tone, "The Good Lord said knock and the door shall open." Sitting behind his desk full of papers now, he said, "Come in." Immediately after noticing the human figure that stepped in from behind the other side of the door, he said with a smile, "You back again, Sister Sarah?"

"Yeah," she said not sure of herself with a smile as she entered the study with her two daughters beside her. "You remember Leesa and Lexe," Sarah said. "Lexe's been away at college and Leesa's still here with us."

"Yes—I know." He said with a lustful smile while looking at Lexe and Leesa, admiring their beauty and their slender, petite figures. The jeans and t-shirts they wore were not doing a great job of concealing their narrow figures.

Suddenly James appeared from behind his wife and daughters quickly and broke Reverend Stevens' negative thoughts. He then said to his wife, "Sarah, we ain't here to talk about the whole family."

Reverend Stevens' eyes quickly moved away from the girls and focused on James. "Well, if it ain't—James Earl Sidney Senior. What a surprise," Reverend Stevens said reaching out his hand to shake James'. James did not seem too friendly about the matter and brushed him off. Reverend Stevens slowly moved his hand away. Sarah could not believe that her husband would not shake the Pastor's hand.

"Y'all come on in and have a seat." Reverend Stevens said with a smile as he proceeded to sit in his chair behind his desk again. "So, what can I do for you all Sister Sarah?" He asked as he crossed his hands on top of the desk.

"Well," Sarah said with a smile as she turned away from her husband. "James wants you too . . ." before she could finish explaining, James interrupted the conversation between her and the preacher.

"Reverend Stevens, I need to know why my boy's memorial service can't be held in this here church?" James asked.

"I explained everything to him at home, Reverend Stevens." Sarah interjected and said.

"I'm sure you did, Sister Sarah. I'm sure you did." Reverend Stevens replied.

"James just doesn't understand, and wanted to hear it from you, just so that he could understand the circumstances of this situation better." Sarah replied. Reverend Stevens could sense the fear in her voice. Was she scared, he thought.

"Sarah, shut up! I can talk for myself. Seeming you couldn't handle all this before." James exclaimed to his wife. She flinched at the loudness of his voice. James then turned to Pastor Stevens and said, "Now, Reverend Stevens, I need to know what's going on around here?"

"Well well—Brother James, I can still call you Brother James can't I? You know Saint Hope hasn't seen you in a long time, bout . . ." Reverend Stevens responded with a smile.

"I ain't here to discuss my absence or saving. I'm here to talk about my son, and I wanna know why my son's memorial service can't be held up in this here church?" He said crossing one leg over the other and placing an arm behind Sarah's head on the sofa.

"Well James, all churches done passed a new law which states that if your child hasn't been to church in 90 days, then his or her memorial service cannot be held in the church. That law applies to us grown folks too." Reverend Stevens replied.

Leesa asked her sister as they were seated on a second sofa, "You hear that Lexe?"

"What!" James suddenly exclaimed. "When y'all pass this new law—cause I ain't heard about it," he said pulling his hand from behind his wife's head and sitting forward on the edge of the sofa as he looked Reverend Stevens in the eyes, "and I ain't seen it or read it in the paper, and I read the paper everyday."

"Well, it was in there, James-published October of 2006—over a year after Hurricane Katrina of course. They said they round here gang banging and they violent and they can't attend church to learn some honest virtues to get their life right—then they gone have to be buried out there in the events of the world that they choose to gang bang in."

"What you mean? Like ain't no events going on up in here." James replied.

"James," Sarah said suddenly to stop him from saying something terrible.

"Look Reverend." James said to correct himself after looking at Sarah.

"Brother James, I understand how you might feel, and I know that it's bad, but James Earl Jr., can't be memorialized up in this church. Now you know that James Earl went for bad, and he had a host of skeletons in his closet."

"Yeah Reverend, but-you know—we all, we all got some skeletons up in our closet. You know if that being the case—don't none of us deserve to be memorialized in a church. And just what is bad these days anyway?" James asked. Sarah flinched at the sound of her husband's voice. "With all the rules these schools, churches, and government coming up with these days, when does anyone know where to draw the line? You should know. You still a politician ain't you?" James said to the Preacher. He then thought about his remark and said, "Oh Lord, I just left the window open for a lie, and speaking of politics, you and Mayor Davenport ain't trying to use my sons memorial as bait to get that new South-Side Train Station are you?" James asked. Sarah could not believe that James actually asked the Pastor that question. Reverend Stevens choked on his saliva as a result of James' suggestion. He needed to fast talk James away from this subject. He and Davenport were up to something, but they did not plan on incriminating themselves.

"Yes, I am still a politician, and I and Davenport would never use your son as bait to obtain alternative favor because of failure. Honestly, I can understand how you might feel Brother James, but as a result, JJ was bad. He did terrible things to good people, so subsequently to law, the line has to be drawn somewhere. Don't you think?" Reverend Stevens said with a slight smile. James didn't find the situation compassionate or funny. His daughters didn't either. "Honestly," Reverend Stevens said, trying to gain the family's peaceful since of humor back, "some of us good people know when and where to draw the line—just like some of us know when to come and get our lives saved. Because Jesus Christ died for our sins, that means yours too Brother . . ."

"I didn't come here to talk about Jesus Christ and my sins. I know Jesus, and I know my sins. I came here to talk about . . . Now look Reverend Stevens, my wife is a member up here at this church. I was one up until this ninety day surprise discovery, and I don't understand why our son's memorial service can't be held here."

"James, it's as simple as this, and it's just like I've been saying all along—his presence wasn't here, that's why his memorial service can't be held here." Reverend Stevens replied.

"This is some bull—and you know it Stevens." James said dropping the title Reverend. "When in the Bible, did you ever hear of Jesus turning any man away?"

"In the Book of Luke, the eighteenth chapter, eighteen through the twenty-fifth verse. Shortly put, when the rich, religious leader refused to sell everything he had and give the money to the poor. When Jesus saw how hard it was for the rich man to do this one deed, He said. "For it is easier for a camel to go through a needle's eye, than for a rich man to enter into the kingdom of God". Now I apologize for this new law, Brother James, but this new law has been approved by a majority—even the head Catholic Bishops said yes, imagine that."

"Imagine what? They did that for y'all, not them. They ain't got nothing to do with Baptist Tradition, and the majority of them is white." James said. Reverend Stevens actually agreed with James in his mind. His face took on an awkward look after James debated his point. James concluded, "They ain't going by that rule—now who the fool?" James asked.

"You might have a valid point. Frankly James, there's no other way around it, honestly and I ain't gone blame it on catholic bishops, I'm tired of families assembling only when a family member dies, and I'm needed to preach the funeral of somebody that I don't even know. It's fairly ridiculous and highly unfavorable in this day and age. I mean, when are we going to really be honest with ourselves here and speak the truth to our families concerning their salvation? Never mind, that is an entirely different subject matter. Now James, I did however tell Sarah that I would preach JJ's memorial service wherever you all decided to have it . . ."

"I don't want to hear that—crap!" James said. Sarah and her daughters flinched once more at the sound of James' voice. "Do you know how many people gone come in and out that train station? People just gone be walking in and saying all kinda mess about that funeral and our son."

Meanwhile, Lexe turned to her sister Leesa and said, "This is stupid. I can't believe that Dad's going to accept this."

"Now James, you're gonna have to abandon your negative attitude. You have to calm down." Reverend Stevens replied to James.

Lexe continued to converse with her sister as she said, "Okay, he just messed up. Daddy's not going to accept this. Jewel Sidney is about to show up." Leesa looked completely shocked, looking around the room for her grandmother. She then asked her sister, "Grandma's here, where?"

"No stupid—in the spirit. Grandma's dead, and you know it." Lexe responded. James and Reverend Stevens continued to converse amongst each other. Sarah was holding still to James' every word. It wasn't doing her any good. By the time she tugged him, the words were already out.

"Calm down. Calm down my ass." James shouted at Reverend Stevens after Reverend Stevens asked him to calm down.

"James," Sarah said truly dissatisfied with her husband's conduct as she had heard enough. This conversation was not going anywhere, she thought. She had to figure out a way to excuse James from the room and soon, but how she thought. It would not be easy, and Reverend Stevens was not making the matter any better. Leesa decided to try and help her father to calm down. "Daddy," Leesa said, holding on to her father's left arm. He brushed her off. Meanwhile, Lexe enjoyed her father's rage, and Reverend Stevens was only shocked.

"Just how is a man suppose to calm down when someone's telling him that his child has to be memorialized at a train station, huh? Just how is it that a Pastor should even bring up the idea to one of his members to even consider memorializing his or her child at a train station? A place in this city that is shot at more than five times almost every month and still holds the deed to remain open for business. Not only that—but strangers wondering if we are crazy and walking in there saying all kinda stuff about our son, and you know it. Some of that mess ain't gone even be true," James said.

"Well James, he did gang bang while he was out there on the streets. In fact, he did a lot." Reverend Stevens replied.

"You are always so judgmental, huh? Then what about, Rehgina?" James asked Reverend Stevens.

"Who?" Reverend Stevens asked.

"James, don't do this? Please don't do this?" Sarah interrupted and said, standing up to try and calm her husband down. She knew where James was going with this topic. He said it often at home, and it wouldn't be a topic that would sit well with Reverend Stevens.

"Your daughter," James exclaimed to Reverend Stevens.

"I don't have a daughter. I have a son and his name is Rehginald." Stevens replied.

"Exactly, that's what I thought you had until six months ago. Imagine that, just how in the hell did you and your wife manage to change a boy into a girl after 19 years? It took 19 years for her to get that girl that she really wanted." James replied.

"What are you saying Sidney?" Stevens asked. Sarah was astounded by her husband's actions.

"Ah, you talking to me? You mean to tell me that God ain't told you that yet? He tells you everything else-at least that's what you claim—and the garbage you keep feeding my wife and daughter."

"Are saying that Reginald is gay?" Stevens asked James.

"God answers quickly—cause that's exactly what I'm saying! Is he going to be memorialized here too? After all, y'all did include sins, right? Or has he repented since last week?"

"James!" Sarah exclaimed as she stood in front of her husband for a brief second-looking into his eyes.

Suddenly and out of nowhere were these words came from Leesa's mouth, "I told you that he was gay! That's why he never called me." She said to her sister Lexe. Her mother suddenly looked away from James and at her. Leesa sat down and looked away from her mother. Lexe was shocked as her eyes widened in surprise.

"Oh, and what about you and Sally?" James concluded in conversation with Reverend Stevens.

At the sound of those words, Lexe asked a general question. She expected anyone with the correct answer to respond when she asked, "So Reverend Stevens and Sister Sally gay too?"

"No child. What are saying?" Her mother asked her. "Just sit down." Sarah then turned back to her husband and said, "James, I think that you have said enough. Now sit down—and stop this nonsense!" James was not listening to Sarah. He was waiting for Reverend Stevens' comment.

Reverend Stevens not sure if he had heard James correctly asked, "Sally?"

"Yes Sally!" James said to reassure him that he was on the right page. Sarah tugged at her husband's arm, once more.

"Stop pulling on me Sarah! Pulling doesn't sound anything like praying-something I told you to do before we left home." Sarah let go of his arm and sat in her seat again. She wanted to leave the room, but what would James do next? What would he say? She thought. On the contrary, James had gone too far, and there was nothing she could do to stop him from trying to save him from himself. At the same time, Leesa and Lexe sat and watched in awe of the show that their dad was hosting.

"What about Sally?" Reverend Stevens asked James. *'How much does he really know,'* he thought.

"Wasn't she just the result of your wipe off a minute ago and many times before today?" He said looking a Reverend Stevens. Reverend Stevens thought to himself, *'he knows too much.'* He was completely shocked by all that was happening and all that James assumedly knew. Reverend Stevens decided that he was not about to let James make him look bad in front of Sarah, Leesa and Lexe. So, he remained calm and allowed James to continue and that's exactly what James did saying, "everyone knows that you two have been fornicating for years, and we don't have to go into detail about it." James stated, suddenly calming down to say, "Look, Reverend Stevens, now all of this can just go away, if you would like to make it right. Nobody's pointing any fingers here. I just want JJ's memorial service at this church, a place of peace and decency. He might have lived a non-virtuous life, but that's not an excuse for him to not have a proper memorial."

'So now he wants to calm down and make the situation less than hostile, I think not,' Reverend Stevens thought to himself before saying to James in a sad tone, "I'm sorry Brother James, but it's like I said. I'll preach the funeral, but it can't be held at Saint Hope." He said thinking of how James' remarks cut him deep. They convicted him all over. Now, hurting deeply, Reverend Stevens couldn't wait until the Sidney's left his office so that he could call his wife. With anger piling up on the inside of him and no break to let it out to entertain a second round with James, he continued by saying, "He didn't give us any hope; therefore, we don't owe him any. Now please leave my office?" He asked.

Very upset by Reverend Stevens' last words, James tried to grab Reverend Stevens. Reverend Stevens moved backward quickly. Sarah grabbed James by the shirt. Leesa had him by the left arm. Lexe continued to watch, standing up now. Not able to grab Reverend Stevens, James exclaimed, "You hypocrite!" Reverend Stevens flinched, blinking his eyes rapidly and backing away from his seat even more. He had challenged the anger in James, and it was unleashed. "Stevens, you better hope that I don't ever get my hands on you." James said as his daughter, Leesa, and wife attempted to pull him to the door.

"Come on daddy. Come on Daddy lets go. Lexe help us get him?" Leesa asked her sister as her father's strength was about to over power her and her mother.

"What! Excuse you! No! Y'all need to let him go." Lexe said as she stood watching her dad with her arms folded. She then said, "Get him Daddy. His mouth done wrote that check today!"

"Lexe Marie Sidney!" Sarah said shock by her daughter's choice of words.

Suddenly, Lexe recanted her words and decided to help her mother and sister with her father. She ran to their aid and called out to her father, "Daddy—Daddy, pull yo-self together and let's go before Ma kills me! What's wrong with you?"

Chapter 7

MORE SAINT HOPE

Even though James frightened Reverend Stevens, this incident would not stop Pastor Stevens from stopping Sarah before she left the room. Sarah wondered if he really understood the bite of the bark located outside of his door. James was no amateur. Usually, what he stated was what he meant. It was nothing for him to slang his two hundred and fifty pounds of flesh around to get his point across. More over, being apart of a family of bully's didn't exactly calm down his attitude. He was loud and vicious. He wasn't afraid of anything and believed everyone to be racists including his own kind. He was angry and not very social unless pressed to be out of respect. Additionally, he loved to get his point across and wanted everyone to listen. He was also forward and blunt. A comedian he was. He possessed all of the qualities, and told great stories that would have anyone crying tears in laughter. Even more, he was an alcoholic. Sarah prayed that he would stop drinking, but he hadn't in thirty years. Sarah imagined that he was self conscious, or that maybe he was afraid to be himself. She could not understand why he drank as much as he did. He was just as much fun with the alcohol as he was without. Meanwhile, she did not believe that he knew why he drank as much either, if so, he wasn't exactly confessing that incident to her, or anyone else—not even his probation officer assigned to him after his second DUI. All Sarah knew for sure, right now, was that while she was trying to play safety for Reverend Stevens, he was trying to take a beating while asking to speak to her alone after he had just managed to piss her husband off.

"Ah—Sister Sarah," Reverend Stevens said nervously-afraid that James would come back in the room. "Can I talk to you alone for a minute?"

"Sure Reverend." She said once James was safely outside the door. Sarah was unsure of what he was about to say.

"Mrs. Sidney, I just want you to know that I am sorry about all of this and the way that it's going down. I guess that the convention didn't really put much thought into the matter—that it would affect good people like you. I commend you for being so strong, especially with that bomb ticking outside of that door. I honestly don't know how you put up with James Earl's attitude like that." He said with a smile, still very scared. "Anyway," he said clearing his throat. "I apologize deeply that your son's memorial service can't be held at this church, but I promise you that I will preach that funeral as best I can even with the fact that your husband does not find me in his favor right now." He ranted on. Sarah nodded her head up and down. She had endured enough for one day. She was ready to go home. Reverend Stevens continued, "but this situation is something that he must understand and you and the rest of the world as well—man out here on the street gang banging and killing one another, destroying innocent lives, marriages, families, and children, they don't deserve to be having nothing special inside of a church. A church is sacred, Mrs. Steven's . . ."

"I understand, Reverend Stevens." She said looking into his eyes.

"A church is supposed to be safe. A church is where all the saints of God gather and commune with one another in a spiritual way to give thanks to God for all that he's brought them through and will continually bring them through, and you just don't disrespect God's sanctuary by bringing something bad or someone bad into his church, hoping that people will just say nice things because they in a church. This is the number one, no, one is price, but number two reason why people choose to host memorials in churches. For people to believe what couldn't possibly be true. But now is the time for the truth to be told, and people should have the right to express their feelings without fear if they don't feel like forgiving just yet and aren't ready to get saved. I mean—I could teach the benefits of getting saved all day long, but if an individual comes and he or she is not ready, guess what happens . . . nothing, because the whole ceremony was in vain."

"I understand Reverend. I understand, but I . . ." Sarah said after giving him her undivided attention. She wanted to know where he was headed in the conversation before he would allow her to speak.

"Hold up, hold up. Now let me just finish. Let me just tell you everything. Now I hate the church passed that new law, and then again, I don't hate it, for the simple fact that sometimes we as people got to learn that bad people belong in bad places. That's the way the world got to be. None of us know all the right, and none of us know all the wrong until it's before our eyes or has touched our lives, but all of us must be held accountable for our misunderstandings, Mrs. Sidney."

Out of no where, Sarah heard James' voice outside the door. "Let's go Sarah. Come on out of there with that hypocrite. Ain't no security in there to help you."

Sarah, impatient with James' attitude said to Reverend Stevens, "I-I know Reverend . . ."

Again Reverend Stevens cut her off, "James Earl couldn't come to church as I told you earlier when I talked to you alone, therefore, James Earl's memorial service just can't be held in this church. It won't look good for Saint Hope. Maybe you can try explaining that again to James Earl Senior. You know it's a lot of people got a lot of mean things to say about James Earl Jr . . ."

"Sarah . . ." James called out to his wife. When she didn't answer, "Sarah" he said again. Reverend Stevens looked at Sarah as though he should finish talking real soon.

"I'm coming James." Sarah said to ease her husbands' impatience and to ease Reverend Stevens' fear. Before attempting to leaving, she said, "I understand Reverend, and I need to go. That bomb outside is about to explode any minute, and I will not risk almost being on the front page of the news again. JJ is enough. But before I go, I really want to apologize for all that happened here this afternoon. If JJ's memorial has to be at the train depot, then that's where it has to be."

"And I'm gone be there to preach it. Now your husband might not like some of the stuff I'm gone say. But it's gone be the truth, Mrs. Sarah."

"Last call, Sarah," James said from the other side of the door. Leesa and Lexe held him tight so that he didn't go back into Reverend Stevens' study.

"Don't mean to cut this short Reverend, but I have to go." Sarah said. A second strike for James would be hell to pay for Reverend Stevens.

"You do understand what I am saying, right, Sister Sarah?" Reverend Stevens asked.

"Yes Reverend. Everything's fine. I can't, honestly, say that I agree completely, but I understand perfectly." She said impatiently, getting a handkerchief from her purse to wipe her face. She was sweating. "And I appreciate you doing this." She said with a smile, trying to end the conversation as quickly as possible. She had kept James waiting for too long. Before she could ask Reverend Stevens the price that he would charge to preach the funeral, James was yelling again.

"Let's go Sarah! You ain't none of Sally. Come on out of there where that no good, hypocrite at." James said. The girls continuously tried to calm down their father, but he would not listen. James became very agitated by the girls supervising him and said, "Look, go to the car, and leave me alone before the both of you be walking."

Leesa said, before letting her father go, "Mom, would you please come on? Lexe and I are tired of holding him out here. He's threatening to make us walk."

"Sarah, Sarah . . ." James continued to call out to his wife. "I know you hear me. I ain't gone tell you again Sarah. Let's go, before I kick this door in. He ain't God. He can't judge nobody, he sure ain't preaching the gospel and doing the Lord's work. He's doing the work of the devil."

On the other side of the door, Sarah and Reverend Stevens came up with an agreement on the charge of preaching the funeral. "Since you are a member of this here church, Sarah, I'll only charge you $75.00. I usually charge more. My fee is usually $200, but you are a member. So it'll just be seventy-five dollars. Is that okay?" He asked.

Sarah thought, *'hell no, and maybe James is right about everything. Besides, Mathew the sixth chapter and twenty-fourth verse in the Holy Bible states that "no one man can serve two masters: for he will hate one and love the other; or else he will hold to the one, and despise the other. Ye cannot serve God and mammon." And Reverend Stevens had a tendency to do just that.'* But instead of citing scripture, Sarah said not certain of why as a member he was charging her, "Sure, sure Reverend—although . . ."

"Good, I didn't think that was too bad," he said interrupting her with a smile. His eyes sparkled at the fact that he was getting money to preach the funeral.

"Well Reverend, I have to go. You do want that door, don't you? I don't want to have to pay for one of those, too." Sarah said with a sly smile as she thought to herself that her Pastor was money hungry.

"Okay—yeah, yeah." He said. Just as Sarah was about to open the door to go out he asked, "Ah, Sister Sarah, and could you make that cash?" He said with a light laugh, trying to be friendly.

"Yeah Reverend, sure," Sarah replied.

"Lord knows that I have enough problems at the end of the year getting my taxes prepared," he said in a low voice under his breath. "And you have a nice day Sister."

"You too, Reverend," she said before closing the door. Sarah had another fight to handle once she got outside of Reverend Stevens' door, and he was in her face and waiting.

"So now you wanna be like Sally, huh?" James asked his wife as she came out the door, closed it and stood before him.

"James, what are you talking about?" She asked with a quizzical look, turning away from her husband.

"You know what the hell I'm talking about-Sarah." He said. Sarah walked away. "Don't you walk away from me Sarah?" Stopping for a brief second in her tracks, Sarah said, "Can we at least make it outside of the church and away from the parking lot before you start to curse again?"

Shocked by his wife's attitude, he said in a calm manner, "Yeah—but you ain't gone like what I have to say then either."

Meanwhile, Reverend Stevens sat behind his desk once more. He was shamed by James' theory concerning his son and his relationship with Sally. However, he was glad that James did not have any knowledge of him actually having a daughter. Picking up the phone, he called home. The phone ranged twice, on the second ring, someone picked up. It was his wife-Lillian. "Hello," she said.

"What did I tell you about Rehginald's mess? He's out, and I want him out before I get home."

"Now Mathew—just wait a minute," she called out to her husband.

"Now!" He said. After he hung up the phone with his wife, he placed a call to another source. The phone rung three times before the female voice on the other end of the cell phone said to him, "What, you want seconds?"

"Ha-ha, uh . . . no Sally, I don't think that you should continue to stop by the church as often as you do anymore. Our relationship is not amiss."

"What? Why? What's going on? Somebody told your wife about us?" She asked with a slight giggle. She hoped so. She wanted Mathew for herself.

"You wish, don't you?" He said with a slight laugh. "How many times have I told you that I am not leaving my wife for you-even if I have thought about it? It wouldn't look good for us or Saint Hope. The ministry does not condone that type of behavior."

"Baby, I don't recall you ever telling me that. People leave spouses everyday, and you've always gave me the impression that you wanted to leave her." Sally replied. Her eyes were glistening because of the formation of the water in them.

"Look Sally, this is not the reason why I called. Just try to stay away from the church as much as possible. Us being together will not look good-let alone rumors that we have been."

"Whatever Mathew, now if you just want to date another member, all you have to do is just say so. You don't have to make up a lie to brush me off. I do know that I am not the only member that you are sleeping with there. And since you seem to be thinking now, and me wondering for some time, is that really your little girl by Sister Betty Dancil?"

Mathew laughed and said, "Of course not." '*Now what bird is chirping in her ear?* He thought. Regaining his composure, he said, "Sally, you are blowing this entire subject out of context. Someone is on to us. This has nothing to do with anyone else. I can't be caught up in any of this nonsense. Now do as I have asked and stay away from the church until you need to pick up the announcements."

Sally asked, "So all of this is nonsense, Mathew?" He did not respond. He had hung up the phone.

Holding the phone in her hand for several seconds after Mathew hung up on her, Sally turned to her close friend, Alice, whom she was visiting and said, "Mathew said that he wasn't leaving Lilly for me. I thought we understood each other. I thought that he would be different from the others."

Alice, knowing that her friend was very naive said to her, "No Sally. He isn't different. Why do you continue to do this to yourself? Of course, he's a man of God, but he's a man as well, and men will lie, and he being a political figure only makes matters worse. I told you before you started this to let it go, but you wouldn't and now look at you. Why don't you for once take my advice and pray and let God send you, your own man." Sally looked confused as her friend confronted her with her mistake. "Mathew doesn't care about you or those other women of that church. His weakness for all of you is why I changed my denomination in the first place. I never wanted him to get the impression that I wanted a piece of the pie as well. Anyway, I refuse to go and listen to someone teach me the word that he or she cannot seem to follow."

"Is that really why you left Alice?" Sally asked her friend as several tears ran down her cheeks after she thought of how much she invested into her relationship with Mathew.

"Yes—I had heard enough of that mess." Alice responded while folding up some towels.

"But running doesn't change anything. You have to study the word for yourself, on your own. Saint Hope won't be held responsible for you going to hell or heaven, you will."

"That's true, and I do study the word. I also abide by it, but what I won't abide by is a hypocrite. Now, that's a word that you should always remember. You cannot be going around calling out people's sins to them when you have sins that you are currently dealing with, Sally, and this is something I have witnessed you do many times. I mean, what makes your sin better than mine. When all is said and done, a sin is still a sin."

"I can't believe Mathew." Sally said, ignoring her friend's advice. "I thought that he was special."

She concluded. Alice was right about Sally; she was always telling sinners what they were doing wrong while she yet sinned herself and knew better.

Alice, responding to her friend's comment said, "He's special all right babe, specially educated. And you—didn't hear a word I just said, did you? But that's okay, you gone wish you had when those same biblical quotes you use come back and hit you in the face. I'm done with these clothes and talking about Stevens. Byron will be home at 5:30 this evening and I have yet to prepare his supper. I have got to get to Brady's Store to pick up some supplies. Now, are you well enough to go shopping?" Alice asked. Sally nodded her head up and down before grabbing her purse from the sofa and getting up. Alice grabbed her purse from the kitchen counter and out the door the two went.

Chapter 8

THE VICTIM

As you will read often, James Earl Sidney Junior touched the lives of many, and it was not in a good way majority of the time. Who was James Earl Sidney Junior? To illustrate, he possessed characteristics of arrogance and conceit, but above all, he was handsome. He stood at about 6 foot 3 inches in height and weighed approximately 225 pounds. Of course, two-hundred and twenty pounds of his weight was pure hell—the only purity about him. He possessed a slim, muscular physic, and his skin was dark, smooth, and always cleanly shaven. He was representative of the word suave but lacking the c-word (*courteous*). His eyebrows were thick with a natural arch, and his eyes were dark-brown. On his right upper arm was the tattoo of a skull and on his left upper arm was the tattoo of a provocative woman. Was JJ sexy? Yes—very. Meanwhile, as stated in the genesis of this paragraph, JJ possessed another side—a side that was disrespectful, ignorant, and strange. He was known for his stupidity, and his immediate family along with the rest of his family could not bear to be within his sight. He was better known as JJ—a combination of the J in James connected to the J in Junior—and he had a powerful weakness. For some reason, he had a problem with women, especially if he felt like he was being disrespected or ignored by one. Additionally, he could not stand the idea of being rejected by one either. For, it would seem as though his power was being challenged.

On a different note, women found him to be rude and very dishonest. They felt like he had an over powering ego and his self esteem was low, because of DEBS, better known as, Daddy Emotional Battering Syndrome, better known as neglect from the daddy-which in literal terms meant that his father never showed or taught him how to love a woman. So therefore, JJ could not beat a woman at her own game, and he had a tendency to lash out at any woman who gestured or spoke of his foolishness, illiteracy, instability, lack of knowledge and negative social attributes. Yes, women did bring out the truth in him, and boy did he hate them for it, but that never stopped him from trying to learn how to beat them at their own game. He felt like women were an enigma.

Additionally, he also found them difficult to understand and very unstable like him, and they were very emotional and socially inclined. Even more, women were experienced speakers, naturally, because they talked much. Now keep in mind, JJ wanted to control women in order to deliver his weakness by them. But what he failed to understand was that without love in his heart, it was next to impossible to retain a woman or mask her. Equally important, if she did not love him back or sensed that there was something terrible that she should pay close attention too concerning him, then the only way that he could win, if he were in fact fictitiously acting, was to cheat as men often do, which brings Jada Wells into this chapter.

Very unlike JJ, Jada was smart, bright, intelligent, and well respected, and JJ loathe the idea of her being everything and awesome. Jada was important. More over, she possessed a natural beauty with no flaws. She was an Eva Longoria look alike, only better with hair that was short, sandy, sassy and curly. But these positive attributes were nothing compared to her honesty and kindness. Without a doubt, Jada was the sun on a rainy day and the wind on a hot day. She treated everyone with the ability to respect—well, and respect was returned to her. Church was her favorite outing and art was her favorite interest. Why, because church corrected her and inspired her, and art conformed and energized her. Additionally, there was something about art. It was the gift of being compassionate, good, honest, and pure, and it was also what the mind imagined it to be. However, one mans love is another mans hate, as JJ rebuked all the unique qualities that Jada possessed. To reveal light where there is no understanding, JJ wanted Jada pure and simple, but not because he was in love with her, now remember what was previously said about love, but because he wanted to humiliate her. Right now, he was humiliated, and he wanted the pressure of wanting her to just go away, but it would not until he had consumed all of her. His mind said for him to get her and so did his heart, sinfully. So, he needed to have her. His obsession with her was viciously weakening him. He needed to conquer her in order to release the madness he felt since first speaking to her. Knowing Jada for an extensive amount of time now, was not exactly soothing his appetite or obsession no matter his consumption of alcohol or marijuana. What he needed was the opportunity to touch her. Jada rode his mind like an innocent man being accused of a crime that he did not commit. She annoyed and agitated him as well as held the proper tools to tamper with his major buttons. Jada was able to do to him what no woman was ever capable of doing; she was able to suppress his tongue and mask his anger. JJ was nothing to anyone when she was around. She disturbed him and figuratively used her interest in art to paint a disturbing picture of him in her company's mind. No one but Jada could do this to him. She never tried to hurt JJ, intentionally. After all, maybe she was his enigma but just did not know it, or even God's way of telling JJ that He had enough of his roughness. Whatever the cause, Jada's only intentions were to allow JJ to understand that his feelings were not the only feelings that existed in the world. Now, the theory that Jada used in order to sustain JJ's terrible behavior when she was around to make him responsible for his actions seemed to be working in the beginning as JJ was starting to recognize the reason behind his weakness—which was smart women. However, Jada's potion was about to be discovered, and the demon suppressed within JJ for so long was about to be unveiled.

Meanwhile, riding around New Orleans with friends and thinking while they were talking as he sat in the back seat and looked at the sky, JJ begin to remember how he was first introduced to Ms Jada Wells. The scene was do to Trei Styles, JJ's best friend. Now Trei was just too attractive for any woman. He was the too in too much. Sexy, light skinned, JJ called him beige. One of Trei's best attributes was his smile, his naturally white, perfect teeth. He could con a con man. One quick smile and the contract was already signed. His experience with women was the same way. Some of them just opted to be Trei's friend, so that they could just kick it to stop from getting their heart broken. Like JJ, Trei too had a temper, but not just for anything and definitely not women. His temper was about getting his money and all of it. If it was not about money to him, it just did not make any sense. You virtually had to have some money to get some of Trei's time unless he needed or wanted you, and today, he wanted Jada. As he and JJ walked up Fifth Street talking about money, something caught his eye, not just something, but exactly someone. JJ captured a glimpse of these features too. They could not take their eyes off this beautiful woman walking out of the library. One part of them opted to let her walk away freely. Another part of them said "bet". Trei and JJ were up to the challenge, and now, it was time to catch up with her before she vanished.

Approaching her calmly after catching his breath do to running, Trei said, "Hi, Ms—". He waited for her to fill in the space with her name as he extended his hand out to shake hers while attempting to capture his breath. JJ was envious of his friend for beating him to the greeting. Jada extended her hand after she managed to gain control of her library books and purse, all while checking both sides of the street for traffic. She did not look happy extending it. Trei was wasting her time.

"Jada Wells," she said trying to brush him off quickly. She did not feel like conversing with anyone. "Now if you don't mind," she said walking across the street after witnessing no oncoming traffic going or coming and the walk light on. She was focused on her research paper.

"I'm Trei, with an E and I instead of an A and Y." He said with a great smile and light chuckle as he hurriedly tried to keep up with her. Jada gave way to a slight smile, which meant, '*get the hell on already*'. Trei seemed content to talk to her, so she said, "Oh really, so tell me something, Mr. Trei with an-E.I., instead of—A.Y.," she said with a timid smile. "What do you want—my body? Cause I know that's why you stopped me." The smile suddenly disappeared from her face. Trei laughed at her sense of humor. He liked it. She could be Mrs. Trei Styles he thought to himself.

Stopping the laugh quickly because Jada was not laughing and JJ, who was standing beside him, did not respond, Trei said to Jada, "Not exactly, what I really want is your mind and heart. Your body will just fall in place." He said with a smile. Jada thought, '*nice teeth but that don't mean nothing.*'

"Oh," said Jada appearing to loosen up with a nice smile, wanting to converse more with Trei. However, she was interrupted by JJ, who decided that it was time for him to talk. "Man—she don't want to hear that mess." He said as he shoved Trei out of his way. Jada was shocked by his behavior. The look in her eyes did not cause JJ to refrain from interrupting her conversation with Trei. JJ continued, "What's up baby? I'm JJ."

"Okay," she said tightening her posture up again, apparently loosening up was the wrong idea.

"So let me guess—you want my body too?" She asked very arrogantly. She was determined to burst his confidence and soon. Trei eyed JJ coldly. He knew that JJ was about to ride down stupid avenue, again.

"Yeah," JJ said to Jada being very direct with an unconcerned smile. Trei thought to himself, '*he's on Stupid Avenue. Man all he needs now is a dead end.*' Leaving his thoughts behind, Trei listened to JJ continue. "It would put an end to all of this yipping and yapping. Honestly, I feel no need to beat around the bush." He said as he gestured with his hands. Trei looked at him as though he was really stupid now. Jada did not like what she was hearing at all. She was listening to the voice of stupidity.

"Um, huh—you are very honest, aren't you?" Jada asked JJ as she looked at him closely, searching him.

"I try to be." He responded as he looked up and down at her body, back at her face and tilted his head.

"I like that," she said, "and very direct too, huh?" She asked.

"I try to be." He said sticking out his chest boldly with a slight rub across it.

"I don't like that." She said. "I must say though—I should say though," she looked at Trei before looking back at JJ. "I like the heart and mind theory better. You gentlemen have a nice day." She said walking ahead of them quickly.

"Man, why did you have to say that?" Trei asked JJ after Jada walked away.

"Man, forget her." JJ said in a low voice as he stood face to face with Trei. "She ain't all that. She gone come in though." He said smiling as he turned to watch Jada walk away. "First impressions ain't always right."

"Now is where you're on Stupid Avenue, again—and you're wrong." Trei said to JJ as he watched Jada hurriedly walk down the sidewalk.

"Stupid Avenue, and just what do you mean wrong?" JJ shoved Trei to get his attention. Trei was focused on Jada.

"Watch this? Come on and learn a thing or two." Trei told JJ before running off. Catching up with Jada and walking side by side with her, Trei said, "Ms Jada—why don't you allow me to carry those books for you? You look like you could use some help." She was skeptical as she looked at him, but eventually, she handed over the books to him—shocked by his sudden impulse to help.

"Oh, thanks. Trei—right?" She asked.

"Yeah, but you must promise me one thing, though?" Trei asked.

"What's that? That I owe you one?" She said with a smile as they began to walk down the sidewalk together.

"No . . . and yes-that's if you would rather look at the situation that way." He said looking at her for a brief moment with a smile. '*Nice teeth,*' she thought. '*You've already noticed that,*' she remembered. Trei continued to speak, "however, what I meant to say was that you should never forget a polite introduction, especially a name. That would be kind of rude to the converser and hurt his feelings." He said stopping in his tracks with an awkward smile, looking into Jada's eyes. She laughed.

"So, in other words, I hurt your feelings?" She asked. JJ wanted to know what Trei was up to.

"That would be correct." He said as he stopped to bow, holding on to her books. They continued to walk together again. JJ, keeping the pace and walking behind them, could not understand why Trei was being so nice, extra nice, especially when he could be rude.

"I'm sorry. But I don't know you. Did you ever give me your last name?" Jada asked Trei.

"No," Trei said. He knew that she had won. He knew that it took more than just your first name to be defined under name. He had not told Jada his last name.

"Then, I don't know you then, do I?" She asked.

"It's Trei Styles." He said as he turned around to see if JJ was still walking behind him and Jada. JJ waved him off. "So, why so many books from the library? Do you have some kind of report to do?" Trei asked.

"Yeah, I have a twelve page research paper due next week." Jada replied with a deep breath.

"On what?" Trei asked.

"Love," she said turning to capture his expression. He was shock but only briefly as he widened his eyes in surprise and tilted his head with a smile.

"What about love?" Trei asked calmly. JJ eyed his friend boldly, trying to figure him out. He couldn't let Trei win the bet. He knew that he had to do something and now was a good time for him to step into the conversation.

"Ahhh," said JJ from behind Trei and Jada. Jada stopped and turned around abruptly to see him behind her. "You don't need all them books for that. I can tell and show you all bout Love." He said while laughing. Some how, Jada could not sense that he was being honest.

"Really," said Jada. JJ nodded his head up and down with a smile. "I don't think so." She replied. Rethinking the matter she said, "On second thought, just in case I cannot be wrong, what could you possibly know about love, with the way that you talk and all?" He laughed at her sense of humor. She laughed as well but only in sorrow. Her humor stabbed him. However, now wasn't the time for him to let her know.

"I know more than you could imagine Ms Jada. Want to explore? Besides, JJ and Jada sound good together, better than Jada and Trei, and they don't call me the love doctor for nothing." He said laughing and feeling foolish at the same time. He was away from his comfort zone. For a guy who was dark and handsome, it usually didn't take this long to win a woman over.

"I'm sorry—was I suppose to laugh? I didn't exactly get that one." She replied. "Honestly, no need to beat around the bush with this yipping and yapping as you so eloquently put it earlier with your consequential euphuism-slang. I cannot imagine exploring anything with you," she said with what sounded like just a pinch of satire in her voice, "not even if you and I were on a hot desert naked and alone and my body and mind urged the touch of a man. And as far as the episode on JJ and Jada, that'll never happen in this lifetime. That is for the birds better known as fools." She said. JJ suddenly stopped with his laughing. She was mocking him in a satiric way. She had gone too far. She crossed over the line of respect to disrespect. She pushed the button that was never often pushed. She was good and bad at the same time and that twisted and turned his blood and nerves on the inside. She continued with a smile, "besides, this report is about re-search. So you have to search for the answers from a professional perspective and back it up with evidence also known as data—although the word you may choose may be proof, and I don't believe that you are a professional." She continued. Trei was stunned at what just happened. He had to stop her before JJ got really mad.

"Okay, you all. Let's stop with all this commotion, ah-ight?" Trei asked.

"I think that you need to teach your friend some manners." She said.

Powerless over what had just happened, JJ started to lash out at Jada. Not only was he losing the bet, but he was losing his power to control the situation. "Hoe, he ain't gotta teach me nothing. I'm my own man." JJ said pointing at his chest.

"Really," she said eyeing him coldly with one hand on her hip. *'Did he just go there?'* She thought. "Hoe, now isn't that a poor choice of words. What happened? Did that mind holding that vocabulary of yours become a little too short?" She said holding short in the two finger sense using her thumb and forefinger.

"Forget you. I don't know why I decided to waste my time with you anyway." JJ confessed.

"You know—I was kind of wondering the same thing-low self esteem, huh? I'm sorry. Have I offended thee?" She asked.

"Girl, shut up before I make you!" JJ exclaimed.

"I would love to just see you do that." She said with a smile while dropping her purse and some of her books to the ground.

JJ, drawing forth one of his hands in an attempt to strike Jada was stopped by Trei. "JJ, stop it man! This whole thing has been blown out of proportion."

"No his anger is what's out of proportion." Jada said very upset by the ticking bomb and holding her position. She was not afraid of the monster threatening her. Even if she were, she was not going to back down.

"Come on Jada. A woman of your educational background should not be picking fights." Trei said. Jada did not like his comment. Trei could tell, so he decided to fix his words into a more pleasing manner. "I'm surprised at you." He said with a smile looking into her eyes as he held on to JJ.

"Well," she said calmly. "He started it, and I don't want him to think that his street attitude offends me."

"Jada, you're doing it again." Trei said.

"Okay, okay, I quit. All of this was prone to happen, but I quit . . ." she said looking at Trei. She then turned to JJ and said, "Look, JJ, I don't particularly care for you right now . . ." JJ was about to speak. "Hold on, before you lash out again, but maybe we can start over and clear all of this up—somehow." She finished with a crooked smile to let him know that she did not mean what she was saying and that anytime he felt like he was ready, she would be also. Looking back at Trei for a second, she said, "I'll take my books now. This is where we depart from one another. I like you Trei—I mean your attitude." She said, looking into Trei's eyes before she glanced at JJ, mocking him with a quick stare she gave. "Why don't you call me," she said turning back to Trei and pulling a card from her purse with her phone number on it. Trei was excited about the whole thing. She had just almost won him a bet.

Taking the card with a smile, he said, "Yeah." As Jada turned the corner to walk away, Trei watched, putting the card in his back pocket.

JJ was not happy about what had just happened. Jada had pushed all of his buttons at once and made him look like the scum under her shoe. Looking both ways to cross the street, JJ said to Trei after he noticed how happy he was, "You know she did all of that just to make me mad. She felt sorry for you."

"Did what?" Trei asked.

"Gave you that card stupid. It wasn't your pretty boy looks and good hair that got you that card. I know what she was doing. I ain't no dummy." He replied.

"Oh, and that's not why she gave me the card?" Trei replied with an arrogant smile.

"Yes—no!" JJ exclaimed.

"I agree. She gave it to me because she saw how quick your attitude would take her down a straight dead end. You did hear her, didn't you?" Trei asked him.

"Like I said before, forget her, and she gone pay for all that mess she started. She wished she did have a well groomed man like me to bow down to her. You do know that a woman not capable of controlling a situation is powerless, right?" He said rubbing his hand down his cleanly shaven beard.

"I believe that saying goes both ways. Why did you let her get to you like that?" Trei asked.

"Man, that incident was prone to happen."

"I believe that's exactly what she just said." Trei replied.

"Anyway, I blame you—trying to act like a gentleman. You know you ain't no gentleman, and just wait til she find out. I'm going to laugh in her face." JJ said.

"JJ, does your brain carry a short vocabulary?" Trei asked, mocking his friend with what JJ had just confessed.

"Man forget you and her. You think—I'm playing. This bet ain't over yet. You gotta get her on your done list first, and I'm gone beat you to it." JJ replied.

"How?" Trei asked. "I don't recall her giving you a card."

"Just don't cry when I do." JJ said with a concerned smile as one of his thick eyebrows moved. Trei knew that JJ was about to play dirty.

Chapter 9

OBSESSIVE OVERLOAD

Trei ignored JJ's intention for months. He expected JJ to still try and win Jada honestly, so that he could win the bet. JJ did not like to lose. He expected to win all the time. Trei was never mad when he did. He always congratulated him. Jada consorted an enemy that day, and she didn't even know it. From that day forward, the closer Trei and Jada got, the madder JJ became. He became obsessed with having Jada first. He envied her hazel eyes and her small slender body. Her naturally curly hair, expressed goodness to him, and her smile haunted him. JJ felt like she was mocking him all the time. She did not take him seriously. He hated the idea that she treated him like a little kid, giving him a do over lesson, and trying to make him grow up and become educated. He did not like what she was doing to him and his consumption of drugs and alcohol was only getting worse.

Meanwhile, Trei stepped in often and broke up the battles between Jada and JJ. Sometimes he grew increasingly exhausted about both of their attitudes. He even thought that meeting Jada was a bad idea, mainly, because JJ could not get along with her and often talked about what he would do to her. His ideas went from killing by stabbing or affixation to running over her with a car. Trei would often tell JJ to let it go, but JJ was persistent and his ideas were continuously growing. Trei could not see any way of calming JJ down as JJ's ideas were becoming a little redundant.

Likewise, things were not in Trei's favor either. He had been talking to Jada for six months now, and she still had not given up the booty. As much as he tried, he was rejected, and he was tired of robbing, thieving, drug trafficking, and carjacking to provide her a luxurious lifestyle, so that he could finally beat his best friend in a bet—a bet that he had paid several times. Trei thought that going to fancy restaurants, walking in parks, attending theatre, and buying expensive clothing, bags, jewelry, and shoes was getting out of hand. He always made sure he took care of himself and not a woman. He had more without Jada than before he gained her. Besides, he felt like a fake. He missed being as terrible as his other gang friends, and his nice guy attitude was beginning to suck. He started to think that she was mocking him and that JJ was right when he said that Jada only felt sorry for him when she gave him her phone number. He imagined that it was his beige, good looks. His thoughts were starting to get as wild as JJ, but not to the point of killing Jada. He had done things for Jada that he had never done for any woman. He wanted what he deserved, her body. He was tired of being romantically involved with other women to avoid asking Jada for sex. He wanted sexual intimacy with Jada, but Jada was too smart to give in. She knew her potential. She was not like any other girl that he had met. She did not feel pity for him when she brushed up against the accident inside his pants. That did not turn her own. Trei thought, laughingly sometimes, when he was alone, high and away from his friends, "She is gay. She has to be to turn me down so many times."

"Six months," he said one evening out with his friends, "And I ain't no closer to getting that than I was yesterday. We still in the kissing mode, and I'm tired of blue balls. I'm starting to think that Jada's gay." He said passing the cigar to Rob one of his friends.

"Whoa! Not Mr. Too Sexy, all the women want me. Anyway, I told you what to do." Rob said.

"What?" Trei asked.

"Put something in her drink to seduce her. Let it come to you." He said with a smile.

"Knawl man, I ain't getting involved in that mess, and she scream rape. She needs to be sober when I tap on her."

"What! Man you already done paid for that." Rob said passing the cigar to Jay, another friend to Trei. Jay inhaled the cigar and passed it to JJ. Letting the smoke out of his mouth, Jay asked Trei, "so you telling me that you been talking to her for six months now and that she ain't giving up the booty with all the money you been spending?"

"Yeah man, she ain't rattling nothing but my pockets," Trei said, nodding his head up and down, starting the chain smoking line over again.

"You got to be stupid." Jay replied.

"He is," JJ said. "I told him that she only using him. I don't understand why he wit her."

"Man, tell them why you don't understand?" Trei asked JJ.

"Cause I hate her—if her mouth was on fire, I wouldn't piss down her throat-let alone throw water down it. You better be glad she chose you, because I would of done took mine by now, and my money from you!" JJ exclaimed.

"So you two made a bet?" Rob asked Trei.

"Yeah," JJ replied, "and I don't know what I was thinking."

"How much?" Jay asked.

"One grand, which he needs to give me five hundred right now," Trei said while looking at JJ.

"I ain't giving you nothing, boy. The bet was for all or nothing. And so far, what you got? Nothing!" JJ responded.

"Man, forget that." Trei replied.

"You know what it is, don't you?" JJ asked while looking at Trei. Trei said nothing. "You too soft man—you need to demand some of that from her or demand yo money back."

"Ain't nobody soft, man—just pass the cigar. You just mad cause she didn't want you." Trei replied.

"And I'm glad she didn't—now I don't have to worry about you getting my money."

Suddenly, Rob decided that it was time to change the subject. He thought that the conversation about Jada had gone far enough. "Say, y'all know her friend Necee having a party this weekend. She home from college. It's her birthday. She stopped me at the store last weekend and asked me to come."

"Oh yeah?" Jay asked. "Man, now that chick's straight up crazy."

"Yeah," Rob said while smoking on a second cigar. "Talking bout bring her a gift. I got her gift. She just can't get enough of Mr. Charlie."

"The singer?" Jay asked. "Yo, that dude can sing." Everyone looked at him strange.

"Hell no, man! Quit playing!" Rob exclaimed. "Are you even paying attention to this conversation? Ain't nobody talking bout no punk ass singer."

"Oh, I got you man." JJ replied to Rob. Everyone began to laugh at Jay at once.

"Yeah, yeah, anyway," Rob said moving his eyebrows up and down looking at Trei. "I'm going to that party, cause you know college girls ain't nothing but freaks once they get drunk." Trei did not respond to Rob's words. "Oh, I forgot-all except Jada that is."

"That's right," Trei said. "Cause she a woman—something y'all may never have."

"Yeah right," JJ replied. "Honestly Trei, I don't see how you put up with her attitude . . ."

"Why she gotta have an attitude JJ?" Trei asked.

"Seriously man, her attitude is a violation—running around here thinking that she better than everybody else, and the way that she be disrespecting you when she want something."

"Hold up now. She don't do that. She ain't never did that." Trei responded.

"Boy please, you a lie. Last week when you promised to buy them shoes and you didn't want too. She made you. And you didn't have a choice because her parents were standing side by side with y'all in Foot Action in the mall at the cash register when Jada said, pay for these. Say it ain't true? I was looking dead at you."

"Now, that ain't exactly what transpired. I promised her those for that scholarship that she got. Besides," Trei responded to defend his manhood, "it saved me some money."

"Boy, you stupid. What about that time that you had to pay her for lying?" JJ asked.

"Oh man, you got to bring that up?" Trei asked JJ. Rob and Jay, relaxing on the sofa now wanted to know what JJ was about to say next.

"What JJ?" Rob asked.

"Man, why you hating." Trei replied.

"We down by Larry and Paul's way, right?" JJ said. He ignored Trei's comment. "All of us outside talking about chicks and first date sex. Paul asked Trei if he had hit Jada yet, and Trei said yeah. Man, we knocking boots all the time. All of sudden, Jada pulls up in her dad's black Lexus. Trei runs over to the car. We didn't know why right," JJ said inhaling the cigar again. Jay and Rob nodded their heads in an up and down motion. JJ continued. "So Sheila, Larry's girlfriend runs outside because Paul calls her out to ask her if she had sex with Larry on the first date. Sheila said yeah, and that she wasn't ashamed either because it was more about her than it was about him. By this time, Jada and Trei walked up, and Paul's girlfriend Diane was coming out of the house. And you know how Paul is, right?"

"Right, always got a punch line," Rob said.

"Yeah, that's Paul." JJ replied.

"Yo, JJ man—why you gotta be telling this?" Trei asked again.

Once more JJ ignored Trei and continued with the story. "Well, Paul said to Jada. So, J, I hear you done resigned from Mary's Secret Club-finally. I don't understand what you mean she said. Paul said, the Virgin Mary. I hear that you giving it up now. Jada looked at Paul funny, right. A look that said, I want to tell the truth, but I've already agreed to lie. So Paul said to Jada, I mean to only Trei that is. Jada didn't say anything. Larry said to Trei, boy we knew you were lying. Jada jumped in and said no he's not. I'm giving it to him. She almost choked. She had to say it cause she wanted her half of a bet that Trei or us never made.

"Then where did the bet come from?" Jay asked JJ.

"If you hold up and let me finish the story, you'll know." JJ replied. He once more continued with the story, "we were all shocked and started to laugh and hit each other around, congratulating Trei. Even I was shocked that he had got her. Trei was grinning hard. All of sudden, Paul took it to the next level. Trei hadn't told Jada about the next level. Trei didn't know the next level. So are y'all on that other level yet? Paul asked Jada. Trei stopped laughing. You should have seen his face. He already beige, imagine him looking snow white. Jada said what. Paul said, you know, that oral level. Trei looked at her funny, and she looked at him. Jada was confused. All of a sudden the thought hit her and she said no. She turned to Trei and said while he was trying to make her be quiet, right. I didn't agree to all of this. You said that you would split the bet with me if I lied about the sex. So every body stopped and looked at her and Trei and said what bet? Trei said nothing. Larry asked again, what bet? That's when Jada asked, so you all didn't have a two hundred dollar bet about us either, me and Trei? No, Larry said. We just asked Trei if you and he were having sex yet. Oh, she was mad and before she could even put her hand out, Beige here," JJ said, pointing at Trei beside him, "was giving her the money. He had to give her two hundred dollars right there and tell the truth. Now say I'm lying?" JJ asked Trei. All at once, Rob and Jay started to laugh at Trei. Trei waved them off.

"Man," Trei said. "I got to go—forget this mess," he said to Rob passing him the cigar. "And you talk too much." He said to JJ as he turned to leave. All of the guys were laughing at him and choking at the same time. Rob stopped coughing for a second and said, "Yo Trei," Trei turned away from the door, "Have you even got off dreaming about it yet?"

"Ha-Ha," Trei replied before closing the door and leaving Rob's house.

Chapter 10

THE PARTY

Being home and away from studying at college this weekend, Jada decided that some good relaxation was just the thing that she needed, until a girlfriend of hers invited her to a party. Jada did not want to attend because she knew what happened at these kinds of parties (there were prone to be many men because her girlfriend liked to hang around them, and there were prone to be many drugs because her friend's, friends like to do them). So Jada declined. But after her friend Necee continued to call and motivate her-and her boyfriend Trei decided to go with her-Jada said yes. Knowing that her rival would attend, Jada decided to do some much needed meditating to calm her spirit. Breaking down JJ took a lot of energy from her. She decided if he had become too much of an obsession tonight that she would just avoid him altogether. It would not be easy. *'Obsessions never are,'* she thought to herself.

Meanwhile, where there is a good girl, a bad girl exists. Necee was that bad girl, very street smart. She could speak of anything on the streets as though she had been there and done that. Jada liked the idea that Necee was her friend because she got much needed advice from her. Necee told her about the streets, however, when Jada tried to educate Necee so that she could improve her book smartness, Necee did not want to hear it. She was content with where she was in her books, and she only attended school because her parents made her. Necee was the go-getter type. If she did not have it, she knew where to go get it. She liked games, and she loved men. Men balanced off her street smartness. Men were her life. Men were her friend. What she knew, she learned from them. She liked fast money and was into drug dealers and anyone else on a quick scheme to obtain money. Her loot was not small. She made her money and was independent. Some men she met did not like her because she could pave her own way, and they felt like they had to respect her. She liked nice clothes and high heels. Boots were her favorite because she liked to use the terminology of kicking someone to sleep in a pair, man or woman. She was very aggressive and was not easily insulted, if anything, people did not like the way that she insulted them. Sex was her favorite subject, and gin was her favorite drink, along with a little marijuana that she smoked on the side. Necee had beautiful chocolate skin and cold, black hair that was shoulder length and often pent up. She was of an average size, and she had a thin waste line that accentuated her hips. She was not a big behind woman, but a woman with a big behind, nice legs and small feet. She was about five foot five inches tall and could walk a runway if she were a model. Necee could be anything that she wanted to be. Guys loved her tom boyish attitude, sexiness, and innovative intentions. Girls loved her defense, street smartness, and ability to shut down the male ego. This girl did not have a low self-esteem. She was very confident and competitive, and nobody encouraged her to do it. She was a woman that did it on her own and was not embarrassed by it-as this weekend was her birthday, and she planned on celebrating the *hell* out of it. Yes hell.

The date was March 13th, 2004 and the crowd at Necee's party was having a ball as Necee conversed with everyone to make them feel special and not left out. The Disc Jockey represented New Orleans by playing music by Cash Money and Little Boosie. But no music was played more than Lil Boosie. Necee felt like her and Little Boosie were on the same level, so the DJ represented by playing all the Little Boosie she could handle, black market Boosie that is, because he was just being discovered world wide. Necee danced around from conversation to conversation, and Rob watched her closely, making sure that he would be in Necee's bed tonight and no one else. There were some handsome men at Necee's party, and Rob was not about to let not one of them still his light. He had to represent for his neighborhood, his woman.

Trei and Jada arrived an hour after the party started, and Jada laughed at how Necee felt confident about herself dancing away from conversations. Sometimes she wished that she was Necee to compete with the streets, and sometimes she did not. For the simple fact, Necee had too many men that she was gambling with, and she was starting to get a bad name, even though she took care of herself. Girls away at college were conversing among each other saying that Necee went both ways. Jada overheard the conversation one day in the bathroom away at school. She did not see Necee as the type of girl that slept with women, especially since her parents were Christians and often had sermons in their church expressing the outcome of homosexuality. Meanwhile, Jada just couldn't understand why JJ had not taken his eyes off of her since she arrived. Every corner she turned, he was there. She thought something was wrong as she looked down at her clothes and in the mirror at her face and hair several times to see if something was on her. It seemed as though each time she put her Champagne up to her mouth to drink, he eyed her coldly. When she eventually gave him a quick, what the hell are you staring at look, he would look away and smile.

Several hours had passed at the party, and Jada's bladder warned her that it was time go get rid of the champagne. Standing by a table listening to Trei, Necee, Rob, JJ, Paul, and Sheila talk, she decided that she had held her urine too long and excused herself after asking Trei, "Can you hold my drink until I come back?"

"Yeah, I got it baby. You going to the bathroom?" He quietly asked her.

"Yes," she said. Necee, a bit tipsy, continued talking to Trei and the others about Rob's attitude as Jada walked away.

"How bout he gone come outside," she said pointing back at Rob behind her, "a minute ago and say ain't no other dude staying her tonight."

"That's not what I said," Rob replied while inhaling a cigarette that he held to his mouth with one of his hands. Everyone began to laugh. They knew how Rob made it seem that Necee wanted him all the time.

"What you say then?" She asked as she turned to look at him face to face.

"I'm high. I don't know what I said." Rob replied. Everyone knew that he was lying.

"Oh, you don't huh?" She asked with her hands on her hips looking at him before she turned to look at Trei. "Um, glad you don't. Let me go over here and see what's up with Favio then." She replied, attempting to walk away to the other side of the room where Favio stood before Rob grabbed her by the arm.

"Man quit playing." He said seriously. Everyone else continued to smile at the pleasant but jealous act by Rob. They knew that Necee had the upper hand.

"Tell'em what you said then?" Necee replied. Rob did not say anything. He just looked into her eyes, and he knew that she was serious. "Oh, you ain't gone tell it? Didn't you say that outside a minute ago?" Everyone waited quietly for his response.

"Yeah man! It ain't no big deal." He replied. Necee laughed. The others did too. Rob did not like being fronted, considering a man of his stature—tall, cute, muscular and just football fine.

"Remember the other day," Trei said turning to put Jada's glass on the stand behind him and reaching into his pocket to get a cigarette. Before lighting the cigarette, he pointed it at Rob and said, "laughing catches. See how it caught you?"

"Man forget all of that," Rob said looking away and taking another puff of the cigarette with a little anger. Necee saw that she had embarrassed him.

"Let me quit playing. I'm sorry baby." She replied as she turned and placed one hand on his face, puckering up his lips and shaking his head from side to side. "You know—I don't want Favio. He's too pretty. Besides, he ain't even like you-at least I don't think." She said, not so sure of herself as she looked across the room at Favio. Smiling and turning back toward Rob, she said, "I need somebody with a little, Lil Boosie in them-like me!" She exclaimed to Rob looking down at her figure. Again, the others began to gesture and laugh. JJ widened his eyes at the idea and eased over behind Trei and the others against the table.

"Don't start again Necee," Rob said. "I ain't in the mood for this."

"For what? A sex lecture?" She asked Rob? "Oh, so you don't want me, all of this?" She was speaking and advertising her body at the same time.

"That's that alcohol that got you acting like this." Rob replied.

"No it ain't." She said.

"Ah man," Paul said. He was a friend of Rob's. "Here we go again. I may as well roll another cigar."

"May as well," Necee said to Paul standing beside Rob. Turning to Rob she said. "Tell 'em you don't want me. Better yet, tell 'em how you sing my name."

"Necee," he called out, "Do we have to do this every time? That's all you talk about."

"Listen at him, sounding like a little girl." Necee said turning back to Rob's friends. "That's the way um suppose to sound! You need to stop spoiling the party and help live it up. It's my birthday! Let me have some fun."

"That's all you seem to be doing, in fact, that's what you been doing all night. I figured you would be done had enough by now. Every time you put that gin in you, you start talking about sex." Rob responded.

"You wanna talk about something else," she asked, blinking her eyes several times at him? "Better yet, hold that thought." She said before calling out to a guest across the room, "Ray, bring me that gin over there."

"See, now that's what I'm talking about. Necee, don't you think that you done had enough?" Rob asked.

Not liking what Rob said, she replied, "No, that's exactly what I don't think. You need to loosen up." Ray soon brought the gin over to her and she said, "Thanks, Ray-Ray. Hey!" she called out to him as he was walking away. "Where's Renee?"

"Jamal's sick. She decided to stay home with him." He replied.

"Yeah?" Necee asked, wondering why Ray was at the party.

"Yeah," Ray replied, attempting to go back to the other side of the room before Necee spoke again.

"Then tell me something, why aren't you home too?" She said lightening a cigarette after she put the gin bottle on the table.

"Don't worry Necee. I got permission, happy birthday." He said with a smile before walking away.

"Ah-ight, now that's what I'm talking about. You could learn a lot from Ray-Ray, Rob." She watched Ray as he walked to the other side of the room where his friends were.

"What? Ray-Ray married and anyway he whipped." Rob said.

Necee looked at Rob with a smile and said, "See, that's why you could learn something from him. You ain't exactly whipping up nothing these days." She said after puffing on her cigarette. Everyone laughed at Rob, and Jada soon returned from the bathroom.

"Save that." Rob said.

Tapping Trei on the shoulder now was Jada, "Baby, where's my drink?" She asked-noticing the glass was not in his hand.

"Oh, here it is." He turned around to the table behind him and picked up the drink.

"I asked you to hold it." Jada responded in a low but careful tone-that was almost harsh.

"I know. I just sat it down to get a cigarette. It has only been a second since I sat it down J." Trei said, giving her the glass of Champagne. Jada was very skeptical about the drink. She eyed everyone around her before attempting to put the chalice up against her mouth. JJ smiled. "I can get you another glass J." Trei responded after observing the look on Jada's face.

"No, it's okay." She said not sure of herself. She began to drink the Champagne. She didn't want to spoil the party for everyone.

After witnessing her friend be a good sport, Necee said, "I'll be back y'all." She needed to go and say hello to some arriving guests across the room. They were coming in through her front door.

"Necee crazy." Paul said about to light up a cigar as he stood next to Sheila. "And where in the hell did Diane go?" He asked after remembering that she was holding his marijuana stash. "Hold this Sheila." Paul said to Larry's girlfriend. "I'm about to find her. She think-she slick. She won't smoke my dope up tonight and then them sluts she call friends don't wanna up nothing."

"Boy, you stupid," Rob said to Paul before he walked away.

"Hold up, Paul." JJ said as he looked away from Jada.

Trei asked Rob when he, Jada, and Sheila were alone. "Man, why you let Necee get to you like that?"

"Man, Necee crazy. You know how she is when she get that gin in her, can't nobody tell her nothing. Even if you had her," Rob said looking at Trei and then Jada to defend his point, "no offense Jada—you couldn't control her, Trei." Looking away from Trei, Rob said to Sheila, "Let me get that cigar."

Sheila passed him the cigar and said, "keep it. I'm going to find Larry. I'm ready to go home. Have you seen him?" She asked Rob.

"He out there by the pool." Rob responded.

"Where them half naked chicks at? Oh, no!" Sheila exclaimed before walking away. Everyone laughed.

"Girl calm down. They playing cards out there." Rob said as he lit the cigar.

"Calm down!" She exclaimed while turning around to look at Rob. "I ain't the one scared to let Necee talk. You whipped too-just like Ray-Ray." She said as she walked away.

"That's a lie!" Rob replied.

"You hear that Necee?" Sheila said, stopping Necee before she made it to her guests. "Rob said he ain't whip."

"That's right Sheila." Jada said with a smile out of nowhere, watching Sheila walk away. "Go get your man." Trei and Rob, both shocked by Jada's attitude, turned to look at her.

"What!" Jada exclaimed, noticing how Trei and Rob looked at her.

"Baby, you ah-ight?" Trei asked. "That champagne ain't doing nothing to you, is it? I mean sexually." Trei said coughing up a smile. Jada hit him on the shoulder. Not even she knew what was happening.

"That's what I'm wondering," Rob said in agreement with Trei.

"I know why he wondering," Necee said walking over and catching Rob off guard. She was speaking on Trei's behalf. "But why are you?" She asked Rob.

"Yeah Necee! That's what I want to know," Trei said, putting his beer bottle down on the table to get another cigarette from his pocket.

"Well, y'all know she ain't," Rob was trying to defend himself, wondering why Jada was acting strange, "Man, y'all know what I'm saying." Confused, he said, "I'm bout to go get something to eat and go outside."

"You hungry?" Necee asked him. "I got something you can eat. It don't come in no can though, and it's already hot, fresh out the microwave." Necee said with a sense of humor. Everyone laughed accept Rob. He did not find what Necee said out loud funny. "Oh, don't act like you never had a hot plate before." Everyone awed Rob and laughed at Necee's sense of humor again.

"Girl, you crazy." Rob said, holding the cigar between his fingers as he scratched his nose. He did not know how to get to Necee. Nothing that he said ever worked. "Yo Trei, you coming with me," Rob asked?

"Trei ain't gay." Necee said to confuse Rob and twist his words, "but I'll come with you." Everyone continued to laugh at him.

"That ain't—what I was saying." He said hesitantly, trying to defend the words he used.

"Then say something else." She said perking her lips with the last word.

"Let's go Trei." Rob said very tired of the conversation with Necee.

Trei turned to Jada and asked after the laugh, "You okay, baby?"

"Yeah, I think that I am going to go get another glass of champagne," she said pointing backwards at the kitchen. "You go ahead. I'm gone talk to Necee. I'll catch up with you."

"You sure you don't want me to get the champagne for you?" Trei asked.

"No, I'm fine. I can get it." Jada responded.

"Yo Trei, come on, man." Rob said waiting for him.

"Better gone Trei, you know yo friend ain't got no sense of humor." Necee said before a strange thought surfaced in her head.

"Man, I coming. Learn how to talk and stop walking away from Necee." Trei said.

Before Trei could walk away, Necee reached out and grabbed him by the arm and asked, "Trei, you sure you a thug?" She was all over him. He could smell the gin on her breath. Jada watched as her friend almost drooled over her man.

"Why you ask that?" He responded with a gaffe.

"Cause, I believe you faking. You know, considering all that gentleman stuff that you do." Necee replied.

Trei found what she said very amusing, "Ah man, shut up girl. You drunk." He said pushing her away from him.

"Seriously, though Trei, Rob needs some training, then I might straighten up." She said before Rob and Trei walked away. She turned to Jada and said, "J, you might need to give that boy some." Thinking of the words she had just said and seeing the expression on Jada's face she said, "On second thought, no! Let's go get you another glass of champagne."

Everyone seemed to be mingling well at the party. No one had decided to throw a fight yet, and Necee did not plan on one. All she wanted to do was chill to the words of Lil Boosie that the Disc Jockey played; hyped by the words of Lil Boosie's song 'Distant Lover' she began to sing, after saying, "You hear that Jay? Yeah! That's what Rob be saying when I'm away at school and not here. He be missing me," she began to sing the words of the song. "I wish that I could touch you everyday, touch you in every way, but you stay so many miles away, distant lover, so many miles away, distant lover, so many miles away," she sang, pouring Jada's champagne.

"Girl, you are crazy." Jada said laughing at her friend. "Lil Boosie has gotten to you." She said as though she was out of her natural state of mind. Necee noticed that her friend's demeanor had changed.

"You okay, Jay?" She asked.

"Yeah, let's go outside and get some air." Jada said not so sure of herself.

"You sure you okay, J?" Necee asked again.

"Yeah, I'm fine. Give me my drink." She said trying to be certain that she was okay.

"How many is this for you tonight?" Necee asked Jada.

"Why, you trying to be cheap?" Jada replied.

"No, seriously, I wanna know. I have plenty more to go around. Ain't nothing about Necee cheap."

"Well, this is my second glass, and honestly, I'm feeling a little tipsy, like I've had something stronger. Is this the kind I always have or did you spike it with something stronger?" Jada asked Necee.

"Yeah, that's the same kind." Necee said calmly, not sure of what Jada was saying, "What do you mean by spiking it and with what? I just opened that bottle. I wouldn't do that to you J."

"Um, huhn, you know that you're always telling me that I am boring." Jada said with a sense of humor. Necee found her new spirit amusing. Jada gave Necee a strange look. "Just kidding girl. Calm down. It ain't that serious," she said waving Necee off with a slow gesture. "Come on. Let's go outside where the fellows are."

"J, can I ask you something serious?" Necee asked.

"What's up?" Jada asked.

"What's up? Now that's something new from you, but seriously have you and Trei done it yet?"

"Nope," she answered, checking out her surrounding.

"Why not," Necee asked?

"Girl, he is not the one. Besides, I feel like once he has gotten it-that he'll be on his way. That's why I'm so hard on him."

"Girl, that's the wrong way to feel." Necee said as her and Jada made their way through the living room of Necee's apartment. "What's wrong with having a little fun before your life becomes real serious?"

"What's wrong with not having a little fun and making your life just what it is-serious. You know Necee, I may be wrong, but I think that the way I feel now is the right way.

Besides, this is sex that we're talking about here-not just a date at the movies, and I want my first time to be just what it's suppose to be, my first time, and not my last."

"Don't go 101 Psychology on me, J. Tell me exactly what you saying here?" Necee asked.

"Well, it's just that I want my first time to be with someone that I love and—"

"So you don't love Trei?" Necee asked.

"Can I finish?" Jada responded. Necee decided to listen. "I want my first time to be with someone that I love and I know that I love him, and I want him to love me back and mean it, every word of it. I just feel like if men want what we ladies have between our legs and that's all, then why don't they just say that? It could ease a lot of heart ache and pain in the long run."

"Because, J." Necee said.

"Because what?" Jada asked.

"It's just not naturally in them to just say it. It would defeat the purpose."

"Do you know how you sound, right now? Like a fool. Like one of them. This is about being honest Necee, not natural." Jada replied.

"Honest, natural, there both the same thing and face it, some women just don't want men, just like some men just don't want women." Necee said.

"That may hold some truth, but in a natural way like God made Adam and Eve, and not Eve and Eve to love one another, I want to be loved by a man. I believe that it makes the whole issue with sex much better, more understanding, and righteous without consequences."

"Forget about all of that for right now. I have no time for it. I chased that dream a long time ago with my daughter's father, and he treated me like crap." Necee said, after noticing that Jada seemed to be behaving strange to her.

"Now Necee, that's the wrong way to feel." Jada said, scratching her neck and checking her arms, strangely. Jada concluded, "Maybe it wasn't love for him as it was for you. See that's what I was saying a minute ago. You loving him, and he loving you and the both of you know it."

"I don't think so J. I don't want love to step into my life right now and no time soon. I wanna have fun, not be tied down to one guy." Necee said as her and Jada stepped out of Necee's patio and into the pool area. Everyone was doing something as she could see-from playing pool, cards, shooting dice, getting stoned, and playing dominoes-to just conversing and laughing.

"Doing what you do, Necee?"

"What do you mean?" Necee asked Jada.

"Let's face it Nene, you don't wanna grow up. You're afraid to gain some courage and spice it up with a little wisdom in your life. You're scared to see what doing right really feels like."

"Girl, what in the hell are you talking bout?" Necee asked her friend.

"Nene, you know exactly what it is that I'm saying. Alexes deserves more than this." Jada said, speaking of Necee's daughter. This rugged, drug life-full of fun-that you want. Selfish was supposed to have been left on that labor bed the moment Alexes was born."

"Has Mr. Rayborn been teaching about this in Psych class? Are you saying that I don't take care of Alexes?" Necee asked.

"I did not say that—of course you do." Jada said, paranoid even more now. Something was wrong with her. She felt dizzy.

"I know—I do. She got more than I ever had as a kid and then some, J. I know some people who don't even buy their kids s nothing. I'm forever spending money on her."

"I'm not talking about that Nene." Jada said as they stopped in front of the pool. The water looked different to Jada. It looked polished and not for real.

"Then what are you saying, J?" Necee said, smoking a cigarette.

"You know what. This is why I don't like to have these conversations with you because you're too sensitive about it. You act like important issues should not be discussed, like its okay for you to judge, but no one can judge you. I'm only trying to be your friend, and friends tell the truth to one another."

"Nope and no, no, forget that Jay. What do you mean by what you said earlier?"

"This is not about your baby's father Nene. This conversation is about you and what you should do for Alexes." Jada said, looking at Necee, or someone for that matter-with her drink in her hand.

"Okay, then what I'm I not giving her?" Necee asked.

"Time . . . time Nene. And how about some love and understanding and not go set your but down sometime, or I'm taking you to mom and dad, or do your homework by yourself, and lets not forget, I ain't going to no PTA meeting, so don't ask. I'll see what the problem is when you bring your report card home." Jada said before continuing, "And you brag about this mess with your so called other friends who have kids, like it's nothing, and what about bringing all these different guys around her? Stuff like that? You're taking that child's guidance and her life. How about giving her a little understanding, so that Alexes can embark and set goals for her own life, not carry on your legacy using the status quo version of my mother did it, so can I. She needs to live to do something for herself, not repeat the history that Nene planned for her, especially if it's bad."

"Wow! That's a lot Jay. You know, this musta been on yo-mind for sometime. I can't believe that you just said all them things to me. You really know how to take someone's birthday away, and I was claiming mine. Forget you. I'm going to play some dominoes." Necee replied. She then walked away to the domino table where some of her girlfriends were playing.

Jada thought that she may have been a little out of line, but she knew that she was right as she thought, '*damn Jay, you managed to ruin you're best friends birthday party.*' Taking a sip of her champagne and then another and standing alone by the pool, she spotted Trei and his friends playing cards across from her. She decided that she would walk over and promised herself that she would not ruin his night as she had Necee's—that is if she could just move from the place that she was standing in. The champagne was really taking a toll on her vision and brain. It seemed that her alcohol level was steadily increasing with every sip. She wanted to keep moving in order to gain her sober consciousness back again. Before she could even plan to put one feet before the other, JJ was behind her, and breathing down her neck.

"So," he said. "Look like you done gained yo-self some downtime, alon . . . ."

"Lay off, JJ, okay." She turned around and said, noticing that she could still move her feet if she wanted to and fast. She then turned her back to him again.

"Oh, I will, and soon. You have fun with that drink. Then again, I wonder what happens to other people's drink when some people ain't responsible enough with it. Maybe you should go lie down before you go over to that card table and dilute Trei's winning spree. You don't look to good, and we know that Trei is no good for you unless he has some money . . ."

"Back off! I left Rover at home to go fetch. Necee has people at this party to play with, not dogs." She said turning to look at him. She could see something bad in JJ's eyes. He turned with a sly smile and walked away.

JJ was the easiest of Jada's problems; at least, that is what she thought. She could not understand what was happening to her. Her body felt weak. Her eyes were heavy, and all she wanted to do was lie down. Something was not right with her physically. She recalled eating before she came to the party, and she could not understand why the alcohol was weakening her all of a sudden. It seemed as though she had taken some kind of a drug. Her head was beginning to ache, and her hearing was in and out as she could feel her heart beating heavily and fast.

Chapter 11

A NEED FOR CONCERN

Sitting at the table, not too far from where Jada was standing, Necee could sense that something was definitely wrong with Jada. She was edgy and moody, and very straight forward tonight and scared, like a psychic knowing that something is about to go wrong. Necee also noticed that Jada was picking on her skin a lot. However, Jada, on the other hand, was in a daze, and it appeared as though someone had turned her body off, like a dummy with facial expressions suggesting that something was wrong or telling a story. Necee saw JJ walk up to Jada, but that's all she saw, trying to keep up with her winnings on the domino table. Jada's demeanor had changed, and it had changed quickly. Taking her feelings into consideration, how Jada had hurt them, once and then twice, Necee pushed them aside and decided to go and check on her friend. Besides, she did practically beg her to attend her party.

"Sasha," Necee called out to a friend, standing across the table from her and waiting to play dominoes again. "Play my hand of dominoes til I come right back. Don't lose or you gone give me back my money."

"Yeah," Sasha said. She was happy at the chance to play another hand of dominoes again, since she had lost a lot of money earlier.

"I ain't playing—you lose-I want my money." Necee said playing a domino and getting up.

"Whatever Nene. Move girl. I got this." Sasha replied before sitting at the table.

"Okay, y'all hear her right," Necee said to the other card players and watchers. That's gone be yo-behind, since you been begging to play to get yo money back. Laugh, and think it's a game. I'm already sized and vested up to put a beat down on you." Everyone laughed. Sasha smiled.

"Whatever . . . girl gone. I got this," she said waving Necee off before she put her cigarette up to her mouth and picked up the dominoes.

"What's up, Tiny?" Necee said to another friend as she walked away from the table.

"What's up, birthday girl?" Tiny replied with a high five and a smile.

"Lil Boosie popping ain't he?" Necee said dancing to the music.

"Yeap!" Tiny said laughing. "Here it comes, cause you a bad chick!" Tiny said, knowing that the Disc Jockey was about to play that song from the sound of the music."

"That's what I'm talking bout, uh, huhn . . . check you later." Necee responded before moving on.

"That Necee crazy bout Boosie." Tiny stated to the others as Necee danced away.

"Yeah," everyone said with an up and down nod.

Dancing her way closer to Jada with a step to the left and then the right and some behind work, Necee was feeling great. She almost forgot what Jada had said to her earlier until she approached her. "J," she called out. "What's wrong baby, you okay?" Jada did not respond. She seemed to be in a trance and slowly coming out of it. "J," Necee called her again, this time tapping her on the shoulder to gain her attention.

"Yeah-huhn?" Jada responded.

"What's wrong wit you? You standing here like you ran into a dead end-and fast. What's up?"

"Necee, something is wrong." Jada replied. She wasn't feeling well.

"I know. That's what I just said, and I'm not mad about what happened earlier." Necee replied.

"No Necee. Something is really wrong with me." Jada said after checking her surroundings.

"So my feelings don't count? What's wrong with you?" Necee said when she sensed that Jada did not care.

"My head is killing me, and I feel a little nauseous. I'm weak all over Nene in some kind of a way, and I'm feeling dizzy and confused."

"Oh, it's just the alcohol kicking in. It'll pass." Necee replied.

"No Nene. You promise that this hasn't been spiked?" She asked, referring to the champagne she held up in her glass.

"No J. I wouldn't do that. You saw me open that bottle inside." Necee replied, trying to defend her honor.

"I know. I believe someone's out to get me." Jada said.

"Girl hush. You just drunk. Stop talking crazy. You ain't got no enemies, not here anyway." Necee said with a hand gesture.

"I don't know Nene." Jada said, moving her head from side to side.

"Then again, JJ is here." Necee said jokingly and looking around for JJ. Jada did not laugh. "However, you have to admit, he been kinda cool tonight on all subjects."

"Something is not right. I can feel it Nene." Jada replied. Her speech was starting to slur.

"Come on. Let me help you inside to go lie down for a minute. You just haven't drunk nothing in a while. You'll be okay. I got some Tylenol in the medicine cabinet in my room. Take two and lay across my bed. Don't . . . Do not-vomit in it. I'll lock the door and tell Trei that you decided to lie down for a minute because you weren't ready to go."

"Maybe, I just need to call my mom and go home." Jada responded.

"No girl. This ain't kindergarten, and besides, that just wouldn't look good." Necee said. She was considering her reputation.

"Why not?" Jada asked.

"Cause they'll say you drunk, and that wouldn't be nice for yo goody-to-shoe image, and it definitely won't be nice for me. You know your daddy already thinks that I am a bad influence on you." Necee said walking out of the bathroom in her bedroom. Jada was sitting on her bed.

"Yeah, perhaps you're right. Besides, I don't wanna be a party pooper for Trei, either."

"Now you talking good. Just take these two Tylenols, and you'll be okay." Necee handed Jada the two tablets. Jada put them in her mouth and chased them down with a drink of water that Necee brought from the bathroom.

"Thanks Nene. Tell Trei that I'm okay, and not to worry. Please don't say that I'm drunk-just say-say, that I have a terrible headache."

"What about, migraine," Necee asked Jada?

"No, just say headache. That's too extreme. I don't want that falling back on me with my dad being a Reverend and all."

"Okay. I got you Boo." Necee said, finding humor in her friend's vulnerability. "I cannot believe this?"

"What?" Jada said, sitting up in the bed.

"For once, yo-ass got drunk." She said laughing.

"I'm not drunk Nene. I feel as though someone has really put something in my drink-like I've been drugged."

"Yeah right, at your best friends party? Even though, you almost ruined it. The only people being drugged here are the ones that want to be that way."

"Honestly Nene. I feel drugged, and it's nothing like the vodka that you put in my cranberry juice two years ago. I did not want to come to this party. My first mind told me not too. Something terrible is wrong." She said before she began to cry.

"Don't start J. I can't deal with this emotional bull today. Catch me next week when I get my period." Necee said to cheer her friend up as she sat next to her at the end of the bed.

"Nene! This is serious." Jada interjected.

"Al-right, just calm down." Necee said. "Nothings wrong. It's all the marijuana lit up around here that you smelled earlier, playing tricks on you. Maybe you got a contact somewhere from it."

"Something is not right. Something is not right. I promise you I did not want to come here tonight because I was afraid that something terrible would happen." Jada replied, still distraught.

"Well, the only thing so far that happened tonight is you chewing me out, and I believe that I took it well." Necee said holding on to the bedroom, door knob now and listening to the music. "Come on J. I'm your best friend. Nothings wrong, and I'm not going to let anyone mess with you. Now go on and lie down. I'll be checking on you, and it's okay. I'm the only one with a key."

"But the . . . ."

"No one's coming in-especially the police. Go on and lie down. I promise to watch over you. You'll be fine with a little sleep." Necee finally convinced Jada to lie down, even though, Jada was still skeptical about being at the party. Jada sat the last bit of champagne she had left in her chalice on the night table against Necee's bed. Her eyelids became stable, and she began to feel at peace. Her body was at rest, and her heart rate slowed down. She imagined that she was over exaggerating and closed her eyes.

Chapter 12

REVENGE

It is often stated that it takes respect to gain respect. No one deserves to be disrespected or violated. For instance, men and women from the street believe that making money entitles them to pay for or take advantage of anyone or anything they want. They honestly believe from a fleshly point of view that everything has a price-when in reality money produces greed which is a sin. With the sin of greed comes evil, and evil that has no boundaries especially when drugs and heated attitudes are involved. This process is a sad situation, and the idea of respect only becomes a distant word profound but often avoided. Today, and even before today, men refer to women as bitches and whores, never thinking that they are so equal to them. Additionally, not understanding that the same God that made woman made man first, and what she learns comes from him and sometimes vice versa. Men and women debating seems like a circle of survival that could be resolved if man and woman worked together to produce the greatest virtue. However, both are often pig headed and selfish and want all of the glory for him or herself. Both would like to render the opposite sex powerless. Both live to possess the word control.

The above mentioned are things that JJ never understood. He was used to having things offered to him or taking things that did not belong to him. He was a violation of everything and constantly walked a thin line. His word was the last word or you would suffer dire consequences. Life for him was all about evil. Money and violence were his heart. What he could not pay for, he took. JJ's family despised his behavior and avoided him, realizing that his behavior was a result of his drug usage and his outside surroundings. As a toddler, he was sweet and innocent. At age 13, sweet and innocent changed to rude and bitter. The streets of New Orleans changed him and showed him a corrupt way to gain things at his own expense. His idea was to be famous. Everyone must know who he was. He was considered a small icon and an important figure until Jada came along, at least he imagined that he was.

Meanwhile, Jada recognized her worth. She was not afraid of this animal or his threats. She recognized that she owed him nothing. Her educational level, contentment and arrogance were weapons that he could not handle and far more powerful than his money and violence. However, even though, she realized her worth, she did not observe what was happening carefully. She needed to understand that she was not in an argument with just any person this time. She was in disagreement with Satan in the flesh, and he was standing right in front of her this time. Her knowledge suppressed his power and frustrated him. She rattled his every nerve when she cut him off in conversation, and she constantly twisted up his words and made him feel stupid and belittled. Now JJ was preparing to come back with a vengeance. He wanted his respect, and he would do anything to get it.

Jada slept peacefully in Necee's bed. The warm room produced relaxation and comfort. The bed was firm, and the sheets were soft to her gentle skin. Her legs felt even better. She almost froze in the short, blue jean, skirt she wore. March wind was not playing, and Necee had a tendency to not turn on the heater. Since Necee did tonight, Jada felt safe and secure from the wickedness of the world as she fell into a peaceful sleep.

Now, Trei imagined that he understood his friend's rage when it came to Jada, but he did not. Again, he imagined that it was just an ordinary game that JJ and Jada played to see who would win each time they argued. Trei believed that JJ was okay, and that Jada was no different from other people that JJ often beefed with. With this feeling in mind, he felt that there was no need to keep an eye on JJ to stop him from hurting Jada. He trusted JJ and believed that he and JJ were best friends. Besides, they had known each other for ten years and nothing could destroy that. However, Trei was wrong and was soon about to learn that no matter how long you know a person, that does not mean that you know what that person is capable of in a desperate situation.

As Necee continued to entertain her guest, JJ was on the prowl. Everyone inside of the house made their way outside to the pool area. The D.J. continued to spin Lil' Boosie for Necee as well as other artists. Drinking and continuously dancing her way from conversation to conversation around the pool, Necee finally found a stopping point with her gin bottle in one hand, a cup in the other, and a cigarette in her mouth. Trei, Paul, Rob, and Dirty, another friend of the pack, were still at the same table playing cards, gambling and talking much manly game. It took Necee to interfere with all of them. As now, it was every man for himself.

"Baby," Rob called out to Necee as he sat at the table. "Let me get five dollars off that shirt of yours." Necee had some birthday money pinned to her shirt.

"No," Necee said sitting her cup on the table and taking the cigarette from her mouth to exhale.

"It's my birthday, and it's my understanding that you ain't gave me nothing-yet," she said to Rob before the next song caught her attention. "Oh, that's my song!" The song was 'Stuntin like my Daddy' produced by the Cash Money Boys. Necee moved her body from side to side with the cigarette in one hand in the air. Rob eyed her figure heavily and then looked down at the cards in his hand. Excited by the beat and words of the song, Necee decided to pull someone into the mood with her. "You hear that Trei." She asked.

"Yeah, girl you wild." He said with a gaffe.

"But you like that, huhn? Yeah, that's what Boosie be saying-every time." She was reciting words and phrases that Lil Boosie often used in his songs.

Rob not caring about the song, said to her, "Come on Necee. Let me get five of them dollars to put on this bet."

"How bout you place a bet on this jelly," she was referring to her behind as she patted it in his face, "and see what you can win?" Sensing some embarrassment by the way Rob was looking at her she said, "You don't like that, huhn." All his friends laughed at him.

"Quit playing Necee." Rob said.

"Baby, all of this is about playing the game," she said after waving her hand displaying the whole outside area and touching the money on her shirt. "Seriously though," she said taking another puff of the cigarette before putting it out, "if you promise me something tonight that will make me shake, quiver, and maybe pass out until I give up, I'll give you a hundred." Necee said. Everyone surrounding her laughed. They knew that Necee was pulling the sex card again.

"Uh, uh," Rob said. "Not for that cheap price."

"Girl-you crazy," Paul said pointing at her.

"Nope, she wild." Trei said after exhaling smoke from his cigarette.

"And you know what that makes Rob," Necee said laughing.

All together with the spirit of their fingers, everyone looked at Necee and said, "Weak!"

"I don't know why y'all edging her on. She ain't gone last anyway with all that alcohol that she drinking." Rob said.

"A lie. I was trying to help you out." Necee said looking at Rob's private area and back at his face. "I thought that would be easy since you know your friend down there won't last long," All of Rob's friends awed him. He was surprised at Necee and a little embarrassed, but he pulled it off with a quick smile and a, "you got me." He said.

"Boy, I know." She said with a smile.

"So it's like that now?" Rob looked at Necee and asked.

"Baby, no offense, but you know that-that's the way it has always been."

"OHHH!" Dirty said.

"So Mr. Charlie ain't taking care of much after all." Jay said standing close to the table. Rob gave him a get lost look.

"Rob," Paul called out. "And let you tell it, it's all good."

"Man, forget that mess Necee talking. Y'all know that's that alcohol. Every-time."

"Um, hum," Necee said still rocking to the beat of the song. "Say you promise me to be quiet?"

"What? What kind of talk is that?" Rob asked.

"Oh, so I stuttered? Promise me something to be quiet or you about to get embarrassed." Necee said. She had not come all this way in the conversation to lose.

"You ain't got nothing to embarrass me with. You know I'm the best, the better, and the goodest, you ever had!" Rob responded. His friends awed him. Necee knew that it was time for some get back. She had to shut Rob up and for good.

"Baby, why you wanna draw some attention to yo-self like this?" She asked. She then changed the subject to something else for a few seconds, asking a friend named Dirty, "Let me get one of them cigarettes?"

"You just had one." He replied to Necee.

"Miss that, this boy done made my body pressure go up," she said. Dirty gave her a cigarette with a smile. The others laughed at her sense of humor. Dirty was ready for what she was about to say to Rob. "As it always do, when he can't please me . . ." Once again Rob's friends laughed at him.

"Now give me a light." Necee said to Dirty, standing beside him now. He put his cards down and lit her cigarette.

"Boy, place yo-bet," Trei said to Rob, who sat with his mouth open.

"So, so—I ain't the best you ever had?" Rob asked Necee. "Say, I ain't?" He asked Necee with a smile.

"Come on man," Paul said, also waiting on Rob to put up his bet.

"Rob," Necee said walking over to him and away from Dirty. All of the guys stopped for a second with the cards to hear just what Necee was about to tell Rob. "I liked you. I was gone let you make it." She said taking another puff of the cigarette and then exhaling the smoke. "You know—make it look like you had some game. Now, how should I put this." She began to think. She then drank a sip of her liquor.

"Just say it," Rob said. "Cause I know what I got and what I can do."

"See, that's just not it. You don't have it, nor can you do it." She said expressing her words clearly and harshly. His friends looked at him guffawing and laughing out loud at him. He was dumb struck at what Necee had just said. She continued, "And you will never be the best, better, and good unless I teach you too. Cause, I'm the biggest competitor you got. I-am my number one-fan."

"OOOOH . . ." All his friends said. Necee began to draw a crowd around the table. Everyone wanted to be a part of the fun.

"She got a point there, Rob." Trei said. "I'm serious right there dawg. Cause don't nobody know me like I know me."

"Right, right." Paul said in agreement with Trei with a cigarette in his mouth.

"What? Please." Rob said in disagreement with Necee. "Who be screaming?"

"Me." She responded, agreeably.

"That's what I thought. Why you out here telling these people all these lies." he said sure of himself, sure he had reclaimed his manhood. "Now! Now player!" He yelled and extended his hand to get some hand clap from Paul. Paul hit his hand. "What I said?"

"For you to move . . ." Necee suddenly said. Rob was hurt by her remark. She continued by saying, "listen here baby. I don't mean to hurt your feelings, but you don't have it in the hips. So I tried to work out a trial basis with them lips." Necee said touching his lips swiftly. Everyone laughed. She continued, "that's why you should of took that hundred dollar hit, so I could see what yo-mouth was working wit. Hello! Can I get some Dap?" She asked Sasha standing beside her. Sasha hit her hand and so did Trei.

"Man," Paul screamed while laughing. "Rob," Paul said pointing at him with a card before he turned to congratulate Necee, "You weak man. You bad Necee! I told you to leave Necee alone. Girl I need you on my team. You ready to get in the studio?" He asked Necee. She moved her head up and down.

"Whatever Necee," Rob said. "Here I was thinking you was on my team."

"I told y'all he be lying on, what you call it again?" Trei said snapping his fingers and looking at Rob for remembrance. "Mr. Charlie."

"Man miss that." Rob lashed out at Trei and said. "I hear you ain't even lying these days."

"This you and Necee's battle, don't be fronting on me." Trei said pointing his cigarette at Rob.

"So," Necee continued to address Rob.

"So what?" Rob asked. "You live to do this kind of stuff."

"You wanna place that bet on broil?" Necee asked. "She can get up to 500. Yo-mouth won't have to do that much work." Everyone laughed. Necee, calm now, asked, "You do know how to work a real woman out don't you?"

"I don't know bout all of that, but if I let you tell me, you'll turn out to be someone else, now, wouldn't you?" Rob replied. He was implying that Necee might turn out to be the male in the relationship.

"Not necessarily, and think what you want. We all got needs. I'm just telling you how to please mine-doesn't necessarily make me the man and in control. And just maybe one day—eventually-you'll satisfy someone else. Cause for the record, we ain't gone be together forever, baby. You might want to get this training in now." She said with a smile and advertising her body.

"Dang man, sounds to me like you ain't been doing yo job, player." Paul said, laughing.

"Paul's right." Trei said playing a card after Rob paid up his bet in the game.

"No, you didn't just say that, did you?" Rob asked Trei.

"Well, when you look at this situation and analyze it correctly, I ain't exactly in the same boat as you." Trei said looking at Rob.

"Well then partner, you ain't exactly looking now as being in the boat at all. Look how long you been paying for that and ain't got it yet." Rob replied.

"So in retrospect, you calling my friend a hoe?" Necee asked Rob not satisfied with his comment to Trei.

"I ain't complaining, and it ain't like I ain't getting some on the side." Trei said laughing at Rob.

"Um hum, Trei Banking Incorporated, I done heard that before." Rob said.

"So you calling my friend a hoe?" Necee asked Rob again.

"Yo-did you exactly hear me say that?" He asked Necee. He was tired of her misconstruing his words. "If anybody is saying that, it's you. All's I'm saying is she was digging for good credit and she found a gold mine in this dummy. The only problem he having now is getting her to pay up." Rob said pointing at Trei with his cards in his hand.

"Honestly Rob, it exactly sounds like hoe fits directly into this conversation." Necee said. "Don't it sound like that y'all?" She asked everyone surrounding her and the guys. They nodded their heads up and down and said, "Yeah!"

"Well, it wouldn't sound like that if you wasn't in my and Trei's conversation, Necee." He said as he looked at her for a brief moment.

"What!" She exclaimed, shocked by Rob's response. "Trei ain't the one that you should be mad at."

Trei intervened and said to Rob, "and for the record man, I gets mine. Don't e-must have to pay for it-three and four women at a time. And that's something you may not never know nothing about."

"Yeah right, from them freaks I assume, as you previously stated?" Rob asked.

"Good girls like Jada too." Trei replied.

"Tell him Trei," Necee said.

Rob wondered why she was instigating so much mess as he said to Trei, "Um hum." He then addressed Necee, "and I thought Jada was yo-friend. You allow him to talk like that around you? Some friend you are."

"Shut-up," she said. "Besides, he gotta wisk somebody with that pressure until he gets her under control. Ain't that right Trei?" Necee asked before laughing. Trei laughed, not sure who's side Necee was on now. It almost seemed as though she was admiring him.

"Like I said, he ain't getting nothing. You know Jada always popping up and cock blocking. He don't have time to do nobody else, and not even JJ will vouch for that. Now that's what's up." Rob said.

"What! Yo-ask JJ" Trei said trying to confirm his sly actions. "JJ" he called loudly trying to find his friend to come to his rescue. JJ was no where to be found. Trei hadn't heard from him for some time at the party. He wondered where he was. He also wondered where Jada was for the first time.

"Whatever, JJ be lying too, and you may as well pay them freaks cause you giving yo money to that virgin for free." Rob said.

"Man, miss that." Trei said with a smile. "Women want orgasms these days too."

"That's right." Necee laughed and said. "Now that's what's up for real."

"So, let me guess. Now you the love doctor, hum?" Rob asked Trei.

"Hell yeah," Necee said. "Didn't I just agree with him?" She asked Rob. All the women agreed with Necee.

"Well," Trei said offering Rob an explanation. "I guess that concludes that."

"Now that's sad, especially with your lack of experience-and your prescriptions must be extra weak cause Jada sho' ain't giving it up." Rob said to Trei before asking

Necee, "Yo-Necee, where Jada at anyway?" He looked throughout the crowd for Jada before saying, "Its time to shut him up for good."

"Like I made you," Necee responded to Rob before continuing. Remembering where Jada was, she said, "Oh, I forgot. She inside. She wanted to lie down for a minute." Necee said to Rob before turning to Trei and saying, "Trei, she said not to worry. She has a slight headache."

"She must be drunk." Rob said. He then laughed and said, "Yo, is she drunk?"

"Nope," Necee said. "Mind yo own damn business."

"I don't have any," Rob said.

"That's why I'm trying to give you some. Now, what's up wit that mouth?" She asked. The crowd laughed.

"Nothing," Rob said.

"Exactly, so let me put something in it." Everyone laughed.

"Girl, I'm serious. You should do stand up comedy live." Paul said while laughing.

"Why? She and you ain't got nothing but sex jokes." Rob said to Paul before saying, "Man, I quit!"

"See what I mean?" Paul said. The crowd continued to laugh at Rob.

"What? I ain't got no mo money to mess up." He replied to Paul before turning to Necee and saying, "You do this mess everytime." He threw in his hand of cards. "And you bad luck," he said pointing to Necee. "I was winning til you brought yo-but over here." He eyed her heavily as he moved away from the table. After he walked away, everyone begin to laugh at him some more. He yelled to Necee, "Oh, and all that I just lost was yo-birthday present."

"Huhn?" Necee asked unsure of what she had just heard and caught off guard while laughing.

"You heard me. Now come on and let's go inside so that we can smoke this cigar together. I need to talk to you!"

Paul, noticing that Necee had gotten the best of Rob, said to Necee in a low voice as she passed him, "Hey Necee, he mad cause you won."

"I always do," she said walking away with a smile. "Wait up baby," she called out to Rob to catch up with him. She turned around to his friends and said in a low voice before tarring off, "he still can't . . ." She was interrupted by Rob as he screamed, "Necee!" Everyone laughed. Rob knew that Necee was still joking from the look he judged on her face.

Immediately after the scene with Necee and Rob, Trei thought about what Necee said earlier and decided that it was time he checked on Jada. He turned to Paul and said, "Yo, I'm about to go check on Jada. I'll be back in a second." Paul nodded his head up and down while he lit his cigarette to let Trei know that he heard him.

Chapter 13

THE PAIN

Life is fun when one has everything under control and can control it, but it can turn into pure hell when everything falls out of balance. When this happens, depression steps in and blocks away any dignity a person has left. Having no conscience motivates many people to do terrible things and having one drives many more people with a strong desire to be good and follow moral guidelines insane, especially when the bad could have been prevented and the good that one has done over the years is not enough to save him or her. Forest Gump stated in the movie 'Forest Gump' that his mother told him that life was like a box of chocolates, "you never know what you're gonna get". Well others say it is about chances or changes (on the other hand, maybe not changes, because the '*Holy Bible*' has a story for everything that is happening today). Parents with children say that life is the existence of two highways, the bad and the good, and it is up to the person making the decision to choose the right one. All of these quotes or once spoken of titles are right. But what happens when one chooses the good highway and something bad lurks around the corner? This is the question. Once there was a woman who became fascinated with the life of luxury, the quick way (drugs). Her new boyfriend was a drug dealer. She liked him and trusted him and enjoyed his money as well as his company. He asked her to take a ride with him one day; others said that she was forced by another drug lord. Anyway, she went on a ride with him to a spot to settle a drug deal that went bad. She was killed. He was too. She was innocent, smart, and beautiful. She is sadly missed. What provokes bad people to do bad things to good people? Even more, what provokes good people to do bad things to good people? Many say that the good deserve it. That the good are going to heaven anyway, *not all the time*. The truth is that the bad and good are very much entangled. It is a cross section and this young ladies life stood right in the middle of it. The other truth, smart people lose some wisdom at a time or too; that's why many are in jail and dead because they felt smart enough to get by.

Previously, Jada was on the very same road as this young lady. She was at a cross section, and she did not know it. She made a mistake attending her best friend's party. She took a wrong turn. Her conscience warned her, and she ignored it. Now she was a prey and the predator was on the prowl. From the moment Jada entered the doorway at Necee's party, things changed in her life as everyone else had a good time. Her enemy had one thing on his mind and tonight was the perfect place to do it. He was destined to win the bet between him and his friend, even if it meant violating the self-esteem of his friend's woman and destroying a friendship.

As Jada rested in Necee's bed, JJ stood outside the door, prying it open before anyone saw him. It took several moments before the door came ajar, and it was just in time as one of Necee's friends was headed toward the hall bathroom. He eased the door shut and found a chair to put under the knob in front of it. Standing at the door, he stared at Jada, sleeping peacefully in the bed. She looked lifeless. He could not fight the urge to have her. He had to have her in order to gain his power and move on. It was his time to win, and he was going to do just that. Moving toward the bed where she lay, his body urges grew stronger. Closer to the end of the bed now, he reached out and touched one of her boots to see if she was really asleep or just resting. She did not move. He walked to the head of the bed and looked at her face. She was beautiful, innocent, pure, and free. He needed her freedom and her purity, he thought, as he reached out one of his hands to trace the baby hair around her face. From this moment on, JJ lost control, "I told you that I was gone get you." He said rubbing down her neck moving toward her chest area. "Trei can't save you now. Necee can't either."

Jada moved one of her arms toward the pillow by the top of her head. JJ, hesitant of her next move, jumped back. She did not move, so he moved toward her again. Ecstasy induced his urge to have her. Fire grew on the inside of him and so did rage. Looking at her lips, like an animal, he rubbed his tongue across them. Now Jada's eyes were slowly opening, but her vision was blurry. She could not quite visualize the figure standing over her.

"That's right. Wake up Jada. It's pay back time." He said. Jada was still unsure of the person now sitting on top of her, straddling her and tearing at her blouse. "Yeah, you gone learn not to ever disrespect me." He said. As the music continued to play outside of the room, Jada was becoming aware of who her attacker was slowly as JJ continued to call her insulting names. She tried to fight him off her, but her reflexes were too slow.

"Shut up," he exclaimed when she tried to scream. Suddenly he grabbed a piece of material from his pocket and shoved it into Jada's mouth. She did not have enough strength to fight him. She figured that the alcohol was affecting her physical strength. When JJ noticed that she could not fight anymore he said, "Well, well, well, can't fight anymore, huhn?" He knew that the drug he put in her drink earlier was working. A tear fell from one of her eyes as JJ cut off her bra with a knife that he took from his shirt pocket. "I ain't gotta worry about you moving. It's all over now. Go to sleep!" He said as he put some kind of wet cloth over her nose. The cloth sent Jada to sleep instantly as her eyes closed slowly.

Meanwhile, JJ gazed closely at her breast before he touched them. Massaging them as though he was a doctor giving a mammogram, he smiled. His power on the inside was growing once he saw all of her nudity. Smelling her neck and chest like a viscous animal, he felt relieved of all the pain that she held over him for months. He decided that it was time to finish her. Behaving uncontrollably, he penetrated her several times. Finally, successful at completing the task and climaxing multiple times, JJ convinced himself to stop before he was caught as he could hear someone trying to open the bedroom door. He was nervous, and he hid himself under the bed. He wanted the persons on the other side of the door to just go away, at least give him an opportunity to escape. His heart was pounding loudly, so loud that he didn't notice that the jingling of Necee's bedroom door had finally stopped. He now heard voices. It sounded like a man and a woman. The woman's voice sounded like Necee's and the man's voice sounded like Rob. Yes, it was the two of them, he thought to himself. Now the door was being jingled again.

"Stop jingling the door. It's locked." Necee told Rob from the other side as she laughed at him.

"Where's the key?" Rob asked Necee.

"I just had it." She said, feeling for the key in her bra. She then checked her pockets. She did not have the key that she remembered putting in her bra. Where could it be? She thought. She then said to Rob, "Come with me to the kitchen. I have a spare in there." Half way down the hall, Necee stopped Rob and said, "I forgot. We can't go in my room."

"Why not?" Rob asked.

"Jada's in there sleeping." She answered as she looked up at him.

"How about we go in Alexes' room?" Rob suggested. Necee did not like his comment.

"Hell no, no man ever goes in there, unless he's ready to die. So, are you ready to die?" She asked Rob. "What's wrong with you?" She asked as she began to walk toward the kitchen again. "That's my daughter's room. How could you even suggest that? And something must be wrong with me letting you convince me to go in my room and I have all these people at my house. Let's just get something else to drink and sit in the living room and smoke." She said after she and Rob reached the kitchen.

Trei was on his way inside the house. After putting his cigarette out on his shoe and throwing the remainder portion in a trash can by Necee's door, a smile appeared across his face. He thought that tonight might finally be the night for him and Jada. Standing outside the door and looking through the visible glass, he could see Necee and Rob playing around in the kitchen while Necee prepared drinks. After entering the doorway, he realized that he had to find the bathroom and find it fast. Entering through the door and approaching Necee and Rob, he asked, "I thought that you two hated each other?"

"It's all a game man." Rob said as he stood behind Necee, holding her. "All an act that all y'all seem to love."

"Yeah whatever, so you enjoy being dominated?" Trei asked Rob. Rob smiled. Trei then asked Necee, "Hey Necee, may I use your bathroom?"

"Yeah, down the hall and to the right—the first right, and do not . . ."

"I already know—pee on the seat." Trei replied before he walked away.

While Trei was in the bathroom relieving his urinary pressure, and Rob and Necee were still in the kitchen arousing one another, JJ eased his way out of Necee's bedroom and out of her apartment. No one saw him leave, just as no one saw him enter the room, no one except God. As Trei exited the bathroom after washing his hands, he noticed that Necee's bedroom door was ajar. He knew that the door was not open before he went in the bathroom, or was his mind playing tricks on him, he thought. He was almost sure that the door was not open. Walking past the bedroom slowly and into the kitchen where Necee and Rob were standing, kissing now, he said, "um, um." They stopped hurriedly and looked at Trei.

"What's up, man?" Rob asked with a smile.

"Did J come in here?" Trei asked.

"No." Necee said. "She's in my room laying down remember. I told you that." She said moving away from Rob and over to a cookie jar hid behind a large vase. "Let me get the key. I'll let you in."

"But the door is open." Trei said.

"No, it's not. I locked it when I came out. Rob and I were just at that door. It was locked." Necee said.

"Yeah, it was. I turned the knob several times myself." Rob replied while looking at Trei.

"Yo, I'm telling y'all that door is open. It wasn't when I went in the bathroom, but it is now." Trei said.

"Are you sure?' Necee asked. She was hoping that nothing had happened to Jada. She told her that she would look out for her.

"Let me go and see if Jada' alright." Trei said about to walk away.

"No." Necee said abruptly while grabbing Trei's arm. "Let me go. You know how she is."

Necee was unaware of how she would find her friend. She was not prepared for what she was about to witness after she turned on the lights in the room. In the kitchen, Trei and Rob continued to discuss the door. Rob told Trei that it was locked and he and Necee could not get in. He explained to Trei that Necee had lost her key and had to get another one from the kitchen. He told Trei that at that moment, Necee remember that Jada was lying down, and they should not enter the room. Trei was wondering what was taking Necee so long to advise him if Jada were okay or not. Walking out of the kitchen and looking down the hall way, he could see Necee pacing back and forward as though she had did something wrong.

"Necee," he called out to her. She didn't respond. "Necee." Trei called again. She turned around and looked at Trei. "What's up?" He asked. She gestured that she did not know with her shoulders. Trei knew at this moment that something was not right.

Quickly walking down the hall with Rob behind him, he was abruptly stopped by Necee. She met him halfway.

"Trei, you can't go in there."

"What do you mean, I can't go in there? What's wrong with Jada?"

"Trei, you have to call 911." Necee replied.

"What's wrong with Jada? What's wrong Necee?" Trei asked. Necee was not talking fast enough, so he shoved her to the side and walked past her. What he saw was too much for one man to see. Necee was already on the phone talking to the 911 operator. Meanwhile, Rob ran outside and asked the DJ to make an announcement. The D.J. did, saying, "If you have anything illegal on you right now, get rid of it because the police are on the way."

Inside the apartment, Necee stood outside the bedroom door looking at Jada, lifeless, laying in her bed. Trei was now holding Jada and asking Necee what happened. He had found one of Necee's robes and covered Jada with it. However, Jada was not awake. Trei was trying to wake her by calling her name. Jada was not responding. Necee's bed was covered in blood. Jada's back, breast and buttocks had bite marks. She had scratches all over her body as well. As Trei sat in Necee's bed holding Jada, tears filled his eyes.

Moments later, the ambulance arrived and took Jada away. The police arrived as well. All of the people left at the party were questioned. The police told Necee that she needed to come down town with them so that they could obtain some more much needed information in order to solve the case. Rob agreed to follow Necee to the station with a friend in his car.

Later, Jada awoke in the hospital, and she had no recollection of what had happened to her, at least not at first.

Chapter 14

THE PAIN

Special Victim's Detective, Paula Anderson was angry when she finally dosed off to sleep in her bed. Her husband was having an affair, and her fifteen year old daughter had just told her three hours ago that she was pregnant and by the boy that Paula advised her not to see anymore. Now, it was 2 a.m., and her cell phone was ringing uncontrollably as she forgot to put it on silent before lying down. Finally, with the phone ringing several more times, Paula decided to pull herself together, turn on her lamp beside her bed and answer the phone. It was a 911 dispatcher advising her of another possible sexual assault, even more the victim was not awake. Paula pulled the cover from over her tired body and got out of bed. It was time to get down to the hospital and pronto before the victim woke up. For some reason, Dr. Stan Hewitt had watched Paula perform this job description for so long; he felt a need to question the patients before Paula got there.

Arriving at the hospital thirty minutes later and before taking the elevator upstairs to question her victim, Paula decided to grab a cup of strong, black coffee from the employee's lounge of the hospital. It would do her some good.

Upstairs and inside room 342, Jada was starting to show signs of waking up. Dr. Stan Hewitt decided to let her come out of the drowsiness on her own as he stood over her checking her vitals. Jada wondered who the brown-skinned, male with short, gray, curly hair was standing over her. He smelled sweet; his smile was bright, and his hands were also soft, Jada thought as he turned her face to her left side to examine it.

"Hello," he said when he noticed that Jada's eyes were open.

"Hey," Jada said, hesitant of why she was in a hospital with a doctor standing over her and her mother and father at her side.

"Do you know where you are, Ms Wells?" The doctor asked. Detective Anderson had just entered the room. Her and the Doctor looked at each other for a second and spoke with their eyes and a smile. Dr. Stan then turned his attention back to Jada.

"I'm guessing the hospital." She said, still suspicious of what was going on.

"Yes, of course you are." He said, listening to her heart now. His smile was still warm. Jada looked at her mother. Her mother looked as though she had been crying and was trying to cover it up with a smile. Jada's father was standing by her mother. He looked different and angry as he breathed deeply and greeted his teeth to conceal his anger. Something was not right, Jada thought.

"How are you feeling, Ms Wells?" The Doctor asked.

"Okay," Jada said with a frown, "but kind of stiff and a little sore." She said looking at the Doctor as he looked at the machine next to Jada's bed. "Why?" Jada asked.

"I'm Dr. Stan." He said looking at her after writing something on a piece of paper that he took from his pocket. He then put the paper back into is pocket. Paula watched and sipped her coffee as the doctor continued to talk to Jada. Dr. Stan then took a small flash light from his coat pocket. He began to check Jada's eyes-as he checked them, he said, "I'm Dr. Stan Hewitt."

"Okay," Jada said. "Now what's going on here?" Jada asked. "Why are you checking my vitals?" She said as she moved her head away from the light. "Is my face swollen? How many times have you all needled me? Do I have on a Catheter?" She asked, reaching up to touch her face, chest, and then pubic area only to be stopped by the doctor.

"Do you remember where you were before here at the hospital?" He asked as he turned off the light and put it back into his pocket.

"Yes, at my friend Necee's apartment for her birthday party—asleep in her bed." Jada said. "Are you going to tell me why I'm here at any point throughout this interrogation?"

"Why? Why were you asleep in your friend's bed?" Dr. Stan asked as he looked into Jada's eyes while he stood beside her bed.

"I had a headache, felt dizzy and nauseous. I also remember being a little upset with my boyfriend and paranoid about a drink that I had." Jada said, looking at the doctor and then her parents.

"Alcohol?" He asked.

"What?" Jada asked.

"Were you drinking some alcohol?" He asked.

"Yes. I had Champagne." Jada replied, extending her right hand to her head to scratch it.

"How many chalices did you have?" He asked.

"I'm not sure, but maybe two to three at the most." She said. "Will you please tell me why I am here? I'm starting to feel a second episode of paranoia coming on." Jada said, looking at the doctor as if she were saying if you don't tell me what is going on, I'm not answering another question.

"Ms Wells, did you drink anything else?" Dr. Stan asked. Jada shook her head no. "Did you consume some other drug or take anything else?" He asked.

"Voluntarily-only some Tylenol, for my headache, that's it. I don't recall taking anything else. Honestly, I have never taken any other types of drugs in my life." She said. Dr. Stan knew that she was telling the truth about the Champagne; her alcohol level was no where close to the legal limit.

"Excuse me for a second, Ms Wells?" Dr. Stan asked. Apparently, Paula had just tapped him on the shoulder. This act usually means that she needs to speak with him about something alone. The both of them walked outside.

Inside the room and alone with her parents now, Jada asked her mother, "Have I done something wrong?"

"No baby, their just running some tests to find out what happened to you." Her mother said. Her father managed to smile again before walking over to the window behind Jada.

"Tests . . . tests for what?" She asked her mother. Her mother looked at her father. Jada waited for an answer.

Outside room 342 and in the hallway, Dr. Stan awaited Mrs. Anderson's question. Mrs. Anderson asked, "Have you all tested her blood yet?"

"Yes, we are in the process of testing her urine now." Dr. Stan said.

"Has she been sexually assaulted?" Paula asked, holding her coffee. If Jada had not, Paula was ready to leave the hospital.

"Yes, she has." He responded

"What did her blood work reveal?"

"That she is no where near the alcohol legal limit, which suggests to me that she has been drugged unknowingly, or has been taking drugs to enhance her sexual desire."

"You have two great suggestions right there." Paula said to the doctor. "You sure that you weren't an investigator in a past life?"

"No." He said briefly before his nurse approached him and Paula. "What do you have Rhonda?"

"Roofies," the short, dark-skinned nurse said, "also known as-easy lay . . . scientific name, Rophynol. It's tasteless, odorless, and colorless, can cause anything from amnesia to aggressive behavior."

"How long after ingestion does it start to work?" Paula asked Dr. Stan.

"Approximately twenty minutes. It can last anywhere from 8 to 12 hours."

"Exactly, but that's not all I found." Rhonda said. Dr. Stan and Paula looked at her. She continued. "Ketamine Hydrochlorine also known as . . ."

"K-hole," Dr. Stan said. "Side effects are lost of time, sense, and identity—can last anywhere from thirty minutes to two hours. This date rape drug is used to render a patient unconscious within seconds. If she were raped, there was no way for Ms Wells to have fought off her attacker with this one. She was unconscious the whole time. She's lucky to be alive. Some people suffer from respiratory failure and die. And guess what?" Dr. Stan asked Ms Anderson.

"What, another drug?" Paula asked.

"No, I believe that Ms Wells was a virgin."

"How do you know that?" Paula asked.

"I've checked out many women. Her vagina looks nothing like a woman who has been sexually active, and I mean never." He said.

"Damn, this is about to make my job that much harder." Paula said.

"Let's go back in and see how far Ms Wells wants to take us with this one. I'm sure her parents don't know what to tell her." Dr. Stan said to Paula as Rhonda handed him the chart and walked away.

Inside the room again, Paula was about to take over the Q and A with Jada, but before she could release another question, Jada, very distraught, asked, "Are you ready to tell me what's going on here?"

"Ms Wells," Paula said. "We have reason to suspect that you were sexually . . ."

Before Paula could finish, Jada screamed, "No—no, no, no, no no. Not me. Me?" She then asked. Her voice was breaking down. Paula could sense the tears coming.

"Assaulted," Paula concluded. "Listen to me Ms Wells, please?" Paula said to Jada. Jada was not listening. All kind of emotions were reacting now on the inside of her. Paula concluded, "Your face is swollen; you've only been needled twice; those other aches that you feel are bit marks from your assailant, and yes you are wearing a catheter because we needed to test your urine for drugs. Do you understand all that I have said to you?"

"Me?" Jada asked again, looking at Paula as she stood beside her bed. Jada's mother began to cry. Her father left the room because his anger had taken another turn. Jada continued, "Not me. I'm a virgin . . ." She replied with a slight chuckle. Paula and the others did not laugh. '*They're serious,*' Jada thought.

At the sound of Jada's comment, Dr. Stan replied, "Oh hell." If she was not a virgin, that would ease the revealing matter, but she was, and the worse was yet to follow.

"You okay Doc?" Paula turned and asked him. He was right, Paula thought, as she looked at him. He nodded yes.

Jada continued, "Virgin's don't get raped. Do virgin's get raped?" She asked not sure of what she was asking. "I'm dreaming right? You tell me I'm dreaming!" Jada exclaimed to Paula, sitting up in the bed with tears in her eyes and rapidly grabbing Paula's jacket-holding to it tight.

"I'm afraid not, Ms Wells." Paula said as she tried to remove Jada's hands. "I'm Special Victims Investigator, Paula Anderson. I handle sexual assault cases. I really need you to calm down and tell me everything that happened to you while it's still fresh in your head." Jada's father returned to the room now.

"Who did this? Do you know who did this?" Jada asked Paula while shaking her.

"No, Ms Wells. Do you remember what happened?" Paula asked as she finally managed to pull Jada's hands from her jacket.

"Let me talk to her Paula?" Dr. Stan asked. Paula moved away from Jada's bed. "Ms Wells, I need you to calm down and talk to me so that we can resolve this matter." He said, sitting next to her beside the bed. Jada was not listening. She continued to hear the word rape and pulled the pillow from behind her head and put it over her face. She was trying to smother herself. Her mother and Dr. Stan's strength was challenged as they both tried to remove the pillow from her face. Suddenly, Jada let go. "Ms Wells," Dr. Stan called out to her once more. Jada closed her eyes. Tears rolled down her face. She wanted to go to sleep and then wake up again without the bad news. "Look at me," Dr. Stan said. She slowly turned her head and looked into his hazel eyes.

"I want you to calm down okay, and tell us everything that you remember happening?" Jada was calm, but she was not consoled. She just wanted to die. Feeling as though her hair was out of place, she reached up to touch it. The water was continuously leaving her eyes. Once more, Dr. Stan said, "Ms Wells." At the sound of his voice, she closed her eyes once more. Her mother tried to hold her left hand, but she snatched it back as soon as she felt her mother's touch. "Let me help you okay. Don't shut down now, and don't shut us out." Dr. Stan said. "Now, will you please help me?" He asked once more. Jada looked at her father. He seemed torn apart. He looked furious. Jada could see the anger in his eyes now. Could her father handle this, she thought? Could her father do what he preached all the time to his congregation? Could he anger but sin not, she thought? Her father was quiet. Noticing the hurt and pain in her father's eyes, she nodded her head up and down to let Dr. Stan and Mrs. Anderson know that she would help them. Jada told the doctor and the investigator everything that she could remember happening. She did not remember much. Dr. Stan told Jada and her parents that she had been raped vaginally and anally. Jada burst into tears once more. The physician also told Jada that she was drugged and that was the reason for her not being able to remember what had happened. After hearing all of this information, she felt alone and sad. Depression was about to take a toll and not for several days but for several years.

Days passed before she could even understand what had happened to her. When she did understand and remember, she had only one enemy in mind-JJ. Additionally, Trei, Necee and Rob too had only one person in mind-JJ and so did Detective Paula Anderson as she checked JJ's record three days later in the system computers at the police station. Meanwhile, Jada's case was about to take a turn for the worse, a turn no one would ever expect.

Chapter 15

THE PLOT

Murderers, killers, life-takers, and life-snatchers do not care to think of how family members feel when death affects the victim's family. It never crosses their mind. I mean, that is bound to be right. Is that not right? It has to be, for if it did and all options are weighed out, then they would not attack as rapidly as they would have with out thinking of others feelings. Life is often what one makes of it, and it's labeled by good or bad deeds or the constant stereotypes. What life is not is a poor choice. All choices made should be rich and logically thought out. No one person is better than the other on this earth, for if so, then God would have labeled all of us. Then why spend a lifetime making everyone else's life miserable because one feels that his or hers is all the time? This is pathetic. Moving on, it is the belief of many that if one cannot take pain, then why dish it. If you are mad, hurt self if hurt exists that bad and not a neighbor for freely speaking how he or she feels. Oh, but that is not right either, for the ways of suicide is hell. Then the only other option for man to do is try to get along because none of us will live forever-and again 'no man is an entire island of his own'. The point being made here is simple; it is time to stop making everyone else's life on earth hard because you feel that you have been short changed. Everyone deserves to live freely and disrespect or my bad is not an excuse for murder. The Holy Bible clearly states that however many times a brother or sister sins against thee that if he or she asks for forgiveness that he or she should be forgiven. It is alright to remember, but forgive and do not fall into that same position again. Some say forgiveness does not exist in their vocabulary, and this is the number one reason where some go wrong.

It is often said that individuals should let God handle the bad or worst. Christian statistics support that no one individual can hurt another individual as bad as God can. However, this belief is left up to individuals, mainly people with a great need to follow moral guidelines. Many others think that it is necessary to carry out vengeance without the assistance of God. Once again, this is where the crossroads begin to confuse the good as well as the bad, producing a thin line and causing confusion.

JJ had finally conquered the right anger in the right persons. He did not know it nor did he care. He was not losing any sleep at night over it either. His extreme enemy was out for vengeance with a devised blueprint in mind. She had waited long enough. She wanted her strength back. With this said, let's focus on the female figure briefly for a second. Women are she devils, seduced by the sliest devil of all. You double cross a woman with a plan, then the best thing that you can do to resolve the matter is divide the situation in half and never at any opportunity convince her that she has lost. She always wins, and she always has a different approach. Now, let's speak briefly about life and death. Only one person can convert an individual from death to life, *at least one person that I know of,* and no one has seen Him. When committing death, one should be certain that that is what he or she wants to do. He or she cannot take it back and must realize the consequences even before committing the act. The ultimate punishment for death is life-an eye for an eye and with that said, now is the time for JJ to die.

"What you crying for?" Kalle asked Diamond as they sat in a red Chevy, SS Impala outside of a convenience store. Sunshine sat in the back seat quietly, very angry at Diamond as the adrenaline rushed through her body. She needed a cigarette.

"I told her to shut up!" Sunshine said to Kalle, who was closing the driver door of the car.

Kalle, ignoring Sunshine's words, said to Diamond, "What you crying for, I said?" Diamond was not responding. She kept sniffing her nose. Fed up with no response from Diamond, Kalle turned around and looked in the back seat at Sunshine. She wanted an answer, so she asked Sunshine, "Why the hell she crying?"

Sunshine was lighting up a cigarette. After she finished lighting the cigarette she said, "I told you not to bring her."

"Miss that Sunshine," Kalle said.

"Look! This is yo mess up." Sunshine said pointing at Kalle with the cigarette between her fingers in one hand and while she took the black skull cap off her head with her other hand. "You gone need that Pepto Bismol you just bought, and give her some while you at it. She just threw up—twice. Now all I need is to get caught up in something with this ignorant, slow—"

"All I want to know Sunshine is why she crying?" Kalle asked Sunshine before turning to Diamond in the front seat and asking, "And you threw up twice, for what?"

"You know she got a slow stomach. Don't digest well or something. Anyway, she crying over that weak punk we just messed up outside the back of that club." Sunshine said.

"Man, I can't believe this. You crying over that trash?" Kalle asked Diamond. Diamond did not say anything, only looked out the window. Kalle grabbed her face and turned it toward her so that their eyes would meet. "Girl, you crying over what just happened to him?" Kalle asked. Diamond did not respond. "Did you forget that he slapped you with a gun two weeks ago and took all of Dominique's money? Oh no," Kalle said letting go of Diamond's face. "I know you ain't doing this to Dominique, me, or Sunshine for that much." Kalle opened the bottled of Pepto. "Let me calm down," she replied before taking a drink of the medicine. "I can't believe you. Look!" She said reverting back to Diamond again. "I need to know that we can trust you? Now you said that you were down for whatever, and now you whining all up in my car like a baby in search of a lost bottle."

Diamond finally spoke up and said, "I'm alright. Let's go!"

Kalle shoved the stomach coating liquid into Diamond's stomach and said before she started the ignition of the car and pulled away from the curb, "You better be."

"Yeah, she better be or she . . ." Sunshine said after taking another puff of the cigarette.

"Shut up Sunshine!" Kalle exclaimed. "I don't want to hear that bull." She said stopping to check for oncoming traffic.

Sunshine replied, "I ain't lying. I'm sick of her always crying and carrying her feelings on her shoulders. She better buy some balls and soon."

"Man, shut up. I'm sick of you. God didn't make me with nuts!" Diamond turned behind her and said to Sunshine after she drank some of the pepto bismol.

"Now that's what I'm talking bout." Kalle said driving the car. She was happy that Diamond was pepping up.

Sunshine, letting the window down a bit and throwing out her cigarette, did not find Diamond's words as amusing as Kalle did. Taking a switch blade from her pocket and putting it around Diamond's neck from the back seat, she said, "Trick, who you whistling at. He might as well had. You imagining being with a woman with some anyway. Now that mouth of yours wanna blow air, instead of vomit. You ain't sparkling so much now-Diamond. I'll cut yo throat out and give it to somebody who don't care. I can hear everybody cheering me on now."

All of a sudden the car came to a halt on the side of the road. Kalle knew that she had to stop Sunshine before she killed Diamond, "Let her go, Sunshine!" She said. Sunshine wanted to cut Diamond to let her know who was in control. "Let her go psycho! I just got this Impala. Do you know how long I been waiting to get it? Not today Sunshine. No, no, no, and not in here. Let her go! Now!"

"I'm sick of her weak attitude, and I'm sick of you always taking up for her too! This Dominique's woman, not yours." Sunshine said. She released Diamond and put the blade back in her pocket. Diamond trying to catch her breath, was gasping for air.

"What?" Kalle asked Sunshine.

"You heard me. And who gave her the name Diamond anyway? She ain't shiny, and she sure ain't gone cut nothing." Sunshine said as she took a cigarette from her pocket.

Diamond eventually caught her breath and quickly turned around in her seat to retaliate. "You tried to kill me!" She said almost able to reach Sunshine before Kallie grabbed her.

"Hold on now, Diamond." Kalle said, holding Diamond tight against her chest. "Let it go."

"Ha, ha, ha!" Sunshine exclaimed mocking Diamond's anger as she began to light her cigarette, "That's what I'm talking bout. Get some act right. I bet you ain't sick now, and you just bought yourself some balls too. Now I only hope that overly, sensitive ego of yours has disappeared for good." She said before taking a puff of her cigarette. "Imagine that Kalle, maybe she good for being something other than a picture on the wall after all."

"Shut up, Sunshine." Kalle said after releasing Diamond and checking traffic before pulling off again.

"Seriously, I like it when she's feisty." Sunshine said, shaking her head from left to right, amazed by Diamond's behavior. "Yeah, maybe she can stop all that crying now. Girl, you might be able to stay on this team just yet."

"Kiss it Sunshine . . . kiss it!" Diamond said while fixing her hat on her head.

"Nooooo, you save all that for Dominique," Sunshine replied. She then smacked her lips to the words of a song Erica Badu recorded that suddenly came to her attention, "wish I could call Tyrone for this one, Diamond finally got them balls off layaway."

"Man, you sick," Kalle said laughingly, followed by the words of one of Lil Boosie's songs. "But I like that, though."

"So you feel what I mean, huhn?" Sunshine asked Kalle.

"Oh, I got you," Kalle said to Sunshine while laughing. Diamond laughed too.

"Man, I don't care what nobody says, you can't mess wit a female wit a plan. A woman with a plan got something for you. But on the real though," Sunshine said. "Excusing all that negativity back there, I'm glad y'all got a sense of humor after what just happened at that club." She leaned back and relaxed in her seat, watching the moon-lit sky from the back windshield. "I couldn't stand JJ. I been wanting to do him-just was waiting for the right time—had to carefully think out a plan. I just couldn't come up with one. Dominique and Vegas did though, and we just did that fool." Sunshine looked at Kalle driving the car and asked, "Kalle, how you feel?"

"What? I feel good since I got that Pepto in me, but you know this ain't no first for me. I know what you feeling." Kalle said to Sunshine. Diamond never said a word. She only thought to herself after glancing at Kalle, *'dang, how many people she done killed?'*

Kalle looked at Diamond and said, "How do you feel?" Diamond relaxed in her seat and looked at the starry sky with both her hands in her pocket. She soon spoke, "I don't know how I feel. I mean—I'm I suppose to feel good? We just killed another human being?"

"O hell . . . lil green horn bout to mess up the moment again. Here she go again with this over sensitive bull," Sunshine said.

"Hold up, Sunshine?" Kalle intervened.

"No, I believe the proper words should be—shut up Diamond." Sunshine said calmly.

"Let her explain, Sunshine." Kalle said driving the car in and out of slow traffic.

"Yeah, I hated him, but I don't get to hate him anymore. That was the final hate, the last hate." Diamond said.

"What in the hell is she talking about?" Sunshine asked Kalle. Kalle tried to understand what kind of point Diamond was trying to make. She was lost too, but she did not want Sunshine to know.

Diamond continued, "I mean, true enough, he did violate and disrespected me."

"You! Girl, save that! We talking bout Dominique and—" Sunshine said while looking at the back of Diamond's head before being cut off by Kalle.

"Shut up, Sunshine," Kalle said.

"Are you listening to this bull?" Sunshine said to Kalle.

"All that I am trying to say is that I don't get to hear him talk stupidly or threaten me or anyone else for that fact anymore." Diamond finished.

"What kind of psychological bull is this trick on?" Sunshine asked. Kalle continued to drive the car. Sunshine had a point, she thought. She liked Diamond because she was calm, conversational and cute, but she did not understand where Diamond's conversation was going tonight. After passing another car, Kalle relaxed in her seat. She scratched her head after removing the black skull cap and glanced at Sunshine in the rearview mirror.

"Kalle, do you understand what she's saying, now?" Sunshine asked. She knew that Kalle was just as lost as she was.

"Honestly, I don't know." Kalle said with a slight giggle. "I never looked at any situation like this before. I just did what I felt was right at the time. I didn't care about no remorse."

"Who said something about remorse? I didn't say anything about remorse." Diamond replied.

"No," Kalle said looking at the car ahead of her and confused by Diamond. "You sure?"

"Look man, both of y'all tripping. That dude back there destroyed many lives. You think that he felt some remorse. No, he didn't feel no remorse. What about my uncle Steel? What about my Aunt? Let's talk about her. She's in a looney bin because of him. He killed my cousin, her only son; ran over him in a stolen car, trying to get away from N.O.P *(New Orleans Police)*. For weeks, he bragged about it. Talking bout, I hit some punk, and I wouldn't bout to go to jail for a stolen car and murder. He shouldn't of been crossing the street. I blew the horn. Then he laughed about it and began to ask his drugged up buddies if they knew what it felt like to run over a body-how the car felt like it hit a slight bump in the road and bounced back up on hydraulics. Man, y'all can cry, but JJ can go to hell."

"That's what I'm saying," Kalle agreed.

"Ain't nobody gone miss him anyway. As for as I am concerned; I just did his mammy and pappy a favor. They don't have to worry no more. I hear his daddy was tired of him anyway. This murder is for all them good people out there who done been violated, humiliated and destroyed by an over powering, snitching, scandalous, quick scamming punk. This is for them people. The person that you would love to get tired of hating, who bullied you all the time, who irritated you, who scared you, who beat on, trapped you, slapped you, talked behind your back and smiled in your face, sneaked up on you, and overall just hated you because they couldn't be you." Sunshine said very content thinking of how he stopped the growth of many families.

"Yep, yep!" Kalle said out loud. Diamond was quiet.

"This is for all the good people he destroyed. Yeah, this for all y'all punk ass!" Sunshine said with a smile.

"Sunshine, why you have to say that?" Kalle asked.

"Cause my daddy always said, help a man up before you kick him down. Anyway, I remember the time that punk took my brother's Jordan's off his feet. My brother worked hard for them shoes. He told my momma, you don't have to buy them cause I'm gone get them, even if I have to save. My brother did that, and I was proud of him because he had some respect for himself. JJ took my brother shoes like he paid for them, and that's why I took his life, like I gave it to him. Y'all just don't know how I feel right now." Sunshine said.

"I know how you feel." Kalle said, glancing at Sunshine through the rearview mirror.

"No, I don't think that you do Kalle. You see—my brother died a week later. He hung himself in our garage. He couldn't tolerate being picked on anymore by his peers over a one-hundred dollar pair of shoes and a bully. A month later, my mother lost her job, unable to sustain. Two months after that, we lost our house because my father couldn't foot the mortgage alone. So, its no accident that I ended up in the projects." Sunshine said.

"Sunshine, we never knew your pain stretched back so far. Why haven't you said something before now?" Kalle asked.

"Just haven't. It's something I never liked talking about. And when I got the opportunity to get him back, all I could hear in the back of my mind was that words of that song that P-Diddy did, when he said, 'do it, do it, do it, do it—do it, do it, do it-do it, do it, do it, do it," she said moving her head up and down smiling, "like revenge of Nike, and I did it—took his light and set his soul free."

"Light? What light? You mean life." Diamond said.

"No, I mean light. Check these out?" Sunshine took a small black bag from her pocket. You wouldn't believe what she contained in it. "Now these are the windows to the soul—better known as the light."

Diamond turned around to see what Sunshine was bragging about, "Oh-my God, she took out his eyes out. That's why she asked me for that crazy glue before we left." Diamond exclaimed.

"Hold up," Kalle said pulling the car over quickly on the side of the highway.

"Oh man! She crazy! It's something wrong with her." Diamond said. She began to drank some more of the pepto bismol.

"Man what's wrong with you?" Kalle asked once she stopped the car. "Why you do that?"

"I have to throw up." Diamond said.

"Diamond, suck that bio up!" Kalle said. She then turned to look at Sunshine in the back seat. Sunshine was admiring the eyes in her hand and laughing. "Are you out of your mind? What's wrong with you? Put those things back in the bag." Kalle said to her. Sunshine put the eyeballs back in the bag and put them in her pocket. She pulled out another cigarette from her cigarette pack seated on the back seat. Kalle stared at her as though she was daring her to do something else, but it was not what Sunshine would do next, it's what she said.

"Man, forget him—and y'all too. Y'all ain't got no real beef in this!" Sunshine exclaimed.

"Who you talking too?" Kalle asked.

"You, and her too,' Sunshine replied to Kalle.

"So, them balls you bought done made you forget who car you in? Cause the balls I got are telling me to take you along way from here and dare you to walk. Now before you continue your boastful mouthing, you better think again, cause you got the wrong trick." Kalle replied.

"I'm cool Kalle. We cool. Just had a flash back that's all," Sunshine said. She knew that she had crossed the line with Kalle.

"Man, I swear to something, you crazy." Kalle said turning around in her seat.

"Let's ride Kalle, ain't nothing else going on around here," she said looking around before she took a puff of her cigarette. "Like Luther said, the sun is shining-ah man-the moon anyway. Can you feel me dawg?" She asked Kalle.

"Yeah, I hear you." Kalle said.

"Knawl, I don't think you heard me! Can you feel me!" Sunshine replied.

"Yeah, I feel you. You saying you got his light. I feel you. Man stop talking bout them eyes," Kalle said.

Sunshine then shoved Diamond on her shoulder and said, "wake up scary." She then slapped the back of her head when she did not respond.

Diamond turned around quickly, "Man why must you be so combative?"

"Shut up." Sunshine said to Diamond. She then said to Kalle, "Pump that Lil Boosie up a bit." She began to rock to the beat of the song 'I'm Mad', saying the words, "I'm mad, I'm mad, trick, you done made me mad."

Kalle laughed at Sunshine's humor. Diamond smiled and relaxed as she listened to the harsh words of the song. She pulled a piece of gum from her pocket and put it in her mouth and began chewing as her friends enjoyed the song.

"Boosie crazy." Sunshine said.

"He'll get you killed too. Ask JJ?" Kalle said.

"Cause we just set it off on him." Sunshine said after laughing and coughing and then placing the cigarette back in her mouth. Kalle laughed and so did Diamond. Listening to the words of the song, Sunshine said, "Boosie gone get himself killed."

"So, now you wanna do Boosie?" Kalle asked Sunshine.

"Is that what I said?" She responded.

"I just asked—cause if you wanna go to the Bottom's, we can go." Kalle replied.

"What's this, pay back time?" Sunshine asked.

"No, I just thought that maybe you had a bone to pick with Boosie." Kalle replied with a smile.

"Boosie cool at least I think, but anytime he get ready to make it do what it do, then I got something for him too." Sunshine replied. Kalle and Diamond laughed.

Kalle replied, "Sunshine—ain't nothing you can do wit Boosie."

"See Kalle, you got your money on the wrong person and you messy. You must didn't hear what I said about a woman with a plan. Man, turn up the radio."

Chapter 16

THE MOMENT

If one hundred women were stranded on a deserted island and waiting to be rescued, ninety-five, no, ninety-nine percent would want to be rescued by a fine, handsome, extremely passionate, respectful, stand up for your woman kind of guy. Why? Because she wants her man to be in control of his manhood and defend her heart. She feeds from his power. She knows that he would do anything for her if he loves her. She understands that he is dangerous and not very wise at times. Because to him sometimes, wisdom does not matter, only what makes his woman happy. She loves this kind of man, for he is not just a man, but a man capable of many qualities. She cannot stand when he ignores her, and he cannot stand when she does not give in to his power. If she has the power to mask his power, chances are he will not give her a chance in a relationship with him out of fear of being controlled by her and losing his real guidance, losing his manhood.

"So check this out," Michelle tells her friend Tessany. Tessany knew that anytime Michelle began a story this way that she was about to talk about a man, but not just any man.

"What? I hope this is not another one of your fantasies. You know that JJ is not that type of man. Besides, out of all those beatings that he's given you, you ought to have some sense. That means that dreams should not exist in there." She said jabbing a finger at Michelle's forehead before getting up from her bed to approach a mirror. Michelle sat at the end of Tessany's bed with a bewildered and confused look on her face. Tessany knew that her friend was in love with JJ. "Anyway, I thought that after you got a child by him that you would stop all of this nonsense. And you just didn't have one, you had two. And what about that jail time that you did behind him. Is it not enough that you his baby's momma now? You are apart of him forever. Now let go."

"Why do you always spoil the fun for me?" Michelle asked Tessany.

"I want you to wake up, Chelle. It's time for you too. He does not love you. He loves those whore's out there in the streets, and they don't love nobody. And until you convince yourself that I am right, you ain't gone be able to move on. Think about your son and how God brought you through all that trouble that you use to get in with JJ."

"Yeah right-but listen to me anyway. True story, no fantasy this time. I think that he's coming around to loving me." She said in a low, sad tone.

"Yeah, I bet." Tessany said applying her make-up.

"He does love me. It's just in his own way." Michelle replied.

"No, I think that it's the other way around." Tessany said applying mascara to her eye lashes. "Chelle, honestly, have you ever thought of it as the fact of the matter is that you may be lusting after him and not actually in love with him?"

"What? Girl—get real. Now listen to my story, at least some of it." Michelle asked.

"I really don't feel like listening to this nonsense, and it's almost never close to being as real as you imagine it to be."

"This time is different." Michelle said.

"And what about all of those other times?" Tessany asked.

"Okay, well maybe I went a little over bo . . ." Michelle said before being cut off while speaking.

"Listen to me Chelle, and then I'll listen to you. Why can't you move on. Ricky across the street wants to offer you and little Jamey Junior the second, a pleasant and peaceful lifestyle. Why is it important that you have JJ. He ain't nothing to nobody."

"He's something to me." Michelle replied.

"Well, you know what I mean. He ain't nothing but trouble." Tessany said turning away from the mirror to face her friend face to face. "I just don't understand you. You rather have nothing than something or someone for that matter. He does not love you Chelle. He never will, at least not now, and if he does—your not going to want him anyway. So let's skip to the end and save your heartache."

"You are not even close to resolving my pain, right now. Just hear me out for a few minutes?" Michelle asked, trying again to tell Tessany her story.

"This is stupid. And what is your excuse for not dating Ricky? He's a good guy." Tessany replied.

"I don't want Ricky. I have nothing in common with him. He's not my type." Michelle said.

"And exactly what is your type because obviously he has something in common with you the way he pursues you." Tessany said. Michelle just looked at her friend. She did not have an excuse to defend herself.

"Can we just not talk about Ricky? You said you would listen. I know that you love me Tess. And all of what you're saying is true and fair. And I know that you want to save me from myself and JJ and the hurt and humiliation that he causes me, but the truth is that I love him, and no one else. Now, is that fair to Ricky, nope. I want to love someone else, but I can't seem to get JJ off my mind. It's like nothing matters to him, and I want something too. It's like I have to convince him that something else does matter besides wrong—like I must convince him to do right before I can move on."

"Oh, that's some psychological bull, and you know it. Now you and I both know that that is not your job. He is not ready to listen to you or anyone else for that matter. Nothing about JJ speaks of change to me, and nothing ever will in this lifetime." Tessany replied.

"You said that you would listen." Michelle reminded her friend again.

"I'm listening," she said turning back to the mirror to fix her hair.

"Honestly, I—I can't describe what it is that I feel for him. Sometimes I wish that some force would intervene and take this matter over, but it seems as though it's meant for me to suffer—at least for a little while, maybe to make me stronger, and not literally to make me look stupid."

"Kinda like God punishing you?" Tessany asked while looking at her friend. Her friend did kind of make some sense. "Yeah, well that could be a possibility, but He's not really punishing you, you are. He's strengthening you."

"Then will you reason with me for a little while? I want this over too." Michelle said.

"I don't think so—because if you were sincere about it, then you would let go and let God help you." Tessany replied.

"I can't—and I don't want too right now, and I hate it. I guess I'm a bit naive, maybe even a little obsessed at this point." Michelle said. Tessany looked at her strange, thinking that her friend may have a point there with the word obsessed. Michelle continued, "Believing that he is honest with me when he say that he cares. I'm just determined to believe him and seeing him smile and tell me something pleasant every now and then, is enough to say to me that he really does care, but he doesn't know what to do. Do you think that he's afraid of loving me? I mean completely?"

"No, I think that he's a fool. I think that you are too, but that won't interfere with me trying to understand what it is that you are going through, saying, mentioning. I constantly try to convince you to move on, Michelle, and the more I do that—the more you love him and want to share these random episodes of love making to him with me. I just don't understand. What has he done to you? It's as though he has some kind of spell on you."

"I think that I'm really in love with him." Michelle replied.

"You think that you are what? Wait a minute?" Tessany said, sighing deeply and looking down at the floor for a second before looking at her lonely friend in the eyes again.

"It's got to be love, don't you think?" Michelle asked, looking at her friend. "Nothing lasts this long but love."

"Heck no. I don't know what this is. Oh, no! Love does not behave this way." Tessany said after seeing a sudden flash back of JJ and her friend fighting each other. "I can't imagine that at all. It has definitely got to be something else." She said reaching for a cigarette on her dresser. "Why are you saying these things? Maybe you're just in love with the infatuation of being in love with him. Maybe you just feel a need to control him for just a nick of time. You know-the reality of going through the motions literally and letting go. You know, having the opportunity to explore something with him and all of it coming to an end one day."

"You think that if I told JJ that I loved him that these feelings will go away?" Michelle asked Tessany. She had not heard a word that her friend has just said.

"No, no and no, I wouldn't do that if I were you. He would only play on your feelings. Don't you think that he has used you enough? And you would think that he would have some sympathy since he has a child by you, and he's responsible for the other one being dead." Michelle could not believe that Tessany brought up Taylor's death again. He had been dead now for two years. Water formed in both of her eyes quickly. "I'm sorry, Chelle. I didn't mean anything by that, by Taylor at all."

"Yeah, I know, but you never do Tessany. You never do." She said as she wiped her eyes clear of the tears. "I wish that you would stop bringing that up. It's not going to change how I feel for his dad. I just need some time to heal that's all, just a little time to heal." Michelle replied.

"What you need is a shrink to listen to you, and these roles that you want to play out with JJ in your life, in your mind. I am not a shrink. I don't have the medication that you need to get well, and I am tired of my only best friend getting hurt by a man that is a beast-and a beast can't possibly love her back because it does not know what love is and can't distinguish the difference between love, control, and survival." Tessany said.

"He knows the difference." Michelle responded.

"Oh yeah! Then how come he almost beat you and the child you were caring to death. Love doesn't behave that way, Chelle."

"He gave a good explanation for that." Michelle replied.

"What kind?" Tessany asked.

"You know Tessany. He was on cocaine then. He just snapped." Chelle responded.

"So—now, our brothers got the right to get on drugs and snap? Is that what you're saying? You should have pressed charges on his behind instead of saying that you fell down some stairs. Those officers know that that is not what happened."

"He doesn't do it anymore, Tess." Michelle said.

"Of course, he doesn't. You two aren't together either. You are so naive. Anyway, did he actually tell you that the cocaine made him snap?" She said laughing.

"Can we change the subject?" Michelle asked.

"Sure, as soon as you stop dating him-like he has you. Do you actually like being abused? Seriously, do you?"

"I saw him yesterday." Michelle said, ignoring her friends comment once more.

"Oh God, you saw him where? I hope you didn't go looking for him." Tessany said.

"No, he was at the gym. I and Waverly were there playing basketball. I think that we were on our third game when he came in with a couple of his friends. I didn't even see him come in. Trei was with him." Michelle said with a smile. She knew how much Tessany liked Trei.

"Forget Trei." Tessany said with a slight laugh. She was mad because Trei would never give her the time of day.

"Anyway, Waverly hissed for me to turn around, and it was like all those feelings that I had been fighting to move away came rushing back when I saw him. I became very nervous and began to shake. You know how you want to walk away, but you don't? And something on the inside of you wants him to say something to you . . . wants him to notice you."

"You did walk away though, right?" Tessany asked.

"I did-this time. I felt good about it too."

"Well, good for you. I commend you. You finally did something decent," Tessany said putting her cigarette out in an ashtray on her dresser. "I bet Trei was looking fine too. He still wit what's her name—Jada?" Tessany asked.

"Yes and yeah. Anyway, when I came out the dressing room with my warm up suit on and my gym bag, he was standing outside the door by the water fountain waiting."

"Here we go." Tessany replied.

"What's wrong?"

"It's a lot more to this story, isn't it, than you just walking away?" Tessany said looking at her friend.

"So he said, Mimi, and I kept walking with Waverly. Mimi, I know you hear me. He said. So I turned around and asked what do you want?"

"What did he say?" Tessany asked her friend.

"He said, where's my son at? I been calling your stupid parent's house, and they won't let me talk to him."

"So what did you say?" Tessany asked, while crossing her legs.

"I said, don't be calling my parents stupid, and that—that he had the opportunity to see his son all the time before he decided to walk out of his life."

"Stupid, stupid, stupid!" Tessany said pointing a finger in Michelle's forehead.

"What do you mean, stupid?" Michelle asked.

"I thought I told your stupid self that you don't ever let a man know where he went wrong if it ain't gone change nothing. No offense, but you should have asked him, which son?" Tessany replied.

"Come on Tess. Let it go."

"You know what? I'm gone get my shoes out of that closet over there." Tessany said pointing to her closet across the room and moving away from the dresser. "You can go ahead and tell me your poetical escapade or fantasy or reality if you want to. But as soon as I pick out the shoes that I want to wear and put them on my feet, I am gone out that door whether you are finished telling that story or not. I cannot stand him. I hate him, and I hate what he has done to you. You had a career in basketball, and you could have been playing anywhere in the United States and anywhere else for that matter, but you had to meet him and mess up your dreams and your goals. Now you sitting in a rut and call yourself in love with something that don't know nothing or want to know nothing for that matter about love or how to love." She said looking for her black Nike tennis shoes on the closet floor. "If JJ died today, it would be my gift to you. How can you still want to be with somebody that almost cost you your life; turned you away from your parents-the only source of income you had; embarrassed and humiliated you; has no respect for you; uses you to survive; plays on your feelings and laughs in your face, and abandons his child to be with his friends-somebody who won't even put his five senses together long enough to make some change? He is a viscous animal. He is not human, Chelle."

"Wow Tess, haven't you hid a brain full." Michelle said. She was shocked.

"You know-I ain't lying . . ." Tessany said, agitated by not being able to find her shoes. "Where are my shoes?" She then said to Michelle, "I promise you, if he died today, he would be doing me a big favor." She said turning back to look at Michelle sitting on the bed. "Why can't you just let go? I mean, what is so hard?"

"I don't know. Letting go is so much easier said than done. It's as though I've lost some of my power-like he has it and I have to get it back. I want to get it back."

"Your what?" Tessany asked.

"Power. I feel like he owes me something. I need some get back. You know, revenge." Michelle said.

"Are you finished," Tessany asked while sitting on the closet floor and looking back at her friend? Continuing, she said, "hold up. What kind of power are you looking for?"

"I don't know, maybe some hurting power. I want him to feel like I feel so that he can understand how it feels to hurt someone who really loves you. I need something that he has—something that revitalizes him or drives him to move on." Michelle said looking at Tessany.

"How about a Voo-Doo doll?" Tessany asked before laughing.

Michelle looked at her friend strange and said, "Stop playing!"

"Who's playing? I ain't playing. We live in New Orleans. We can find you a hook-up on every corner." Tessany said. Michelle was not laughing. So Tessany decided to be serious. "So you want some kind of a hold on him because he took your kindness for weakness?"

"Exactly," Michelle said looking at Tessany. Tessany got up from the floor and sat down beside Michelle on the bed while putting her shoes on. "Okay, I never thought of it that way. You may have something there. You know it's something about a naïve woman losing. When she incorporates a source of strength, you better get back. My grandma told me about that. So, you still want to finish telling me what happened between you two?" Tessany said after putting on her tennis shoes and looking at her friend before tying them.

"Nope-somehow now I don't feel a need to. All of it was nothing anyway." Michelle said. She looked distant.

"Good, because I think that you just may have found the remedy to release JJ's spirit from you. You know what? Then again, maybe, you just need an apology—if he apologies for all that he has caused you to endure, you could move on. And then again, maybe you are standing at the door of a break through, girl. I think that you should open it." Tessany said as she finished tying her shoes. She patted her friend on the back.

Confused by Tessany, Michelle asked, "An apology? And what else did you say?"

"See that door?" Tessany asked Michelle while pointing at her bedroom door.

"Yeah," Michelle said. She was not sure of Tessany's relevance. She did not understand.

"Get up—open the door and let's go. Break through—that's what I mean." Tessany said. Michelle laughed. She thought to herself, *'my friend just played me.'*

Chapter 17

PREMEDITATED

A man in control of his own power is fearless, very confident, and satisfied. Respect is his demand; money is his influence, and his friends are his servants. Nothing else matters as he is like a Libra who has tipped the scales; a Leo, picking a power trip fight, or a Scorpio, exploding like a nuclear bomb in bed. Nothing affects him. He can be anything. His power pushes him to the edge; drives him to higher heights, and throws love aside. He learns not to need anyone and to buy everyone. Greed, wrath and pride are his side-kick sinners. He lives to degrade and his actions can be down right ignorant and stupid if he lacks social skills. Change is an understatement to him, and he looks to statistically injure the status quo. He is alone and cannot be trusted-this is his work ethic. You say that the wine bottle is empty, and he says that it can be refilled. He see's what you cannot and does what you will never attempt to do. He is not afaid of his conscience and there is a knife in his heart, maybe from some part of the past. His soul does not rest, even in death. He constantly roams and lurks for danger. His mind visits the most unusual places, watching fear, money and power. He knows that he cannot capture love only pretend that it is what it is. All of this is control which is associated with power.

Power is what JJ desired-the power to do as he pleased. Fear was not an option, and everyone was a target that he was out to mask and control. Yes, JJ was on a power trip and nothing was going to stand in his way, not even his own family and never love. He had everything that he wanted, but he had lost his soul, and his days on earth were numbered.

Riley had just been released from jail, when he picked up JJ. *'Of all the people,'* he thought. Not wanting to give JJ a ride, he gave him one anyone, just to keep down trouble. Honestly, he did not want JJ to know that he hated him like everyone else. Riley wished that someone would call him. He thought of his mother, his sister and his father as he drove with the phone in his hand. He was so desperate to get away from JJ that he hoped that his baby mother would call and curse him out or do something. No one called. Riley pressed a button on the phone every few seconds for the screen to light up. JJ, noticing Riley's behavior asked, "Hey man, you waiting on a phone call or something?"

"Naw man-just a habit, I got." Riley said. "Anyway, where you going," Riley asked? He and JJ were riding through the projects. JJ said nothing. He was looking for someone. Spotting the person that he was looking for, JJ said to Riley, "hey man, turn right here." Riley did. JJ said, "There goes Dominique, and she better have my money." Three apartments down, JJ spotted Dominique. She was wearing shades and had her long, dark hair pulled to the back in a pony tail. You see, Dominique wanted to be a man, but she was a light-skinned woman all day long. Surprised? I thought you would be. Men wanted Dominique to be a woman because she was good looking and sexy. Women enjoyed her being a man because she was very attractive and sensitive. JJ said to Riley as the car approached the apartment, "pull over here." Riley parked on the street of the apartment complex where Dominique was sitting on the porch. Dominique was surrounded by women of all different shapes, sizes, colors, and each one of them revealed a gifted characteristic from God. Dominique had a woman for any type of man. She built an empire and nobody was lacking anything. Spotting JJ, getting out of the passenger seat of Riley's car, Dominique said, "Now, this just what I need to mess me up the rest of the day."

Trish, one of Dominique's sweethearts said, "And why is Riley riding around with that fool in his car anyway."

"I don't know, but I ain't putting up with his bull today." Dominique said calmly. She turned to another sweetheart and said, "Yo Lady, give me a cigarette." Lady brought the cigarette over to Dominique, put it in her mouth and lit it. JJ proceeded out of Riley's car with a smile on his face as he looked at Dominique and her entourage. Lady eyed him coldly before walking away from Dominique. The rest of the women surrounding Dominique began to scatter. Dominique said to Diamond, who was standing beside her, "Go in the house." Dominique knew why this conflict was about to take place amongst her and JJ.

"Well, well, well . . . what's up Dominique?" JJ asked. "Hoes," he said gazing at the women, who were scattered around. The looks they gave JJ did not frighten him.

"Man don't come over here disrespecting my ladies," Dominique said. "Now, what's the business?" She asked. All of the ladies who were scattered at first, decided to go inside where Diamond was. They did not want to be bothered by JJ.

"Yall ain't gotta go in the house on count of me," JJ said with a smile.

"They know that, but seeming your mouth can be a little over rated, they just decided to avoid conflict. So again, I ask, what's the business?" Dominique said.

Before JJ could speak, Riley, after turning down his radio, hollered from the car and said, "Yo Dominique, where that fine Diamond go?" JJ laughed. Diamond was the reason for his dilemma now. Dominique said to Riley after inhaling a puff of the cigarette, "Why? You got some money yet?"

"I'm still working on that," Riley said with a gaffe. "And why you always shielding her?" He asked.

"Cause, I'm still waiting on you to come up with the right amount of money." Dominique said with a smile. "Come holla at me when you get some?"

"Ah'ight," Riley said before turning the music back up.

Suddenly JJ said, "Hey Dominique, you got that money that you owe me?"

"What money?" She asked, putting her cigarette up to her mouth.

"I ain't for yo bull today Dominique. I want my money." He said as he took a cigarette from behind his ear, put it in his mouth and lit it.

"What money punk?" Dominique asked. "Yo, why you keep coming at me with this?"

"I got yo punk, and you know what money. You might got all these tricks round here scared, but you got me messed up." JJ said. Riley watched Dominique and JJ arguing from his car.

"Didn't I tell you that you ain't getting no refund. What you got amnesia? You played my girl man. You know what you did was wrong." She said inhaling the cigarette once more before putting it out.

"That wouldn't the deal, Dominique, and you know it. It was Diamond for everybody, and she dipped on us."

"Yeah right, JJ. I would have too. Man, you had your chance, and you blew it. My girl wasn't going out like that. You know you had to have a grand up front. You threw her 250 for you and three of your boys. She a business woman, JJ. She ain't stupid." Dominique said.

"The truth is she bounced-with my money, and she didn't do nothing. Great business women invest wisely." JJ said.

"Man, get away from here with that bull. I'm tired of everywhere I see you, you bringing up the same situation. What's today? Go get Dominique day? You need to gone with that. Anyway, did you forget the part where you pulled a gun on her? Naw man, I don't owe you nothing." Dominique said.

"Oh yeah," JJ said finishing up his cigarette. Dominique had a way with words, and it was time to shut her up.

"That's what I said ain't it! I don't owe you jack, boy. Now get on—my patience short, and I don't want to deal with you today. Running round here talking bout I'm dodging you, for what punk? I ain't scared of you. I don't owe you nothing. Yeah, I said it. I wish I had one time to be Trei, not 2 or 3, just one-the way you messed that man up. Ain't no way I would have killed myself, and you wouldn't have gotten away with raping not one of them in there." Dominique said. JJ provoked her for too long.

Vegas, one of Dominique's friends on the inside of the house and looking out of the window at Dominique and JJ said, "It's time for somebody to do that fool. He want it bad." All the women on the inside of the house were shocked by Vegas' comment as they eyed her.

"What you wanna do then Dominique?" JJ asked full of rage.

"It's whatever boy." Dominique stood up and said. Riley still seated in his car with the music up loud, was not sure what was taking place with JJ and Dominique.

Dominique looked angry, and she had just took off her shades. JJ was closely walking toward her. Riley turned down his radio to listen to the conversation between the two. JJ noticing that the music was lowered said to Riley while looking at Dominique, "Yo Riley, Dominique done bought some balls-looks like that dil-doe done grew on her." JJ said pointing at Dominique's pants. Riley laughed.

"You wish you could have what I got." Dominique said.

Laughing at Dominique's hardness and caught off guard, JJ said, "What?"

"You heard me sweetness. Ain't that yo penitentiary name? The blacker the berry the sweeter the juice," Dominique said with a smile. Something was about to go all wrong and Riley sensed it. He needed to get JJ away from Dominique. If anybody had the nerve enough to push some buttons, it was Dominique.

"Charge that man, and let's go." Riley said to JJ.

"Naw, naw, I ain't going out like no punk—and Dominique done messed with me for the last time." He said. "Now look man, boy—or whatever you is. I want my money or you need to send Diamond on out here." He said with a finger pointed at Dominique. Dominique did not care about his finger. She was just as much serious as he was.

"Hell no, um-um, and ain't no way. So do what it do. It won't take long for me to tag you like the way I use too." She said, standing. "Anytime, young soldier, anytime." She said angrily looking at JJ as she flipped her cigarette bud.

Suddenly, out of nowhere, a gun was pierced in Dominique's side. Riley knew that his point of relaxation was over. He had to get out of the car now and quickly. King Kong and Godzilla were about to make a mark in the projects. "Hey JJ, put the gun up man." Riley said rushing toward Dominique and JJ to resolve the problem. Dominique was quiet. She had not judged JJ correctly. The women inside the apartment watched as JJ and Dominique stood eye to eye.

"Man shut up. This trick trying to get rich off of men—done crossed the last line. Yeah I said it! Say something trick, say something? Matter fact, sit down. I tell you what, how bout I take you instead of Diamond?" JJ asked. Dominique sat down in the chair. Out of all the things that JJ did, she was not about to let this go.

"Boy, you'll never have enough to hose me down. You better ask yo mammy about me." Dominique said looking at JJ.

"You know, ordinarily, now is where I would have shot you, but I'm gone let that one ride." JJ said before Diamond stormed outside.

Diamond, not wanting her friend to get hurt, came outside the door and said, "What are you doing? Put the gun away JJ."

"Go back in the house! All this yo fault. You gone learn how to handle your business right," JJ said.

"JJ, come on man. Kids are out here. They don't need to see this." Riley said standing beside JJ.

"Man forget them kids. This ain't nothing new to them. And shut up whining like Diamond. Dominique know what the deal is," he said eyeing her heavily. He wanted to shoot her. He could see himself pulling the trigger, "Running that smart mouth to my friends talking bout how she ain't gone pay me. Oh, she gone pay me. She gone pay me today." JJ said with the gun to Dominique's head now. Diamond was in tears. "You can go in the house wit that. Won't none of them tears falling stop this from happening." He said to Diamond.

"Let her go JJ. Let her go, and put the gun down." Diamond said.

"What happen to your tears? Girl, shut up. I should just smoke you now. All of this could have been avoided. Naw, you wanna run out." He said to Diamond. "Let me ask you something. With all these men on earth, why do you feel the need to be with a woman, and you a woman, huh? Tell me that?" He asked. Diamond did not respond. She was looking at the barrel of the gun pointed at her friend. "Well now, let me guess," JJ said to Diamond when she did not respond, "cat got your tongue?" He laughed quickly and then recanted what was taking place.

"Man just stop all of this and let her go!" Diamond said while walking toward JJ. "Why you pull a gun on her anyway?" Diamond asked JJ.

"Shut up, trick!" JJ said before slapping Diamond with the gun. Dominique was about to attack but JJ put the gun back on her and said, "sit down!"

"JJ," Riley said. "Shoot man-not the gun, though," he said to clear up his mistake. "Let's go. All of this is unnecessary. Man, I'll pay you man." Riley said pleading to JJ.

"Nope, that's too easy. It's the principle of all of this. Besides, I'm getting my money from this Dominique and right now." He said to Riley before speaking to Dominique, "I oughtta make you eat this gun for labeling me all them punks a while ago. You must don't know who you messing wit Dominique. This ain't little JJ no more. I ain't taking no beat down." He said. Diamond looked as though she wanted to react. JJ said, "Don't plan on wanting to be that froggy that leaps today Diamond."

"Diamond," Riley said. "Just go back in the house." Riley then turned to JJ and said, "Man, lets go. You know Mrs. Helen got 911 on speed dial. Do you hear them sirens? Man I just got out of jail this morning, leave this alone. You proved your point."

JJ did not hear any sirens. He did not hear Riley. What he did hear were the words about to come out of his mouth. "Give me my money!" He told Dominique. "And I want a full refund." Dominique reached into her pocket and pulled out some money. She had several one hundred dollar bills. She began to count out two hundred and fifty dollars for JJ. JJ snatched all of the money in Dominique's hand. He decided that he wanted more than what she owed him. With all of the money in his hand, he said to Dominique, "this for making me act a fool." Dominique only looked at him with much anger. She did not believe in crying, all she could see was revenge as she bit her lip. "Big bad Dominique, look at you now." JJ said. "I told you Riley. Didn't I say that I was gone get my money. Let's go eat and put it on Dominique's tab. She gave us a tip." JJ said as he walked backward toward the car pointing the gun at Dominique with a smile. Dominique did not flinch. She watched as JJ got in the car with Riley and left.

After JJ and Riley pulled away from the curb, Dominique looked at the sky and then back at the ground. Her body guard, Kalle, had witnessed the whole episode from inside the screen door, and she could not do anything. *It was okay though*, she thought, because she like no other had a plan. Talking to her friend from inside the screen door after the whole episode, she asked, "Dominique, you okay?"

"Yeah," Dominique said. "Tell Diamond to come here."

On the way to get Diamond, Kalle heard Dominique calling her again. "Yeah baby," she said, after hurrying back to the screen door.

"Bring me a cigarette. That thief took my cigarettes too. Can you believe it?" Dominique said gazing across the street with a smile. Sunshine, Dominique's California girl, was about to light a cigarette she held in her mouth. Kalle snatched the cigarette from Sunshine's mouth and took her lighter from her hand.

"Hey," Sunshine said getting up from the sofa.

"Now is not the time. Shut up California." Kalle said. She proceeded into the kitchen, where she witnessed Diamond going to earlier. "Let's go Diamond?" She said. Diamond was sitting at the kitchen table with some ice in one hand and rubbing the bruised side of her face with her other hand while holding a cigarette. She looked at Kalle as though she could not believe that JJ had really hit her. Kalle noticing the pain in Diamond's eyes said, "I warned you that this business wasn't nice. You regret it," Kalle asked as Diamond walked toward her?

"Nope," Diamond said pulling the cigarette away from her mouth.

"Anyway with your shine, you'll heal up just fine. You probably should have let JJ have his way with you, though, cause now we gotta murk him." Kalle said walking side by side with Diamond. Diamond knew that she meant murder. "It's time to spoil some flesh, and I'm ready. What about you?" Kalle asked Diamond in a low voice as she pulled her inward and rubbed the side of the face JJ had bruised. She then kissed Diamond on the cheek and smiled.

Diamond replied, "I'm down for whatever."

"That's what I like to hear! Now let's see what Dominique wants." Kalle said slapping Diamond on the behind before they walked out of the kitchen.

Chapter 18

THE BODY

The body of man is very unique and well created. It is complex but organized enough to understand. God created man in the image of Him, and He filled man with knowledge, understanding, and wisdom. Well, he filled him with knowledge and understanding. Wisdom was something that man almost had to buy in literal terms. A man without wisdom has almost nothing. A man with God and wisdom has everything. Without God, nothing is possible. With God, all things are possible. Evil lurks around every corner, and God is the only One that is able to strengthen one enough to resist it and be shielded from it. Satan is always working to gain more power and strength, and when one betrays him, death is the card dealt.

To JJ, life was nothing. He never thought about it or how much it meant to be a part of the world. In his mind, he was only here because his mother and father created him, and that was it. Life can mean so little when one is partying and having a good time all the time, but on the other hand, life can mean so much when one knows that it is about to be taken from him or her and there is no time to get right with God, or God has not cross his or her mind until the last chance, the last second, the last breath. Sometimes God visits to see if one's heart has changed, but He is often turned away; pushed aside, and thrown out. God works through channels, the channels are known as people. Has something or someone good ever entered or approached you and you turned it or him or her away; something or someone that you thought or imagined that was too much and too smart and too bright for you; something or someone dying for a chance to make your life easier and his or hers happier? If so, this person was being used by God. God was maneuvering a new way and a new life for you, since you did not know where to belong. Life is not hard, with a little bit of love and understanding it can last what is known as a lifetime and come to an end without commotion and destruction, promoting celebration. If you have never experienced what it is to really live, how can you expect to understand what it really means to die? JJ was one of these people. His baby's mother was not good enough. His best friend was not good enough. His high was his existence and what strengthen him. His high was what killed him.

Patrick woke up to a ringing cell phone, which was doing nothing to reduce his hangover. He had avoided the phone ringing for sometime, but after the eighth ring, he figured it must be important. It was his homeboy Tony.

"Yeah," Patrick said answering the phone.

"Hey man, they said-they found JJ's body." Tony said.

"What you said?"

"Man wake up! They said-they found JJ's body." Tony said.

"For real?" Patrick asked.

"They said that fool been dead three days."

"Hold up man? Wait a minute. Don't call me playing on the phone. If you want some weed, just ask for it. You ain't gotta be making up no stories." Patrick said to Tony. Tony knew how to lie when he did not need too.

"Man, I ain't want no weed! I'm for real this morning. That fool been dead three days. You know ain't nobody seen him." Tony said.

"Man quit playing. So he dead for real?"

"Yeah, he dead." Tony said with a brief pause. Patrick was quiet. "Man they said the maggots was eating . . ."

"Man kill that sickness." Patrick replied.

"Man they said the maggots was eating up that fool body, and his tongue had been cut out. You know that gold out grill he had in his mouth. It's gone. And his grill was straight loaded. His tongue was gone man. Man, his right hand was cut off like, I guess that meant he was stealing. Man, people saying that the mafia did it."

"For real?" Patrick asked.

"That ain't it. His eyelids were glued shut with some crazy glue and when the coroner finally opened them up-check this out? He didn't have no eyeballs."

"Knawl, no way!" Patrick exclaimed.

"And guess what was carved in his chest? The word dead."

"What's that suppose to mean?" Patrick asked Tony.

"Dead fool. Shoot—that's what he was. Then again, I don't know. Probably whoever did it saying they got the last word. You know once you dead, you dead—can't nothing else be done about it. Man, I'm talking they had time to straight up murk him to carve that in his chest. They say that fool was messed up, stinking, corroded, funky . . ." Tony replied.

"Al-right man, I see the picture." Patrick replied.

"I know he went for bad, but he didn't deserve to die like that." Tony said.

"Fool say something else?" Patrick said.

"That's all I can say. Whoever killed him done said it all. Man—they cut that fool hand off, man. Cut it off. Not the left one, the right one. Stick and balls ain't been cut off." Tony said

"Maybe he didn't have much to cut. Man this is crazy. I don't understand who could have done this." Patrick said.

"I don't either. I know JJ and dude got into it, him and Flip a couple of weeks ago, but they squashed that, and drunk a twenty pack of beer together. They got into it bout Flip's sister, how JJ disrespected her on the block the other day. Flip let it go cause JJ apologized to his sister. Talking bout he didn't know that was Flip's sister. It didn't matter who sister she was. You don't yank down nobody skirt in front of a bunch of males." Tony said.

"Man that fool was always disrespecting them females. He just robbed Dominique about two weeks ago. Anyway, I don't care about him being dead when I think of it. He wasn't no kin to me." Patrick said. "He was bad about saying that he was drunk or high too just to get out of some mess. That fool wasn't drunk. He wasn't high. He was just disrespecting. That's all he was. That's all he was." Patrick said taking a cigarette from his pants laying on the floor beside the bed.

"All I know is that he made the wrong person mad this time. Body missing for three days, three days, didn't nobody know he was dead man." Tony said.

"What about his momma them," Patrick asked?

"His own family didn't know he was dead, man—til the police said tap, tap, tap on the door and told them that they need them to come and identify the body."

"You lying!" Patrick said while sitting up in his bed.

"Man, I ain't lying—cause they use to say that JJ was known for disappearing from home for days. They use to him always just showing up, though. I bet that they never would have imagined that they would have to go downtown and identify his stinking body, a body maggots almost done savored." Tony said paying close attention to the police car passing by his house as he sat on the front porch.

"Ah, man, that's messed up. I wouldn't want my momma to see me like that, man." Patrick said inhaling the cigarette.

"Yo momma, you know how my momma is. Anyway, you'll be dead. It wouldn't make any sense to you. This just proves that sometimes you gotta stop gambling bout every thang, and let some stuff go man. I don't know if I wanna get saved or testify right now man." Tony said watching the cops get out of the car in front of his home.

"Fool that's the same thang," Patrick said. He then laughed at Tony.

"Man, I gotta go. The cops at my doorstep-again. I ain't killed no body." Tony said while hanging up the phone with Patrick. As the policemen approached him, he said, "What y'all want? I ain't killed nobody. Yeah, I'm on house arrest. And I don't know nothing."

Chapter 19

HOME

Sarah was exhausted after ripping and running and making arrangements for her son's funeral. The long, hot bath she took seemed to do her arthritic hands some good. Turning the covers back on the bed, she relaxed beside her husband, who was reading the sports section of the newspaper. "Ahhh, James, I-am-so tired." She said calmly, laying her head against her pillow. James said nothing. He kept reading the stats in the paper. "It's been a long day." She said quietly. James still said nothing, only shook the wrinkles from the paper a bit. Sarah assumed that James did not feel much like talking, so she turned over on her side and closed her eyes. A few minutes passed and Sarah could feel her husband gazing at her as she opened her eyes and found him breathing over her. "What?" She asked as he moved away. He closed the paper, folded it, and laid it on his lap on top of the covers.

"I just wanna know a good answer to one thang." He said to his wife as she slowly turned over to console him.

"What James?" She asked.

"Train Depot—I just can't get it off my mind. Joe called today. And you wanna know what he asked? James, where JJ funeral gone be at anyway, St. Hope, he asks? I says no Joe. Now you know my brother crazy, right?" He said with his arms folded behind his head.

"And you ain't?" Sarah asked with a smile.

"So I tells Joe that the funeral was gone be at the Southside Train Station. You know what he did? He laughed, and said, quit playing bro. Moments later Sam called, like Joe ain't told him what I said, and I told him the same thang. He too thought that I was kidding. He laughed. Asked me why not the church, and you know what I told him. You know what, as a matter fact Sarah, everybody who called while you were out taking care of the funeral, laughed at me!"

"James, please, don't start. Let's not get into this again." Sarah said about to turn back over on her right side.

"Naw—naw, listen to me?" He said turning his wife over to face him again. "Do you know that I thought that that mess was a joke? This new bill passing and stuff? Two weeks ago, I heard about some people having their sons memorial service in their back yard—cause, cause the preacher wouldn't let them have it in their church, and they didn't want people mocking them, so they had to bury they son in the back yard to avoid criticism. Well not bury him in the back yard, but you know had his memorial service back there. You know, in the back yard. Now that same bit of stuff done stepped in our household-you know-done passed on to us like a freaking virus, contagious and stuff . . ."

"James," Sarah said quietly, "let it go."

"How can you say let it go? Do you understand what is happening here, Sarah? I mean . . .

this is sad Sarah. It don't make no sense. Our son gone be having his memorial service at the—train station. Who came up with that mess anyway?"

"Just think of it as a going away party." Sarah said.

"Forget that! I wanna know who came up wit that law? It's sad, and it's bad enough when you don't know that your son been dead three days. Then you got to find out that he can't be having his memorial service in a church, where that hypocrite, no good, skank, scandalous . . ."

"James!" Sarah exclaimed. She did not agree with her husband's remarks.

He continued, "preacher at."

"O-kay," Sarah said. "I get the point James."

"That sucker ain't nothing. Yeah, I said it. You go to that church and tell that fool that I said, he ain't nothing. Forget him! We don't need him to preach our boy's funeral anyway." James said, briefly pausing before continuing, "I tell you what—I'm just gone go downtown tomorrow and get a pine box to put JJ in. We gone bury him in the back yard. No memorial—no nothing. We own this land. We can do it."

"We can't do that." Sarah said.

"Why not," he asked his wife?

"James, you acting simple." She replied.

"Simple—Sarah. You know what's simple, all this bull that's going on now. Okay, okay, okay, yeah-you-you right. We probably can't do that, but this what we gone do. Put him in a pine box, don't invite anybody to anything and pay for a spot at the grave yard. How bout that?"

"That's funny James, really hysterical." She said.

"Why? I'm quite serious, Sarah. Before today, people did that yesterday. Anyway, that no good fool don't need to be preaching our boy's funeral, and you know it Sarah. This don't make no sense. I ain't saying that the boy wasn't bad and all, but he don't deserve to be memorialized in a train station. He don't deserve this and then these nosy, sorry, no good neighbors staring in yo face all the time, asking, 'Is there something I can do for you?' All the while they saying behind your back, who ever heard of being memorialized at a train station. Oh, I been hearing what they saying. Why no fool . . .

ain't nothing you can do. Can you bring me a good son back, an obedient one, who will die and have a proper burial? If not get out of my face!" James exclaimed.

"I hope that you won't say that. Rationalizing on things now, you're where he got that attitude from." Sarah said.

"From me," James asked his wife?

"Yeah, you are where he learned how to disrespect women." Sarah said

"No, no, no—that kid, didn't learn nothing from me. Not nothing like that."

"So now he's just another kid and not yours. He got that attitude from you-and the way he degraded women." Sarah said.

"No, I don't think so." James said looking at Sarah.

"And why not?" She asked moving her head on her pillow.

"We didn't even get along. Anyhow, if I were that bad, how come is it that you married me?"

"Honestly, I don't know James. You know sometimes I ask myself exactly the same question, and you wanna know what myself always tell me? It's cause you too smart for him, and he needs someone to teach him how to be smart." She said before she started to laugh.

"What? That's a lie." He said with a smile.

"No—it's not James, and it wouldn't surprise me at all if a dang woman killed JJ."

James laughed at his wife's sense of humor and said, "Sarah, you do know you just cursed?"

"I did not. That's what you heard. Go to sleep," she said turning her back to him.

"I knew you could still be a sinner if you wanted to be." James replied.

"Oh yeah, and the only difference between yours and mine is I know how to get forgiveness, and you don't." She said before closing her eyes.

Chapter 20

THE INVESTIGATION

The police had all the evidence they needed to convict JJ of rape and battery. However, the evidence did not stick, not because JJ was innocent, but because the evidence confiscated was either lost during Hurricane Katrina, used up, or had never been recovered in the first place. JJ's defense team made him look like the victim and very innocent. A terrible picture was painted, concerning Jada's credibility. Many people testified that JJ left the party early and that there was no way that he had raped the twenty-three year old virgin. However, no one seemed to know what time he left. The semen collected in the rape was lost, and the bite marks on Jada's body were never photographed as evidence. These two sources were the prosecutions biggest pieces of evidence along with Hurricane Katrina carrying evidence away with her. JJ's bloody clothes were never found. Jada's case was a mess also because a new rookie detective assigned to the case with no experience did not confiscate or handle the evidence well.

Honestly, no one in the police station was really concerned about the rape case. In fact, they hoped that Hurricane Katrina carried more than Jada's case with them. Besides that, JJ's defense team said that Jada could easily have drugged herself and taken her own virginity both ways and set JJ up, since her and the defendant did not get along. The new detective on the case recorded the timing of the rape all wrong as well. Jada's story had many inconsistencies and if that was not enough, Sarah testified that her son was at home at the time when the rape had supposedly taken place. Additionally, several people at the party testified that JJ and Jada did not get along well and was always competing for strength. One girl testified that Jada said that she would use rape as a method of ridding of all her altercations with JJ once and for all. The jurors believed what the young lady said, and JJ walked away calm and free. There was no way for Jada to win, at least not now.

All methods of victory for Jada were gone, especially when her best friend, Necee, testified that she locked Jada in the bedroom alone. Necee also testified that she was the only one who had access to the room. The defense lawyers also put the doctor on the stand who evaluated Jada, and asked the doctor if Jada even knew that she had been raped. The doctor said no and that only three days later she claimed to remember what happened after being embarrassed. So with no evidence and no witnesses for the prosecutions side, JJ was exonerated.

While JJ was found innocent of all charges do to his gang members, family, friends, and Hurricane Katrina. Jada was slowly dying on the inside. She knew that JJ had raped her, but her quick approach of depression was telling and showing her that maybe she could be wrong. She gave up school, God, and was giving up on living. Her constant suicide attempts made her look guilty, and JJ powered-up when he heard about them. She was alone, and she trusted no one. Necee was no longer her friend as Jada pushed her away, and Trei was no longer her boyfriend. Somehow he believed JJ and not her about the rape. He wanted to believe her but the gang that he was involved in was one for all and all for one. Trei missed the presence of Jada and often cried at night thinking of her. On the other hand, Jada hated Trei for not standing by her side. She hated him for not knowing what kind of friend he had. She never knew that deep down on the inside, Trei questioned his friend's credibility too. The incident caused Trei to fall into a depressive state as well. He used alcohol regularly to move on from day to day. It stopped the pain sometime. He wanted to ask JJ what really happened when they were alone together sometime, but he never did. He wanted JJ to tell him first without him having to ask. Thoughts of Jada drove him crazy, and he was now an intoxicated fool. He could not release the conversation with his mother that he had six weeks after JJ's trial, "You're guilty, just as much as that JJ, gang member friend of yours. You know as well as me that he raped Jada." His mother said.

He said to her, "I'm sick of hearing that mess, Ma."

"Look at you," his mother said, standing, talking to him with a bag of groceries in her hand by the porch where he sat smoking a cigarette and holding a bottle of beer. "You've become just the son that I despise, consuming all that liquor and doing all them drugs. Just look at you."

"Yeah, yeah, yeah," he said to her after taking a puff of the cigarette. "Leave me alone."

"And that's exactly what I'm gone do, Trei" she said as she started to walk up the steps to enter her house, but before she went inside she turned and said, "You know, you may as well have raped that child yourself, Trei. You let that demon seed get away with it. You chose his lies over her innocence. She'll never be the same again. And she can never physically be a virgin again."

"Man, let me go," he said getting up from the porch and walking away.

"You always remember that." She said.

'When you gone preach a different sermon? You know-I'm tired of hearing this one. Jada not virgin, Jada not a virgin, JJ raped her." He said mocking his mother.

"Yeah, gone on around that corner with that bottle, I just hope the law round there waiting on you," she said. "You want be as lucky as that friend of yours, and I ain't coming to get you," she said opening the screen door.

"Whatever, I don't need you. I got some money." He said pulling some money from his pocket and flashing it at his mother.

Once inside the house she said, "Lord, he has become a drugged out, drunk, arrogant fool because he's afraid of the truth, please help him?"

Chapter 21

DOING THE TIME

Trei always believed in the idea that there were two tales to every story; he just did not understand the rules as to how to be able to tell what or who to believe. In this worst case scenario, he chose not to believe Jada because he knew it meant death for him. He also knew that his mother would never lie to him, not intentionally. But what could he do? He had known JJ for ten years and Jada for only six months, and he knew how well Jada could shut-up JJ quickly, causing him to become entangled in his own words and confused. He questioned the idea of Jada telling the truth. He also questioned what his mother said to him about how his best friend of ten years was guilty of rape. The score 2-2, besides, he had witnessed how his best friend cried before him behind a jail cell saying that he was innocent and would not do something so bad to hurt him. He also remembered JJ saying once for him not to cry when he got Jada. Trei saw the tears on JJ's face that day; listened to the heart felt plea in JJ's voice that day; and watched the swearing hands that JJ presented before God almighty. Yes, JJ was capable of violence and had done many things, but never had he sworn before God that he was innocent of a damaging act that he had committed.

Two years had passed, since Jada cried rape. JJ was still involved in many altercations since then, but never convicted of anything, not robbing the Asian American's store for two hundred dollars; carjacking a 2005 Hummer from some visitors; pulling a gun on a Jehovah's witness lady for telling him the word of the Holy Bible; cutting his pregnant girl friend across the stomach because he did not want a child, or burning down a Methodist church because a juror in his domestic case was threatening to convict him to make him an example in all domestic cases. No, he was never convicted. He ran away from all the charges pending against him. Why? Because he knew people that knew people who could get close to people. It was as though, he was being shielded from all the wrong that he committed. Trei almost wanted him to get caught so that he would suffer from something deep down inside. He prayed that if JJ had sexually assaulted Jada multiple times, that he would suffer soon, but JJ never did, and Trei only believed that maybe JJ had not raped Jada and that it was a scheme to land his friend behind bars. Nevertheless, Trei was not normal either. He was with his friend when the crimes happened. He was the one often jailed for the crimes, and being pretty behind bars was not good for him, not at all.

Behind bars many times, men saw him as a woman, and Trei often had to prove his manhood. He did not hesitate to stoop low once when a cell mate asked him to get on his knees and open his oven (mouth). He did it, but it had consequences because his teeth were his weapon. Two episodes of that gave Trei a reputation, and he was never approached that way again. His second victim was not as lucky as the first one. It took several guards to pry Trei's mouth open. They did not have to pry for long because Trei had bit it off. The cell mate almost bled to death. After those two unfortunate incidents, Trei decided that he would shave his head bald. He did not want anyone to be imagining him or fantasizing about him being another Halle Berry. He did nothing that looked like it was the ways of a woman. He learned not too. It almost got him raped six times. Hair was a no-no; wearing a bandana was a no-no; keeping his lips moisturized was a no, no; crossing his legs, wearing tight clothes, and keeping himself well groomed like he did with the ladies was a no, no. He was a man, and a man in jail-if he is a real man-has one thing on his mind, and that is survival-like man against nature under the worst conditions.

Meanwhile, while Trei was dealing with the ways of man on the inside, locked up, JJ was enjoying the ways of man on the outside, freedom. He never once paid his friend a visit when he was in jail. Trei wondered if JJ was truly his best friend, or if he was that asshole that his mother often warned him about. This was the third time that he was locked up in two years for something that was JJ's idea in the first place. Cell mates on the inside told Trei that JJ was a snitch, said that he worked for a corrupt cop and judge, and that was the reason he often beat the charges brought up against him. That was not the only thing that was said. They said that the two times that JJ was convicted for crimes, he was raped in jail. They even showed Trei and introduced him to the guy that did it. Trei asked the guy if it were true, and the six-three, muscular built man said, yeah because he needed Trei on his team for some prison deal that was going down. Apparently, the guy needed a new contact on the outside to bring something on the inside without the guards suspecting something was wrong. Trei could not believe that his friend, that was so hard on the streets, had been raped in jail. Maybe that was it. Maybe that explained JJ's attitude. He had been taken advantage of, then again, Trei thought that JJ was not the first and that he would not be the last; besides, Bible history, American history, and Western Government states that men have been sleeping with men since the beginning of time. That it is nothing new. It's just something that God, Himself, was never and is never happy about and often warned and is still warning man about. Greek history mentions it often, I guess because it was the idea of men spending much time away from home and in war or in some kind of religious organization that prohibited sexual desires with women or ruled out sex period. Consequently, the idea of it and history teaches that man lying with man is an abomination. This idea is presented to both man and woman alike.

Trei was trying to piece together the puzzle of his best friend's attitude. Maybe, his cell mates were telling the truth about his best friend; especially since, he was asked by the police to set JJ up in exchange for a lighter sentence or some house arrest time. When he refused, he was sent straight to jail for three months. He was tired of jail. He was sick of it, but yet, he would not lead a virtuous life and every time he was out, the same trouble was knocking at his mother's door. And what did he do? What that trouble wanted done at his expense.

The whole time that he was in jail, he could only think of two people, his mother and Jada. His mother because she gave him life and often warned him about trouble and about getting in it, and Jada because she was a good woman with goals and dreams ahead of her and one incident swallowed that up. He often dreamed of Jada. The dreams seemed so real and innocent and happy. Jada haunted and lived in his spirit every day. She tormented him with her beautiful smile and warm eyes that could be cold when she was mad. He thought of her shiny hair and its sweet smell. He never once had a dream where he made love to her. The only dream he had of being close to her was standing in the room and watching while his friend raped her, and he was able to do nothing to help her.

The day had come once more after one year, when the guard approached Trei's cell door and said, "Lets go styles. You're out of here." Outside his mother waited and two days later, trouble was at the door again, knocking to come in to his life. He welcomed trouble, pushed his mother and her advice aside, and accepted the alcohol and the drugs again. The drugs never made him feel totally better, but they helped him to cope. He could not understand why he had not overdosed between the thoughts of Jada and getting high, because both were killing him slowly. The ecstasy pills were messing up his heart and brain; the cocaine was burning up his noise and his brain, and the alcohol was killing his liver, kidneys, and his brain. He was a medicine lab on the verge of self destruction. Heroine was almost his next choice, but something, some urge pushed him away. It was like a super power ego inside his brain that kicked up a notch and told him, 'hell no, I have had enough. You are going too far'. Trei's life to him was clueless. He did not know what was next. He just lived day for day. If hell was his destiny, then he decided that he would soon be there.

Chapter 22

ANOTHER CHANCE

Three years had passed since Jada's rape. The anniversary of the incident was quickly approaching, again. No matter how many times Trei called Jada's house anonymously to calm his own nerves and release his pain, hoping she would answer the phone, she never did. Her mother Lauren always answered the phone. Trei would hang up quickly, and then he would cry; even though, Jada's mother Lauren was saved and would possibly forgive him. Additionally, he would drink more alcohol to soothe his pain, and he would cry some more. He wanted to knock on Jada's door, but he could not. He had hurt her too much. He knew that he had. However, even though she was mad at Trei for not believing her, she could not understand why he had not come to comfort her or try to help her, and she hated him for it.

Each time Trei built up the nerve to make that phone call, he was disappointed. His eyes watered with anger as he would sometimes gaze into the open sky with his drunken spirit and then walk away from the pay phone. By now, the Trei that Jada once knew had disappeared. He was disfigured, nothing like he use to be; unshaven, small, and his full, handsome filled, face was only skin and bones now. He retained the bald head that he started in prison, and his long goatee stayed platted, reaching his chest area now. The women who use to love him now refused his company, advances and calls. It did not phase Trei though. He was a human bomb, walking, talking, and ticking away into the very crevices of Satan's hell. His attitude was terrible, almost worst than JJ's.

While everyone else pushed Trei aside and refused to be around him, JJ embraced him. He liked the person that Trei had become. JJ just did not know who this person was really becoming or why, and the day had come when Trei realized that it was time to beat JJ at his own game. He had to know the truth about Jada before his life came to an end. And even though the truth came with a price, Trei refused to pay for it this time.

In the drug business, there are ups and downs. For months things were looking good for gang 186. '*Yeah, that was our gang title. We took on the name 186 because we were one number short from being dead.*' Trei use to love the easy money along with the good times he had with the fellows, but something went wrong, and Trei was not feeling the way he use to feel about the gang, and he definitely was not feeling JJ. While in jail the last time, he had become suspicious of his best friend. Word in jail said JJ was a snitch. Jealous birds were talking and all their talk was JJ. Trei found it hard to believe that his best friend was a snitch, especially since, he and JJ had pulled off the last two drug deals with no problem with the police. But now things had changed as fate revealed to Trei that his instincts were just the right instincts. It appeared that all the jail talk was true, and Trei realized now that the reason for JJ never being on the inside was because the cops needed him on the outside.

It was Thursday morning and around the seven-o-clock hour, when Trei received a call from JJ. JJ told him that he was on his way over with the food. Food was the undercover word for drug supply. Minutes later, JJ arrived. Trei opened the door and accepted the drugs after letting JJ inside the house. He and JJ spoke briefly before Trei told JJ, "hey man, I'm gone grab a shower right quick, and I'll meet you at the spot later." JJ said, "ah'ight . . . see you soon." He fist pounded Trei and then left. Trei raced upstairs to the bathroom to prepare for his shower after locking the front door. About to look in the medicine cabinet for some aspirin, he noticed JJ was still outside as he spotted him while he looked out of the bathroom window. JJ looked suspicious. Trei watched as JJ turned his hat backward and got in his SUV and pulled away. *No, Trei thought to himself. I'm just paranoid.* Flipping the hat to the back is the way that the 186 gang let someone know that a deal has just went down and the drugs were in place. The only thing about this picture was, who was JJ warning? Seconds later, undercover cops were coming from no where. Trei raced out of the bathroom and down the stairs, trying to recover and rid of the drugs before they were found. He was too late. As he made it down three steps, the cops kicked open the door. The door fell to the floor and with guns, the police told Trei, "Get down!' Trei thought, *"where?"* before saying out loud, "Damn!"

Trei was glad that his mother left hours earlier. He did not want to put her through the cruel episode of getting down on the floor. It was only seconds before the police found the drugs. The cops went exactly to the spot where only JJ and Trei knew the drugs were, under one of the carpeted steps leading upstairs.

"Where the rest of the drugs at Styles?" Detective Rumsfield asked Trei.

"What you mean rest? I didn't know those were in here." Trei said while being handcuffed.

"You a lie. It don't matter though. We got you anyway?" Rumsfield said with a smile.

"Whatever man," Trei said as he tilted his head to the side.

At the police station, Trei was offered the opportunity to get out of jail for free. But he had to agree to do something for the cops first. He had to deliver the main guy pushing the weight. Trei was not about to do that, so he said, "What? JJ ain't snitching enough for yall?"

"Shut up Styles. This ain't about no JJ. This is about you." Rumsfield said as his partner looked on. "Now sit down."

"Why can't you call me Trei?" Trei asked Rumsfield as he sat down.

"Because I like calling you Styles better, Styles," Rumsfield said. "You know you gone for a long time with this one. You might want to talk."

"Naw man, I think that I'm gone let JJ keep that job." Trei said sitting at the table.

"Boy, piss on JJ. We about to nail him too." Rumsfield's partner Carter said. Rumsfield was busy lighting a cigarette.

"Show you right," Rumsfield said, agreeing with his partner. Apparently, JJ was not delivering enough, and his free passes were at an end. His snitching had started to stink.

"I'm serious Styles, ain't no come back this time. You gone for life with this." Rumsfield said relaxing in his chair. "You might oughtta take some time and reconsider our offer. Yo boy want you to disappear."

"Man, save all of that—I ain't no snitch." Trei said. "Just like them ain't none of my drugs."

"Oh yeah, let's see what this audio tape says and what these pictures look like." Carter said standing, holding something in a manila envelope.

"Let's see then!" Trei said standing up.

"Sit down punk. Who you think we is?" Carter said. Rumsfield looked at his partner before looking at Trei again.

"Look Styles, we trying to do you a favor." Rumsfield said after puffing on the cigarette.

"Naw—man, y'all trying to kill me. What? Let me guess, y'all aint got nothing? That's why we doing all this talking?" Trei asked.

"Here man. I know you could use one." Rumsfield said trying to offer Trei a cigarette.

"Naw man, I'll pass. I don't want you weak cigarette." Trei said. "You won't get no DNA today."

"That's it! You on your way back to jail!" Detective Rumsfield said, getting up from his chair.

"Let's see the pictures and hear the tape!" Trei exclaimed.

"I promise you that you will never get out again!" Rumsfield replied while hitting his fist on the table.

"The pictures, the audio . . ." Trei exclaimed. This time the police would have to show him that he was guilty. "I done been down this road too many times, and this time I promise I ain't going without seeing the evidence."

"Carter, show him the pictures." Rumsfield said. "Show his punk ass we ain't lying."

"Naw, this punk ain't gone talk." Carter said.

"Carter, the pictures and play that tape," Rumsfield said.

Carter dropped the manila envelope on the table. The pictures slid out. Detective Rumsfield grabbed the audio tape and pressed play. Trei could hear voices, but was it his voice he thought. Soon he heard the voices clearly and recognized that it was him on the tape along with JJ. The pictures revealed everything that took place in the house. Trei thought to himself, '*this fool done ratted me out, and he has being doing it for sometime now.*' Detective Rumsfield could see the anger in Trei's eyes. He knew that he had him. Trei did not know that the police had more on him until Rumsfield said, "This is only the icing on the cake. The worse part of all of this is, simply the cake. Additionally, you are facing more federal indictment charges on 2 counts of conspiracy in drug related activities, and the delivery of drugs within several feet of a school yard. I don't think that your gang friends would be too happy with a snitch in their family."

"Man, miss that. You and I both know that I ain't no snitch." Trei said.

"Oh, but I don't know that. Now you listen to me, you slick, scum, scavenging the streets, drugged up punk." Rumsfield said before being cut off by Trei.

"Yo man, why I gotta be all that? Why all the name calling?" Trei said. He knew that Rumsfield was already upset. He wanted to make sure that he pushed all of his buttons.

"Shut up, punk," Rumsfield said after putting out his cigarette. "You got three days to help us lock that JJ up and find the source responsible for the distribution of all these drugs on the streets in New Orleans! After then, and you still ain't talking, you belong to us. Now you either gone do it or get with it. It don't make us no difference. Do I make myself clear?" Rumsfield asked Trei as he leaned into his face from across the table. Rumsfield then took a piece of paper from his pocket and said to Trei, "here." The paper was a pink slip, similar to that of a receipt a jailer receives when he is bonded out of jail by a bondsman. Rumsfield continued by saying to Trei, "consider your self out on bail, on me." Rumsfield's partner, Carter, was standing by the door. Rumsfield then said to Carter, "Let that punk out." Trei, walking toward the door, briefly stopped in his tracks when Rumsfield said, "Oh and don't try to run."

Carter said, holding the door and looking at Trei, "Cause it won't take long for us to find you." Trei eyed him suspiciously before leaving the room. Carter shut the door behind him and said to Rumsfield, "you think he gone run?"

"Naw, he got a big decision to make and by the time he makes that decision, he'll be dead. And we'll have just what we want." Rumsfield said lighting his cigarette again.

"What's that?" Carter asked.

"Are you always this slow, Carter?" Rumsfield asked his partner. "One less brother off the streets." He concluded.

"Oh," Carter said hitting himself on the head. "You one bold white man to say that to me, but that's okay." Carter said. He had something up his sleeve. Rumsfield would pay for that comment. Carter couldn't stand his racist attitude. He needed to throw Rumsfield off, so he said, "I forgot that we house over fifty percent of jails and only account for six percent of the population. Yeah, the white man quick to lock us up." After Carter made the statement, he left Rumsfield in the interrogation room alone.

Chapter 23

AT MY WORST

It seemed that everything JJ touched was dying. He was entering and withdrawing people from his life quickly. Jada had been raped and Trei was going insane, but Trei had a way out. Rumsfield had given him three days to give up JJ and his drug source. With one day almost over and two more to go, Trei had to figure out a way to possibly avoid the matter all together. Jail was not an option. He was not going back. Snitching was definitely not an option. He was nobody's snitch. His consumption of drugs and alcohol was on the rise as he gazed at the figure in the mirror he had become. He was nothing like he used to be, six-eight, light-skinned, healthy and good looking with hair. He was now bald headed, skinny, weary and depressed. Trei thought to himself, '*I have to do what is right*'. At that moment, Trei had reached a decision. He had to fix all that he messed up. First, he had to talk to Jada or try. Second, he needed to talk to JJ. Picking up his cell phone, he dialed Jada's number. The phone rang several times before someone picked up and said, "Hello." It was Lauren Wells, Jada's mom as always.

"Hey Mrs. Wells." Trei took a deep breath and said, "If it's possible, will you please let me talk to Jada?" Deep down inside, she wanted to say hell no, but the power of the Holy Ghost made her say something better. See, Mrs. Wells believed in conclusions and making things right. She believed in everything being finalized and forgiven even if it took some time to do. She believed in doing what God commanded her to do, and right then, God said for her to put Jada on the phone.

"What took you so long son?" She asked Trei.

"Mrs. Wells, I guess that you can claim the devil and me on this one. I've always called, just didn't have the courage to say something. Mrs. Wells, if it is any consolation, I really want you to know that I am sorry. I'm sorry for everything." He said.

"I know son, but I must tell you, Jada probably won't talk to you. She lost a lot after what happened-tried to kill herself six times. Oh, but I prayed and rebuked that beast." Lauren said. Trei wondered if the beast she rebuked stopped him from getting raped six times in jail or was it just mere coincidence?

"I know. I wish that I could go back and change everything. May I speak with her, please? I have to let her know that I was a fool and stupid." He said.

"Yeap, you were that, even if it is not my place to judge you. Hold on? I'll see if I can get her to talk to you." Lauren said after wiping her hands on her apron after rinsing a dish.

Staring out of her bedroom window, Jada thought of how things would have been different. She would be finished with college by now, and her career would have just begun. Looking down at the grass for a brief second, she walked away from the window. She could hear her mother calling her from downstairs, opening her bedroom door, she yelled, "yeah."

"Would you please pick up the phone? Someone wants to talk to you." Lauren yelled from the bottom staircase.

"Tell Micha that I will call him back. Don't want to talk right now." Jada said about to close the bedroom door.

"It's not Micha honey. Will you please pick up the phone?" Lauren asked, hoping that Jada would not ask who it was.

Jada was not sure if she should pick up the phone or not. Instinct said to her, answer it. Closing her bedroom door, she picked up the phone and said, "Hello."

The voice on the other end was silent. Once more Jada said, "Hello." Lauren had not hung up the phone downstairs yet. She could hear Jada saying hello. Lauren thought to herself, *'say something son'?*

Trei spoke, "Hey J. How are you?" Jada could not believe that she was hearing the voice of the very person who did not believe her. She waited for him to call her years ago and apologize and now he was calling today. Jada did not know how to perceive the call. The part of her that hated him decided to react first.

"Why are you calling me? Shouldn't you be supervised by your buddy now?" She asked.

"Okay, I deserve that and whatever else you're going to throw at me. So, you go first and then if time and you permit, I will speak second." Trei said. Jada was shocked by his words. She wanted to go first, but his words caused her to refrain and listen. There was a brief silence in the conversation. Trei not sure if Jada was still on the phone asked, "J, you still there?" Jada did not respond. "J," he said again. Once more he called out to her, "J, please be there? I don't know if I'll ever call again." Downstairs, Lauren sensed that it was time for her to hang up the phone.

Tears rolling from her eyes, she said, "Don't worry—I'm still here." Trei released a sigh of relief. "Why Trei," asked Jada? "Why did you abandon me and make me look like a liar and a fool?"

"My status, situation—environment then J. Those were the only reasons, but I am so sorry Jada. Not once did I not believe you in my heart. I always believed you. I did." He said.

"Then why didn't you help me? You stood by and let you friend get away with humiliating me. You said nothing. You walked away as if you had never met me, spent time with me or held me." She said.

"And believe me, you. I am paying for every bit of it right now. I was stupid okay, J. I was really stupid and foolish. He and everyone else had convinced me that he was innocent, and I listened and thought that he was in my mind. But in my heart, I knew that he was guilty. I could feel it. I just couldn't prove it."

"Prove it! What was there to prove to you? I was your girlfriend. You were supposed to believe me. You were supposed to be there for me. I was in the hospital for two weeks and you never once came to see me. My face was a mess, my body worse. I had to wake up to the most devastating news about me. Did you even think of doing the right thing?" She asked sitting on her bed.

"Of course, I did. He was my best friend. I mean, what was I suppose to do? I didn't know what to do." He said.

"You were supposed to do what was right. You were supposed to step back and look at the situation for what it really was. Your friend raped me vaginally and anally. He beat me and left me for dead. And you ask me, what you were supposed to do as if all of this were my fault?" Jada replied.

"You know what I mean J. What I'm saying is if I believed you, it would be as if you were trying to set him up. If I believed him, it was as if he was trying to set you up. I had known him for 10 years then, and I had only known you for six months. I didn't know who to believe at first. You two were always at each others throat. Honestly, I was confused." He said.

"And apparently stupid—So, are you confused now? Because if you are, this conversation is so over," she said.

"No I'm not confused now." He said in a low tone, relaxed on the sofa. "I'm angry. I'm angry at myself for being so naïve and angry at him for allowing him to use me! Now I know what it feels like to be the one asking the question why. I'm dying Jada-on the inside that is. I've been dying for a long time."

"What are you saying?" She asked.

"Nothing, just a figure of speech," he said. "Jada," he called out to her.

"Yeah," she said.

"Have you forgiven me or will you ever forgive me?" He asked.

Quiet for several seconds, she said, "Yes and yes," while taking a deep breath.

"Do you hate me?" He asked.

"I did, but I got over it," she said.

"Do you still love me?" He asked while looking up at the ceiling in his mother's house.

"Boy, do you dig deep. No, I don't love you anymore, but I do still care about what happens to you if it's any consolation." She replied while tracing the flower print of her comforter on her bed.

"I can respect that." He said as a tear rolled down his cheek. He tried to wipe it away, but more tears were falling. Trei took a deep breath to remove the lump in his throat. Jada had just told him that she did not love him anymore. What other reason did she have, he thought? He quickly answered himself saying, *'a lot.'* But he could not hang up the phone with Jada just yet. He had to tell her how he felt. He had to be honest with her. After many moments of silence, Trei said, "I still love you Jada. I always have. One stupid mistake just messed me up for a lifetime. I remember the first time I saw you. I said to myself that I deserved you and that you could be Mrs. Trei Styles. I said if any right was in me that you would make me right. Seeing your face while I was in jail was the only way that I got through. Every fight that I fought was for you. I soon realized that I was fighting the wrong fight. I had only one enemy to defeat, but I was too busy embracing him as a friend. God, I feel so bad now. My life is a complete downsize. If I don't rat JJ out tomorrow to the police, then I'm going to jail for the rest of my life. If I do rat JJ out, I'm dead. So you see Jada, I'm getting just what I deserve. I wouldn't save you. Now, I have no one to save me." He said. Jada's eyes filled with water. She felt sympathy for him and recognized that she could not save him. Trei had to pay for his own sins. It was only her job to forgive him, and she had done just that. Trei concluded by saying, "You know Jada, all I really wanted was an opportunity to love you completely with no one around, to hold you and laugh at your corny jokes. I feel like if it were another time and place that I could do just that-I mean granted if you would allow me a second opportunity. Man, I messed up—bad, but I won't ever get over you. I wish that I could hold you just once more, at least see you, but I know that that's impossible. Anyway, thank you, Jada. I needed to know that you had forgiven me. I thank God for the opportunity that both you and He gave me. I love you, and I wish you the best for always—Good bye." And just like that the conversation came to an end. Jada held the phone for a few seconds before hanging up. She wanted to save him by grace, but her spirit just would not allow her to speak. The next day Trei was dead, and she wept for him.

Chapter 24

THE NEWS

Jada's mother stood outside her daughter's door, thinking of a way to tell her daughter that the stranger that haunted her for four years was finally dead. She didn't know if she should break it down gently or say it harshly the way that she wanted too. She read her bible often and no matter how many times she read the word forgiveness, she could not find it in her heart to forgive JJ. She wanted to take his life herself and relieve all the pain and humiliation that she felt and dealt with on the inside. The police had screwed up the investigation and so did Hurricane Katrina, and her daughter's name was scandalized. Jada had heart broken scars that seemed to show that she was not healing anytime sooner. Lauren talked to her daughter often to try and strengthen her, but it never did any permanent good. Anytime JJ's name was mentioned, she would feel ill. Jada's skin was pale, and life worth living on the outside became life worth living on the inside for Jada. Her mother wanted her to go back to school and finish her education. Her father wanted her to go back to church. Jada was not listening to either one of them. She found a new world, and it was on the inside of herself, and she was not about to let anyone, not even the dead spirit of Trei and their last conversation interrupt her.

Listening to gospel music, preferably, Donnie McClurkin and his song 'Stand', Jada decided to turn down the radio in her room because of a distinct sound she thought she heard. Someone was knocking on her door. It was her mother calling her name.

"Jada—J—Jada," Lauren said after not hearing a response from her daughter.

"Yeah," she replied.

"Can I come in for a sec?" Her mother asked.

"Yeah, come on in."

"Is today any better?" Her mother asked-a question that she asked often.

"A little bit better than yesterday," Jada said with a graceful smile.

"You say that everyday girl. How you really doing?" Her mother asked sitting at the end of Jada's bed.

"And everyday is a little bit better than the next." She said with a smile again.

"Well, Micha stopped by a while ago."

"Yeah, I noticed his car in front of the driveway. What was he here for? Better not be another trial, my name has already been statistically recorded." Jada said.

"Well, you know that name that we promised not to mention in this house anymore?"

"Don't want to talk about it. Didn't you just hear me? I refuse to go through another trial and lose."

"We don't have to anymore." Lauren said to her daughter with a smile.

"I'm not surprised. What? Have we ran out of chance finally?"

"Yes and no. He—he's dead Jada." Her mother said. Jada stopped folding the blanket that she had only retrieved moments earlier from her bed. She was quiet for several minutes. "Jada," her mother called out to see if she was okay.

"Yeah." She replied. She looked unsure of her mother's response.

"Did you hear me?" Her mother asked.

"Yeah. Did you just say that JJ's dead?" She asked.

"Yes I did. Your father's on his way home so that we can celebrate, if you want too." Her mother said clutching the morning paper in her hand with a bright smile.

"Is that what I'm suppose to do?" Jada asked.

"I would like to think so. Micha also brought the newspaper to prove that he is dead and so that we could read where he will be funeralized at."

"Let's just hope it's not a church. Lord knows, he does not need to be remembered in a church."

"It's not. Would you like to see the paper?" Her mother asked.

"No! no—and I don't feel much like celebrating either. So why don't you call dad back and cancel?"

"Jada! He's dead. This is what we wanted, no matter how he died."

"No! It's not what I wanted. And saved women shouldn't speak that way even if they think it."

"Better said aloud than in mind, either way it's a sin. Remember, so as a man thinketh then it is?"

"Forget about all of that! And understand this, just because the bell has tolled for him that does not mean that my life will be any easier. I wanted to see him punished, dying is easy!" She exclaimed.

"Jada!" Her mother replied.

"I'm sorry mom. I mean . . . does anyone care about how I feel? I have to live the rest of my life with this rape, torture and humiliation. Gosh! It seems like I'm never going get out of this house-not for sanity's sake. He should have killed me! I feel like I'm dead anyway!" She said throwing the folded blanket on top of her shelf against the wall.

"Now Jada, that's enough. We love you, and we of all people definitely care about how you feel. You can get past this. You're just not . . ."

"Trying enough—I get it Ma. I've heard that before. I mean, did he even leave a written apology or a guilty plea. I mean . . . did he even write down the words, Jada I am sorry?" Jada replied while standing and looking at her mother.

"Now Jada, it's time you sucked all of this up. You're just gonna have to be encouraged and get out of this depression state and get back out into the world and live again. It's not good to be cooped up in a house for the rest of your life. This house is not going to save you from the sinful acts commited in the world by man everyday. You have to make your own destiny and not live it out in here. You need to know what's going on in the world."

"I guess he didn't," she said referring to JJ's apology, "and I do know! I watch the news, and I log-on to the internet."

"That's not the destiny you create for yourself. That's someone else's destiny pointed out to you. And those are someone else's facts."

"It doesn't matter who creates it, if you like it, then you can borrow it." Jada replied.

"For what reason young lady, plagiarism when you don't use direct quotes—you need to get out and gather your own facts, Jada. Living through someone else's eyes isn't always the wisest choice. Come over here and sit down?" Her mother asked.

"And, why not? I didn't choose this life." Jada said as she walked over to the bed where her mom was sitting. "It was the one dealt to me, so technically, I can live through someone else's eyes."

"Jada, what is wrong with you? Why can't you let this go? Do you actually think that you are the only woman in this world that has been taken advantage of, the only virgin too—for that matter? This has happened to many women before you and after you. It ain't gone stop with you. The truth is that, there are good men and there are bad men who are animals and wild predators waiting to fulfill their sexual desires and increase their power, and if you want them to continuously do this, you just sit in this room and fulfill your destiny, and they will. They will Jada. Now you can be like me and confront your hurt and pain and get over it and live again, or you can sit in here and do nothing and feel sorrow for yourself. And frankly, I am tired of you feeling sorry for yourself."

"So in other words, you want me to celebrate his death and go out there in the world and humiliate myself so that this can all happen again?" She asked her mother while looking into her eyes.

"No child. I want you to celebrate your life and gather your own facts, strengthen your weaknesses and build you a stronger bridge. Help someone else's pain to feel easier by helping yourself? Stop being afraid and re-gather your power. Don't ever let anyone belittle you and control you. In case you didn't hear me earlier, I too have been taken advantage of, but I got over that honey. No, I made it up in my mind that that unfortunate incident was not going to beat me. And no, I didn't do it alone. I met your father, and he was patient and gentle and understanding with me, and that helped me to become even stronger. I didn't want to tell you this until the time was right, and right now is the time too. I love you Jada, and I love myself." Her mother said as she touched her daughter on the shoulder. "Not for someone else to love me, but for me to love me. Forget the negative things that you have said about yourself and get away from this rut. Life is not worth it. If you die like this today, you would be of no help to anyone. Step away from yourself and let God have control. Please baby, push this thing aside. Let it go. You have suffered long enough. And you know what they say, what doesn't kill you only makes you stronger, and baby, I am strong, you hear me?" Her mother asked.

"Yes—you are. You really are." She said looking up at her mother with a smile.

"And you are too. We are going to celebrate, and we are also going to that funeral to throw away this pain once and for all."

"Momma, why didn't you tell me all of this stuff about you before now? And who took advantage of you, if you don't mind me asking?"

"I didn't tell you before because you needed to fall into the bottomless pit and get back up again. I also didn't tell you because I was afraid that if you didn't experience the pain that you would regret it later. You needed to understand your pain, child. You helped me to build a bridge again Jada, and it was my father who raped me. Once upon a time, I wished that it had been a stranger, but now I understand that it does not matter who does it, it's the pain and humiliation that kills your self-esteem and changes your life. But in the end, you regain your power back—that's only if you want to claim it, and nothing feels as good as that."

"You know, now that I think about it, you and dad could have saved a lot of money on my counseling if you had talked to me first."

"Yeah, we could have, but neither one of us would be healed. It helped me too Jada."

"I love you momma." Jada said.

"I love you too."

"So, I'm I really suppose to be happy that JJ is dead?"

"No, you're supposed to be happy that you are alive, um-um," her mother said clearing her throat and getting up from the bed beside Jada, "so that we can celebrate his death! And maybe we'll think of forgiving him." Her mother said. They began to laugh.

Chapter 25

WHAT REALLY HAPPENED

Knowing that Jada was okay was only half the confirmation Trei needed in order to move on. There was no need for him to question himself anymore concerning that matter. She had forgiven him, and she seemed alright. The other confirmation that Trei needed was from JJ and why. He knew deep down inside that JJ had done something wrong. That something wrong was attacking Jada and almost leaving her for dead, but the question was why? Did he want to win the bet that bad or did he just want Jada? Meanwhile, Trei's time with Jada was fun. She was a friend, teacher and comforter. She kept him balanced and had a way of showing him life from a different point of view. She inspired his mother to be the best that she could be at budgeting, working, and as a religious figure. In fact, she convinced his mother to join her father's church. You would not think that a person of Jada's status, so young, would not be so beneficial to older adults, but she was. Two of Trei's cousins were sure that they were going to drop out of high school. Jada counseled them; opened their eyes to a brighter future, and both of them went on to graduate with honors. Jada was awesome when she was awesome. The only person that Trei ever witnessed her being mad at was JJ. Sure, she had her ups and downs with her parents, but being Christians, they got over that quickly. They were not the type of family to lie down with conflict over their heads because tomorrow was not promised to either of them. Even though, Trei was talked about and criticized by his friends for buying Jada so much, it never really bothered him. It felt good to take care of someone other than himself for a change. Besides, he loved Jada, and he did not care about prices when they were together. Each time he looked at Jada, he saw beauty. She was beautiful all over. He felt safe looking at her, and he was comforted when he had the opportunity to hold her in his arms. Deep down inside, he honestly believed that Jada wanted to help JJ. But JJ was full of so many mixtures of demons. When Jada quieted one, two more would appear. She could not save JJ. He was too much. She was willing to let Trei go in order to avoid him, but Trei couldn't accept that. By holding on to Jada, he had pushed her into another door to face something that was almost tragic.

Jada wanted her life back. Trei could hear that in her voice as he talked to her on the phone. She needed her life back, and it was time for him to help her.

Trei thought. 'Two days over was weighing on my heart heavily. I knew what I had to do. I knew what I was going to do. I invited the fellows over to my mom's house to play several games of dominoes in the basement. I hoped Detective Rumsfield did not mind. In fact, he should not have since I was about to give him all the information that he needed in order to confiscate at least half the drugs on the streets of New Orleans. Just in case you do not understand where I am going, I decided to wear a wire after all. Everything was fine. Nobody suspected anything. We all laughed and told many jokes up until twelve midnight. Rob and Paul decided that it was time for them to bounce. I and JJ were left alone, and the party was just getting started. I decided that tonight was the night to find out what kind of friend I had. I locked the door after Paul and Rob left. I then proceeded to the bathroom to take a leak and to put a fresh tape in the recorder. The small problem had been taken care of, but the bigger problem was in my house, in my basement, at my table. Leaving the bathroom, I retrieved two beers from the freezer. JJ was sitting at my mom's table, rolling a cigar and laughing at Mike Epps, who was playing Day-Day in the movie 'Friday. Handing a beer to JJ, I sat down across from him at the table. He was sealing the cigar now with his mouth. He then dried the cigar with a lighter. The night before, I thought of many ways to engage JJ into a conversation concerning Jada. It had to be good. Nothing was to look suspicious. Everything must be as it always was. Watching Mike Epps on television and then JJ, I had decided that now was the time to end all of this. So, I slid one grand in front of JJ. He looked confused when he observed the money before him'.

"What," he asked? "You wanna gamble?" Trei shook his head no with a smile, and JJ lit the cigar.

"I owe you that," Trei said.

"For what," he asked?

"That's a g-right there." Trei said.

"So," JJ said while inhaling the cigar. "What the hell you want me to do with it?"

"Oh, how we forget so easily now, man you remember Jada." Trei said. JJ looked puzzled. "The bet," Trei replied to ease JJ's confusion.

"Oh snap. Yeah, you never did get that did you? Let me get that out you dog." He said. JJ then put the cigar in his mouth before he proceeded to count the money.

"Yo man, it's all there. No need to count it." Trei said.

Taking the cigar from his mouth, JJ responded, "I'm sure it is. But I'm still gone count it."

"Look JJ, all jokes aside now, tomorrow-I'm gone, and all of this gone be over and behind me for good, so I need for you to be honest with me." Trei said.

"Gone, where you going? Does everybody else know that?"

"Naw man—I'm going back to jail, again." Trei said. JJ acting shocked, stopped counting the money.

"For what," JJ asked? Trei said in thought, *'nigga like you don't know.'*

Taking a cigarette from a pack on the table and lighting it, Trei said, "Man, I got 3 indictments pending against me, and N.O.P said the only way to beat all three is to give you up plus our main source."

"What?" JJ said. Choking on the cigar, he could not believe what Trei had just said.

"Now, I ain't no snitch, but if I don't set you and Chinks up by tomorrow, then my life is over." Trei said. There was a brief moment of silence. JJ did not speak. Trei continued, "I can live with my life being over, but what I cannot live without is your trust. So what I need to know is if you raped Jada, the way everyone assumes you did?" Trei asked. JJ was not calm anymore. He decided that it was time to put the cigar down and possibly talk to Trei, man to man.

"Everyone like who," he asked?

"That doesn't matter? Did you do it?" Trei asked.

It was time for a drink. JJ opened his beer and took a swallow before saying, "Man, all of that happened three years ago. I'm a free man baby. So what's up with this now?"

"JJ, I'm your boy, your ace, your side walk by the street. I need to know." Trei said.

"Man, you know I ain't raped that girl." JJ said.

"What about what sources say, and how you bragged about it round town?" Trei asked.

"Sources telling a lie. I did not rape that slut. I told you this three years ago behind them bars. What? You don't believe me all of sudden?" JJ asked Trei. Trei could see the anger in his eyes. The real JJ was about to surface.

"I don't know what to believe. There are too many inconsistencies in this story. I mean, where were you man when I was calling your name at Necee's party?" Trei asked.

"What do you mean? You calling me a liar? Man, I don't believe that you of all people throwing this guilt trip on me. You messing up my high with this. Didn't you hear what the witnesses said in that court room? I left that party early." JJ said.

"Forget about the witnesses. I wanna know where you were. Just tell me the truth, man? You owe me that much."

"Fool, I don't owe you nothing. Now come on let's finish up this cig." JJ said.

"Man, I don't want that mess. I've had enough of that for one night. Just tell me the truth. I can't go to jail like this man."

"Like what, fool? I already told you that nothing happened." JJ said while gesturing with the cigar in his right hand.

"She haunts me, JJ, for taking your side in that courtroom. Look at me, man. I'm nothing like I use to be. I'm stressed out over this mess. I want peace of mind and the opportunity to move on. I need to know what happened that night. I have to know." Trei said relaxing in his chair and taking a deep breath.

"Man you sick. You sound like you in some kind of a horror movie. Man, let that go. Jada is still alive ain't she?" JJ asked.

"The truth, JJ?" Trei asked again.

"Man, you don't want to know what happened."

"Yes, I do." Trei said leaning against the table with a cigarette in his hand.

"No, you don't!"

"Yes I do!" Trei exclaimed. The whole matter had taken a toll on him. JJ could see Trei's eyes filling with water.

Faced with telling the truth or a lie, JJ decided the truth and said, "Okay man . . ." He took a deep breath and continued, "the truth is that you are weak like I've said all alone Trei." This was the typical JJ. He had to criticize before being revealed. Trei wanted to hit him, but he could not. He was fearful that JJ would not reveal what happened. "Especially telling me that she haunts you. I mean, look at you." JJ said, laughing at Trei. "You barely take care of yourself since that happened. You look dead-like kung fu on crack. Why do you torture yourself with the past? The guys and the girls don't want to be around you because rumor has it that you have Aids. That's why all your ex-girlfriends call me now."

"Man, forget them freaks. As far as I am concerned, they can think what they want. They just mad cause I didn't want them, and they didn't get half the opportunity Jada got. Come to think of it, you one of them haters too—right man?" Trei asked JJ. JJ did not see that coming. Trei took a swallow of his beer, content to get the truth out of JJ.

"Naw dog," JJ said before he put the cigar in his mouth. "Ain't nothing bout me got hater in it." He said after inhaling the cigar smoke. He spoke again, "Now the real answer is, she didn't want you Trei. She was using you. I thought that I did you a favor."

"How," Trei asked?

"I just did." JJ said. Things were not going as Trei predicted. JJ was not confessing. It was time to use another method.

"Look JJ—a while ago, I asked you to tell me the truth. That time has passed. Now, I'm demanding the truth! Now what's up man. I've known you for thirteen years, and you can't even be honest with yo boy for once?" Trei said drawing a gun from his back and pointing it at JJ.

JJ shocked, said, "Man, what's wrong with you?"

"See man, you don't understand. I told you before that I have nothing to lose. I want the truth or this gun is going off."

"Come on man. Quit playing? This done gone on long enough." JJ said putting out the cigar.

"Did you rape Jada?" Trei asked.

"Trei, put the gun down man?"

"Did you rape Jada?" Trei asked again.

JJ could see the seriousness in his friend's eyes. He said, "No".

"Then what happened?" Trei asked.

"She gave it to me man. That's what happened."

"Yeah right, she didn't even like you-boy!" Trei said.

"I'm serious. Ya girl was on something." JJ replied.

"She didn't take drugs JJ. She hated it when I took them."

"She took something that night! Now man, put the gun down!" JJ exclaimed.

"I don't believe you JJ." Trei said holding the gun to JJ's head now.

JJ saw the perfect opportunity to take away the gun. It was a trick he and Trei had learned while watching the movie, 'Rush Hour'. JJ did not understand why Trei had moved so close to him with the gun. Within and instant, JJ said, "Give me that gun. You weak punk!" The gun was now in the possession of JJ's hands.

"Man just be cool," Trei said with his hands in the air.

"Cool, you done messed up my high. Why after all these years, you got to bring this mess up again? Get over that slut man. Let her go. That's the past." JJ said pointing the gun directly at Trei.

"I can't man, somehow, my conscious won't let me." Trei said rubbing his head with the cigarette in his hand.

"I wonder why?" JJ asked. "Man you weak. I cannot believe you." Seeing that his friend was desperate for an answer, he said, "Okay, okay, yeah, I had sex with her, but before you blow up all in the chest, you said that you wanted the truth. You said that you needed it. Well here it is. Man you know how she constantly cut me off when we were arguing. She was constantly on my back, and I got sick of her. I wanted to teach her a lesson. She call it rape. I call it even."

"You call rape, even?" Trei asked. "Did you drug her JJ?"

"I didn't," he said with a smile and then laughed at the idea of really doing it. "Okay I did, but I left after I did it."

"Why JJ," Trei asked? "I thought you were my friend."

"Man, get over her!"

"Was she really nothing to you, JJ?" Trei asked.

"Yeap, I hated her. Let me tell you how much. Everything that I did to her, she deserved. She wanted it, man."

"So, what happened, JJ?"

"What happened was, I wasn't gone do it at first. I was gone leave, but she constantly provoked me. Every time she caught me staring at her at that party, she would wall her eyes or look at me strange, like she couldn't stand my guts."

"She couldn't." Trei replied after exhaling smoke from his cigarette and placing the bud in an ash tray.

"Yeah, I soon figured that out. By the way, where were you when she was calling your name and I was on top of her? Huh, where were you Trei? Oh, I forgot, you were outside playing cards wit the fellows."

Trei suddenly stood up from his seat. JJ said, "Sit down. Don't bite me." He cocked the gun. "Yeah, that's what she pretty much told me that night when I walked up behind her by the pool. How did she say it? Oh yeah, she said back up; I left Roover at home. Man, can you believe that? She called me a dog." He laughed. "That's when I knew the pill had kicked in on her. As a matter of fact, she was looking at you across from the pool, playing cards. Moments later, when I walked away from her, Necee approached her.

I just sat back and watched. She kept asking Necee if she had spiked the Champagne. Necee said no. Then she complained of a headache. Necee said that she would help her inside to lay down-something bout taking two Tylenols. So, I beat them in the house, right, and hid in the hall closet. Honestly, Jada felt that something was going to happen to her. Necee assured her that she was overreacting. Necee told her that she would keep an eye on her and convinced her to lay down. Jada decided that she would apparently. Necee locked the door and left the room. Jada was really scared. It's a shame that you were no where around to help her." JJ said pointing a finger at Trei with a smile. "So, I waited about 20 minutes and got out of the closet. I almost went to sleep in there. By the time I came out—everyone was outside. So I knocked on the door. She didn't say nothing. So I knocked on the door again. She still didn't say nothing. I knew it was all over then. I pried the door open. I almost got caught. Some girls were running toward the bathroom. I made my way inside the room just in time and closed the door slowly. Jada was passed out on Necee's bed." JJ stopped talking about the subject matter and said, "Hold up, let me re-light this cigar." Trei was boiling over on the inside. He wanted to kill JJ, but JJ had something worse coming to him. Ready to talk some more, JJ said, "Okay."

"Man," Trei said. "Put the gun down. I ain't gone do nothing."

"You must think I'm a fool like you? I ain't stupid." JJ said.

"Man, put the gun down. Let's talk about this honestly without violence involved. You know—I'm your boy."

"Naw, naw, forget that Trei. I ain't nothing like them tricks you use to pimp." JJ said.

"Did Jada know that it was you?" Trei asked.

"Not at first. She thought I was you. She was gone give it to you that night. She kept saying, Trei, Trei, help me, help me-putting my hands all over her, right?"

"I don't believe that bull man. That don't even sound right." Trei responded with anger.

"Yeah, you right. She was asleep." JJ said.

"So what really happened?"

"If you shut up, I'm gone tell you."

"But you been telling me for the longest and somehow you keep saying lies. So why don't you tell the truth and clear up this mess-all of it!"

"Shut up punk. She moved okay, after I touched her. I jumped back. When she didn't move anymore, I just went crazy. I don't know what happened. My body was on fire, and my hands and mouth was everywhere."

"You sick man." Trei said.

"I know that now. I had popped about two x-pills. My hormones were on edge. I made it up in my mind that it was gone be her stuck up but. I needed a challenge as strong as those two pills. Jada was the challenge I needed. Ah man, I wish that you could have seen that body. God gifted her. Them breast, a nice brown like fresh baked cake and the size of Florida oranges-not tangerines—but oranges. You ever seen 'em?" JJ asked

Trei. He knew that his friend had not. Anger filled on the insideTrei. "Oh, I forgot, you ain't never seen her naked." He said with a light chuckled. "Her body screamed, come get me. I got her too. It took some time, but I got her."

Trei could not take anymore. Tears fell from his face. JJ laughed and asked him why was he crying? JJ confessed to Trei that he had raped Jada vaginally and anally. Trei threw up in a trash can by the table. JJ called him weak once more. He also thanked Trei for the money for the bet. He told him that he owed him more, but that he would charge it to the game. Additionally, he told Trei that after he finished crying and feeling sorrow for himself and Jada and had calmed down, that he could come and get his gun. Finally, before leaving the room, he said to Trei, "One more thing, Jada would have never felt my wrath if you hadn't put her glass down that night. You gave me the opportunity, and I took it. Holla!" He said before closing the basement door.

Trei paced the basement floor for several minutes, trying to take in all that happened. Jada had told the truth three years ago. JJ repeated everything that she said had taken place. Trei was trying to swallow all the pain of that night, when his basement doorbell ranged. Cleaning up his face, he walked over to the basement door and opened it. It was Detective Rumsfield and his partner Carter.

"Talking about bad timing," Trei said to Rumsfield.

"Naw, talking about evidence," Rumsfield responded as he closed the basement door.

Chapter 26

RAGE

Anger that is explosive, furious, extreme, intense, diseased, passionate or desired is also known as rage, a word after pain and before trouble. Words of the King James Bible states that one should just turn the other cheek; but how many times must you ask? It states that as many times as your brother or sister sin against you and ask forgiveness. Many people trust and follow the law of the Holy Bible, letting countless events with man destroy their sanity and letting God empower them eventually. Others are not quick to follow these laws and believe in the process of an eye for an eye. JJ was one of these people. He was selfish and arrogant and overall down right ignorant and stupid when he could not have matters his way. He did not care about anyone or anything. He was a passenger on this earth with borrowed time. Could anyone agree that rude individuals have no place in society? If you were to ask a Libra this question, your response would probably be yes and no. No, because rude people stop the world from evolving into something great, and yes, because if rude people did not exist then how would one determine what respect would be characterized as? Rude people are designed as a study, and the question often asked is why? What made him, her, or it commit such an unforgiving act? Why was good overruled by evil, a viscous content to attack and destroy any obstacle that appears better, looks better or acts better.

JJ could not possibly understand the word better, let alone, comprehend anyone or anything giving praise to such a word. It was not because, honestly, he lacked understanding, but it was because he felt in his nature that his job was to instill fear on his prey in order to gain power. Deep down inside, JJ was a weak little boy and hated himself for not being the best of the best. The only enthusiasm he relied on in life was the forceful impact he used on his prey to gain power and influence. He wanted to conquer the world, but he was not ready or willing to give up the world in return. His sins out weighed his good. The one thing he hated most was a clean, honest virtue. Just as any other man, he looked in the mirror at himself, but not often because he loved what he had become and hated what he could not have. He had become a missile that with the touch of one button, he could strike. No one wanted to be around him because of his evil content to cause trouble. His job was to make everyone's life miserable because his was, and misery loves company. It was almost as though he wanted to be the king of pain, to have it so that people would only cling to him to avoid being hurt by him. Yes, he laughed and talked with friends but they hated him. They ran from his company. If JJ did not see them, they would hide from him. He was avoided constantly, that's how much of a terrible person he was or could be. He chose seriousness over happiness and respect over love. His family did not even like his attitude, mostly his mother and sisters. His dad was never around but when he was, JJ was not. They did not see eye to eye. They were almost alike and fought for power often, which usually ended with JJ storming out of the house and not returning for several days at a time. Sarah never worried, and James did not care because he knew that if JJ had gotten into any trouble that an emergency call was coming from the police department. His son's attitude was terrible. Sometimes, James wished his son was dead. JJ's sisters loved him for taking up for them, but hated him for beating them consistently when he was around. He degraded his sisters. They were nothing but sluts and hoes. His teachers could not calm him down because they were afraid. His principal in high school threatened him everyday, so that he would quit school. After JJ quit, he set the principal's car on fire, and threatened to kill his wife and kids after he served six months in a detention center for rehabilitation. The principal and his family moved away from New Orleans. JJ's girlfriend at seventeen only liked him because she was afraid of him. Her name was Michelle Tolenslee. She became pregnant with their first child and threatened to leave him if he did not stop beating her. He came home late one night high on cocaine and tried to cut the baby out of her stomach at six months. She and the baby both survived because the wound was not deep enough. Afraid of JJ, she did not press charges. His second child by Michelle was killed in a drive by shooting between JJ and another rival gang. JJ did not attend the funeral and blamed Michelle for the incident because she was at work while he was stuck babysitting. He physically abused Michelle often. Michelle started to think that she deserved it. She was losing her mind, her life, and the child that she had left. Very vulnerable to her prey, she turned to drugs and violence. Her violence was against other women. She was JJ's prodigy. With a new attitude and reputation, her parents decided to push her away because of her constant disrespect. They even tried to take her child, but did not succeed. The honest friends she had, walked away from her and became her enemy. The streets became her body, and JJ claimed her soul. She lost her self esteem and self respect. Her family hated JJ, and JJ hated them. Michelle had lost her innocence, sense of direction and guidance to someone who did not love her-someone who did not love himself. By the time JJ was done with Michelle, she had lost a child, and all of her friends except one; a basketball scholarship; her parents; her job, and was on the verge of losing her freedom.

Everyday for JJ was a struggle, but only because he made it one. He was constantly on a power trip. If a cashier slammed his change on the counter, he or she was threatened, often told, *'you don't know me, I'll set yo ass on fire and then put lighter fluid on you'*.

He was known all over the Bottom Streets of New Orleans. Everyone was warned about his behavior. They knew that he was explosive. He constantly warned people who crossed him to watch their back, that he would be back. He always went back, even if it meant murder for him or them.

Trei was probably the only friend JJ had. He could compete with JJ as well as let some things go. He was the only one who could keep JJ under control or talk him down. Now Trei was dead. No one ever really knew what happened; the coroner called it suicide. Anyway, JJ felt no remorse for Trei. Trei was just another person to him. When JJ found out that Trei had killed himself, his only comment was, '*I told that nigga that he couldn't handle the truth or me. He just never would believe it. Now look where he at, 4 feet under. Katrina had more heart than him, but not even that hooker could kill a real man like me.*' Everything JJ touched was dying, if not in spirit, definitely in the flesh. JJ was hated by men and women alike, but if you asked them who JJ hated the most, the answer would be women. Why? Because he never cared about any of them-not even his own mother. If you asked JJ who he hated the most, he would tell you himself.

Chapter 27

PREPARING TO SAY GOODBYE

James Senior was very frustrated trying to put on his tie. As he looked in the mirror at the angry lines in his face, he saw his son looking at him. His thoughts were, *'that nigga looked just like me, but what happened to his personality?'* He suddenly turned away from the mirror and tried to fix his tie. Sarah, coming out of the bathroom wearing a black slip and black sheer stockings with her hair still tied up in a handkerchief, observed her husband trying to fix his tie. She could see the frustration in her husband's face, even though, she could not sympathize with her husband. She did not want to imagine how he was feeling. She was certain that she felt no sympathy for her son's death. She did not know what to feel. It was as though a mute feeling came over her. Honestly, deep down inside, Sarah was happy that her obtrusive son was dead, and she vowed to keep that a secret between her and God. Walking over to her husband, she witnessed as he moved his tie hurriedly from left to right. He was angry. Trying to calm his spirit down and reaching for the tie, she said, "let me help you with that."

"I got it!" He said, moving her hands away.

"I said—let me help you with that." She repeated while moving James' hands away from the tie. James could see that she was not about to take no for an answer. He dropped his hands to his side and looked away from her. Staring at the dresser on his wife's side of the bed, he noticed an envelope. Suspicious of the envelope, he said, "Sarah."

"Yeah James," Sarah replied.

"Did the mailman already run this morning because when I checked the mailbox, nothing was in there?" Sarah looked over at the dresser. She was planning on putting the envelope away before James saw it. James stood still waiting on her to answer him.

"No," she said while finishing up with his tie.

"What's in that envelope then," he asked? "It wasn't there last night." He said walking toward the dresser. Picking up the envelope, he noticed that it was addressed to Reverend Stevens. Sarah knew that James was about to lose his cool once more when he looked inside. Looking inside and seeing several twenty dollar bills, James exclaimed, "What the hell is this?"

Picking her dress up from the bed now, she answered, "It's the money we have to pay Reverend Stevens for preaching the funeral."

"What? You have got to be kidding me. You mean we have to pay him too?" He said. Sarah slipped her feet into the black dress and pulled it up. "Now Sarah, this just don't make no sense. Now enough is enough and too much makes me want some get back. Why do we have to pay him? He preaches other funerals for free."

"Well JJ's funeral ain't no ordinary funeral." Sarah replied.

"Huh. What do you mean?" He said backing against the dresser and folding his arms with the envelope in his hand.

"It's out of the church James. The church will not pay him for preaching funerals not held at the church unless approved in advance by the Board!" She said raising her voice a little. "Can we just not talk about this?" She asked, reaching in the back of her dress for the zipper as she looked in the mirror at James.

"No Sarah! That's what we just gone do! Talk bout it!" James said walking up behind her to help her with her zipper.

"Okay, but without the yelling. I am simply not up to it this morning. I have enough on my mind, and Lord knows that I can't wait until JJ is in the ground and this whole episode is over with." She said, taking a deep breath as James finished zipping her zipper. She walked over to the walk in closet to obtain her heels. James just looked at his wife. He was shocked by her words.

Finally, after being quiet until she put on her shoes, he asked, "Sarah, are you high on something?"

"What?" She exclaimed.

"What, is exactly—what I'm trying to understand? You got to be high on something, seeming how you moving about around here, acting as though everything is normal. Our boy is dead, Sarah!"

"Oh, don't start that again James. JJ is dead. I mean—must you continue to remind yourself of that?" She said, removing the head scarf away from her head.

"No, I feel the need to remind you Sarah. Reverend Stevens is charging us to preach our son's funeral at the Train Station, and you're a member of that church." The whole ordeal made James shake his head before he sat at the end of the bed. "At a Train Depot, Sarah . . . I mean, what in the hell is going on here?"

"I see you haven't got over this new development yet. So . . ."

"So what Sarah? Ain't nothing about this sitting easy with me. God can't be happy with all of this mess . . ."

"James!" Sarah said while combing her hair.

"Hurry up! Hurry up, you hear me?" James said standing in front of his wife now and looking into her eyes. "I can't take no more of this mess. If I don't tell him off today, my mammy ain't dead." James then grabbed his jacket from the bed and put it on.

"But you've done that already, James." Sarah said, looking at her husband.

"Oh yeah, well this time, I plan on acting it out nonverbally—with my fist, better known as whooping his ass! You like that one better Sarah? Um Huh, I thought you would." James said before walking out the bedroom door.

Chapter 28

UNCLE SAM

Samuel Sidney sat on his front porch, fully dressed for his nephew's funeral with a cup of coffee in his hand. Rocking backward and forward in his rocking chair and staring at the sky, then railroad tracks, and then street, he could only imagine how his brother's family was feeling. No one wanted to put up with JJ. His whole attitude was disgusting. Sam thought of all the times he tried to help his brother with JJ. James often told his brother that he stated to the Lord often, '*this world is too small for JJ and me. One of us has to go.*' James Senior complained about JJ's behavior all the time. He could not go anywhere without someone telling him what his son had done the day before or the same day in general. As a father or mother, parents sometimes are tired of hearing everything that their children are doing wrong all the time. It is upsetting and makes the parents' feel like failures. James would often tell his brother Sam how he wished that he and Sarah had never had JJ. He said that JJ was a problem from the time he learned to walk and talk. Sam did not agree with his brother's attitude in the beginning about JJ, but it did not take long for him to witness what his brother James Sr. was saying all along. JJ was terrible. He was a piece of plague. If he was not destroying something, he was creating something to destroy. It was one thing for Sam to actually believe what others said about his nephew, but it was another thing to actually witness his nephew's behavior in person as JJ was the reason why Sam had a prosthetic left arm.

Sam wanted to forget the incident. He tried on many occasions, but he soon realized, how can you forget and forgive someone for doing you wrong, when that very same person every time an argument takes place would rub the incident in your face? Yes, the Holy Bible speaks of the act of being angry but sinning not, but JJ had a way of making an individual sin. JJ always pushed all the wrong buttons. Sam remembered how the coil wire wrapped around the lower left half of his arm and took it off. Blood was gushing everywhere as Sam felt a pain that he had never in his life felt before. He did not think that one small shove would cause so much damage; after all, he was trying to save James Senior, JJ's dad. They were all at work, Sam, James and JJ, in a small Industrial Plant called Project Loco. This plant manufactured electrical products. James and JJ were arguing before getting work prepared in their area. James was furious at JJ for causing him to be late in which this time the incident resulted in a write up.

Just as the discussion got a little more heated and out of control, Sam stepped in the middle of the two and was shoved by JJ. James Senior acting on impulse by reflex now, slapped JJ. James and JJ began to shove one another. Neither one of them were aware of Sam's arm being grinded in the machine, until an associate screamed for help. James quickly hit the emergency stop button on the machine, but by then, it was too late. Sam's arm was gone. Very upset by the matter, James said to JJ, "Look at what you just did?" JJ replied, "That's what he gets for always trying to step in a save somebody." James was very angry at his son for the incident and lashed out at him again. Co-workers around them broke up the matter before it escalated any further. The main priority was Sam. Losing his left arm was devastating for him. He fell into a state of depression after the incident. For three years, he was addicted to pain killers. Sam could not forget or forgive. He wanted his arm back, but he knew that it was next to impossible. He attended rehab to get off the pain killers. After losing the pain killer issue, Sam had to attend counseling for five years to relieve the anger he felt in his heart. Sam always dreamed of the day that JJ would ask his forgiveness, but JJ never did. Now JJ was dead, and Sam could stop dreaming, so he thought. Sam wasn't sad about the passing of his nephew, neither was he happy. He felt relieved and calm.

Sam, almost done with his coffee, wondered what was taking his wife so long to come out of the house. He had started the car; turned on the air condition to cool the car; finished his coffee, and his wife still was not ready for the funeral. Very impatient with her tardiness, he yelled to her while she remained in the house, "Fay, bring yo but outta there. The car been running fifteen minutes, and you still ain't ready. Now unless you got some gas money or expecting to call a cab, you better come on outta there cause you bout to get left."

"Fool, I ain't worried bout none of that. You know you don't have any license. Troy already done told you that if he catch you driving again, that you going to jail. Don't let the day be the day that you be made an example of. Anyway, that car is not cool yet, and you know that I'm allergic to heat. Besides, it takes that car fifteen minutes to cool off."

"I just told you that it's been running for fifteen minutes. I been out here fifteen minutes, Fay."

"Liar, it's been eight minutes. It has not been fifteen minutes Samuel. I looked at my watched when you went outside. You've only been outside approximately eight minutes." She said watching the local news on television.

"Lord, are you about to start with that Law and Order attitude?"

"Whatever Samuel, you know that I cannot stand the heat. It irritates me and drives me crazy. Besides that, I began to itch uncontrollably. I am not about to wet up my make-up with sweat. Even you know that it has not been fifteen minutes, because that is how long it takes for you to finish a hot cup of coffee." She said.

154

"It has been fifteen minutes. I am done with my coffee woman."

"Um, hum, so I guess that your mouth is irritated also?" She remarked. His mouth was irritated from blowing and drinking the hot coffee at the same time. Fay knew this incident happened every time her husband was in a hurry. "Samuel, we have six minutes left until that car is fully cool. I am not about to step out in that heat until then. Like I said before, I am allergic to heat."

"All heat or just that stove in there?" Sam asked his wife.

"Whatever fool," she stated.

"You know, yo own momma told me not to marry you. But did I listen, no, no, no. I had to be hard-headed and marry you anyway."

"My mama told you what?" Fay yelled.

"Nothing! On second thought, she said that you was lazy Fay. And she didn't lie. You always have been. How you gone tell me of all people that you allergic to heat, when all you do is feed on it? Remember, I am the one who lives with you every day. It ain't but two things yo wide but allergic to, that's work and being on time." Sam told his wife.

Irritated by his words, Fay said, "Like that arm of yours? Forget you, Samuel. I did you a favor. If it were not for your steady income, you would not have me."

"Leave Fay, you don't have to be here. I don't need you."

"Yeah, all of that is easy to say now, ain't it fool?" She asked standing at the front door looking down at Sam in the rocking chair. "I just so happen to remember another Sam just a couple of years back, crying on my shoulder about an arm he lost and how much pain he was in. Oh, but how quickly do we forget to be charismatic when someone else is in those shoes besides you. Fool, I don't care what you are my mother say about me. Like I said, I am just . . ."

"Yeah, I know." Sam said. "Allergic to work and rude-how can you use my weakness as your defense?"

"You used my weight as your defense." She said in her defense. Fay was not fat, on second thought; she was not all that healthy either. All she had was a beautiful face with no body. Her best feature was sitting down. When she stood up, all hell broke loose.

"You know what Fay? I was just sitting here thinking while you were talking that I bet that you and lazy don't have no trouble with one another. Why? Because y'all both on the same team." He said while laughing.

"Let's go Sam," she said locking and closing the front door after retrieving her purse. "The car is cool."

"I told you that five minutes ago . . ." He said walking behind her. "Oh, and by the way, I'm gone drive today."

"Sam, you cannot drive. You don't have any license. Did you forget what I told you about Troy? And he is definitely on duty today. You will go to jail."

"Forget Troy and you too. Don't nobody care about your nephew. You always try to run over me, and he like it too. I know how to drive my own car. I have the right to drive my own car, Fay."

"Yes you do, but with a license. Yours is suspended. Pay the city and state and get them back. What are you going to tell the police when you are pulled over and asked for your driver's license, fool?"

"I'm gone say—you mean to tell me that you done lost them too? The last time I checked, y'all had them." Sam said. Fay eyed him coldly. He was terrible. His attitude was terrible, she thought to herself while getting behind the drivers seat of the car. She knew that Sam did not want to go jail. She knew because he was headed for the passenger side of the vehicle after he stated that he was going to drive.

Chapter 29

MORE NEWS

Steel Johnson laid his newspaper down on his car seat before he went inside the mental hospital to visit his sick wife, Lucille. He hoped that the news that he had to tell her would help her recover, and she would come home to him. Inside the hospital, he approached the front desk nurse and asked, "Is she awake, yet?"

"Yeah, Mr. Johnson," the nurse said while she was on the phone, "you can go right in to see her."

"Has today been good or bad?" He asked the nurse.

"So far, she hasn't hit anyone today. She's been kind of quiet."

"Thanks Judy." Steel said.

"Sure." She replied before getting back on the phone.

Steel watched his wife for a few seconds from the doorway before he went in the room to tell her of the news that he had heard. She was in a rocking chair, facing the window, talking to someone in the room, but no one was there. Steel figured that it must be his dead son, Terrance.

"I don't know. They said the impact of the car is what put you to sleep." Lucy, Steel's wife said.

"They say that's why you didn't wake up—said you would sleep for a while." She was quiet for several seconds before saying, "remember, I told you that I was going to stay here until you wake up."

Steel did not see anyone in the room, but he knew that someone was there, at least, his wife said that someone was there. She said that it was their son, Terrance. Terrance was hit by a hit and run driver, racing to get away from the police. The driver was JJ in a stolen vehicle.

Steel could not stand to watch his beautiful wife, Lucy, talk to a person who was not in the room, a person who did not exist anymore. Timothy Terrance Johnson was dead, and his mother wanted to believe that he was just sleeping.

"Oh, so he's punishing me Terrance? Well, what did I do son? Terrance, you should really come back to me. You've been sleeping for a long time."

"Lucy!" A voice from behind her said. Steel could not stand the idea of his wife talking crazy. When she did not respond, he said, "Lucy—Lucille."

She turned around to face the direction of his voice. She looked up to see her husband staring down at her. "How long you been standing there? Were you eaves dropping on me and Terrance like you always have?"

"No, I just came through the door." Steel replied.

"Um, huh. Terrance said, you been standing there for three minutes. He says that he was looking right at you."

Caught off guard and smiling at the idea of his son looking at him and being alive, Steel asked, "me?"

"Yes you." She said.

"O' hell! Lucille, Terrance is dead." Steel said after realizing that his son was dead and could not be looking at him.

"No, he is not! He's standing right there against that window talking to me."

"Lucy, how many times are we gonna have to go through this? Terrance is dead. He is not alive. He's Dead!"

"No, he's not! And don't you say it again!" She replied.

"Alright, al-right, then tell him to leave so that I can talk to you for a minute."

"I will not. He says that he wants to talk to the both of us." Lucy replied, looking at her husband.

"Lucy, please, please stop this? You're making me crazy."

"Are-you-saying, that I am crazy?" She asked, pointing a finger at herself

"No, no—heaven's no." Steel said walking closer to her. In his mind, he said, *'hell yeah, but you can change.'*

"Then, why are you here?" She asked.

"I came to tell you something." He replied. He became exhausted with his wife's illness.

"Are you okay?"

"I'm fine, Lucy. Is it alright if I sit down?" He asked standing beside her bed.

"I guess."

"Lucy, that kid . . ."

"What kid?"

"That kid, who ran over Terrance and killed him." He replied.

"Terrance ain't dead."

"Well, that kid who ran over him is dead." Steel said, irritated by his wife's remark again. "His body was found two days ago. His funeral is in a couple of days, I came to see if you wanted to go . . . and"

"And what?" She responded.

"To see, if you would regain your senses back and stop torturing me with this nightmare by thinking that our boy is still alive. I wanted to see if this would be enough to change your mental state, so that you could come home again, and love me again . . . so that we can be happy again." His wife's eyes began to water. She could feel that he loved her and missed her. "You said that if that boy was not punished that nothing would stop you from going crazy. Well he's being punished now, and I want my wife back and sane. So, can this craziness stop?" He paused to hear a response from her. She did not say anything. A tear fell from his eye, and he looked away from his wife for a second and at the window where she said that their only son was standing. "Terrance if you are there, please convince her to let go? Go rest son? So that she can heal. Your killer is dead. It's time for your soul to go home. It's time that you rested for good and stopped roaming." At the sound of those words, Terrance returned to the spirit world. His mother had several rose plants growing in her room. A petal from one of her roses fell into her lap after Terrance vanished, but not before he said to her, 'I love you mother, forever and always. I'm okay. Goodbye."

Chapter 30

AN UNTIMELY DISCUSSION

For two days, Reverend Stevens questioned the idea of how he would preach James and Sarah's son funeral. He knew all that he wanted to say, but he did not know how to put his thoughts in order. After shaving the hair from his face, he went to the kitchen where he greeted his wife every morning with a kiss on the lips, sat down at the kitchen table, and took a sip of his coffee. However, this morning, there was no coffee waiting for him; it could mean one of two things, either his wife had left him because she found out about all of his affairs, or she was mad for some reason or another about something that he did not do. Looking over at the counter, not sure of how he should act when he entered the doorway of the kitchen area, he spotted his wife with her arms folded by the sink. He paused and wiped his hand over his face, where two minutes earlier, he had a beard. He decided that he would not say the first words this morning because usually he was wrong when he assumed what his wife was thinking. She did not say anything. She just stared at her husband as though she was trying to read his mind. After several minutes, Mathew decided that he had had enough of the admiring her and her, him, he said calmly, "Good morning." He then decided to walk into the kitchen and kiss his wife as he usually did every morning.

This morning, Lilly did not feel like being pampered by her husband, so before he leaned over to kiss her she said, "Don't even think about it, this morning." Her hair was pulled back in a pony-tail and the arch on her eyebrows were not hard to read what kind of a mood she was in. You see, Lillian usually read over her husband's notes in the morning to proofread for errors that he may have made unnoticed. This morning was no different from any other for him, but it was very different for her as she yelled, "Mathew Levhon Stevens! I can't believe that you are gonna say the words that you have written on that paper over there at that child's funeral."

Now that he knew what his wife was thinking and what kind of a mood she was in, he walked over to the kitchen cabinet beside the stove to obtain some coffee to make.

"So—I guess this means no breakfast or coffee?" He asked with a strange look at his wife, who was standing with her arms folded watching his every move.

"Do you even remember what you have written on that paper? Were you drinking that wine last night when you wrote all of that? Are you going to say that mess?" She asked.

Holding the coffee can in his right hand, he said, "Every messing word of it."

"Mathew," she said, hoping that he would change his mind once she said something.

"Look Lilly, this is not up for discussion." He said as he walked over to the coffee maker beside the stove.

She walked toward him from the other side of the room, "Mathew, this is very debatable. This is serious. We need to discuss this and what the outcome will be."

"It's not that bad," he said preparing the coffee to be made.

"It's just that bad! Now, I wrote something well presentable over on the table that you can say without embarrassing that family. The train station is bad enough, especially on the Southside. Wait a minute, did you and the Mayor plan this to get that new train station that you two have been fighting the city about for the last two years?"

"Of course not, politics has nothing to do with this." He said nervously, trying to hold his composure so that his wife would not see. *'What bird has been chirping in her ear, James Senior?'* He thought.

"Um huh—yeah right. I've heard that one before. You and him always plotting a way to get something new approved in this city. Now—the both of you have been advised on the new budget for this city, and ain't nothing in it saying anything about approval of a new train station. I just hope that you two aren't trying to get the insurance to do just that as an alternative. Now look Mathew, you better remember that you are a preacher before a politician. You need to let them politics go. You know what happened to Sister McGill and her husband last year." She said looking at her husband. Mathew was thinking while making the coffee, *'who told her about this?'*

"Look Lilly, we ain't the McGill's. You haven't heard of me taking bribes from anyone. And if I do decide to give up my council position, who's gonna represent our Ward better than me?"

"You sure, you ain't trying to use Sarah son's memorial as a means to gain a new train station on the Southside?"

"Of course, I'm sure. Now, would I lie?" He turned toward his wife and asked before pressing the start button down on the coffeemaker.

She looked at him heavily and asked, "Are you asking me that from a politician perspective or preaching perspective?"

"What's that suppose to mean?"

"You'll figure it out. Now about that speech over there, like I said, that's bad Mathew."

"Lilly, what I wrote on that paper ain't bad enough. So, this is why you have no breakfast and coffee ready this morning? I am prepared to say everything that I have written on that paper over there. Now . . . you've wasted your time writing me a speech." He said pushing the start button down on the coffee maker before looking his wife directly in the eyes again and asking, "And can I get some toast?"

Walking away she said, "Mathew, that ain't right. Now I know that there's a thin line between right and wrong and that's wrong. You are not justifying the reason for that kid's wrong with insults."

"Justifying," he said watching his wife walk away, "nobody cares about his past or the reason that he should not have died to violence because he was a terrible person. This is not his personal biography. This is his funeral, and he was a terrible person, and I mean every d—. Girl, you almost made me say the wrong word in this house. Now, I'm going to say every word on that paper over there Lillian. That kid was overly sensitive and hot headed. He raped, stole, and killed. Hell Lillian, he destroyed a lot of families."

"No need in swearing, Mat. This is all irrelevant to his funeral." She said taking a loaf of bread from the bread holder. "Funeral's help prepare victim's families, so that they may understand or have an understanding of what or who they had a part of their family and reduces the idea of the family having to distinguish if their family member went to heaven or that awful hell."

"Lilly, that is only the general idea of a funeral. The truth is—he's going to hell, anyway, whether you and they want to admit it or not."

"How do you know that he's going to hell?" She said sitting at the bar after she pressed the start button down on the toaster and looked back at her husband. "He probably asked for forgiveness before he died."

"Ha, ha—yeah, right!" Mathew said with his arms folded as he waited for the coffee to finish. "That kid? That's a lie, and I refuse to believe that bull."

"He probably did, Mat. You don't know if he knew God or not."

"Oh, I know!" He said looking at his wife. The coffee was now finished. He walked to another cabinet to obtain a coffee cup. "And I'm sure that I ain't far from determining who he did believe in."

The toast were now ready as they popped from the toaster, Lilly placed them on a saucier that she pulled from the cabinet earlier before sitting at the counter. "No, you don't Mat. Only he and God knows that. It's almost impossible for you to know that."

After taking a sip of his coffee and stopping by the bar to look his wife in the eyes on his way to the kitchen table, he said, "That kid did not talk to God. That kid did not know God, if that kid knew God, he would not have committed all those sinful acts."

"That does not mean anything, Mathew." Lilly said.

"Yes, it does," he said as he was preparing to sit at the kitchen table. "It means that that kid ain't human. He sure ain't nothing God made. Speaking of made, when Rehginald left, did he take my tool box with him, the one that he bought me last year for Father's Day? I was out in the shed last night looking for it, and I can't find it."

"I don't recall him taking anything other than his clothes when I informed him that you wanted him out of the house." Lilly replied.

"Where's the phone? I think that I should call him and see."

"Can we please finish talking about your speech? If Reghinald did take the tool box, he had a right too."

"And if he did, he's going to hell too and not for that tool box, but sleeping with men. Now that's what's bad."

"Mathew! Did the same God who made you, make me? Cause you don't sound like it right now." She said looking away from the toaster.

"Listen Lilly, I need that tool box so that I can fix the garage door this weekend, and as for who made me, I was a man before I became a Pastor or a Politician."

"And Sarah's son?" Lilly asked while Mathew was getting a few things off of his chest.

"Well now, that kid was an animal untamed, a complete demon. Satan had a cut in everything that kid did," he said picking up the morning paper. Lilly walked over to the table where her husband sat with his toast and some butter in her hand. Mathew opened up the paper and began to read it. Putting the plate down, she decided that she would prepare herself a cup of coffee. She needed it to deal with her husband's attitude. She had spent so much of the morning fixing her husband's notes for the funeral that she had run behind schedule. Mathew continued to look at the paper, not noticing that his wife had brought him the toast.

Grabbing a cup from the cabinet, and fixing her coffee, Lilly said, "Mathew, why don't think about considering what I wrote for you to say?"

"Are we still debating that subject? Nope," he responded while busying himself with the paper. "I will not Lilly. You always try to sugar coat the truth, and I refuse to mask this kid's bad with good."

"Please," she asked. "If Sidney Senior heard about what you were going to say at his child's funeral, he would fire you right after beating you. Besides, there's enough bad on the front of that newspaper in your hand about that child."

Mathew flipped to the front of the paper quickly. "Where?" He asked.

"Top, left corner," she said before taking a sip of her coffee.

The words that he found were, *'Local Family: The Second, To Memorialize A Family Member Outside Of A Church Because Of New Law Passed By Churches.'* Under the title were these words, *'Nothing good to say about victim. You name anything bad; he done it; Murderer, Thief, and Rapist. He leaves behind his mother, father, two sisters, and one son, whose names they want to remain anonymous. The victim's name was James Earl Sidney Jr. He was thirty-five. His memorial service will be at New Orleans Southside, Train Depot in the open ballroom, and the Reverend Mathew Lehvon Steven's, the second, will be affiliating the service. Service will be at 10:00a.m., Tuesday, the 19th of July. James Junior is the second person to be memorialized outside of a church due to the passing of the new Religious Union Bill past last year by the Pastors Convention. For more information on the Religious Union Bill, go to www.religiousbill.gov or any Baptist church.'* Amazed by what he just read, Mathew asked his wife, "So you read this?"

"Of course, I did." She said putting her coffee down on the countertop to look him straight in the eye's from across the bar. "Now, will you reconsider my revision of your speech for tomorrow? The paper has made a spectacle of this nonsense already."

"It's not that bad. I mean at least his family's names were spared and his son, even though, James Senior's name and address should have been mentioned with that fowl mouth of his, and just knowing that James Junior has a kid only introduces another demon to follow in his footsteps. They should have written more about this kid. This is nothing."

"Mathew!"

"Look Lilly," he said. "I'm gonna say what I wrote on this paper. If I don't, someone else will. I have to say this. The world has gone long enough without the truth being told at funerals. All of this sugar coating must stop. This needs to be heard, so that families can stop coming to church when someone in their family dies and just come period." He said after he took a bite of one of his toast.

"And why must you be the hero?"

"Heroism got to start somewhere." He said while chewing the toast.

"That's sad, Mat. That's really sad, and who's gonna save you from the bad history that you have at Saint Hope? I mean, shouldn't you for at least one second consider not being judgmental. From the looks of things lately, JJ and Rehginald aren't the only ones on their way to hell."

He almost choked on his bread, after coughing a couple of times and clearing his throat, he said, "What do you mean, Lilly?"

"You want me to say it?" She asked while pulling her coffee cup away from her mouth. Mathew did not respond. He just looked at her as she moved away from the counter and walked toward him at the table. "I'm talking about your whorish ways, Mathew," she said snatching the paper from his hand. "You know the scandalous affair with sister Sally, Sister White, Sister Katherine, Mary, McCarty, Nelson, and Richards, and the girl child that you couldn't give me that you have by sister Betty, and using church funds for unrelated church activities, and once a year going to strip shows in Vegas with your deacons and politician friends. You wanna hear some more, because I can relate to more. No, you may not be a murderer or robber or rapist etcetera, but where I come from a sin is a sin no matter how big or small. I guess all of these years you thought that I was a fool, at least, you tried to make me look like one. I can't believe you, thinking that you had me in the dark with all these secrets. I should of done been left you."

"Now Lilly, you are behaving radically." He said after drinking a sip if his coffee. "What has put these vicious thoughts in your head?"

"Oh, so now you want some understanding? You need to remember that the Lord does not only talk to you these days—and don't you try and counsel me. I wish my daddy was still alive. I cannot believe that I married you when I think about it sometimes."

"Then, don't think about it, Lilly." He said with a sly smile. She was not in a humorous mood.

"Oh, I won't since you wanna play these animalistic games. But on the other hand, you better be thinking. It's time I done something that I should have done a long time ago."

"And what's that? Call your friend, Cheryl, and get out of the house for a couple of hours to cool off." He asked.

"Knawl, Dog—I'm gone call my friend, Cheryl, and get out for good. Now hero, you can save all them sluts that you want to save." She confessed before walking away. Mathew was dumb struck by his wife's words. He was a preacher, and he could not tolerate his wife leaving him with his current status.

"Lilly! Lillian! Come back here. We need to talk about this." He said calling out to her as she walked out of the kitchen and down the hall.

"Nothings up for discussion, Mathew, remember? I'm prepared to do everything that I just said."

Chapter 31

MEDIA COVERAGE

JJ's death was a mystery. The police had no leads other than JJ's friends telling the police that the last time that they had seen JJ, he was talking to a girl named Diamond. It was up to the police now to use whatever information that they could to bring JJ's killer to justice. They thought they maybe interviewing people outside the club where JJ was last scene would produce some leads. So, they asked the local news station to stop by and ask some people at the club the next Saturday night if they had witnessed anything in particular outside the club that night. The police wanted to study the demeanor of the witnesses to see if anyone of them may have been the killer. They only leads that the incident brought forth were honest feelings from individuals who did not care much for the victim. Several people choose not to speak, walking away from the camera. Others said that JJ was no one of concern to them and walked on. One young man just could not help himself. He had something that he wanted to say when Anchor Michelle Witley asked him if he knew the victim; the man said 'yes.'

"What is your name, young man?" She asked.

"My name is Frank-Frank Mizer."

"Frank, what can you tell us about the victim who was found dead here outside the back of this club four nights ago?"

"Besides, he deserved it?" He asked while looking at the reporter.

"Excuse me sir."

"You heard me. He deserved it. Everyone around here knows that. They just don't have time to be hauled down to the police station about it."

"Why is that, Frank?"

"Because New Orleans police are corrupt, they'll put anything on anybody no matter the condition or person involved. And for JJ, oh, he got just what he deserved. That bastard raped my aunts daughter; stole my uncles car; killed my cousin running from the police; sold drugs to my niece and she has four children in custody of DHS now, and put all four of my tires on flat because I would not let him have the rims off my car; pulled a gun on me, and then took my rims. So that bastard deserved to die."

"And there you have it New Orleans," The female news anchor said, "another witness that JJ's death is a blessing and a relief to all—another death diminishing us all."

At home and watching the news, James and Sarah shook their heads at the broadcasting of the investigation. Sarah soon changed the channel. She decided that she would rather watch FOX News, John McCain and Hillary Clinton lie about Obama than listen to some mess about her own son. Anyway, it didn't matter, Obama was gone win President of the United States, and several months later, he did. And who decided to work for him? Hillary Clinton.

Chapter 32

THE INVESTIGATION

Some people are born naturally with good intentions. Some are born naturally with bad ones. '*In any case both are born*', Vegas thought as she looked out her apartment window with a cigarette in one hand and listening to her friend, Diamond sing. Diamond had great intentions as she was capable of being good again, but Vegas' life was a different story. She did not believe much, and what she did believe, she nine times out of ten witnessed or carried out. Today, she felt confused, alone, and abandoned as she thought of JJ's murder. Diamond's mind, on the other hand, was far from murder as she pampered herself and carried on a tune.

"Girrrl—what are you doing?" Vegas asked Diamond after she hit a high note in the song. She had interrupted Vegas' thoughts, and she was disturbing Vegas' nerves as well.

"Singing, Beyonce's new song, 'To the Left'," she replied.

"And that's just the direction you're voice is going in." Vegas replied.

"What? I can sing." Diamond proclaimed.

"Sing what?"

"Anything that I feel that I can sing." She said holding the nail polish brush in her hand while looking up at Vegas.

"That's why you'll never make it."

"Vegas, are you saying that I can't sing?" Diamond asked.

Vegas motioned her head up and down with her cigarette in her left hand and said, "That's exactly what I'm saying." She then put the cigarette up to her mouth again and continued to look out the window. Something was happening outside.

"Girl, I know—I can sing. All I need is to go down town and audition—and I bet I'll get a singing contract. Master P is looking for a new singer to re launch his production company. I believe that I'm what he's looking for."

"Oh yeah," Vegas replied while turning to look at Diamond again away from the window.

"Yeah. Don't believe me? I got the audition sheet right here." Diamond said, reaching for the paper on the night stand beside her bed.

"Diamond, kill that Master P mess okay," Vegas said after she almost choked on her cigarette. Regaining her voice, she said, "There's something that I always want you to remember." Diamond closed her fingernail polish remover and moved her feet off of the bed to pay close attention to Vegas.

"Whitney can sing. Pattie can sing. Mariah can sing, and that girl that was voted off American Idol before Fantasia's time—that girl coming out in that movie, 'Dream Girls'. What's her name?"

"Jennifer," Diamond said. "Jennifer Hudson."

"Yeah, that's her. She can sing." Vegas said standing at the window with her back turned to Diamond.

"So what's your point?" Diamond asked Vegas.

"Hold up?" Vegas moved away from the window and looked at Diamond sitting on the bed. "Let me finish making my point," she said. "Even Christina Aguilera can sing, and Reverend Ducksworth down at the church. My point is that they can really sing and can save you from a life and death situation. Now people like you and I and, forgive me, Ciara, Beyonce, and Kaliz, and Jennifer Lopez, well, we only have a commodity that sells, a body, some dance moves, a clothing line, some perfume, some make-up, an acting career, etc—that probably won't last a lifetime and when the commodity expires, were finished—and until we realize that—I mean you and them, y'all being a singer is only false."

"I can't believe that you just said that. You need to speak for yourself. I can sing, and all of those ladies can sing that you just criticized. Anyway, how can you count Whitney with all the drama she been apart of lately."

"Sure they can sing Diamond, nobody's denying that, and trust me—only a fool wouldn't count Whitney. She's coming back, mark my word. It's just that the others can sing in their own way, bout like you said earlier, sing what you feel you can sing." Vegas said pointing to Diamond.

"But they can't sing period—only a few can. It's time for people to realize that everyone that comes out with a video can't sing. It's two kinds of singing or rather two categories . . ."

"And what are those Ms Professional?" Diamond asked.

"Now, Ciara, Beyonce, Kaliz, and Jennifer Lopez fit under the category of a ticket-temporary saving and short fix. They can give you a quick fix-just for the moment. Meanwhile, Whitney, Patty, Mariah, and young Jennifer from American Idol, and Luther, well, they fall under the category life saving and long fix. They can get you off crime stoppers, murder she wrote, diagnostic murder, even death row-they can even make people believe that you went to Heaven. So—who would you choose to sponsor you when you find yourself into some trouble?"

"I don't know. It's kind of hard to choose because I like them all." She said while thinking for a brief second. "I'd have to go with the second group if I had to choose one of those situations."

"Good—cause you gone need them. It's some cops that just pulled up, and they downstairs waiting to question you about that JJ mess." Vegas said, walking over toward Diamond and putting her cigarette out in the ash tray on Diamond's night stand next to the bed that was next to the door. "Don't let Dominique down. You know what to do. No hard feelings about those quick fix ladies either. They don't deserve that, just like that singing contract you plan on getting wit Persy." Vegas said before she opened the door and walked out. All of sudden, Diamond felt nervous all over again, like she did after JJ's murder two weeks earlier.

Chapter 33

THE BEGINNING OF THE END

So she says that she is a victim. He says that he is a victim as well. No one ever wants to think of victimization in this way. When researching the matter, the victimization process can fall either way. The victim can be the plaintiff or the defendant. It is all the same, just defined differently. Pitfalls fall on both side of the fence. Today may be your chance and tomorrow may be mine. The point being made here is if you dish it, then almost twenty times out of twenty you will have to take it back. It may not be tomorrow, today, yesterday, an hour, a minute, or a second later, but you better believe that the disadvantaged will come back to win the title back. No sins will go unpunished, no matter how big or small. You kill today and it will be your chance to die tomorrow. You hurt someone today, and you will hurt tomorrow, and if you dig a ditch for someone else to fall in, then you better dig one for yourself because you will fall along side them if you don't fall alone. So, why then do people not think about this before they commit such sinful acts? The answer to this is that none of us, once again, are perfect, and some of us would much better prefer to be doing the wrong thing than the right, which will continuously cause the world to reproduce history speeches and critics to research and remain debatable about new methods of evil reasoning. In other words, nothing is ever bad until it happens and once it happens, then, and only then is it judged. The question is always why? The answer is why not, for the bible says that nothing that's happening now is new, nothing. It is repetitive human history that we cannot seem to get right—the power of good verses evil, and the mystery of the human mind, very sinful.

All day long, Kallie, Sunshine, and Diamond had murder on their mind. It was time for revenge. JJ felt like he had the last word, the last action, but his enemies were right around the corner waiting and ready to lavish out all of the hate and hurt that they endured from him. Today was just an ordinary day to JJ. Nothing went wrong, and he had everything his way. He slapped his baby momma earlier because she had not cooked or cleaned the house, called her nasty and walked out of the house; took his dad's last beer from the fridge and lied about it when his father asked. He and his father got into an argument and JJ left as he always did. Gambled with a few friends on a car bet and when he lost, he said that he did not bet. His friends were upset over the matter. He called a cashier a bitch at the Mall because she called security because she suspected JJ of stealing. She had reason too, he often walked out of the store with some shoes or a jacket or a hat. There was nothing about today that convinced JJ that he should slow down and check his role. Today was full of criticism and pain as everyday was for JJ, and he loved it. Death had never crossed his mind. He did not plan on dying anytime soon. He did not plan on dying today, no one ever does.

Six miles away from 'Club New Orleans', some women were dressing very seductively to web their prey. They desired to have him, desired to have his blood on their hands. It would be the perfect crime, in the perfect place, at the perfect time. He could scream, but no one would hear him. He could run, but he could not run far. A dark shadow was being spawned into potion and the soul she claimed tonight would be her reward.

Inside 'Club New Orleans', JJ was getting stoned, as he did every Saturday night. It was no different from the rest as he imagined that he had some real go getters on his team to help him out of any trouble that was about to go down with anyone in the club who wanted some drama. When he was not in the bathroom or at the bar for seconds, JJ was chilling on the dance floor with his friends watching women shake their thing on the dance floor. He was creating much static as every now and then he would reach out and grab a handful of some girl's behind. Many of the women did not like the way that he was behaving and left the dance floor, but not before leaving him with a walling of their eyes or a turn up of the nose. As usual, JJ would call them a bitch or whore when he could not get what he wanted. His friends grew tired of his behavior and decided to leave the dance floor. JJ noticed when Brian tapped him on the shoulder and said, "Come on man! Let's go grab a table! These women don't like yo-dumb attitude tonight."

"Man, forget them freaks . . ."

"That's what we trying to do, but you messing it up for the rest of us. Now come on. Man, you need to stop taking all them drugs. Letting them mess with yo-brain and stuff."

"What you said?" JJ asked.

"Fool, you heard me. Stop blocking opportunities for the rest of us. And why you always got to take something. You act like you ain't never gotta ask for nothing. This ain't JJ's world. We all live in it too. You ain't no different from the rest of us."

"Man, what's wrong with you?" JJ asked Brian.

"Ain't nothing wrong with me?"

"Oh yes it is. You act like one of these complaining females when they period on. Ain't gotta be nice to them freaks if I ain't want too. Forget them! Just like I said!"

"All women ain't freaks—JJ."

"Oh yeah, my bad, then they hoes."

"No offense, so you saying Mrs. Sarah is a hoe?" Brian asked.

"Yeap! She ain't no different from these in here. She a she ain't she." He said with a smile.

"Man, it's something wrong with you. Calling you own mama obscene names. You got to be sick, but what I can't figure out is on what. Is it ecstasy, cocaine, weed, or alcohol. Yo-body showing mixed signals. You need a drug intervention program to clear up yo-side effects."

"You know Brian, just cause you all educated and whatever, that don't make you no different from me. You just know how to use better words to get what you want—and I say what I think and feel. Now all these hoes up in here hoes just like I said. I mean the word you use 'women' but its freaks to me. It ain't nothing serious. I just like saying hoes."

"Sit down, man. It's serious to them." Brian said.

"No it ain't, and I'm gone prove it. Watch these two coming over here by our table. Now they don't like them over there. Listen?"

The two women stood against the wall where JJ and his friends sat. They were two brown skinned women. One had short red hair and the other long black hair. The red head said, "Look at that hoe, she thinks that she going home with Black tonight, but I'm gone slide him right out of her hands." She said while laughing.

"Hoe, that's her man." The long, black hair chic said.

When the long haired girl had finished speaking, JJ turned to Brian and the other's and said, "I win—my point exactly." The two women looked at the men sitting at the table and walked away. JJ yelled, "Come back freaks, or is it hoes. We free tonight!"

"Has it ever occurred to you that they use that language because men like you continue to call them that?" Brian asked JJ.

"No man. They use that language because they hoes." JJ said while laughing. The other guys laughed as well. That was until Diamond approached them. '*Very attractive,*' Brian thought. '*Damn,*' JJ thought. '*All I need,*' Clay thought, and '*all I want,*' Kent thought. Yes, Diamond had all of them eyeing and eating out of the palm of her hand. Her dress was red, short and tight. Her hair was pinned up. Her legs were glistening as though she had pulled them straight from a tub of oil and water. Her smile was bright, and her eyes were like sharp needles. Diamond knew how to get what she wanted. She knew how to make sure that no one at a party missed her. All of the guys were practically drooling over her.

"So JJ," she said after laying her purse on the table and walking close to him. "How about you buy a real hoe a drink?"

"Yeah—okay." JJ said, still eyeing her seductively.

"Say Diamond—why don't you allow a real man to buy that drink for you?" Brian said with a smile.

"Maybe some other time baby—I want JJ to buy me one tonight." She said with a smile.

"Why me?" JJ asked.

"Why not you? Word on the streets baby that you got a black jack the police can't hold back. Besides, I need some maximum security. Dominique ain't treating me right." She said seductively. JJ laughed. All the other guys smiled and hit one another.

"Yeah—I think that we can get you something to drink then. But I'm telling you right now, I ain't up for that bull you pulled on me the last time-Diamond!"

"Everything's cool, baby. Now, let's go get that drink. I'm really thirsty." She said grabbing her purse from the table as she stood close to JJ.

"See Diamond, you ain't right. Had you let me buy that drink, all of that with JJ could have been avoided." Brian said, checking out her figure.

"Some other time—okay baby." She replied after rubbing his face and walking away.

"Yeah, and I want you to look just like that-with baby blue instead of all that red." Brian said as Diamond and JJ started to walk away. "That red look all right though," he said to himself before turning to Kent and Clay for approval. "Damn—she done messed me up for the rest of the night." Brian replied as he watched Diamond and JJ walk away. Kent and Clay looked at Brian. They were shocked by his comment. Brian never talked this way about a woman. As Kent and Clay continued to listened, Brian said, "Whoever, I meet tonight, if she ain't close to looking like that, she may as well get on." Kent and Clay laughed at Brian.

Chapter 34

THE FUNERAL

The Sidney Family along with Reverend Stevens was the first to arrive at JJ's funeral. James, Sarah, Lexe, and Leesa sat on the front row on the right side as Reverend Stevens busied himself at the podium. Everyone was quiet and no one said a word. JJ's casket was open. His body in plain view of his family, but yet, no one visited the casket. Sarah thought of all the times she saved him from going to jail, all the times she lied to prevent it. The thoughts took a toll on her as several tears ran down her cheek. James busied himself with his tie and checking the inside of his suit coat pocket. Lexe watched as Reverend Stevens read his Bible. Leesa, after keeping a close eye on her mother, decided to get up and view JJ's body. Everyone watched as she just stared at JJ. Everyone wondered what it was that she was thinking.

Within minutes, people started to fill up the Ballroom of the Train Station. First to show up were JJ's gang friends along with others. They bought with them gifts to put into JJ's casket. Some had guns, others jewelry, others money and shoes. Reverend Stevens watched as the gangsters placed the items into JJ's casket. The Sidney family watched as well. James wondered, '*what in the hell*'. Sarah did not notice what was going on at first, but when she did, she knew that she had to speak. '*JJ's funeral is not about to be a Mardi Gras,*' she thought.

As each guest arrived, right to JJ's casket each was headed to view JJ's body. Each took notice of the white sheet, covering JJ's body all the way to his waist. His hands were not visible. Many thought, '*it must be true that one of his hands is cut off*'. JJ's gang friends stood against the wall. No way were they going to sit down; they had to watch their backs. Within twenty minutes, JJ's funeral was packed with strangers and family. The guests conversed and wondered:

'*Is it true about his eyes?*'
'*Were the maggots really eating him*'?
'*Is his hand really cut off?*'

'They say he was found dead in an alley.'
'JJ was something else.'
'Man I hated to see him coming.'
'I'm just here to make sure he's dead'
'I'm just glad he's dead.'
'I'm here to witness his biography.'
'What biography?'
'The wicked one.'
'I was sick and tired of him.'
'This is unbelievable.'
'Yeah, he's really dead.'
'Did you notice all that stuff in his casket?'
'Was it made that way?'
'No, his gang friends put that in there.'
'And his mother allowed it.'
'I thought his mother was a Christian.'
'Is this a funeral?'
'Yes.'
'Why wasn't it allowed at Saint Hope?'
'Ain't his mom a member there?'
'Yes.'
'Then why isn't the funeral there?'
'The Pastor wouldn't allow it, something about gangs, violence, safety and charity.'

Reverend Stevens watched as the guests filled the room and conversed with one another. On this day, he wished that he could take up an offering. Meanwhile, as Reverend Stevens watched the guests, James watched him. James paid close attention to the Pastor's every movement. He watched as Reverend Stevens watched all the different kinds of women. He watched Reverend Stevens as he hugged and kissed many of the women on the jaw as he greeted them. After several minutes of greeting, gossiping and viewing, Reverend Stevens decided that it was time to start the funeral. "Hello everyone—if each of you will be seated, we will begin with this morning's ceremony."

Everyone calmly scrambled for a seat at the sound of Reverend Stevens' voice. Reverend Stevens imagined that no more than one hundred guest would attend JJ's funeral, but he was wrong as he looked at the crowd. There were over two hundred. Some of them were mad, some sad, some angry, some happy, some disappointed, and some just plain messy. The room was quiet after everyone took their seats. Some of the people had to stand until more seats were gathered.

"Well, well, well," Reverend Stevens said with a smile. "If we had a turn out like this every Sunday morning at Saint Hope, there would be less gang funerals to attend as well as criminal activity to reduce. I tell you—the south side of New Orleans will have overcome many obstacles." James as well as the gang members eyed Reverend Stevens coldly because of the remark.

"Amen," several Christian guests said.

"Speaking of gangs, it is only necessary that I get something off my chest before we began." Reverend Stevens said.

"Reverend, if you don't mind," Sarah stood and interrupted. James and many others wondered why she was standing and so soon.

"Go ahead, Sister Sidney," he replied.

"I'm sorry guys," she said looking in the direction of the gang members, who were JJ's friends. "But I'm going to have to ask you to go get your things out of that casket before we start. This is not the Mardi Gras. This is a funeral, and James Junior does not need any of that stuff where he's going." The gangsters eyed Sarah coldly with smiles. They didn't move. Sarah sat down. Reverend Stevens agreed with Sarah as he eyed the gangsters coldly. He thought, *'this just one reason why this funeral ain't at Saint Hope. These niggas are disrespectful.'*

James, irritated by the gangsters not moving, stood and said, "Did y'all here my wife. Get yo stuff." The gangsters still didn't move. "Now!" James yelled. The gangsters decided to move. "You better be glad the police ain't in here. All of you would be locked up. My son already going to hell. What y'all trying to do—send him there to shoot Satan, pay him, deliver some jewelry or run? Get yo stuff, and get it out of here—right now-if you planning on staying at this funeral."

"Thank you brother James," Reverend Stevens said. "You handled that much better than I would have." He concluded as three other Pastors walked behind him to sit down. It was two of his Associate Pastors and an invited Pastor.

"Don't thank me. You thank God." James said, sitting back down and mumbling, "You hypocrite." Sarah looked at her husband in disbelief. Leesa and Lexe smiled. The rest of the family surrounding James laughed.

After the Pastors took their seats, Reverend Stevens said, "I would like to welcome each of you to the Funeral Service of the late Mr. James Earl Sidney Junior, just in case some of you don't know where you are. If you are in the wrong place, now would be the time to leave or an excuse you may use to avoid being shot." Reverend Stevens said with smile. He figured that he would get one back on James, but no one found the joke funny. Everyone stared at him. "Just kidding everyone—only exercising a little enlightenment before all seriousness breaks loose, however, if you feel like you are in the wrong place, now would be the best time to leave before interrupting this service." No one moved. Everyone was in the right place accept some travelers who watched until their train came. "If you all have your programs in front of you, please turn to page three. There, you will find this morning's agenda. Also, if you have a comment for the family and you've filled out your sheet, you may place it up front before leaving in this box by the casket." All whom had programs began to turn to page three. "If you do not have a program, I'm sure that your neighbor will allow you to look on with him or her, or you may raise your hand and the Ushers will get one to you." Reverend Stevens said as he looked at his program before he began to read the agenda out loud, "First, we will have the Lord's prayer by a very special friend of mine, Reverend Luke. Then, there will be an opening of the memorial with a song by Sister Annie Watts. Next, we will have memories and confessions by who all wants to speak. Each person wanting to speak is limited to 30 seconds, again, if you don't plan on speaking or don't feel like it, you may fill out your sheet and place it up here in this basket. Following memories and confessions, will be today's sermon, by yours truly, who is I, Reverend Stevens. After the Sermon, we will conclude with a song and the benediction. So let's began with the Lord's prayer lead by Reverend Luke along with the congregation."

Reverend Luke approached the large podium and spoke the words, "Hello everybody." No one said anything. "Let me try this again," he said, turning to look at Reverend Stevens. "Everybody seems a little uptight." He turned back to the crowd and said, "Hello Everyone!" This time, the audience responded and returned the greeting saying, "Hello."

"No need to be upset and so uptight. Today—is another day that the Lord has made, and I'm surely glad about it. Touch your neighbor and tell them to wake up." He said with a smile, looking at the audience. "Each of you are still here. Now I don't know about the God you all serve, but the God I serve doesn't make mistakes." Reverend Luke said with a friendly smile. It was something about his voice that made the audience feel welcome. Reverend Luke looked and sounded confident and sure of himself when he spoke, as sure as the weight he carried around. His voice was bold, strong and sincere. "Sure he's dead—sure he's gone," Reverend Luke said to the crowd in reference to JJ as he pointed at the casket. "But our God is a man of his word. You know what He said? He said that all things must come to pass. With that said, forever ain't promised to any of us." Calming his voice and reducing it to a low tone, he said, "shall we all bow our heads in repeat of the Lord's prayer?" Everyone bowed their head and closed their eyes. "Our Father, who art in heaven, hallowed be thy name. Thy kingdom come, thy will be done, on earth as it is in Heaven. Give us this day, our daily bread and forgive us our trespasses as we forgive those who trust past against us, and lead us not into temptation but deliver us from all evil. For thine is the kingdom and the power and the glory, forever, Amen. Now we will hear a song of praise by Sister Annie Watts." Reverend Luke said.

Sister Watts moved away from her seat on the front left row and stood behind the microphone closest to her. She sang "Precious Lord".

> *Precious Lord, take my hand,*
> *lead me on, let me stand,*
> *I am tired, I am weak, I am worn;*
> *through the storm,*
> *through the night,*
> *lead me on to the light.*
> *Take my hand, precious Lord, lead me home.*

When my way grows drear, precious Lord, linger near,
when my life is almost gone,
hear my cry,
hear my call,
hold my hand lest I fall.
Take my hand, precious Lord, lead me home.
When the darkness appears and the night draws near,
and the day is past and gone,
at the river I stand,
guide my feet,
hold my hand.
Take my hand, precious Lord, lead me home.

Through out the song, Sarah and her girls shed tears. They couldn't hold back. Many of the guests were touched by the song as well. Annie sung the song with such patience and grace. The words to the song made the impossible, possible. Her voice was sweet, innocent, searching, convicting and sure. Annie, a short and petite woman, needed no music for the song. Her voice assured the audience that all was well, even for a short time. God was in the room and he comforted many. Suddenly, those who were angry loosened up. Those who were sad began to smile. Those who were happy began to cry. Those who were disappointed were relieved. The song was peace and understanding. After Sister Watts concluded with the song, Reverend Stevens approached the Pastor's podium ready to proceed with the agenda, and once again, God walked out of the building. All that was before the song, was back again.

Once Sister Watts was seated, Reverend Stevens said, "Thank you Sister Watts. Oh, you did a fantastic job. I tell you that was simply beau-ti-ful. Y'all want to hear some more of that kind of singing, then come to Saint Hope on Sunday morning at 10:30 am. Yes, Sister Annie knows how to get God to show up and show out."

"We know that Reverend," a strange woman said. "And you know how to make him disappear." All laughed.

"Ok, ok. Now, we'll hear JJ's biography, written by his mother, Sister Sarah Sidney, and read by his sister, Sister Leesa Sidney." Leesa in all her black, smiled at everyone as she stood before them. She began to read the paper in front of her. "James Earl Sidney Junior was born November 7, 1975. He weighed eight pounds and five ounces at birth. He is the son of James Earl Sidney Senior and Sarah Sidney. His is the brother of Lexe and Leesa Sidney. As a child, James Earl Junior also known as JJ was very active; as a teenager even more active; as an adult, active, disruptive and violent. JJ was no Beaver from 'Leave it to Beaver, and he certainly was no Opee from the 'Andy Griffith Show'. He was no Saint. He was JJ. The happiest moments that I and my parents remember with him, were his birth and toddler years. The worst years we can never forget. For those of you thinking that he should have been punished, JJ was punished. He went to church in his early years. My mother took him every Sunday as a child. He went to school, and he had great parents, but none of that encouraged him to be a better person. So for those of you who think that we don't understand your pain, we just want to say that we do. Thank you." With that said, Leesa left the microphone to return to her seat.

"Now," said Reverend Stevens standing at the podium again. "We want to exercise this as hurriedly as possible. We will hear responses from each of you wanting to speak. The family welcomes the testimony of all wanting to speak and apologize for all and any endeavors that JJ has placed on the heart of each of you. Remember, only one may speak at a time, and your time is limited to 30 seconds. No one at anytime is allowed to disrupt this part of the ceremony unless motioned to speak. Now, who would like to speak first?" The first person to stand was Michelle, the mother of JJ's alive and dead son.

"I just want to say that this whole incident is unbelievable." Michelle said before being interrupted. Tessany seated beside Michelle, looked at her strange.

"Unbelievable," a guest on the row behind her said. "Please, sit her down."

"No disruptions please, ma'am." Reverend Stevens said.

"Yes, unbelievable." Michelle said. "I mean, he's the father of my son, Taylor, and the father of my other son, Jamey, and the family didn't even mention my sons in this obituary." She replied while holding up the obituary.

"Is she serious?" Another guest replied from across the room. "Do you really want us to know that, Beyonce wanna be?" She was referring to Michelle's weave and her attitude as well as her short, black dress and stiletto heels.

"Like we care," Dominique said from the back row. James thought to himself, *'this was a bad idea, allowing the audience an opportunity to speak.'*

"Quiet please," Reverend Stevens said again. "Everyone who wants to speak will have an opportunity to speak when the time comes."

Insulted by the negativity surrounding her, Michelle said, "Since I can't speak in peace. I just want to conclude by saying that JJ's actions, which were negative, were the result of my-our, first son's death and our second son being abandoned. In death, he is rejoined with our son Taylor. He is survived by me and our son Jamey. I will truly miss him as he was the love of my life. Thank you." Michelle said before she sat down.

Dominique, seated on the back row, leaned over to Kalle and said, "She is so stupid . . . survived by her, yeah right. She and JJ were never married. JJ must of beat the senses out of her, and then she had the nerve to say that she loved him. How could anybody love a beast like that?" Dominique said before standing.

"What you doing D?" Kalle asked Dominique, nervously.

"I'm bout to speak." She replied.

"About what?" Kalle asked, apparently still nervous.

"It ain't what you think Kalle, calm down." She said. As Dominique was about to speak, Reverend Stevens waved her off to allow someone else to speak before her. Next to stand was Sonya, mother of Trei, JJ's best friend. Dominique didn't like what Reverend Stevens did at all.

"Hello everybody, I just want to say that my thoughts and prayers are with the Sidney family. My name is Sonya Styles-my son, Trei, and JJ were friends for thirteen years. They did almost everything together. Just last year that friendship came to an end because of rape, lies, drugs and betrayal. Yes, all of this happened between my son and JJ. All of this ended with my son committing suicide. I must say that JJ destroyed my son's life. He was my only child. Now he's gone. All of this is terrible. First, I had to bury my boy, now I'm attending the funeral of the reason why he's dead in the first place. Rest in peace Trei." She said before sitting down

"What was that?" James asked his wife.

Jada seated across the room was sympathetic to her ex-boyfriend's, mother's speech as tears ran down her cheeks and her mother comforted her. On the other side of the room, Dominique was ready to speak. "Can I speak now Reverend Stevens?" She asked aloud. Everyone turned and looked at her.

"This is about to get ugly," JJ's uncle Samuel said seated next to his wife.

Dominique continued, "It ain't like you do things decent and in order anyway."

"Excuse me," Reverend Stevens said.

"I told you." Sam said to his wife. "Why is James and Sarah allowing this mess to take place?" Sam said to his brother Joe who was sitting beside him.

"Just hush Sam," his wife Fay said overhearing the conversation between him and his brother.

"Yeah, hush Sam," Joe said in agreement with Sam's wife. Joe knew that the situation was about to be anything but orderly.

"Excuse Reverant," Dominique asked? "You know what I'm saying." She was confident and content in her tone. She knew Reverend Stevens, and she also knew his desires. "To the Sidney family, I wanna say that my thoughts, whatever those may be, and prayers are with you too. But y'alles boy JJ, now that's another whole different set of chips. Y'all son is in hell and . . ."

"Mrs. Hellieam," Reverend Stevens yelled. "You have no right to condemnation."

"I forgot to say this earlier, but now I believe that I will, in fact, I'm sure I will say it now. Sit down, Mathew. Don't nobody respect you. That is—nobody but your church members. You going straight to hell too, and they with you if they don't read they bibles."

"And you Mrs. Hellieam?" Reverend Stevens asked.

"I got an appointment to talk with God about that this week-maybe even today." She said. Everyone laughed. "Anyway . . ."

Joe finding humor in Dominique's confession said to his brother Sam, "I like her. She going over thirty seconds. I can feel it. This whole scene right here with her is what's fixing to blow everything out of proportion."

"No, I'm afraid all of that happened when the arrangements were made." Sam replied. Fay overhearing her husband and his brother said, "So you two could have done better, I'm guessing?"

Sam looked at Joe, and Joe looked at Sam before the both of them said, "Hell yeah—pine box."

Seated on the front row and not pleased with the funeral arrangements, James said to his wife Sarah, "See, what did I tell you Sarah?"

"About what?" She asked.

"Being dumb—that there is the reason why we at the Train Station in the first place." He said while pointing backward at Dominique. "I told you that all of this mess was going to happen. But did you believe me, oh no. You had to go listening to him up there. Now all of us look like fools."

"Shut up James." She replied.

"Ain't no way. I ain't gone take too much of this. You hear me Sarah. I just want you to know that. All this mess done got on my last nerve. I'm one and a half second away from lighting up this place like them gangsters out there been doing," James said looking at his wife and pointing at the window.

"Will you please hush?" She asked.

Dominique continued, "and I hope that y'all know that. He was always into something. To name a few things: robbery, rape, murder, gambling, violence and that was mostly against women. In fact, his violence against women is the number one reason why I came to this here funeral in the first place. You know what your son did a couple of weeks ago? He put a gun to my head and robbed me, all over lack of control of a situation with one of my female friends. I hated y'alles son, and I'm glad he dead."

James knew in his spirit that he would not hold his peace for long. Joe and Sam watched as James hurriedly got up from his seat and turned to Dominique and said, "Hold up. Wait a minute." James captured the attention of all of the audience members. "Now this here bad enough," he said concerning the environment he and his family were in. "Being at a Train Station and having a funeral. Y'all done lost your minds if you think that I gone sit here through all this mess. If I have to stand up again, all y'all motherless . . ."

"James, sit down." Sarah interrupted and said.

"Fools gone clear out of here." James concluded.

"That's right. Tell 'em Bro—cause our momma didn't raise no punks." Joe said, looking down at the floor.

"Shut up Joe." His wife Nancy said.

"Sit down now, James!" Sarah yelled.

"What are you yelling at Dad for?" Lexe asked. "She started it." Lexe said referring to Dominique.

"Don't start. Stay in your place Lexe Marie." Sarah said.

"Man, this is some straight up bull. This ain't no funeral service. It's judgment day for us and JJ. And how she gone judge somebody anyway back there? She the ring leader of a female sex pool operation. That's the problem." Lexe said to her sister Leesa.

"Girl hush, for the last time," Sarah said to her daughter Lexe. "We don't have the right to judge."

"Man, this is ridiculous," Leesa said to Lexe.

"Shut up Leesa." Sarah replied.

"I was talking to Lexe." Leesa replied to her mother.

"And I don't care . . ." Sarah said before she was cut off by Dominique.

"So y'all think that I like feeling this way? Huh?" Dominique asked. James was still standing. He turned to look at her.

"Feeling like what, a man?" Lexe said in a low tone where only Leesa and a few guests surrounding them could hear. Sarah looked at Lexe, so did James. Leesa laugh at her sister. Some of the guest found humor in the matter too.

"I don't like feeling this way." Dominique said looking at James and unaware of what was happening on the front row.

"Oh, now she don't want to be a man. I'm confused." Lexe said. The men and women surrounding her began to laugh. Sarah didn't find what her daughter was saying funny. She eyed her coldly. Lexe witnessed her mother's stare and looked away. She then began to admire a ring that she wore on her finger to avoid seeing her mother stare at her.

As far as James was concerned, Dominique had spoken enough. It was time to sit her down. So he said in response to her feelings, "I don't care about how you feeling. I just ain't going to listen to all this bull all y'all came to throw at my family. Now who ever you is, Dominique, Diamond . . ."

"No, I'm Diamond." Diamond stood and said at the sound of her name. Everyone looked at her, even Dominique, and she sat down quickly.

James concluded, "Different, Dog or whatever. I agreed with you in the beginning, especially about Pastor Stevens, but now you crossing the line."

"Crossing the line? That's all yo son ever did. He was terrible. Didn't nobody want to see yo son come around. He was a bully, and he was controlling. He wanted everything his way and was always on a power trip. Now, I'm sorry that you are left to defend the true person he really was, but I am not about to apologize for hating him. I feel safer knowing he ain't around anymore. Majority of us in this room do." Dominique said. Many of the people nodded their heads up and down in agreement with her.

"All right, Mrs. Hellieam, you are well over your thirty second speech." Reverend Stevens said to Dominique

"Shut up!" James exclaimed to Reverend Stevens. "You the reason for all this. All you had to do was have this funeral at Saint Hope. No, that was too much for you, and I dare you to walk out of here. If you do, you better leave all my wife's money on that podium. I'm sick of you man, always seeing spots in every ones eyes except yours. Your own house ain't even in order-parading these whores all over town and many of they husbands too. All of it look homosexual to me, no wonder why yo son don't know which way to go, or are you the only one that's in denial?" As James spoke, Sarah tugged on his coat and asked him to sit down. However, James was not listening to his wife. This time, Reverend Stevens did what was told of him. He took his seat. James then turned back to Dominique, who was still standing in the back and said, "Young lady, I appreciate your feedback, expressions, examples, opinions, and all of that, but will you please sit down, and allow someone else to speak before I lose my mind? I can't take no more from you. Now I got about a hundred more people, including some of my own who would like to speak, but I ain't gone listen to no more than two. After them two, he gone speak," James said pointing to Reverend Stevens, "and we all gone pray and Amen JJ's ass to the ground."

"James," Sarah called out to her husband once more.

"I'm serious Sarah," he said looking down at his wife before he sat down. "We already been here too long. All these people wanna tell me about the demon I already know. I gave birth to."

"I gave birth too, James," Sarah replied.

"You know what I'm saying." He responded.

Chapter 35

THE FUNERAL

New Orleans', South-Side train station was on fire and the only thing burning was the attitudes inside at JJ's funeral. James Senior had done exactly what he came to do and that was to stay in control of his son's life even after death. The audience was ill tempered when arriving; comforted when Sister Watts sang; and then ill tempered again. Attitudes were circling all over the room. Eyes were roaming and rolling, and facial expressions came in all shapes and forms. The idea for everyone affected by JJ negatively was to tell everyone what JJ did and to tell JJ's family a piece of their minds. There was so much evil in the ballroom of the train station, that it could be smelled when coming through the doorway, even travelers was suspicious of everything that was going on. Some people did come to actually support the family, but as soon as they reached the doorway to enter the memorial, their tolerance level went from neutral to negative by mathematical powers. Ninety-five percent of the people at the funeral believed that JJ was evil and cruel. Five percent believed that he was good, but that five percent would take no chance at his defense with all the hatred surrounding them. The audience was focused on each person speaking from beginning to end. Everyone was alert and in awe of what was happening, and James would allow only two more people to speak. He was fed up with the way the funeral was turning out.

Jada decided that she would be next to speak. As she slowly stood, everyone watched. "Hello," she said to everyone hesitantly. Clearing her throat she said, "My name is Jada Wells." At the sound of her name, Sarah turned back to look. Sarah was surprised. Trei's mother, Sonya, also turned to look in amazement. At the sound of Jada's voice, Sonya's spirit was comforted. Within seconds, all eyes were focused on the lovely young lady speaking.

Jada continued as she rubbed her hand through her short, curly hair and rested it on her neck for a second with a smile, "I bring you all greetings from Christ Love Ministries. My purpose for speaking is to tell you all that I too was angry at JJ for a long time. Why, some of you may ask? Some of you already know." She said looking at Dominique, then Sonya, then to the front row at Sarah. "I attended a friend's party and was raped in more ways than one—and yes, JJ did it. You see, we didn't get along well. At the party, he slipped a date rape drug into my drink. A drink that I asked my boyfriend then, Trei, to watch while I went to the bathroom; several minutes later, I began to feel agitated and out of my comfort zone as well as dizzy. I was also paranoid. My best friend thought that I was drunk. She offered to let me lie down in her room and sleep it off. I did, and I woke up in a hospital bed to bad news and shame. I tried to kill myself six times after JJ got away with the incident. I also dropped out of college, and quit going to church. That is until a strong willed woman, my mother, realized that it was time for her to stop being nice to me and tell me to wake up and get over it. And that's why today is a new day for me, a stronger one; and as Reverend Luke said earlier, a day that the Lord has made, as we should rejoice and be glad about it. People, please understand that nonsense is no cure for ignorance. However, knowledge and wisdom is, and in my wisdom, I stand to say that I forgive JJ. I forgive Sonya and Trei, and I forgive the Sidney family. My personal advice to each of you today is a Bible saying, don't let the sun go down on your wrath. It's JJ today, but it could be any and all of us tomorrow. Thank you." She concluded. After Jada sat down, her mother hugged her, kissed her on the jaw and said, "well done, my angel, well down. God is pleased." Her father seated on the other side of her patted her on the knee before looking at her with proud eyes and hugging her.

Tears rolled down Sarah's face as she listened to Jada's speech. Sonya couldn't hold back her tears either. Both mothers were releasing tears of joy and peace, as both were relieved.

Forty-five minutes into the funeral, Steel decided to speak. He thought, '*if I don't speak now, I never will*'. He did not want to speak; in fact, he was not going to until he heard Jada's speech. Steel needed to heal his family, so he decided to speak on behalf of his wife Lucy and dead son Terrance. Already, Steel had heard so much bad about JJ, and like the others, he too was angry and mad at the young man. Compelled to speak, he decided to stand and release his testimony. Everyone stared at him. It seemed as though he received more stares than anyone. Some of the stares were cold; some warm; some fierce; some impatient, and some shameful. Steel wondered if he left some food on his beard as he rubbed his hand over his face. Looking down at his hand and seeing nothing in it, he thought, '*it can't be my beard*'. He was ready to speak, but he was in a state of shock. Caught off guard by the stares for a brief moment, Steel thought of sitting back down. Was it just him that received the stares or was it everyone, he thought.

Reverend Stevens, not sure of why the man was standing because he had not spoke, decided to end the suspicion by asking the guest, "Are you going to speak, Sir?"

Steel, nervous and trembling, pulled himself together and said, "Yeah. My name is Steel Johnson. I wasn't going to speak," he said nervously before clearing his clogged throat with a cough. "That is until the young lady over there did." He said pointing in the direction of Jada. "Anyways, I came to speak on behalf of myself, my wife, Lucy, and my son, Terrance. A few years back, my son was killed. He was crossing the street on Fifth and Palmer. He was me and my wife's only son. We were told after his birth that my wife would not be able to bare anymore children."

Seated on the back row beside Kalle, Sunshine became aware that the man speaking was her uncle Steel. He was the uncle she told Kalle and Diamond about on the day that they killed JJ. Tears filled the corners of her eyes as she listened to her uncle talk, soon her eyes were over filled and the tears rolled down her cheeks. Kalle, confused after she finished scrolling through JJ's obituary for the third time, looked to her right to find what looked like tears running down Sunshine's face. At first, she thought that it was sweat, the train station was kind of warm. But with a closer look, she noticed that the water on Sunshine's face was in fact tears. Reaching out to her friend she said, "You okay?"

"Yeah," Sunshine replied. "Bad allergies—that's all."

"You sure? Them don't look like allergies to me," Kalle replied.

"And how would allergies look to you Kalle?" Sunshine said to her friend as she wiped her face with a tissue.

"I'm just saying, it look like you crying to me."

"If it look like I'm crying, then why you gone ask me if I'm crying?" Sunshine asked in a terrible mood.

"To be sure," Kalle responded.

The look on Sunshine's face said for sure—and I'm not so pleased with you. Kalle knew what the look meant. She decided to leave Sunshine alone.

Meanwhile, Steel continued, "He was 22. So after my son's death, everything with my wife and I all went down hill. She decided that she would live with our son in the imaginary world, just to have that relationship that they had before his death. She refused to accept that Terrance was dead. She told everyone that he was just sleeping. She did it for six months before I had to admit her into a mental hospital. JJ killed my son Terrance, and as a result of his death, drove my wife crazy."

At this moment, Kalle knew why Sunshine was in fact crying. Diamond on the other side of Sunshine knew as well. Vegas looked down the row at Dominique. Apparently, they were the only two who did not know what was going on.

"You see, JJ was on a high speed chase with N.O.P (New Orleans Police) behind him. I asked God many times why Terrance and why before I or my wife. JJ took the two most important people in my life away from me, well for sure one, as I had taken them for granted. My answer today is that God don't make no mistakes. He said that he would move through your children to get your attention. And he did, because for years, I wanted nothing to do with my son. I put everyone before him. Honestly, I was ashamed of him because he was a homosexual." With that said, Reverend Stevens looked down at his bible in front of him. He also thought about his wife, Lilly. "Anyway," Steel concluded, "to make a long story short, I still have my wife. She is now recovering and doing well." With that statement, everyone clapped. "That's why she's not here today. She regained her sanity after JJ's death and the return of my son to the spirit world. Being inspired to speak by I believe Ms Jada, I too want to say that on behalf of the Johnson family, I too forgive the Sidney family. I let the sun go down on two wraths. I can't afford to let it happen three times. Thank you." Steel smiled and said before he took his seat.

Relieved that Mr. Johnson's speech had come to an end, Reverend Stevens said, "All right, thank you Mr. Johnson. We-do-appreciate-your-testimony as well as the rest of you who spoke. To those of you who were inclined to speak and weren't afforded the opportunity, I can only say that there will not be a next time." He said provoking James. James holding on to Reverend Stevens' every word, got the memo and asked, "just what in the hell are you saying Stevens?"

Reverend Stevens almost regretting that he used the tone looked confused and fearful.

"James hush, please," he wife said.

"Sarah, I'm sick Mathew and this whole situation." James said throwing up one hand.

As the debate between James and Sarah was taking place, Reverend Stevens attempting to speak again was interrupted by Reverend Luke, who tapped him on the shoulder and said in a low tone, "My apologies, but clearly this father has a lot of animosity against you, and he's upset. If I may, I would advise that if you want this to go down easy, you should probably consider letting one of these Associate Pastors behind us finish this funeral, or even me for that matter."

"Do you know this family, Pastor Luke?" Reverend Stevens asked.

"I do now." Luke said as he had heard much from the audience and the family.

"Then yeah," Reverend Stevens said making sense of the advice and his Associate Pastors, "you're probably right. I'll let you speak though. Have you ever heard my Associates speak?"

"No," replied Pastor Luke not sure of Pastor Stevens' relativeness.

"Trust me, and you don't want too." Pastor Luke looked confused. Pastor Stevens looked sure as he then said, "let me announce the change, and I'll let you take over." He concluded by saying, "Great looking out Pastor." He then patted Pastor Luke on the back. Pastor Luke walked away after saying, "Yeah, no problem."

Suddenly from no where, cops swarmed the train station. Everyone was shocked and surprised. They also wondered what was next, considering JJ was already dead, or was that him in the casket. Dominique, Diamond, Kalle, Sunshine, Vegas, and the rest of the Dominique's friends on the back row stood up. Many other guests stood as well once the officers walked past their row.

"What are they here for?" Kalle asked Diamond. "Or shall I ask who?"

"I don't know, but I already know the story. No need to repeat it. I don't know nothing." Diamond replied.

James suddenly sprang from his seat when he witnessed the officers and yelled, "What's this?" The officers walked back and forward searching each row. "What's going on here?" James asked a second time. No one answered. Everyone kept a close eye on the police. Some of JJ's friends who had returned to the funeral after putting away their treasures, hid behind some of the innocent standing guests standing beside them.

In a matter of seconds, the officers had found what they were searching for. A Hispanic officer yelled to the remaining officers, "Here he is right here," he said. He found who they were looking for in the fifth row on the left. "Let's go Rumsfield." He said.

Sunshine asked Kalle, "What is he here for?"

"My question exactly," Kalle said. "He's been mighty quiet up there too."

Rumsfield knew that his day was coming, but he did not think that it would be so soon, and definitely not today, he thought. Thinking to himself, he said, *'Carter just had to breakdown and tell Internal Affairs everything. I knew he was weak, but I never knew that he was really dumb'*, Rumsfield thought to himself as he rubbed both of his hands up and down his well creased pants.

"Rumsfield," Detective Sanchez said. "Lets go now!" Detective Rumsfield eased out of his seat at the call of his name. He fixed his jacket once standing. Sniffing his nose and wiping across it with his fore finger and his thumb, he preceded pass several people sitting in the direction of Sanchez.

James still suspicious as to what was going on asked, "Um, um. Did any of you hear my question? What's going on in here?" Sarah, Lexe and Leesa all agreed with James as they looked in the direction of Sanchez.

Reaching Sanchez, Rumsfield said, "Well, of all my friends, they had to send a rival after me."

"Is that right Big Boy?" Sanchez asked Rumsfield as they stood face to face.

"Yeah, that's right," Rumsfield responded.

Rosenthall, another officer, approached Rumsfield and said, "Have you asked for that forgiveness yet? Captain is waiting, and he wants you in his office ASAP, before we hand you over to Internal Affairs."

"No, I ain't asked for that forgiveness yet. Only three people done said that they forgive this family out of this entire crowd. I thought that you said that Baptists were quick to forgive with Martin Luther King practicing that turn the other cheek in all?"

"Naw white boy," Rosenthall said in a low tone, "what I said was eventually, and you might be dead when that happens, but forget, not ever. Come to think about it, and they will take it all back too."

"Now you tell me this. Man, I can't go to jail like this. How will I be able to hold up?" Rumsfield asked.

"You should have thought through all of that before. Now you got five seconds to do what you came here to do before these handcuffs show you what thinking is all about." Sanchez said. James still with no answers to what was going on and upset, walked over to Detective Rosenthall and said, "Man this here is my son's memorial service. What's this all about?"

"Stop playing! A funeral? At a train station?" Rosenthall laughed. The other officers laughed too. The audience did not laugh at all. "Honestly, who's he going to visit?" Rosenthall asked while laughing. Some of the other officers laughed with him. He quickly stopped laughing and said, "Shut up and go back to your seat. All will be explained soon."

"Do what? You do realize that you still black right, and a cop?" James asked. "Man this is my son's funeral—ain't nothing funny about this!"

"Yeah, yeah, and unless you plan on going with him, you better have a seat. We are dealing with official police business right now." Rosenthall replied. "This ain't got nothing to do with being a black cop."

"Freaking cops," James said. "Always on a power trip. What the system don't know is the mess they made when they gave y'all a badge and a gun. They just added a license to y'all super ego, like the flash light method wasn't enough."

"Oh yeah, and you about a second away from getting some act right." Rosenthall said to James.

Sam not wanting his brother to end up in jail while his son's memorial was taking place called out to James and said, "Come on and sit down Bro. You know a brother quick to lock another brother up when the white man's around, and they ain't gone give second thought to it when a Hispanic is around either." Sam said. James began to walk back to his seat.

Sanchez after James walked away and Rumsfield was handcuffed said, "Listen up everybody. Rumsfield has something to say, and we'll end this disruption. Speak up." He said to Rumsfield.

Rumsfield, a little distraught, decided to speak, "look everybody," he said. "I know that y'all can't stand me, and I can't stand some of y'all, but that's cool. Cause now I'm about to pay for my portion of the trouble that I've caused." Turning to look at Sonya, who he was seated two seats from earlier, he said, "Mrs. Styles, I owe you an apology as well as the Sidney and the Wells family. JJ did not cause Trei to kill himself. It was me. He was suppose to give me some evidence I needed to close a case. He refused to give it me. We tussled . . ." He said before being interrupted by Sonya.

"What?" Sonya exclaimed.

"How?" One of Trei's gang friends yelled out.

"Why?" Jada exclaimed.

"Hold on," Rumsfield said. "Let me finish, and you all will have the answers to your questions." He turned back to Trei's mother and said, "Mrs. Styles, you also have another death certificate to pick up at the Police Station. You see, Trei did not kill himself either. I killed him and made it look like a suicide. It was an accident. I tried to get him to calm down, but he refused."

"What?" Sonya asked again.

"Just say the word Mrs. Styles," one of Trei's gang friends interrupted from the other side of the room. "We got a beat down to give away."

"Shut up, punk!" Rosenthall said. Rumsfield continued to talk.

"He wanted a second chance with the young lady Jada over there," Rumsfield continued. "He wanted to make things right with you Mrs. Styles, and he wanted to forgive JJ. Trei was supposed to rat out JJ and his source to me. He wouldn't do it. I stated to him that his only other option was jail and this time for good. When I visited Trei on the night he died and after JJ left, he expressed to me that he was not going to rat JJ out or anyone else, and also that he wasn't going back to jail. The whole idea freaked me out. One thing led to another and I strangled him with a rope lying on your basement floor." He said to Sonya before all the excitement of the incident caused her to black out. The ushers rushed to her aid.

"All right," Sanchez said. "You've said what you needed to say as your priest advised."

"Hold up Sanchez," Rumsfield said as he looked across the room at Jada and then to the front of the church at the Sidney's as they stood. "I'm sorry that all of this had to happen today, but its going to be all over the news tomorrow. I ask now that the Wells and the Sidney family both forgive me as I have trespassed against them both by covering up Jada's rape by JJ."

"Now you know you need a beat down!" Jada's mother yelled as she tried to make her way to Rumsfield. Her husband was shocked and so was Jada by her mother's attitude. "Do you know what my family went through?" She asked trying to get to Rumsfield. Her husband was on her heels, finally he caught up with her and held her so that she could not attack the ex cop. Jada was in shock as she sat down in her seat.

"Let's go Rumsfield," Rosenthall said after checking the caller ID on his phone. "Captain's calling again."

"Somebody, stop him for me please!" Jada's mom yelled as her husband held her. "Somebody, please do something." She exclaimed before she too fainted. Rosenthall and Sanchez guarded Rumsfield as the other officers followed them out of the station. As they walked, Sanchez asked Rumsfield in a low tone, "Now how many times did you really call Carter dumb?"

Rumsfield fearful of being hit by one of the funeral guests, looked behind him before saying, "I don't know. I can imagine a lot." He said, thinking of the gun gestures he had just witnessed from the gang members.

"Yeah," Sanchez said before they walked out the door. "And that's just how much time you looking at. That's if you survive a trial."

Chapter 36

THE FUNERAL

A memorial service at the Train station had turned into a court case full of defendants, prosecutors, judges, and surprise witnesses. The funeral held one surprise after another. If anyone felt bored or isolated before attending, both were gone now. The audience welcomed all new and future conflicts. Once again Reverend Stevens decided that it was time to settle down the crowd as no one could believe what had just happened. Sonya was awake now and alert and so was Jada's mom, Lauren. Both women were being fanned by the Ushers.

Sonya sat calmly in her seat, thinking to herself about her dead son. 'Yes, Trei was dead', she thought, and she missed him, but she would not miss being broke. She struggled to provide a living for Trei since her divorce. She was tired, and many times she felt like giving up. But now she was blessed. Her Life Insurance policy on Trei would not pay for suicide, but it would pay for murder and double.

Across the room and two benches over was Sony's sister, Leslie Rae-Styles, and her husband Mike. They watched as Sonya was fanned by the Ushers. Mike wanted to reach out and comfort Sonya earlier when she fainted, but Leslie would not allow him to do so. Leslie and her sister, Sonya, were long enemies. Not because of Sonya, but because of Leslie. Leslie being the younger sister, took Mike from Sonya and married him. Mike was Trei's father and also, he was married to Sonya before Leslie. Sonya and Mike obtained a divorce after Trei's first birthday. Mike later married Leslie. The incident created animosity between the two sisters and their mother, who was always on Leslie's side. Leslie only supported Trei because she loved Mike, but now with Trei out of the picture, she felt all her problems were gone as she did not have to suck up to Mike to keep him anymore. Now she was having second thoughts as she watched her husband looking across the room at her sister, his ex-wife.

"Why are you looking at her?" Leslie asked Mike. "She is fine. She has plenty of people surrounding her to keep her secure. A faint is not always a cry for help." She exclaimed.

"Are you saying that she faked it?" Mike asked his wife. "She's my ex-wife Leslie, and the mother of my only son. I don't hate her, you know?"

"Correction, now dead son! Anyway, what I do know—is that you are unbelievable," Leslie said. "She didn't faint because of Trei. If you weighed what just happened a while ago on a scale of one hundred, only ten percent of what happened would be about Trei, the other ninety percent would involve her. And as far as her relativeness to you is concerned, she is my sister, and I know her all to well. You are ridiculous."

"Why?" He asked. "I'm only being concerned."

"And for what?" She asked. "She does not want your concern or your sympathy. She's comforted fool. Did you not hear what that Ex-Detective Rumsfield said a moment ago? She has another death certificate waiting for her. Your ex-wife, simple minded, is the sole beneficiary of five-hundred thousand dollars from your son's death. Your job is only going to pay us fifty thousand."

"Well, that's better than the nothing we started off with." Mike said looking at Leslie.

"And who says so?" She asked. Mike knew that it was time that he shut up from the look in Leslie's eyes. He also needed to shut up because the people sitting next to he and his wife were enjoying the argument.

Chapter 37

The Funeral

Once again, Reverend Stevens asked for everyone's attention. So much was happening and so fast. There was one outburst after another. Each time the crowd was settled down, something else happened. Stuff was happening, and the strangest thing about it is, the guests knew something was to be unexpected, but they just didn't know when.

"Okay everyone, let's try this again," Reverend Stevens said holding his hands up as a sign of 'be quiet or I surrender'. Either the case, the crowd once more became silent. "We will once more proceed with the agenda." He said before moving away from the subject at hand and saying, "You think JJ is pleased with today?" He asked with a laugh. Some of the audience laughed. Many did not, especially the Sidney family. "Okay, okay, just a little humor before we continue. I apologize. Now, before the finalization of this memorial proceeds again, I must make an announcement concerning the remaining agenda. Now, as I and as you all have witnessed," Reverend Stevens said placing one hand on his chest for a brief second. "Mr. Sidney has so un-eloquently disrupted and clearly stated that he doesn't like how . . ." Pastor Stevens said before being interrupted.

"I really don't," James said out loud. The audience laughed.

"James," Sarah replied.

"How I've handled this situation, and how he's not impressed . . ." Reverend Stevens continued again before being interrupted by James a second time.

"I really ain't," James said out loud again. Sarah looked at him. The audience laughed.

Reverend Stevens continued once more, however, James would interrupt again, "impressed with the way this situation has turned out even before now. Even more, I'm reminded of his negative attitude to accept . . ."

"I really can't," James replied.

"Sidney Senior." Sarah exclaimed.

"accept certain change," Reverend Stevens continued. "Anyway with all that has been said and not much being accomplished thus far, in order to speed up and finalize this process. I must under the respect and advisement of my Brother and friend in Christ, allow Pastor Luke to complete this ceremony." Reverend Stevens said extending a hand of welcome to Pastor Luke.

"Good," James stood and said. "Because honestly Stevens, if you ain't never wore a beat down, the day was gone be the day. Ask Sarah? I told Sarah before we made it here that I was gone get you." The audience laughed. All pain was gone now.

"James Earl Sidney Senior!" Sarah exclaimed before James turned to her and said, "Shut up, shut up, and for the last time HUSH!" He said to Sarah. Several audience members laughed in agreement with James and the Reverend Stevens matter. Many of them knew that Pastor Stevens deserved it.

Shocked by James's out burst, Reverend Stevens swallowed his pride and said, "Now with no further a do . . ." He was about to welcome Pastor Luke to the podium when he was interrupted once more by James.

"Stevens sit down," James said.

"Must you continue to be so disruptive?" Mathew asked James.

"Sit down. Pastor Luke don't need no help fixing this mess you done made." James said fanning his hand several times, waving Reverend Stevens off. James then unbuttoned his suite coat once more and sat down beside his wife, who eyed him coldly. He eyed her back for a brief second and then turned his attention to Pastor Luke.

Within seconds of Pastor Luke walking up to the podium, an Asian male and his wife appeared in the aisle of the two rows, separated from one another. Reverend Luke close to speaking was shocked and confused by what was taking place now. He was suddenly silenced. The audience turned their attention to the two individuals as they were guided by Pastor Luke's eyes and the surprise in them.

A petite, Asian male, looked in the direction of James and said, "You son robbed me store. Me want money today." His wife nodded her head up and down with a nervous smile.

"Oh hell, what's going on now?" Joe asked his Brother Sam.

"What is . . . ," James said. "Where them peoples come from? White people we can expect to show up, but Mexicans and Asians, now this something new." He said to Sarah after he stood.

The Asian male continued, "We see JJ on news. DEAD! We want money, today. You pay" The man said pointing at James. Reverend Luke relaxed. The audience was shocked, yet again.

"Who me?" James asked pointing at his chest.

"Yes, son robbed me store. You pay two hundred dollar." The man said. His wife moved her head up and down in agreement as she smiled at the crowd nervously.

"Sarah, what is this?" James asked his wife in a low tone. "Is this a joke?"

"I don't know, James. You told me hush, remember?" She replied.

Reverend Luke in an effort to calm the situation down said, "Sir, would you and your wife like to take a seat? This funeral is almost over, and I'm sure you can speak with Mr. Sidney concerning the matter after then."

"No. We want money now. We no John the Baptist," the Asian man said to Reverend Luke. He then said to James, "You pay us. We go. Police on the way."

Everyone laughed at the Asian couple. Reverend Luke decided to intervene, "Lets quiet down everyone, "he said before slightly laughing himself. Regaining his seriousness, he said, "lets quiet down, please." The audience continued to laugh.

The Asian woman embarrassed said, "Chan, these people laugh at us. This bad idea."

"You called the police? Who they coming for? JJ dead." James said.

"Yes dead. You father. You pay." Chan said to James.

"A lie." James exclaimed. "I didn't rob you. I ain't giving y'all a dime."

"No, no dime, two hundred dollar." Chan's wife Lee said, looking at James and then the audience around her.

"It's amazing how y'all try to speak English, but can't understand it." James said. "Now—I said, I ain't giving you nothing."

"The police on way. We wait, then" Chan said.

"Wait where?" James asked. The audience could not stop laughing.

"Wait here—on floor. No new to us—tradition in China." Chan said before he and his wife sat down and the building was stormed by police for a second time. The police came in with there guns pointed. The skinny, tall officer said to the Asians as he pointed his gun, "Get down! Get your ass on the floor!" The officer then turned to the crowd with his badge in his other hand and said, "Don't be alarmed folks. We will be out of your way in no time." It was Detective Carter. He was dressed in civilian clothing.

The second cop, known as Red said to Chan and his wife, Lee. "Didn't we tell you on the phone not to come down here? You and your wife are under arrest for failing to obey a lawful order and business disturbance. Put your hands behind your back, both of you now." The officers handcuffed Chan and his wife and helped them to their feet.

"Let's go!" Carter said.

"No, no, no." Chan said. "He son robbed me store. He pay two hundred dollar." Chan said looking at Red, the detective.

"So he paid you two hundred dollars?" Red asked Chan.

"No, he pay two hundred dollar." Chan said to Officer Red.

"That's what I just said. He paid you two hundred dollars." Red exclaimed. Chan had confused him.

"No, no. He no pay! He no pay for son!" Chan said. His wife, Lee, nodded her head up and down.

"Bring yo no English speaking but on. I told you over the phone that you needed to file a civil suite. His son is dead. Now tell me how you expect a dead man to pay you?" Red asked Chan after grabbing him by the right arm. Carter looked at Chan to hear his answer.

"In my country, father pay." Chan said looking at Red face to face.

"See—now is where you are mistaken. This ain't China. This U-S-A." Red said, mocking Chan and his wife's broken down English. Red continued, "And in this country—fathers may not pay, especially child support. Got it—now let's go." He concluded before reading the Miranda rights to Chan and his wife while they were escorted out of the building.

Chapter 38

THE FUNERAL

James in his mixed and mad emotions could not handle another interruption. He thought to himself, sitting beside his wife once more, *'this is exactly what I was afraid of happening'*. He then rubbed his hand across his forehead several times before glancing at his wife Sarah. Somehow Sarah found peace in the whole situation. Leesa, her youngest daughter, was quiet as well, but not at peace, frustrated. However, Lexe was on edge like her father. Almost everything that happened so far was wrong. Throughout the memorial service she wore a frown on her face, and she had held her peace long enough. It would only take one more outburst to send Lexe off edge. Within seconds of her last nerve being frustrated, one more person decided to stand up. Now her last nerve was pinched as her eyelids took the last flutter to draw back tears. Her feet became relaxed and something inside her moved, telling her that it was time to speak.

"Well," said a Caucasian man standing with glasses on, white shirt, and a black dress coat from what Lexe could see. He was smiling, "I guess no one would object to . . ."

Out of no where came the words, "Sit down! Sit down! And shut up!" It was Lexe, standing and full of anger.

Sarah caught off guard and shocked yelled, "Lexe!"

James also caught off guard yelled, "Lexe!"

"Ah hell," Joe said to his brother Sam on the second row.

"Shut up, shut up and Hush!!" Lexe yelled to everyone around her. Leesa was in complete shock but happy.

"Yeah, James her daddy," Sam said to his brother Joe.

"I was about to say the same thing," Joe agreed.

Lexe continued, "We supplied each of you with a comment sheet when you first walked in through the door. The idea was for each of you to fill out that sheet, if you had something terrible to say of course, and drop the sheet in the basket up here," she pointed next to JJ's body, "for the family to read La—ter. Late, get it! Instead," she said pointing a finger, "ignorance has yet again made its statement. Now this is my brother's funeral. Aren't we allowed to grieve in peace? Every since the news aired JJ's death, y'all been talking, and you still talking! When is all this going to end? Now I and my family want this funeral over. How many more of you want to stand up and express your hurt out loud?"

Joe, in a low tone on the second row, said to Lexe, "Wrong question baby girl."

"You think we don't know he was bad? We know. You think we don't know that he was a murderer, rapist, thief, bully and snitch?" She said as she looked at his gang friends at the mention of the word snitch. She then looked back at the crowd. At the sound of those words, JJ's gang friends looked at Lexe. "We know." She concluded. "We had to live with him, argue with him and defend ourselves against him. We too have nothing good to speak of him, and yet we are forced to sit here and be silent to listen to all of you." She said, looking around at everyone. While looking at everyone, Lexe noticed that the man who had interrupted the service once more was still standing and smiling. The stranger standing was one thing, but smiling sent Lexe's attitude in a different direction.

"Why are you still standing? And why are you smiling?" She asked. The Caucasian male sat down. He had no choice. Lexe refused to stop looking at him until he sat down.

Once more, Lexe continued to speak, "Now this is it! We will not allow anyone else to speak about the hurt and pain that JJ caused. We too have nothing good to say except he got on our last nerve too and we hope he knew the God that we know." Lexe said sitting down. Her entire family searched her over with their eyes. Everyone was shocked by Lexe's words. Everyone except one person of course, the person she forbid to speak. The mystery guest had held his peace for too long. He could not remain silent anymore. Lexe would just have to tell him to sit down once more, but only after he confessed, he thought before saying, "Young lady," while standing once more. The crowd wondered why he was so eager to take another chance after what had just happened.

"Now I let you speak out of respect. I'm not ignoring your message, but I need to speak." The mystery guest said.

Lexe was about to stand and speak but was interrupted by Reverend Luke. Reverend Luke could see where the matter was going and he said, "Sir," to the mystery man, "no one else is permitted to speak. You heard the family. Now they want this whole ordeal over."

"But wait," the man replied, trying to get his point across.

"No sir. Now if you continue to interrupt, we are going to have to ask you to leave." Reverend Luke said while looking at the guest.

"But you don't understand, JJ did . . ." the guest replied once more.

"That's it. You have to leave Sir. I asked you to be quiet out of the respect for the family, but you have refused. You have to leave-now."

Reverend Luke refused to listen to the guest. The guest acknowledged in his mind that the pastor was not going to listen to him, so he decided to reach out to the family, specifically saying, "Mrs. Sidney, if you would permit me to speak—just for a moment, please?" He pleaded with his hands. "It's about your son." The guest said as he was making his way out of the pew. Sarah looked at him and motioned with her head no.

"Alright," Lexe said while seated. "Now you heard the Reverend-leave."

With no one to listen to him or stand on his behalf, the guest blurted out before leaving, "Mrs. Sidney, your son was saved. This is what I've been trying to tell you."

Sarah not sure of the words, turned and looked at the stranger and asked, "What did you say?"

The guest standing in the aisle now and looking at Sarah said, "He was saved three months ago. He repented for his transgressions, all of them two weeks ago. I can tell you that he is right with God, and you already know what I can't tell you."

James not so sure of the man's words stood and asked, while buttoning his suite coat again, "Who are you? And what can't you tell?"

"My name is Father Michael. I bring you this news from Saint Mathews. I was provided the opportunity to hear JJ's confession and pray for and with him."

"Yeah, I know that part. Now, what can't you tell?" James asked. The crowd was in tuned to every word that was being said.

Sarah comforted and secure wiped the tears from her eyes and said to James. "What he can't tell you or us, is that if everyone JJ sinned against has forgiven him. The bible teaches that when you sin against someone that you should ask forgiveness of that someone and God. JJ didn't ask the people that he sinned against for forgiveness, at least we don't know."

"That's right Mrs. Sidney," Father Michael said. Everyone looked at the Father. Some were astounded; some confused; some comforted, and many in disbelief. The majority of the audience hearing the words JJ and saved conversed with their neighbor their disbelief. They believed that JJ being saved was next to impossible. It was hard to believe that JJ was saved and had repented recently, they discussed amongst one another. Even Reverend Stevens found the message hardly true, not only him, but all of the family except Sarah. Many convinced themselves that Father Michael just felt sympathy for the family and the whole outburst was a flake. The idea was hard for many to accept, but only one person stood to protest the matter.

"Hold the hell up!" James' brother Joe yelled. "Why come JJ would go to a Catholic Church? I mean we Baptist. You are Catholic right? 115 and Albuquerque, right?"

"Yes, I am Catholic, and I don't know why he chose our church." Father Michael said.

"Here comes the drama again," Sam said to his wife Fay.

"Now this don't make no sense to me." Joe said before asking the crowd, "Do this make any sense to y'all?" Some shook their heads no, and others said, "No."

"See, F.M. It . . ." Joe said to Father Michael before being cut off.

"It's Father Michael, not F.M." The priest said in reference to his name and title.

"Same thang. Look at you a mist all these black folk with an attitude. Anyway, these people agree that you are lying. Now why would JJ choose a Catholic Church, I ask you again? He was not Catholic. He was Baptist."

"Like I said, I have no reply to that question. I never asked him. But if I had to guess—maybe because of the foolishness and money issues associated with Baptist churches." Father Michael said.

The crowd was insulted by the Father's remark and so was Joe as he said, "Oh yeah, and maybe its because of the idolism and little boys associated with Catholic churches." Everyone laughed. Joe was mocking the Catholic Church.

"What are you saying?" Father Michael asked Joe.

"What are you saying?" Joe asked Father Michael.

Sam, tired of the whole issue at JJ's funeral said to his wife, "Damn, this is about to go bad again. Now remind me why we need a Pastor here in the first place?" He asked his wife. She looked for confirmation around her. She could not find any. Sam continued, "He's not keeping this in order, none of them are. James should have took my advice and put JJ's ass in a pine box, in his backyard and four feet under. This is a mess. I ain't never been in no mess like this before."

"Sam," his wife replied.

"This is ridiculous. Are you at the same funeral as me?" He asked her. "I'm going to have a smoke."

"Sam, that's not a good idea. You do know that this side of town is not safe." She said.

"A lie. What's not safe is the mess going on in here. If damn Asians ain't afraid to visit this side of town, you think I should be scared and of my own kind. I'll be back soon, soon as all this here over that is. Where are the car keys?"

"Sam—Asians know how to fight. You can't, and you can't drive either Sam. I've told you that too many times." She replied.

"Exactly, too many times. What? Is your nephew Troy patrolling this side of town too? Give me my car keys." He said.

"You are going to jail if you move that car, and when you do, I don't have a clue as to how you gone get out."

"That simple question has a simple answer." He replied.

"Oh, and what's that Sam—because I won't spend one red cent of my Disability Check trying to get you out." Fay said while feeling for the keys in the bottom of her purse.

"You ever heard of pro-bono, which can be equal, charity, or pay back. If I work my way in there, then equally, I will work my way out. It's just that simple." He stated.

"And how you plan on doing that with one arm?" She asked.

"Boy, I tell you. You don't mind reminding me of my handicap, do you? I'm gone do it with one arm, one movement at time. Now, you think that maybe you can put your other hand in there and dig up them keys? You worried about what I can't do with one arm, when you don't even remember how to use two." Sam said after Fay handed over the keys.

"You and your mouth," she replied. "If you only knew how to keep it closed until you had something nice to say. You better not move that car." She replied once more as Sam was about to move out of his seat.

"And you say that I can't say nothing nice," he said to Fay before leaving her side.

Meanwhile as Sam and Fay ended their debate, Joe and Father Michael continued. Joe still was not happy with what was happening concerning JJ's repentance. He felt that Father Michael must convince him of the matter as he stated, "Man, I still don't believe you—as far as I'm concerned. You just mouthing off to make Sarah fell better, cause the rest of us don't care. So unless you got some facts to back up your story, you need to leave."

"What kinda facts you gone have that a man has been saved Joe, when he's clearly dead?" Sarah stood and asked her brother-in-law while pointing at JJ's casket with him in it with one hand and holding a Kleenex in the other.

"Yeah," Leesa stood in agreement with her mother.

"I don't know, but he," Joe said while pointing at Father Michael, "ought to have something in writing." Joe replied to Sarah.

"Joe," Sarah replied, "you don't save a man in writing. You save a man in the name of the Father, Son, and the Holy Ghost. It's done by confessing thy sins, believing that Christ died for them and receiving prayer, which in the end exercises deliverance. The whole procedure is done orally, not written down physically."

"Yo, sister law, that sounds good and all, but we live in a world today where verification is proof of occurrence, and unless he got some proof that JJ is saved, did talk to him, and did confess, then I can't believe him and a lot more people in here agree with me." Joe replied to Sarah. Noises from the crowd approved of Joe's statement. "See." Joe said to Sarah, "they agree". Turning to Father Michael, Joe asked, "So like I said, do you have some proof?" James stood up to here the Father's reply. Joe continued, "Cause the JJ that I knew was incapable of caring about his fate."

Father Michael could not believe what he was hearing. It seemed as though no one really believed in God. Everyone wanted proof, except Sarah.

"I'm sorry Joe, but . . ." Father Michael said to Joe before being cut off.

"That's what I thought. You don't have no proof, do you? It's time for you to go F.M.". Joe replied before Father Michael could respond.

"For the second time, it's Father Michael. And I have to disagree with you." He said taking an envelope from his pocket. Joe looked surprised as he walked toward the priest.

"Is that the proof?" Joe asked Father Michael.

"Yes, it is," he replied to Joe. "I must say you took on a great risk to ask for evidence. Do you ever read your Bible, brother?"

"Yeah, I read my Bible. Why do you think that I asked for that evidence? Satan has all kinds of disguises." Joe said with a smile.

Father Michael smiled as well and replied, "Yes, he does Brother. But if you would have been reading your Bible—even after reading the words 'be ye not deceived', you would have also read the words that 'faith is the evidence of things not seen'." Joe was shocked by the words. The Priest caught him off guard. Father Michael continued, "You see, my brother, even if I didn't have this evidence and you were a true believer of Christ, you would have believed me anyway. All of you who doubted me would have," Father Michael said looking around at all of the people before looking back at Joe. Reverend Luke still standing behind the pulpit podium smiled. He was touched by the Father's words, even he too for a second had stopped believing.

Joe standing face to face with Father Michael now, extended his hand out to collect the evidence that Father Michael had in his hand. Father Michael said to Joe after seeing his hand, "However, I can't give this evidence to you Brother." Joe's smile all of a sudden went to a frown. "Why you may be wondering?" Father Michael asked Joe. "Because God takes care of his kind. You be blessed." He said to Joe befoe walking away and toward the front row where Sarah and her family stood. Joe went back to his seat. Before he could sit down, his wife said, "See, I . . ." she could not finish her statement as Joe said to her, "shut up, shut up and hush!" Joe then sat down in his seat.

Sarah accepted the envelope from Father Michael. She then sat down and placed it inside her Bible. Father Michael exited the building at the nearest side door. Everyone wanted to know what was in that envelope. The envelope contained written and signed confessions in JJ's handwriting. He admitted to all of his sins, and in the end, he asked for forgiveness of all his family, friends and enemies. Sarah smiled after reading the letter later that night at home while she was alone.

Chapter 39

THE FUNERAL @ LAST

James eyed the envelope in Sarah's Bible for several minutes before looking at Sarah. He wanted to know its contents. Leesa and Lexe and the rest of the family looked at Sara also until Reverend Luke spoke. It was finally time for the funeral to be preached and over.

Reverend Luke began by saying, "With the grace of God and the holy spirit appearing once more and again, I must conclude that all interruptions are complete except one." At that moment, he witnessed Sam returning to rejoin the rest of the family in the conclusion of the funeral. Every one was quiet. You could here the sound of Sam's shoes as he walked down the aisle. Reverend Luke looked at Sam and gave him a smile. As Sam found his seat and sat down, he waved his hand for the Pastor to continue.

Reverend Luke proceeded, "now let us turn to a word of the Father." He said. Everyone began to pick up their bibles and open them, while waiting for the Reverend to say out loud the scripture. "I'm not going to hold you all too much longer.' He said.

"Ain't that what all of 'em say before they keep you a long time?" Joe asked Sam. Sam smiled.

"Let's lend an ear to the book of Proverbs, and let's lend an ear to the book of Psalms. Now before you get your eyes all crossed up and your breath frantic. I don't want to do Proverbs without the Psalmist. My heart will not let me break away from either. I seriously wish that I could read the whole good book to all of you," he said with a laugh. No one laughed back. Everyone was ready to go. "However, understanding and attention limits that decision. Instead, based upon my audible senses of what has taken place here, I must direct the attention of mine and yours to Proverbs the 6th chapter and the 12th through 23rd verses. And we are going to look at Psalms the 36 and 37th Chapters. Now don't be dismayed, we are only going to briefly touch on the scriptures for those of you who are wondering if I'm going to preach from all of them. With that being said—shall we all stand in reverence to God's bread of life?"

Reverend Luke continued, "Proverbs the sixth chapter, verses 12 through 23 reads as thus. A naughty person, a wicked man, walketh with a froward mouth. He winketh with his eyes, he speaketh with his feet, he teacheth with his fingers. Frowardness is in the heart, he deviseth mischief continually, he soweth discord. Therefore, shall his calamity come suddenly: suddenly shall he be broken without remedy. These six things doth the Lord hate: Yea, seven are an abomination unto him." At the sound of those words, Dominique and her girl friends all looked at one another. Some of the guests looked at them as well. Reverend Luke continued, "A proud look, a lying tongue, and hands that shed innocent blood." Now all of the people looked at JJ's casket and at one and another. "An heart that deviseth wicked imaginations, feet that be swift in running to mischief. A false witness that speaketh lies and he that sowed discord among brethren." Sonya looked across the room at her sister after Reverend Luke read those words. Reverend Luke completed reading the scripture and said to all, "You all my be seated. Did you all hear those words from the scripture? The bible says that a naughty person, also known as a wicked person, walks with a froward mouth. You know, their mouth is turned side ways, crooked, up, down, and in and out, figuratively but almost literally. Now, if I have read correctly, majority of the scripture that I have read just now was pertaining to JJ. Would you all agree?" He asked the audience. Many said Amen, others said yes and others nodded up and down. "Then how many of you agree that the scripture is speaking to you as well?" Reverend Luke asked. The room was quiet. "Oh, y'all didn't see that one coming? Well, I have news for all of us. At least one of us are one of those things that God hates if not all. Notice, I didn't say that he wouldn't forgive this type of man, but I said that the Lord hates these things. Not you, but these things. Now JJ won't be the first to carry out all of these things and God forbid, he won't be the last. Some of you in here are going down the same path. Not me you may say. But yes you. You just don't see it yet. The bible says that 'let him who is without sin cast the first stone'. Again, my question to you is who in here has not sinned and missed the mark? Some of us are still sinning and mostly the same sin. You know what they are hypocrisy, fornication, adultery, murder, disobedience. Those are only a few. But who of you all has recognized that sin before tardiness, before it was too late, like JJ here? Which of you knew that your transgression had gone too far? With that said, let's understand the word transgression. Lets turn to Psalm's the 36th chapter. Does anyone know your transgressions?" Reverend Luke asked as he flipped the pages in his bible. Passengers waiting on their train to come began to take heed to the Pastor's words. Looking up at the crowd, Reverend Luke asked while pointing to his right side, "Do you know your iniquities?" He then pointed to the left, "Do you know your iniquities? Some of you are asking, what are you saying Reverend? I am saying—do any of you recognize your sins? Do you recognize your sins? Better yet, do you control your sins or do they control you?" He repeated. "Let's stand again in reverence to God's bread?" He asked the audience. "Psalm the 36th chapter reads as thus, 'the transgressions of the wicked saith within my heart, that there is no fear of God before his eyes. Let's stop for a minute and briefly clarify. Guest what people? If you don't recognize your own sins, you don't recognize God. You want to know why? One answer to that in the flesh is because you are ignorant. You are not wise. Another answer to that lies in the scripture and reads as thus, 'For he flattereth himself in his own eyes, until his iniquity be found to be hateful. The words of his mouth are iniquity and deceit, he hath left off to be wise, and to do good. He deviseth mischief upon his bed: he sitteth himself in a way that is not good. He abhorred not evil.' Guest what people? He loves evil. He does not hate it at all." Reverend Luke said. "You all may sit. Now David," Reverend Luke said, while observing the crowd and the passengers, "says that a wicked man has no fear for God in his heart. In other words—one, he does not acknowledge God, and two, he does not care. All that matters is what he wants and how far he's willing to go to get it. God does not scare this type of man. This type of individual places God in the category of just like any other and no different from another. This type of individual believes that Luke is like God and God is like Luke." Reverend Stevens said as he referred himself to God. "This individual is very boastful. He's proud. He tends to believe that he is in control. Even more, he has a tendency to laugh at himself. He laughs at himself. No one's special to him. Now David adds, that a wicked man loves himself. He finds humor and satisfaction in himself, un-til guess what? His iniquity is found to be hateful. Oh, now look at this," Reverend Luke said secretly. "Something is wrong. Something has went wrong-either voluntarily or forcefully. He's tired of the same thing; the same lie; the same wrong. Let me give you an example. You ever been addicted to something or someone so much until you started to hate it or he or she? For some of you it's a man or a woman, alcohol, drugs, rape, murder, money and so on. Have you all seen the news lately?" Reverend Luke asked while looking at the crowd and gesturing with his right hand to clear up his point. "How that Bernie Madoff man, swindled honest, hard-working, individuals out their money for years. Well, Madoff became tired of that and turned himself in voluntarily only after being forced too, right? You see, his addiction was cunning investors out of their money to invest in stocks under his company, in exchange he was suppose to make trades for the individuals and possibly return to them a profit for their investment. Turns out, every thing was a 65 Billion dollar joke—a scheme, and this man was not trading anything at all-only getting rich. The point that I am trying to establish is that soon your addiction becomes your enemy. You see. You hate it because of the addiction to it, and you love it because you think that you can control it, only to find out, that you never really had control at all. The bible says that all things will be revealed. No way of the way that we live today is new. All that happens today, has already happened. Don't believe me? Just take some time and read your bible and watch how God will reveal some things to you."

"Amen," the Associate Pastors said behind Reverend Luke.

"But I have news for all of you fearless, addiction haters. God can fix it. God-can-heal-you. David says that the transgressions of a man are sin and lies. He says that the words of his mouth are iniquity and deceit, hidden sins, lies and sin, sin and lies. Wisdom and good are not his allies. A wicked man plans and plots mischief and evil and wrong. He venues himself right in the middle of it. He surrounds himself with it. Even more, he-loves-it. So the bible warns us of the wicked man. You see, JJ is nothing new. None of you and your sins are either. But does anyone want to know how to overcome evil is the real question? You see, just as the bible warns us of evil, it confesses the overcoming of it. There's no need for us to be angry, loud, or confused. Just as there's no need for us to examine JJ, for judgment is that of our Father. Condemnation is that of our Father. You wanna know what the bible says that we should do to over come evil? Then stand and look with me at David again?"

"David," someone said from the audience.

"Yes, lets look at the book of Psalms once more, Chapter 37." Reverend Luke said.

"Oh," the stranger on the third row to the left said to her neighbor. She didn't know that David was a product of the book of Psalms.

Reverend Stevens continued, "Now David said, 'fret not thyself because of evil doers . . .'"

"Amen," some believers of the bible said.

"David said, neither be thou envious against the workers of iniquity. For they shall soon—be cut down—like the grass, and wither, as the green herb. David continues by saying, that the seed of the wicked shall be cut off. You all may be seated once more." Reverend Luke directed the crowd. "So what does the Lord do to evil doers? He cuts them off, plain and simple. Some of you may ask, just like he did JJ? And the answer is yes, and just how he will do some of you, us. You know what else the Lord does? You ever heard some one say that if you wanna make God laugh, just tell him your plan. That theory is true. God laughs at us in our wickedness. He laughs. Don't believe me? Then read the 13th verse of this chapter. Do you know what he does for the righteous, he upholds them. He keeps them as they shall inherit the earth. So you see, ladies and gentlemen, just when you thought that the worst was the worst, it's not. God has a remedy for your hurt, pain, deficiencies, and delinquencies. God has a remedy for your loneliness, fear, misunderstanding and confusion. It makes no difference who you are or what you've done, because no one lie is bigger than another. When I was just a Junior in Community College, I remember reading a poem in one of my literature courses, that spoke of a man and an island. Its title is 'Meditation 17: From Devotions Upon Emergent Occasions' and it was written by literary figure, John Donne. I remember something about the tolls of a bell. Now I can't remember the poem in its entirety, but what I do remember as I am reminded at this moment are these words, 'no man is an island of his own'. I said um, after reading those words, what relativeness is that? I didn't understand in the beginning, but that's why the instructor was there. Later on, I read the same words in one of Dr. King's speeches that I chose to do for my 'Marriage and Family Course', 'no man is an island of his own' were those words again. I said um, all of these subjects are connected. And I liked those words because they sounded good, and I studied those words to found out why they sounded so good because the words seemed to have an infinite meaning-a meaning that goes beyond understanding. And low and behold, they did. You see, I prayed and asked God for understanding and

He heard me. Are any of you familiar with the words, 'no man is an island of his own'?" Reverend Luke asked the audience and the Associate Pastors behind him before turning back to the crowd. Some raised their hands. Many did not. "Does anyone know the meaning of such words?" He asked once more. Several raised their hands. He asked only one to express the meaning. He asked Lexe to explain. "Tell everyone what those words mean to you?"

"The expression of the words from my understanding is if one dies, a part of all of us dies. We are all affected by one another as a whole, whether dead or alive." Lexe responded.

"Exactly. Why are we all here? Because JJ died, right? He touched all of our lives in some way or another." The audience smiled knowing the meaning of the words now. "Maybe JJ didn't do everything right, but in the end, he did what was of the utmost high. He asked for forgiveness, and he asked to be saved. The bible says, 'train up a child in the way he should go, and when he is old, he won't depart from it'. James and Sarah took him to church, and they prayed that he would receive understanding. But then JJ became older and his sins were of himself. He strayed away, but in the end, he went back to the Lord for help. And, his family was comforted. Yes, they believed that they lost him, but he went back. The important thing is he went back to that island to all he affected. Thank you and Amen." Reverend Luke said concluding his sermon. "I'm gonna turn the rest of the service back over to Reverend Stevens now."

"Stop," James said when he heard this statement. "You conclude the service Reverend Luke. Reverend Stevens need prayer—and I do too. In fact, a lot of us do and we don't want Reverend Stevens to pray for us. My wife and those ladies over there maybe, but not the rest of us. Reverend Stevens need to rededicate himself to God's ministry, that's the only way he gone regain some of our trust. And I want you to pray for his associate pastors too, that whatever corruption they've endured will cease. Now I wanna be right Reverend Luke. I recognize every word that you said, plain and simple. I'm a hard man to get too, but you got to me with that 'no man is an island of his own'. You made me proud when you asked the question and my Lexe knew the answer to it. I now recognize that when I do wrong, I wrong my family and my neighbor. Now if you are about to start the benediction, I and my family wanna be the first to come."

Reverend Stevens and his Associate Pastors were shocked by James' announcement. However, James was right. Pastor Stevens was misbehaving and his Associate Pastors were not being educated in the doctrine well. They couldn't preach. They didn't know how too, and Reverend Stevens would not tell them their weaknesses or rear them past them. He only continued to let them make fools out of themselves.

Reverend Luke, on the other hand, was glad that James pointed out Reverend Stevens and his Associate Pastors, but he was even happier to be praying for and saving an entire congregation. Pastor Luke with a sincere smile turned to James and said from the podium, "Yes and yes—I see Brother." Reverend Luke said to James with a smile. "Then let's have another selection from I believe, Mrs. Watts, and then I'll open the doors of this afternoon's event to anyone requesting prayer or wanting to be saved." Mrs. Watts' next selection was "Be Encouraged" by Donald Lawrence. This time she would add something new to her presentation. She decided to add 'Spiritual Mind Dancers'. She had six women in white, long dresses to perform. The women stood up in front of the audience-all had their hair pinned up and make up applied, softly but neatly. Around their eye area was white lining that accentuated their eyes. They were beautiful as each stood with bowed heads, until Mrs. Watts started to sang the song. Many of the audience members did not know what was about to happen, as they had not been in the company of the spiritual world for a long time. Mrs. Watts thought, *'if I can't convict or bring them to you with my voice alone Lord, then I will deliver them to you with your art'.*

Verse 1:
Sometimes you have to encourage yourself.
Sometimes you have to speak victory during the test.
And no matter how you feel,
speak the word and you will be healed;
speak over yourself,
encourage yourself in the Lord.

Verse 2:
Sometimes you have to speak the word over yourself,
the pressure is all around,
but God is present help.
The enemy created walls,
but remember giants, they do fall;
speak over yourself,
encourage yourself in the Lord.

Bridge:
As I minister to you, I minister to myself,
life can hurt you so,
'til you feel there's nothing left.
(No matter how you feel),
(speak the word and you will be healed).

Vamp 1:
Speak over yourself.

Vamp 2:
I'm encouraged.
I'm encouraged.
I'm encouraged.
I'm encouraged.

Vamp 3:
I'm encouraged,
I'm encouraged,
I'm encouraged,
I'm encouraged.

(Speak over yourself),
(encourage yourself in the Lord).

The dancers along with Mrs. Watts did a magnificent job. The audience was in awe of everything going on as some smiled, some cried, and some did nothing at all. Everyone was encouraged. After Mrs. Watts took her seat for a second time, Pastor Luke called everyone to the altar. James along with his entire family went for prayer. Reverend Stevens and his Associate Pastors did too. Many more followed until all stood in need of prayer. When Reverend Luke finished praying for everyone, he shook James' hand and the hand of Pastor Stevens and his Associate Pastors. Yes, hell went into the South-side Train Station, but peace reigned out, and Mrs. Watts had fulfilled her duty to the Lord.

Chapter 40

AFTER THE FUNERAL

JJ's funeral was a victory for some and a defeat for others, mostly the immediate family. They took as much as they could and decided to stop all the hurt, pain, and agony before it went further. Now, the funeral was finally over, and James and Sarah could not wait until all the visitors departed from their residency. Most were there for the food and never stopped James, Sarah, Lexe, or Leesa to offer their condolences.

JJ's uncle Joe did not care much for JJ still. It took all the strength in him to not stand up and tell how his nephew stole from him on countless occasions, and Sarah took up for him. Joe could not say what he wanted to at the train depot out of a small bit of respect for his brother James. He enjoyed the strangers' attacks and decided that he would save his comments about JJ until later.

Now later had come and Joe was ready to talk to somebody as he said, "While everyone was expressing themselves, I started to tell how that foolish nephew of mine stole my brand new gold watch, Nancy bought for our tenth anniversary; a lawn mower that my boss gave to me—almost spanking brand new, and twenty dollars out of my wallet while I was in the shower, and that was my last twenty. It was suppose to last me through the week. Nancy thought that I gambled it up." Joes said talking to his wife Nancy, his brother, Sam, and Sam's wife, Fay. They were standing by the kitchen at James and Sarah's home.

"Now Joe, you know you wrong. You don't know those things for sure." His wife Nancy said.

"Oh, I know, especially that twenty situation. He was the only one around when my watch and twenty dollars came up missing." He said before taking a puff of his cigar. "JJ didn't have no money that morning that my money came up missing. My money came up missing around twelve-o-clock and he was eating candy around twelve ten."

"He was only ten then, he ain't no nothing bout no stealing." Nancy said to her husband.

"Whatever—that's when kids know about stealing, Nay." Joe said. "Them fools even know that they ain't held accountable for it—that their parents is until they reach twelve. And, anyway, Sadie's son Mike said he saw him wit my lawn mower, and now that I think about it, that kid was only good for messing up.

"Joe!" his wife said.

"Every time he came over to the house, he stole something." Joe said

Sarah was now approaching her in-laws, as she passed by, Joe asked, "Everything okay Sarah," as he took another puff of his cigar? Nancy was fanning the smoke as she managed a smile at Sarah. Sarah walked by them all with a piece of cake on a saucier in her hand for a guest, "Just fine Joe," she responded as she kept walking.

"Good, good." Joe said with a smile to his sister in law. Thinking that Sarah had went on about her business, he turned back to his brother Sam and sister in law Fay and he said, "I know she is since that no good kid dead."

"You know that you are not allowed to smoke in this house, Joe." Sarah said to Joe before walking away. She had caught him off guard. It was a kick in the throat for him as he attempted to put the cigar out in front of Sarah. Sarah had heard his negative remark. She knew that Joe did not care much for James Junior. She thought for a moment of all the times Joe accused JJ of stealing something from him or his house. And it seemed that each time he accused JJ, he was right. It was hard to suck down the pain of someone being right about JJ. For once, she prayed for the opportunity to tell someone that they were wrong about her son.

"Joe!" his wife exclaimed. Nancy knew that Sarah had overheard Joe's remark. "Now . . . of all the words to say, that was a poor choice of words." Joe looked at his wife for a brief moment and put the cigar back into his mouth. He re-lit it as well. "Joe, she asked you not to smoke in here." Nancy said to her husband.

"What-ever!" He said to his wife. He quickly restarted the conversation about JJ. "It's something wrong with ya'll. JJ was bad at ten. He was even worst, not to forget, ignorant at twenty-five. To be honest, James and Sarah just wasted a nut on that kid."

"Joe!" His wife said again. She had heard enough.

"What!" He exclaimed.

"Now that's enough," she said.

Suddenly, Sarah appeared out of nowhere again, this time with a plastic cup filled with water and said to her brother in law, Joe, "Put the cigar out now, Joe!" Joe dropped the cigar in the cup that Sarah was holding.

"Oh, yeah, yeah, I forgot." He claimed.

"I'm sure you did," she said after he dropped the cigar in the cup. She then walked away.

"And I'm suppose to be feeling some sympathy for her," he said watching Sarah as she walked away.

"Come on bro . . . her son is dead, and the least you can do is respect her house-our brother's house for that matter." Sam said.

"Yeah whatever—Save that. Now I know that Nancy and I ain't got no kids, but if we had that one that was just buried, I would have been done murdered him myself. That's one that I would have reluctantly taken a prison ride for. Give me my commissary, bed and a television. Not even Nancy would matter."

"Oh," said Sam's wife Fay. She could not believe that Joe had just said what he said.

"Whatever Joe, society wouldn't miss much either." Nancy said

"Bro, . . ." Sam said with a light chuckle. "Now where did all of that come from?"

"Nancy, I was only hypothetically speaking. Anyway, God could not have offered me that kid. Uh um, I don't care how bad me and Nancy wanted one. I would of told God, Himself, no offense, but no."

"Oh, Joe-that's terrible. I can't understand why you would say that. Why don't you try looking at the situation from your brother's point of view?" Nancy asked.

"Hell no, and it's not terrible—I told James to get rid of him a long time ago. JJ was Satan in the flesh, and I say that that gangster was guilty of all that them people said at that memorial service." Joe said. He glanced across the room to see James and responded, "And look at James over there. He should of let them people said all they peace, all of them."

"No Joe. Memorial services are supposed to define the good in people. I don't blame James for stepping in. People are supposed to express positive dying wishes or actions that a person has taken as well as remembrances, not negativity and insults."

"Tweet that Nay to someone who cares," Joe said to his wife. "If people continue to tell the truth at these funerals, even mine, then people will change. What, you think he need to go in peace, and he caused hell on earth? Nope, I don't think so. And I don't care what that Priest said, JJ was not saved. I'm gone refuse to believe that until Sarah let me read them papers."

"Yeap, you a crazy man." His wife said.

"Knawl, that's real talk, as them young people would say." Joe said. Sam and Fay listened and smiled at some of the guests.

"But bro," Sam questioned his brother's attitude.

"Bro-nothing. I already know where you are going with this." Joe said.

"Knawl, let me speak." Sam said.

"Not if you don't agree with me."

"Is that necessary, Joe?" Nancy asked. "Let him speak. You ain't always right, you know."

"Look, ain't no other way round it." Joe said overlooking his wife's words. "Now Fay," Joe said turning to his sister in law for her opinion, "wouldn't you want to tell a person that caused you hell . . ." Fay was about to answer but refrained when she noticed Joe's hand in the hold that thought position. Joe continued, "and pain a piece of your mind if you had one last time too."

Again she began to speak, saying, "I, uh—" Joe knew that she was about to justify the idea, so he cut her off again and stretched the idea a step forward.

"Wait, wait a minute before you speak. Cause you look like you don't agree with me right now. If a sucker shoved a gun down Sam's throat and slapped you, wouldn't you have something to say?" Joe asked Fay.

"No—that sucker would be doing me a favor," she said. Everyone gave her a quick stare. "Just kidding," she said with a laugh. "But yes, Joe, I probably would have several years back before I got saved."

"Probably nothing, sometimes God uses mediators."

"No Joe," she continued. "It's a way and time to do and say something." Fay said. "God knows how to handle these matters best himself."

"At that moment, ain't none of what you just said would count. At that moment, there ain't no time to think of a way and a place, things suppose to happen right then—instant reflex baby. That's all I'm saying." Joe said taking another cigar from his pocket. Thinking of what Sarah said earlier, he put it back and said, "That service did him just and good."

"Joe." Nancy said to her husband.

"Shut up, Nancy. You better start taking this world for what it really is. All of us ain't wise. Some of us some dumb motherless . . .

"Don't you use that word?" His wife said.

"Freaks," he concluded. "Y'all know the word. The point is we don't mind being dumb. Somehow it excuses our carelessness and sadistic behavior. Leaving us with the presumption of believing that we are smart, when deep down inside, we are ignorant as the hell we are on our way too."

"Did you not just receive prayer for the very same things that you are discussing?" Nancy asked her husband.

"Yeah Nancy, but I ain't truly sanctified yet. God knows my heart." Joe said.

"Does he Joe? How?" She asked her husband.

"He knows, because I haven't truly confessed my sins yet."

Sam, Fay, and Joe's wife Nancy looked at him in disbelief. Nancy asked her husband, "And just what were you doing while the Pastor was praying for everyone."

"Standing outside; Smoking me a cigar. That's why I let your hand go. Please, y'all cannot tell me that he got to y'all with that no man and island mess. My philosophy is if you mess up, then you mess up on your own. Not if I mess up, I mess you up. Who wrote that stupid ass Lit., anyway?"

"You're going to hell!" Nancy told her husband before walking away. Fay and Sam joined her. Sam looked back at his brother, who was about to put a cigar in his mouth. Joe noticed Sam's stare and eyed him widely before rocking on the back of his shoes and turning away. Just as Joe turned away with the cigar in his hand, Sarah walked by and grabbed the cigar.

Chapter 41

WAKE UP

You know what's worse than dying? Dying for nothing. It is not wrong that makes life bad and sends you to hell. It is the idea or action that you did nothing to make your life right so that you could meet God in heaven. Everyday, if it is not us, it is someone that we know that continues to live on the edge. What part of God made man in the image of Himself do we not understand? Man is capable of doing many good deeds. He chooses not too. Greed is a sin, so help your neighbor. Honesty and good are virtues along with patience and understanding, so gain some. Ignorance is bliss and wisdom is only an age difference away. We have all heard our mother's tell us that life is not just a good time. We have heard many others say that it is what you make it. Both statements hold some truth, but what life really is about is choices, making the right one and being thankful that you did, and making the wrong one and becoming wiser from that mistake. We all have power. Not one of us is weak. Life is what you choose, and not a gift certificate handed out to you randomly to set yourself free of evil deeds or super ego incriminating events. We all must answer for our sins, whether we believe in God or not. I'm alive because I woke up and choose God and my family and the good that man can do. That means earning an honest days work, being nice, sharing and caring and loving someone else besides myself all the time. Selfish deeds only presents sinful acts, and hell is only a foot step away. I did some evil deeds. I hurt a lot of people and now is the time for me to make it right.

JJ awoke to a beautiful day and the smell of pancakes and bacon. His mom prepared this kind of breakfast only on Sunday before church. "Damn, "he said getting out of bed. He had not stayed at home for several months now. "That's a nightmare that I don't plan on letting come true." He said after brushing his teeth and washing his face, he headed down stairs for some pancakes and bacon. He planned on surprising his mom this morning by going to church. The table was set for four. JJ wondered if his mother had forgotten about him.

"Thank you Mr. Sidney for going to Revival with me all this week." Sarah told her husband, pouring him a cup of coffee.

"Your welcome baby, I'm glad I went too. It was time that I let some of that hell go." James said. JJ could not believe that his parents were not arguing. His father looked relaxed, and his mother was happy.

His mother yelled, "Leesa, Lexe—breakfast is ready," before she sat down. JJ still didn't have a plate or utensils.

"Ma, where's my food," JJ asked?

"You know James," Sarah said after sipping her coffee. "I remember when I had three names to call on Sunday." She said.

"Yeah," James said laying down the morning paper. "It's been two years since JJ's death."

"Death, what do you mean? I'm standing right here. That was all a dream." JJ replied.

James continued, "I just thank God for giving me a second chance. JJ messed up so many lives and families. I never thought in a million years that he would leave before me, especially have a memorial service at a Train Depot. It took him dying to make me live. I thank God for his grace and mercy, and I thank God for a woman like you too Sarah. I Love you Sarah," he said looking at his wife.

"Love you too," she said to her husband before Leesa and Lexe sat down at the table.

"So, I'm really dead! Man, I thought that you gave me a second chance to make this right?" JJ said, looking up at the ceiling. He was talking to God. "So all of this really happened to me and to them?" JJ asked. His spirit was then escorted out of his parents' house by two angels. JJ looked behind him at his family. Everyone seemed to be doing okay. His father looked like a changed man. His mother looked extremely happy. His sisters looked as though they never had a brother in the first place. In fact, all of his family looked as though he never existed. JJ thought, *I really messed up*.

Yes, JJ did mess up, but he had given all of his enemies' and his family an opportunity to build a closer relationship with God—an opportunity that no one took for granted.

JJ's assassins turned themselves in after the funeral. Everyone was shocked by women committing such a terrible act-everyone except Sarah. James looked at Sarah after Dominique and the rest of the women confessed what they did to JJ to Pastor Luke. Pastor Luke called the police for the women to be picked up. Three months later, each of the women were sentenced to 25 years in jail. Each had the opportunity of parole as well for turning themselves in. Each of the women, along with Dominique, decided to let the street business go as well as the Lesbian activity. It was time for each to do right by God, and their minds were set to do just that.

Executives of the Train Station did not get what they bargained for, nor did Reverend Stevens and the Mayor, but Reverend Stevens did not mind. He was too busy thinking of a way to get his wife back home. The Executives thought that by allowing JJ's funeral at the train station that they would gain a new station. They thought that the station would be damaged by gang members. That didn't happen, and they realized that not even a funeral of a dead gang member would get them a new train station.

Months later, the law that led up to an absent member not having a proper church funeral was banned. The Religious Convention overturned the matter because they had no way of determining when and where an individual had been saved, repented, or offered some kind of charity to a church while living. Pastors just agreed to continue to let the families have the funerals if the family was known or had been affiliated with the church or Pastor asked to perform the ceremony.

Sonya received her money from the insurance company and bought her a new home in New Orleans. Her sister, Leslie, divorced Mike a year later. Leslie and Sonya became close again and so did Sonya and her mother.

Jada returned to school in the fall of the year of JJ's death. She also returned to church and began to teach Sunday school and sing in the choir. She let go of the past and married a well educated English Professor who really loved her. A year later, she received her master's degree in Criminal Justice. After gaining her license to practice, she took a job at a high paying law firm in New Orleans, called 'Jacob and Swarts'; five years later, the firm was titled, 'Jacob, Swarts, and Wells'. She looked for Necee for years, but could never find her. Later, by messenger, she was delivered the news that her best friend of so many years had been murdered in Harlem. The news was devastating, and Jada wanted to know in detail what happened as she planned on soon finding out.

Gang 186, the ones who were left, decided to shut down its operation. The members formed and Mission for the Lord. They were educated on Christianity and Reformation, and soon went out into the streets of New Orleans practicing peace and deliverance. Their purpose was to bring sinners to Christ and to show them a different mentality of thinking. Their organization was a success as they saved hundreds of lives within their second year of operation. They also reduced the crime rate in New Orleans significantly.

Michelle soon got over JJ's death with the help of her parents, Tessany, and Ricky. She realized that it took JJ dying in order for her to live honestly. She also gave Ricky a chance. Turns out, Ricky was just what she and Jamey needed. Jamey respected Ricky-thought that he was his real father, and Ricky made it apparent that he was since Jamey never really knew his biological father, JJ, personally. Looking over her past and standing face to face with her best friend's advice now, Michelle wondered how she could be so naive and foolish. She soon realized that she had to go through something to get to something—her blessing. Soon basketball came back into the scene for her as she was granted an opportunity to coach for a non profit, youth league, called Respect.

Patrick and Tony decided to testify and get saved. Both the gentlemen's parents were extremely proud. They didn't stop using drugs within that moment, but they did after getting a hold on the wrong drug and losing their minds for one day. The incident scared them so, that both decided to repent for their sins and for real this time.

Rob, Jay, Dirty, Paul, and Larry, all went back to church. The gentlemen took several training courses on male etiquette and responsibility and decided to form a non profit organization called Respectful Men. The mission of the organization was to assist young males with proper training and responsibility concerning God, etiquette, and work. They recruited young adult males from their neighborhood. The process was slow in the genesis phase, but it soon became successful in ten states other than New Orleans. The men soon realized that they were missing something and decided to cohabitate with female leaders. Sheila and Diane decided to join the fellows. They were educated just as the fellows were and soon enlisted hundreds of young females to join the organization. Now the Organization took on the title Respect, and it was a success. It was nice to finally see young women and men learn how to respect one another as well as to just agree to disagree at times without violence. Patrick and Tony, needing positive feedback, so that each would continue on the straight and narrow, decided to join the organization. God, this organization and work, proved to be just what the guys and Michelle needed in order to be virtuous. The Organization soon became successful nationwide.

"No man is an island of his own'. All of us are affected by each others change no matter the circumstance. When JJ died, a part of all of us died.

THE END

John Donne's: Meditation 17
From Devotions upon emergent Occasions

"*Perchance he for whom this bell tolls may be so ill as that he knows not it tolls for him; and perchance I may think myself so much better than I am, as that they who are about me and see my state may have caused it to toll for me, and I know not that. The church is catholic, universal, so are all her actions; all that she does belongs to all. When she baptizes a child, that action concerns me; for that child is thereby connected to that head which is my head too, and engrafted into that body whereof I am a member. And when she buries a man, that action concerns me: all mankind is of one author and is one volume; when one man dies, one chapter is not torn out of the book, but translated into a better language; and every chapter must be so translated. God employs several translators; some pieces are translated by age, some by sickness, some by war, some by justice; but God's hand is in every translation, and his hand shall bind up all our scattered leaves again for that library where every book shall lie open to one another. As therefore the bell that rings to a sermon calls not upon the preacher only, but upon the congregation to come, so this bell calls us all; but how much more me, who am brought so near the door by this sickness. There was a contention as far as a suit (in which piety and dignity, religion and estimation, were mingled) which of the religious orders should ring to prayers first the morning; and it was determined that they should ring first that rose earliest. If we understand aright the dignity of this bell that tolls for our evening prayer, we would be glad to make it ours by rising early, in that application, that it might be ours as well as his whose indeed it is. The bell doth toll for him that thinks it doth; and though it intermit again, yet from that minute that that occasion wrought upon him, he is united to God. Who casts not up his eye to the sun when it rises? But who takes off his eye from a comet when that breaks out? Who bends not his ear to any bell which upon any occasion rings? But who can remove it from that bell which is passing a piece of himself out of this world? No man is an island, entire of itself; every man is a piece of the continent, a part of the main. If a clod be washed away by the sea, Europe is the less, as well as if a promontory were, as well as if a manor of thy friend's or of thine own were. Any man's death diminishes me, because*

I am involved in mankind; and therefore never send to know for whom the bell tolls; it tools for thee. Neither can we call this a begging of misery or a borrowing of misery, as though we were not miserable enough of ourselves but must fetch in more from the next house, in taking upon us the misery of our neighbors. Truly it were an excusable covetousness if we did; for affliction is a treasure, and scarce any man hath enough of it. No man hath affliction enough that is not matured and ripened by it, and made fit for God by that affliction. If a man carry treasure in bullion, or in a wedge of gold, and have none coined into current moneys, his treasure will not defray him as he travels. Tribulation is treasure in the nature of it, but it is not current money in the use of it, except we get nearer our home, heaven, by it. Another man may be sick too, and sick to death, and this affliction may lie in his bowels as gold in a mine and be of no use to him; but this bell that tells me of his affliction digs out and applies that fold to me, if by this consideration of another's danger I take mine own into contemplation and so secure myself by making my recourse to my God, who is our only security."

John Donne
1572-1631

From the Author,

Thank you, Lord, for the finalization of this work-as I am not perfect, but a work in progress. Writing has always been in my heart and a part of me as a whole. It never left me when I was up or down. It was always here. I ask now that you open the door to many more great works written by me as well as bless me with the company of great spiritual advisors to aid me in this endeavor. I also pray and ask for that of understanding to follow this work; that it may open the minds and hearts of many whom read it, and that it will be used to inspire change. I pray that many are blessed through it and by it, and after all seriousness is gained from it, I ask that the readers be comforted, inspired, and filled with joy. Meanwhile, bless my family, not just personally, but abroad with a heart of support and understanding; fill them with knowledge and reduce all foolishness. As always, I will continue to give you the honor and the praise. I love you Lord, and I thank you in advance in your son Jesus' name, I pray. Amen

Are you ready for more published work by Lorraine Ducksworth-Rogers? Then look forward to her next book, titled, "Selfish Heart: Sinful Pride".

Made in the USA
Columbia, SC
24 July 2024

39261246R00124